D0850186

The Armageddon Game

The Armageddon Game

A NOVEL OF SUSPENSE BY

MARK WASHBURN

G. P. PUTNAM'S SONS, NEW YORK

SBN: 399-11934-5

Library of Congress Cataloging in Publication Data

Washburn, Mark.
  The Armageddon game

  I. Title.
PZ4.W3132Ar   [PS3573.A788]   813'.5'4   76-58425

PRINTED IN THE UNITED STATES OF AMERICA

For TC and the Durham gang,
and for the folks on Electric Avenue

The Armageddon Game

1

The explosion went off about two yards from my left foot.

I was lying on the beach being lazy and reading the *Herald-Tribune*. Heidi soon proved to be far more interesting than the *Trib*, and I spent more time looking at her frolic in the sea than at the gray global news. Anyway, I was wearing my sunglasses, not my reading glasses. I didn't need them to see Heidi, who wasn't wearing her reading glasses either, or much else to speak of.

The Mediterranean surf does not make much noise, not at Torremolinos, so I heard the brief *fssst!* before the sharp crack of the explosion. It was a sound I knew, and the familiarity of it softened the shock. Somehow, I wasn't even surprised by it.

I felt a quick surge of heat on the soles of my feet and then the stinging shrapnel spray of sand pelting my legs.

The charge of gunpowder was very small, tightly packed in a paper wrapping: a firecracker. The bang was authoritative, not like the staccato snapping of the Spanish crackers at the bullring. This was an honest, full-bodied bang that took me right back to a Fourth of July in Iowa twenty-five years ago. A cherry bomb—the atomic bomb of firecrackers in that somewhat smaller world I knew then. And here it was again.

The sand also spattered into my newspaper, which shielded my face from the blast. I stared at the paper a moment more, considering the event. I decided it had to have been someone's idea of a calling card. It had caught my attention, but not my interest.

I put down the *Herald-Tribune.* A heavyset man in his forties plopped down onto the sand next to my beach towel, grunting from the effort. From the baggy, formless cut of his swim suit, I could tell he was an American. His skin was turning pink under a smeared coating of lotion, so he was new in town. Below a slightly bulbous nose, his mouth was arranged in what, for him, must have passed for a smile. He was chuckling softly, but he didn't bother looking at me. He peered out toward the sea through his opaque Foster Grants.

He didn't say anything, and I was in no rush to find out what he wanted.

"Nice day," he said after a few moments.

"Lovely," I agreed.

"Pretty girl. Yours?" He nodded his head toward Heidi, who was still attempting to body-surf.

"Mine."

"Good for you. Your life seems to be going well."

"It was, until a moment ago. Look, I know what you want, and I'm not interested. So why don't you go back where you came from?'

"I just got here."

He was glib, like other visitors I had encountered over the years. The glibness was part of the package, a clue to the way they saw themselves. Even the ones who probably know better fall into it and find themselves speaking lines from old Warner

Brothers films. And they get upset if you don't feed them straight lines. So I did.

"Do what you want," I said. "I told you, I'm not interested. And I'm especially not interested when the proposition comes from some idiot who thinks a cherry bomb is a cute way to say hello."

"Perhaps it was a little melodramatic. I wanted to get your attention.

"You wanted a hell of a lot more than that."

He turned toward me and smiled suddenly. "You're right, Boggs. And I'm going to get it."

"Don't count on it."

He was still grinning. "Oh, I'll get it. And I'll tell you why." He paused. He was very sure of himself, a man who was obviously accustomed to getting his way. He had the placid confidence of a shark among sardines. His grin bared teeth that were white and well kept, like those of any carnivore.

"So tell me why," I said.

"Okay, Boggs, get ready. You won't believe it, but I'm going to make you an offer you can't refuse." And then he laughed like a maniac.

I had never met one like this before. He seemed to be enjoying himself, and that worried me. Usually they spoke in self-important conspiratorial tones, without a hint of humor or irony. The gravity of style was important, because it kept them from realizing how ridiculous they sounded. But this one seemed to know that it was all a game, and that made him more dangerous than the others. I knew he was dangerous, because already he had me wondering what the proposition was going to be.

He had stopped laughing at this little joke, and his features fell back into a narrow smile. His nose was big, red, and peeling, giving him a clownlike look. From behind the dark sunglasses his eyes gave away absolutely nothing.

11

"Are you from an employment agency?"

"I think you know where I'm from. But if it helps, of course you can think of us as an employment agency."

"It doesn't help at all. Why don't you just trot on back to Snelling and Snelling and tell them to get someone else? I don't need a job."

"But the job needs you, Boggs. Skill and experience. That's what you've got, and that's what we need."

I had them, all right. Skill enough to be one of the best at my profession. And experience enough to be wary of propositions from strangers who laughed too much.

"Face it," he said. "You're going to do it. You're like Fred Astaire singing 'I Won't Dance,' and all the while everyone knows he's he's going to dance. You'll dance, Boggs. You could save us both some time if you stopped pretending that you don't need the job."

"I don't."

"You've got exactly thirteen thousand dollars in your account in Zurich. I can't remember the number offhand, but I can look it up for you."

He wasn't supposed to be able to know that.

"Thirteen thousand will last me quite a while," I told him diffidently, like Rockefeller discussing the market.

"A year," he agreed, "maybe two, if you give up your expensive habits." He glanced in the direction of Heidi.

"Fine," I said. "I'll see you in two years."

He picked at some dead skin on his nose for a few seconds. Some people shouldn't spend time in the sun.

"Okay, Boggs," he said suddenly, forgetting about his sunburn, "let's cut the horseshit. My name is Stover. I work for people who want to purchase your services. We can pay you more money than you ever dreamed about. Enough so that you won't have to keep taking half-assed little jobs like that fiasco in Portugal last month. You didn't even get paid for that one, did you?"

"Don't you know?"

"Your contact was foolish enough to let himself get stomped by an angry mob. That's what comes from working with amateurs. Sooner or later, they'll get you killed, Boggs, or on the inside of some rat-infested European jail that hasn't been cleaned since Charlemagne was a boy."

I was beginning to realize that Stover and his people could make absolutely certain that I landed in that dungeon.

I stretched out and adjusted my sunglasses. I needed time to think about how to lose myself so rapidly and so thoroughly that even Stover's people couldn't find me. At various times and places I had done some damned convincing disappearing acts, but there was a difference now. To vanish, I needed fake papers and passports, transportation and lodging, maybe even a disguise or plastic surgery. And I would need help for all of those things. When you want to hide from the government, you get that help by going to people like Stover. But who do you go to when you want to hide from the Stovers?

"You were going to make me an offer I can't refuse," I reminded him.

Stover smiled. "I told you that you'd dance."

"I don't even hear any music yet."

He leaned close to me and carefully removed his sunglasses. I took mine off. People seem to hear better when they're not wearing glasses.

"Okay, Boggs," he said, "here it comes. One million dollars."

I put the sunglasses back on and sank down to prone position. That childish cherry-bomb shtick should have alerted me.

"I'm serious, Boggs. One million dollars, deposited in the Swiss bank of your choice."

"I'll find one that gives free toasters to new depositors."

"I figured you'd have a little trouble believing me. But I really am a very truthful man." He reached for his rolled-up towel and started to unwind it. "Just to prove to you that I'm serious, I've brought you a small token. In addition to the one million, of course. It's because we think you're such a swell guy and we like you."

In the middle of the towel there was a small green package, the same shade of green they like so much down at the Treasury Department. Of course, from behind the sunglasses everything looked green. I removed them again to make sure. Stover handed me the bills, ten of them.

Grover Cleveland was on them. I had to read the fine print to discover that it was, in fact, Cleveland, and not, say, Benjamin Harrison or Rutherford B. Hayes. Cleveland would have been a lot better known if they had put him on the twenty instead of the thousand.

"I have to apologize," said Stover. "We wanted to give you nice crisp new ones, but they don't print them anymore. These are a little worn, but you'll find that they're still good."

I took one of the bills out of the wrapper and held it up in the sunlight.

"It's real," Stover assured me.

"I believe you."

"That is exactly one percent of what you'll get. Guaranteed."

"Stover, at first I thought you were some kind of joke, and I didn't want anything to do with you. Now that I know you're for real, I want even less to do with you. Anything worth one million dollars to you scares the shit out of me."

"We're willing to pay less if it will make you feel any better."

I played with the ten grand, riffling through the bills and admiring the portrait of Grover Cleveland.

I tried to envision one thousand Grover Clevelands staring back at me.

"What in God's name could I possibly do that's worth one million dollars?"

The half-smile disappeared from Stover's face, and he looked at me very evenly. "You won't like it, Boggs," he said. "But you'll do it."

"What?"

"We want you to build an atomic bomb."

Heidi emerged from the waves.

Stover and I watched as she came up the beach toward us. She moved like the girl from Ipanema, swinging smooth and swaying gentle, a samba in motion. Ballerinas study for years to learn to move that way, flowing and graceful. But Heidi was a natural.

She was tall and slim, but not gaunt in the manner of fashion models and Park Avenue ladies. Her straw-blond hair, wet now, dropped halfway down her browned back. The hair went well with her eyes, which were the color of the Mediterranean sky, azure and empty.

She looked questioningly at Stover, then turned to me. Heidi knew what was going on and wanted to find out if she were welcome.

"Heidi, say hello to Mr. Stover."

She looked at him suspiciously, made her judgment, then brightened.

"How do you do, Mr. Stover?"

"I do fine, kid," he said. He looked at me, scowling.

"It's okay," I assured him. "Heidi knows what I do."

Heidi nodded in agreement. "Sam's a mad bomber."

I slapped her gently on the rump and she grinned back at me. Heidi didn't mind my profession, or if she did, she was smart enough not to let me know it. Reality for Heidi was

15

selective; she accepted the things she wanted, and ignored everything else. It didn't matter to her what I did for a living.

But all Stover saw was a blue-eyed blond in a bikini. He didn't want to discuss nuclear weapons with her.

Stover rose ponderously to his feet. He brushed sand from his hairy legs as if swatting at hostile insects.

"I'll talk to you later, Boggs."

Stover trudged up the beach past the baking hordes. A Spanish hawker tried to interest him in some ice cream, but Stover ignored him.

Heidi got down on the towel with me and put her arms around my shoulders. She dripped saltwater all over the *Herald-Tribune.*

"Sam, honey," she said in her most seductive, wheedling voice, "I thought you weren't going to take any more jobs for a while?"

"So did I, babe."

"You're not going to take it, are you?"

"I don't know. I sure as hell don't want to."

"Then don't." That settled it for Heidi, and she concluded with a salty kiss. She settled comfortably onto her stomach, unfastened her top, and closed her eyes.

After a while, though, she turned to me and murmured sleepily, "What did he want, anyway?"

"He wanted me to build him an atomic bomb."

"Oh," she said, as if things like this happened every day. She had just one more question. "Could you do it? If you wanted to, I mean."

I looked out at the blue, blue Mediterranean and told her, "I don't know."

But I did know. Dammit, I *knew.*

2

It's funny how you get into these things. Or maybe not so funny.

Aeons ago I was an assistant professor of chemistry at the University of California at Berkeley. Perhaps if I'd been at MIT or Cal Tech, none of it would have happened. I might have written high-school textbooks or invented a new formula for floor wax. I might have won a Nobel Prize. As Heidi and I made our way up the winding stairway from the beach to the shops and restaurants of Torremolinos, I mused that the thing to do might be to take my million dollars and establish a Boggs Prize. It would be even more prestigious than the Nobel, since old Alfred merely invented dynamite, while my fortune would be built on split nuclei and whizzing neutrons.

I was in Berkeley in the early sixties, a time and place where you had to choose sides. Long before Princeton preppies and Columbia political-science majors started burning draft cards and punching out cops, the revolutionary fires were burning at Berkeley. Mario Savio fought for free speech, the Port Huron statement was debated as if it mattered, wild-looking people espousing strange causes proliferated. We all came to know the pungent aroma of tear gas.

In Berkeley, you could find Trotskyites and Stalinists and Maoists and Fidelistas, Old Lefties who had fought in Spain and New Lefties who had marched in Selma, anarchists who read Ayn Rand and anarchists who read Bakunin, placid surburban SANE members and smoldering urban SNCC members, blacklistees with bitter memories of the fifties and scared FDR liberals who had crapped out under McCarthy, One Worlders, Third Worlders, conscience-smitten men of God and Hell's Angels, and intense young men with fingers blue from mimeograph smears handing out Leninist leaflets and speaking urgently and rapidly of the revolutionary vanguard.

You could also find earnest young academics with fresh Ph.D.'s and juicy government grants. I was one of them.

I was a scientist, and scientists are not supposed to care about politics. I had liked Jack Kennedy, and I was beginning to dislike Lyndon Baines Johnson, but then, so was everyone else. I registered Democrat and voted when I remembered to, and had even passed out a few pamphlets for Brown when he was running against Nixon. But I really didn't care about politics, because there were no neat, crisp formulas for dealing with it. I didn't understand how there could be more questions than answers. Equations must balance.

Chemistry, I did understand. I also understood that government money paid for most of the exciting new work that was being done in my field. Federal grants were the wellspring that watered and kept fertile the sheltered Valley of Science. And I was as willing as anyone else to stand in line and fill my bucket with those polluted waters.

18

My field was plastics. Plastics were soon to symbolize everything that was wrong with our society: people were plastic; jobs were plastic; politicians were plastic; homes, families, schools, communities, churches, television, and McDonald's hamburgers were all plastic. And a new type of bomb was also going to be plastic.

Plastics do not occur in nature. They are synthetically produced substances generally created to replace something that does occur in nature. Far from being evil, plastic, to me, represented a genuinely beneficial advance; if we used plastics, we could let all those rubber trees and whales go on living. Surely, that was good.

Actually, I probably didn't think that at the time. Chemicals were ethically neutral; the same chemicals that in one form could fry a Vietnamese village, in another form could power your car. That was the way I probably thought about it then, if I thought about it at all. Ethics were the exclusive property of the Philosophy Department, and I was in the Chemistry Department.

The jet set used to come to Torremolinos, but then the jet set left, and that's when I arrived. The beautiful people left behind them a jungle of cheap, half-finished cliffside condominiums. Some would never be finished because the jet-setters had moved on to Ibiza or Puerto Vallerta or some unsuspecting little fishing village on an unspoiled tropical shore. When Torremolinos was still "in," there were never enough rooms, never enough ways to shake loose still more dollars and francs and kroner. So they began building high-rise matchboxes and ritzy cabanas and cheap hamburger joints and kinky little bars, thousands of bars, bars for the Americans and bars for the Germans, and even pubs for the English.

And suddenly the place became tacky. It looked too much

like Atlantic City, New Jersey, and there were too many fat, loud Germans, and fat, loud Americans, so the slim, discreet beautiful people deserted Torremolinos and found other places to despoil.

But people still come to Torremolinos. The glamour and glitter are gone, but the sun still shines on the Costa del Sol. Every two weeks a new supply of Scandinavians would arrive, and I would watch them as they turned from white to pink to bright red to golden brown, just in time for them to leave and make room for the next shift.

Torremolinos was an ideal place for me. No one paid much attention to who came and went, and no one who stayed was likely to know me. All the kids I had known were no longer kids, so I was safe among the young drifters and degenerates, while on the other hand, the Spanish police would never think of bothering a prosperous man in his thirties when they had all those hippies to hassle.

We stopped at an outdoor sandwich stand and bought a small paper cone full of salty French fries. We walked on up the mall, past the boutiques and record stores with their blaring hi-fi systems and American music.

Heidi absently nibbled on a few fries. She was in one of her quiet moods. Heidi usually matched her moods to mine— flighty and talkative when I was feeling loose, quiet and supportive when I wanted to think, and lustfully uninhibited most of the rest of the time. Now she was silent and morose, and I realized that it meant that *I* had been silent and morose during the long walk up from the beach.

I didn't want to think about what I would do with one million dollars, and I didn't want to think about what I would have to do to get it. I knew how my thought processes worked. Once I started thinking about an atomic bomb, I would get engrossed in the finicky technical details and not even consider the implications, the very scary implications, of building such a weapon for the likes of Stover.

No, I would wonder exactly how I would go about it. There was the question of materials. They had dropped a uranium bomb on Hiroshima, a puny little U-235 device that was obsolete even before they loaded it aboard the *Enola Gay*. It was fantastically inefficient—only about one percent of the uranium fissioned—but also marvelously simple. Just two subcritical blocks of enriched U-235 rammed together as fast as possible. Any high-school kid could build a Thin Man bomb, given the uranium and a little technical know-how.

I would probably build my bomb, given a choice, from plutonium. It was difficult and dangerous to work with, but you could build better bombs with it. They used plutonium on Nagasaki. A plutonium bomb has to be well designed if you want it to work properly. You have to build a very good casing for the stuff so that it will implode properly. A plutonium bomb is simply an appropriate conventional bomb made from good old blasting powder or, better, plastic C-4 to put around the plutonium. But you had to be careful because of the neutron absorption and reflection qualities of the explosive. I didn't know about C-4, but it would be easy enough to check. . . .

I threw the French fries at a garbage can and missed. I was doing it. I had known that I would—just as Stover had known it.

Heidi glanced at me but didn't say anything.

"Well?" I demanded.

"Nothing," she said coolly. She slipped her arm around my back and gave me a reassuring squeeze. I wanted to fight, but Heidi had just surrendered. Or won. I wasn't sure.

Heidi had come into my life four or five months ago. She sat down next to me on the beach, lugging a canvas backpack and dressed in sweatshirt, Levi's, and hiking boots. She looked about the same as every other young American with a knapsack and a Eurailpass.

She laboriously unlaced the hiking boots, then peeled off her long gray woolen socks. She wiggled her toes at me. "Feels good," she said.

"I'll bet it does," I agreed. "When's the last time you had them off?"

She made a face at me. "Okay, so they smell. I've been on the road from Barcelona for three days. There weren't any convenient bathtubs. You wouldn't happen to know of one, would you?"

I thought about it. When you're underground, caution is the prime motivating factor. She was American, and that was a definite minus. American girls want to know where you're from and where you went to school and how long you've been here and how long you're staying and what you do for a living. I couldn't answer any of those questions.

She looked about twenty, but it was hard to tell for sure. Take her out of her hippie togs and dress her up in Paris originals, and she might look a sophisticated twenty-seven. At any rate, she was younger than I was and wasn't likely to have known any of the people I had known, or to have been in any of the places where I had been. When I was at Berkeley, she had probably been in a junior high school.

I looked her over. She was dirty but pretty, perhaps even beautiful. Her sweatshirt concealed her torso, but from her tight, low-slung Levi's I could tell that she had a nice ass. A nice ass ought to count for something.

What she wanted was a bathtub and a bed. If the bed included me, that would be all right with her, since I could be counted on to provide a certain amount of food and entertainment as well.

"I think I might be able to find a tub for you. Anything else I can help you with?"

She smiled. "I'll let you know," she said.

That night, she thought of something I could help her with. Having gotten her bathtub, she found that she needed someone to scrub her back. I was happy to volunteer. By the time we were finished, that girl was *clean.*

She was shameless and guiltless, the way the younger generation claims to be but seldom is, and she asked me no questions, so I told her no lies. She didn't volunteer anything about herself, and I didn't ask. After she had been using my tub for about a month, I got curious.

While she was at the beach one afternoon, I checked her belongings. Her passport told me that she was twenty-two and had been born in Venice, California. That was bad news, but California is a big state. The passport had been stamped by customs officials of France, Italy, Switzerland, France again, the Netherlands, Egypt, Libya, Tunisia, Algeria, France once more, and Spain.

Quite a world traveler. I found a book of traveler's checks, badly depleted, with a hundred and fifty dollars left in it. She might have had a thousand dollars when she started. Or more, since she may have had another book of checks. Say, two thousand dollars. It seemed reasonable for a girl of twenty-two to have two thousand dollars and spend it all on a European vacation.

Other possessions: a guide to European youth hostels, and membership card for same; a road map of Spain; an address book containing seven names and addresses, five of them in the States and the rest in the countries she had visited; a bottle of Dramamine; a diaphragm; some toilet articles; a pair of leather sandals purchased in Barcelona; two pairs of well-worn Levi's; a yellow cotton dress from J. C. Penney; three pairs of bikini panties; two T-shirts, one labeled "Keep On Truckin' ";

a sweatshirt; a blouse; and miscellaneous trivia including a wallet card with a map of the Paris Metro, a key, loose change from five different countries, and something that appeared to be an Egyptian roach clip. Also: a bikini from France and a caftan from Algeria, both of which she had taken to the beach with her.

As far as I could see, this did not add up to a field kit for CIA agents. Nor did it add up to anything else except what it appeared to be. Heidi was not an undercover Stalinist out to do me in for revisionist thinking. She wasn't from the Central Intelligence Agency, the Federal Bureau of Investigation, or even the Department of Housing and Urban Development.

Heidi, it appeared, had no ulterior motives. She loved me for my own sweet self.

I carefully replaced her things. I didn't want her to think that I had been checking on her. In fact, I was a little disgusted with myself. My paranoid life-style may have been necessary, but it wasn't very pleasant. I kept remembering things like Leon Trotsky with an icepick in his skull and Joey Gallo blown away between the antipasto and the linguine. I had played for two of the toughest teams in the league, and when they bench you, it's for keeps.

But Heidi was the real thing, it seemed. I forced myself to relax.

Heidi was good for my nerves. For a time, I even stopped jumping at sudden movements and staring suspiciously at strangers in bars. I smiled more often, and eventually made friends with some of the people in Torremolinos. Bartenders and waiters always had a quick smile and innocuous chitchat for Señor Dobbs and his blond friend. I was Dobbs these days, because it sounded like "Boggs," which was safe and convenient, and because I loved Fred C. Dobbs. Given my expatriate life-style, Richard Blaine might have been a more appropriate name, but Rick had an unfortunate streak of integrity in him, and I didn't want to be trapped by any of my own games. Fred C. Dobbs fit me better, scoundrel that he was. Of course, my passport said Samuel Dobbs, but I fancied that I was Fred's long-lost and equally unprincipled brother. Fred was all the family I had.

Except Heidi. We were lazy and loose together, like Adam and Eve or Tarzan and Jane. Heidi turned a golden brown all over, or nearly, and I took on the look of the idle rich. I found an English bookshop and treated myself to a noncredit course on the Great Books, while Heidi seemed content to laze on the beach during the day and go out drinking at night. We conquered all the pinball machines in town, one by one, then took the bus into Málaga to find new victims.

We returned to my apartment one night to find it occupied by two brooding young men with a look of starvation about them. I was not surprised, but annoyed. Heidi clung to my arm and said nothing.

One of them stood when I entered, the other sat on my couch and watched. "Mr. Boggs?" asked the one who was standing.

I shook my head "I'm afraid you've made a mistake. My name is Dobbs."

He grinned apologetically. "Boggs, Dobbs, it's all the same, is it not? We have a need of you." I couldn't identify his accent.

Heidi looked up at me questioningly. "Sam? What's going on?"

I patted her shoulder gently. "Just some business I have to take care of. Why don't you go back over to Tina's and have another drink? This won't take long."

"I want to stay," she said firmly.

"The señorita does not know?"

25

"The señorita does not know," Heidi affirmed, "but she wants to find out. Sam? I don't know what you do, but I've figured out that it must be something kind of weird. I don't care what it is, it won't make any difference to me. But I want to know."

I kept my eyes on our guests. Heidi wasn't stupid, and I wasn't perfect. I had probably given her dozens of little clues and inconsistencies to wonder about. That was the problem with staying too long with one person, in one place. Dobbs/Boggs was too complex a person to get away with too simple a deception.

I could kick Heidi out or let her stay, and if she stayed she would have to know. If she knew, she could destroy me over something as petty as a lovers' quarrel or one incautious moment when someone was listening. If she left, she already knew my name was Boggs, and that could be fatal. And I thought of how empty my days would be without Heidi.

"Okay, kid," I said. "If you want to stay, you can. But if you do . . ."

"I'll keep my mouth shut. You can trust me, Sam."

I don't know what she thought she was getting into. Maybe she had had some romantic notions about Etta Place and the Sundance Kid on the run in Bolivia. Or maybe she just didn't care about anything but the two of us. I kissed her lightly.

They were from Portugal. They had a job for me.

There was a time when I would have asked them which of the many Portuguese factions they belonged to. I would have questioned them on matters of ideologies and allegiances. Now I only asked them, "How much can you pay?"

"We are struggling," one of them explained. "We can only offer you a thousand dollars American."

I felt offended. "Would you offer Brando a thousand dollars to do a soap commercial?"

"What? I do not understand."

"For a thousand dollars, I wouldn't throw a firecracker in a urinal. Find someone else."

They had a hurried conference in Portuguese. The one who had been doing the talking spoke very rapidly, and the other one grunted a lot.

"It will strain our resources, Mr. Boggs, but we can offer you twenty-five hundred dollars. That is as high as we can go. Please say you'll take it."

"I'll consider it. Tell me what you want."

They wanted me to blow up their own party's offices. They needed an outrage to scream about, and the other parties weren't cooperating, so they decided to hire me to provide the outrage. The explosion had to look convincing but not kill any of their own people. It would also be nice if their office equipment were not badly damaged, as they needed the mimeograph machine and the typewriter.

"We were told that you were the right man for this job. Manuel Perez recommended you. He said you were the best."

"Manny would know," I agreed. I had blown the wall of a Moroccan jail to free him once, back in my careless youth. Now he was back on the outside, peddling guns, dope, and information. I wondered how much my name was worth these days.

I questioned them for an hour. Heidi poured us wine and listened intently.

I asked them to describe their offices, the building, the floors above and below. How many people would be in the office and how many would know about it.? How thick were the walls? What time of day would be best? Were the police or the army watching them? How many doors in the building? Windows?

I told them I would need a floor plan. I wanted to be able to get in and out in two minutes. I wanted precisely timed

27

transportation in and out of the country, with no chance of a delay at the border. And I also told them that I wanted five thousand for the job.

"Five thousand! But I thought we had agreed—"

"I agreed to listen, that's all. Now that I know the setup, my price is five thousand, take it or leave it."

"But it's such a simple thing, Mr. Boggs! Why, I could do it myself!"

"Then do it. You'll find out how simple it is. I just hope that you don't have any close friends working in that office."

He didn't know how to handle it. He was a kid playing at revolution; five years ago he had probably been a fisherman. I scared him because I was a pro and knew more about this business than he could ever guess at. The easy job he had dreamed up now seemed terribly complicated and dangerous.

"But why? It is just a small bomb . . ."

"You don't want a bomb at all. You want a shaped chemical explosion that will expend all its force in one predetermined direction. You don't do that with a stick of dynamite and an alarm clock. In fact, *you* don't do it at all, because you don't know how. That's why you need me, and it will cost you five thousand to get me."

He consulted his partner, glancing anxiously at me every now and then. He was wishing he had never thought of the whole thing in the first place. But he had gone this far and he would look bad if he returned empty-handed.

"Okay, Mr. Boggs. Five thousand." He was sweating badly and looked very frightened.

"Fine," I said. "Make the arrangements. I'll want half of the money up front."

"Half!" He was beginning to realize that he was going to have to empty the party coffers just to blow up his own office. Sooner or later, someone else was going to see what a dumb move it was, and that would be the end of my friend's career as a revolutionary. He would probably run to the opposition or the police and spill his guts. This would undoubtedly be my first, last, and only job in Portugal, which was just fine with me.

I didn't want to push him too far. "Okay, give me the original thousand now and the rest after the job."

Relief spread across his face.

"And just in case you have any ideas about not paying, remember this. If I can blow up your offices once, I can do it twice. And the second time, I won't worry about your mimeograph machine."

He nervously assured me that I would get every centavo that was coming to me. He and his friend made a quick exit.

Heidi had been sitting silently on a wooden stool in a darkened corner of the room. I had almost forgotten about her.

"Far-out," she said simply.

"Too much for you?"

"No. But it's kind of strange. I thought you were a hit man for the Mafia or maybe a Russian spy or something. But throwing bombs! That's just kind of wild."

"Heidi, I don't throw bombs." I was offended by the suggestion. "I create specially designed chemical reactions to achieve certain desired results. Try to think of it that way."

Heidi began pacing around the room. "Chemical reactions, huh?" She gave a short, snorting laugh. "Don't bullshit me, Sam," she said earnestly. "You could get killed."

"Listen. I'm the best in the world at what I do, Heidi. I only take the jobs I want to take, and I never take anything that looks too chancy. And no one—*no one*—has ever been killed by one of my jobs. I'm a chemist, not a murderer."

It seemed to reassure her. She came into my arms and hugged me very tightly. "It sounds so dangerous," she whispered.

"Not really. There's always an element of risk, but if you

29

know what you're doing, you can keep it to a minimum, and believe me, I know what I'm doing."

"What about them? Do they know what they're doing?"

"Of course. They hired me, didn't they?"

Heidi wanted to come along, as if I were on a business trip to Chicago. I told her she would have to see Lisbon another time.

The flight from Málaga was short. I had no problems with Portuguese customs, checking my camera equipment through with barely a glance from the inspector. I travel as a photographer, and with Nikons strung around my neck, I am about as anonymous as it is possible to be. I think I might be even more invisible if I were Japanese, for they are everywhere now, clustered in smiling groups on every European street corner, shooting prodigious quantities of film. But Americans with high-priced photographic equipment are no novelty, either.

I checked into a medium-grade hotel, as arranged. Revolutionaries and anarchists are traditionally supposed to hide out in fleabags and storm cellars, but since those are the first places the cops check, I prefer touristy places with a modified American plan.

This hotel even had stationery. Without really planning it, as soon as I was checked in I sat down and wrote a letter to Heidi, care of American Express, telling her the number of my Zurich account and how to get the money if she needed it. She usually checked American Express once a week. If everything went as planned, I would be back before she could read it.

Then I sprawled on my bed and waited. I had no desire to see Lisbon. I had already memorized three alternate escape routes on a map of the city, and that was as far as my curiosity extended.

The phone rang sometime after midnight. I recognized the voice of my frightened Portuguese contact.

"Mr. Dobbs? The matter we spoke of? We can meet you in front of your hotel in fifteen minutes."

"That would be fine. Do you have the item we spoke of?" I strongly doubted that our cryptic conversation would fool anyone who might have been tapping the line, but I was willing to play the game.

My friend hesitated. "We have it, but . . . there have been problems. When we meet, I will explain."

"You'd better explain now, or we're not going to meet. I told you what I wanted."

"Mr. Dobbs, please. You will get everything we agreed upon, I promise you. But we have had, uh . . . disagreements over the matter."

"Sorry to hear that. Perhaps we can do business when you get your problems straightened out. Good-bye."

"Wait! Mr. Dobbs, please! We have your money. It is just that the job has changed slightly."

"How slightly?"

"I will explain when we meet. Please."

By now my stomach was churning. Someday I'll have big, juicy ulcers. My stomach just wanted to get the thing over with.

"Fifteen minutes," I said, and hung up.

They met me in a battered little Toyota. Perhaps that's why there are so many Japanese around; they come to visit their automobiles. My contact (I still didn't know his name) was out of the car before it had stopped rolling. He clutched my arm and pulled me with him into the back seat of the Toyota. There were four of us in the car; the two in the front seat turned to look at me. They were cut from the same mold as my friend—dark, intense, scared. The one who had been with my contact in Torremolinos wasn't along for the ride. Perhaps he had been purged, or arrested, or killed. If he was smart, he had gone back to his fishing boat.

31

We pulled away from the hotel with a very unconspiratorial squeal of tires. The one riding shotgun kept staring at me. I stared back for a while, but soon lost interest. He wasn't all that pleasant to look at.

"Do you have what you need?" he asked me. All I had brought was my Nikon and accessory bag.

"Do you have what you owe me?"

He snorted. "Money. That is all we have heard from you. We were told that you were devoted to the cause of revolution, but all you talk about is money. Is this how they will fight the revolution in America?"

"Very likely. Do you have it?"

My friend in the back assured me, "Yes, yes, it is here. And you will have the rest after you finish the job."

"And what about the job? What are these slight changes?"

He tried to explain, but never quite got started. The man in the front cut him off.

"Marcelo is an idiot. He wanted you to blow up our own offices. Sometimes I wonder what side he is really on." He glared at my friend.

"As long as you are here," he continued, "we felt that your talents could be put to a better use. Your task will be essentially the same; only the offices will be different."

I had expected somethings like this. "That's not the job we agreed on. Save your money. Take me back to the hotel."

Marcelo grabbed my arm again. "Please, Mr. Boggs—"

"Dobbs, dammit."

"Mr. Dobbs," he amended, "it is a simple thing we want. It is exactly what we asked of you before, what you agreed to do. We just want you to do it to someone else's offices."

"Then it's not exactly the same. The people in that other office might not like the idea. They might even try to shoot me. And I'm not interested in killing them, even if they do try

32

to shoot me. I blow up things, not people. If all you want is a big boom and don't care who gets in the way, then do it yourself. Even you could handle that." I glanced at the one in the front. He didn't look very happy.

Marcelo was still trying to earn some points, but neither the man in front nor I was interested. He was right, Marcelo was an idiot. He pleaded with me for a few moments, then gave up, trailing off into fretful silence.

"You want more money, is that it?" The leader thought he had my number.

"I don't want the job. For any amount of money. It's stupid and dangerous and will do you more harm than good. You're new at this, aren't you?"

His eyes widened a little. In the dim illumination of the passing streetlamps, he looked slightly unsure of himself.

"I have been in the party every since 1970, when Salazar died. And before that, I—"

"—sat around reading Lenin and Bakunin. Yeah, I know all about it. You know the theory, all right. But you don't know shit about *doing* it. None of you do. You just fart around talking about historic inevitability and blowing up each other's offices. Lenin would be ashamed of you. Hell, even Stalin would be ashamed of you."

I still knew how to talk a good game. If you can outleft the lefties and outcool the mafiosi, you usually get your way.

He didn't know what to say.

"Your original idea wasn't bad, you know."

I thought I saw his eyebrows lift a fraction of an inch. "How do you mean?"

"Getting sympathy by setting yourself up as a victim. I did it once in West Germany a few years back, and it worked like a charm. Minimum damage, maximum outrage. If you kill people, everyone is just glad that it wasn't them. But if you just miss killing people, everyone is scared and angry because it almost *was* them."

He considered it for a few moments. In the middle of his confusion was the awful fact that his position as a leader was being undermined. He was supposed to be decisive and visionary, and he was acting as fumblingly as poor, incompetent Marcelo. Courageous action was required here.

"You are sure you can do it?"

"Guaranteed."

"Then we will go back to my original plan."

Suddenly it was *his* plan again. I couldn't believe it. I had just talked him into blowing up his own offices. I felt like laughing out loud.

Their offices were on the second floor of an old four-story building not far from the center of Lisbon. The stucco front of the building was crumbling in places, revealing naked bricks. It would not take much to blow out a wall or two.

We went in through a back door and up a creaking wooden stairway. At two in the morning, there was no one in the office or even in the building, I was assured.

Their offices looked like the editorial room of a college newspaper. There were mismatched desks, chairs, filing cabinents, two ancient Underwoods, and the prized mimeograph machine, which looked to be valuable only as an antique. The walls, cracking on the inside as well, were adorned with revolutionary posters and slogans. Most of them were in Portuguese, but I saw a couple of familiar socialist-realist portraits of Lenin exhorting a crowd of workers to move forward to communism.

My employers wanted to watch me work. I didn't enjoy the audience, but I thought it might strengthen their resolve if they were impressed with my expertise.

I asked them some questions about the office routine, who worked where, and the like, then settled on a desk in an isolated corner. I manuevered it to an angle I liked and opened a few drawers to find the best spot.

I opened my accessory bag and took out four film canisters. I tossed one to Marcelo. He dropped it.

"Go ahead, open it."

Marcelo unscrewed the lid and inspected the contents. "Plastique?" he asked.

I nodded. The French had turned the use of plastic explosives into an art form during the Algerian fracas. I had learned a lot about it from an old communist who had been blowing up buildings ever since the Spanish Civil War. He and I were in Paris for the May Day celebrations in 1968, and we exchanged a lot of shop talk between explosions. He claimed to have known Hemingway. Plastique was safe even in Marcelo's hands. You could wad it up, roll it, mold it, or bounce it without any danger. It was light, easy to carry, easy to hide, and easy to detonate.

For my purposes, it was ideal for shaped charges. If you look at explosions as just big bangs, they are pretty chaotic; I looked at them as chemical reactions. Chemical reactions are very orderly. By shaping a charge and placing it carefully, almost all of the force of the explosion can be expended in one direction. Theoretically, a person standing a few feet away from a well-planned blast is relatively safe, while on the other side of the charge concrete walls come tumbling down. However I had no desire to test that theory personally; that was Marcelo's job.

After I had set the charge, I told them what I wanted. "Marcelo, at exactly eight in the morning, I'll be standing on the corner down there. You'll be standing at this window. Do you understand?"

He nodded . I would have preferred having his fearless revolutionary leader at the window, but Marcelo would have to do. My man with the quick mind and firm resolve had to be somewhere else in the morning.

"I'll have this camera in my hand. When I hold it up to my eye to focus, that will mean that the sidewalk is clear and we're ready to go. If the office is clear as far back as that third window, you scratch your nose. That's all, just scratch your nose."

"You will see it?"

"I'll see it. After you scratch your nose, you've got five seconds to get far away from this desk. That will be plenty of time, so don't run."

"Five seconds?"

"Trust me."

They took me back to my hotel and gave me an envelope. I counted a thousand dollars in fifties, twenties, tens, and even some soiled ones. It made a thick bundle.

"And I get the rest of it back here at ten, after the job, agreed?"

"If all goes well," said the leader. He was having second thoughts already. I decided to give him something else to think about.

"My friend," I said, "if all does not go well and I don't get my money, I'll come back and do the job again. For free."

I was up early. I had no intention of hanging around Lisbon one minute longer than necessary. I was also a little wary of my revolutionary friends. At ten o'clock, I would not be in the hotel, but across the street from it. If Marcelo brought along some associates to help him deliver my money, I was not going to stay to collect it.

Five minutes before eight I was on the sidewalk diagonally

across the square from the soon-to-be-renovated offices. I mingled with the early-morning crowd, just another American with a camera.

It was an interesting camera. The Nikon people would have been amazed. I had paid a German electronics expert to build it for me, and he had done an excellent job. The Germans are great for that sort of work; they'll build any device you want, no matter how lethal, just out of love of money and sheer fascination with technology. Like me, I suppose. Instead of a roll of film, my Nikon contained a powerful little transmitter with an effective range of two miles. Built into the 350-mm lens was a directional antenna. The lens was functional, so I could use it to sight and aim. When I clicked the shutter, the receiver-detonator in the plastique would say "cheese."

I pretended to be taking snapshots of buses and pigeons and passing Portuguese. I still had the queasy feeling that something was going to go wrong. I did not like Portugal.

A good reason for not liking Portugal suddenly appeared a hundred yards down the street, coming my way: a demonstration. I had no idea what they wanted or who they were. One of the marchers carried a sign that seemed to explain everything, but I couldn't read Portuguese. It didn't really matter. I couldn't tell how many there were, for they were still flowing around a corner like a viscous mass of protoplasm. Angry chants floated through the morning air like cheers at a distant football match. They carried banners, they waved signs. Their line of march was going to take them right under Marcelo's window.

If I was lucky, the demonstration could work to my advantage. People on the streets stopped to stare, and there was no one under the party offices. And the people in the offices would be drawn to the windows at the far side of the building, away from the charge.

Marcelo suddenly appeared in the window. I drew a bead on him in the viewfinder. Through the 350-mm lens he seemed close enough to touch, He saw me, saw that I had the camera raised, the streets were clear. We were ready to go, as soon as he scratched his damn nose.

But Marcelo spread his arms in a gesture of helplessness and bewilderment. He tapped his wristwatch with his index finger.

I looked at my own watch. It was two minutes before eight. I had said eight, and Marcelo intended to stick by the schedule. In two minutes a thousand angry demonstrators would be directly beneath the wall, and a crowd of taunting party members gathered around the window. But Marcelo wanted to keep the schedule. I didn't know if it was party discipline or native stupidity.

Marcelo stood there, looking nervously from me to the marchers, to his watch, and back to me. When he looked my way again I frantically scratched my own nose. Seen through a 350-mm lens, it's a fairly distinctive gesture, but I was the one with the camera. He didn't see me.

I was angry enough to click the shutter and let Marcelo take his chances. I might actually have done it if I hadn't had a record to keep intact. It was like having a no-hitter going.

At seven-fifty-nine, Marcelo's nose showed no signs of developing an itch. The marchers were about fifty yards away.

One of them hurled a bottle at Marcelo, who made an inviting target. I was sorry to see it miss. But Marcelo was frightened by it; at this precise moment in his life, Marcelo was probably frightened by everything, and rightly so.

He glanced swiftly at his watch, then raised his arms and screamed so loud I could hear it above the demonstration, "*Mr. Dobbs!*" He scratched his nose with a gesture so emphatic that it must have drawn blood. He disappeared abruptly.

I gave the incompetent son of a bitch three seconds. Then I

pressed the button, just as another bottle smashed into the window.

It was a masterpiece of timing. Anyone watching would have sworn it was the bottle that exploded. A loud, satisfying BLAAAMMM! rocked the square. Suddenly the wall of the building was in the street, and marchers were screaming in panic.

Inside the office, which now looked like a cutaway room in a dollhouse, loyal party workers were picking themselves up and staring dazedly at the damage.

I allowed myself a smile. I had delivered exactly what I said I would, much to my own surprise. I had given them an outrage, and the marchers had unwillingly provided a scapegoat. It had been one of my better efforts. Where it went from here was not my business.

And then it began to go wrong.

Marcelo was firing rubble with both hands from the edge of the shattered floor. Around him his comrades were screaming curses at the marchers and aimlessly racing back and forth in confusion and panic. In the street the demonstrators were getting organized again.

Another bottle sailed toward Marcelo, and this time it really was a Molotov cocktail. Marcelo might have gotten his offices bombed even without my help.

The bottle smashed into a broken remnant of wall two feet from Marcelo. It exploded with a muffled *wummpf,* spraying him with flaming gasoline.

Marcelo yelled in agony and then staggered off the edge. He fell twenty feet to the street, trailing orange flame behind him like a downed fighter plane. The mob in the street backed away and watched him burn. I could see only the greasy black smoke, but that was enough.

It was enough for the mob as well. Their blood lust was

satisfied, and the police would be here any minute. They broke into scared, running clusters, anxious to get far away from the sight and smell of their victim. Some of them came toward me.

Somebody grabbed my camera strap from behind and nearly wrenched my head off. He was jabbering something frantically to his comrades, and I knew what it had to be. Cameras have never been welcome at demonstrations, not at Berkeley in 1967, not in Washington in 1969, and not in Portugal now. Pictures taken at rallies end up in thick, comprehensive files. People who take the pictures work for the government.

They wrested the camera from my grip, almost tearing off both my ears as the leather strap was pulled over my head. I grabbed for it but missed, and instead got a knee in my groin. The air went out of me like an untied balloon. I crumpled to the ground. Somebody's foot caught me in the ribs. I smacked my head against the curb, then lay there sprawled out over the sidewalk and street. I was surprised because I felt no pain, none at all.

When I came to, I was still in the street. All was as before, except that pain had been added. The pain didn't make the sky look any prettier, so I tried to move, and suddenly had a good view of the gray sidewalk.

In time, I made it to my feet. People were standing near me, watching with great interest. I expected them to break into a round of applause when I finally craned myself up to an angle close to ninety degrees, but they didn't.

I wandered around the streets of Lisbon for a few hours. Eventually I found myself back in front of my hotel. I wanted to sleep, but not there. I decided it made sense to be back home in Torremolinos with Heidi.

So that's where I went.

3

I brooded about Portugal, about Stover, about nuclear physics, all the way back to my apartment, a comfortable place on the ground floor of a solid pre-jet-set building. Heidi took a shower while I sat on the couch in the living room and stared at the walls. After Portugal I had returned to Torremolinos, bruised and shaken, and sworn to Heidi (and myself) that I would not take another job until I absolutely had to. I no longer enjoyed my work. I allowed myself to think and behave like an invalid while Heidi nursed my wounds and tried to ease my mind. After years of being on my own, I finally needed someone, and Heidi was there.

Without Heidi, I might have given up the whole thing. She kept me going. She let me brood in mournful silence for hours at a time or get so drunk that it was all she could do to get me back to the apartment. She even let me ignore her at the times when she wanted me.

Somehow, she kept me from hitting bottom. Maybe it was

41

just her presence; a man doesn't want to fall apart in front of his woman. She watched over me without really seeming to, like a protective dog. If I needed her, she was there; if I didn't, she would wait. I wondered what I had done to deserve her.

And what terrible thing had she done to deserve me?

One night I suddenly came out of the fog. Heidi lay next to me, breathing deeply, regularly, hypnotically. I leaned close to her, pulled a long strand of blond hair away from her face, and kissed her gently on her cheek. I thought that somehow she would know, even in her sleep, what I was trying to say to her. It might start a dream for her, a sweet and happy dream that would explain everything.

She stirred, stretched, and came into my arms as if she had been waiting for just this moment. We made love softly, trying not to damage or frighten. We found a slow, underwater rhythm, floating and sliding, surrounded, until at last we glided to the surface.

When I awoke in the morning, she was still beside me, awake and smiling. "I'm sorry," she said. "I didn't get your name last night, stranger."

"Sam Boggs, the Mad Bomber. Pleased to make your acquaintance, ma'am."

"Are you still the Mad Bomber, or are you just going to be Sam Boggs for a while?" She propped herself up with an elbow on the pillow and stared at me.

"They are one and the same."

"Are you sure?"

"No."

"Sam, I think we should talk."

"About what?"

"About what it's going to be like from here on."

I rolled over and fumbled for cigarettes from the nightstand.

"I don't know what you mean," I told her.

42

"Yes, you do. You just don't want to think about it. But I want you to think about it—now, before you start brooding and staring again. Whatever you want to do, Sam, you know I'll stay with you. No matter what, as long as you want me. But I need to know how it's going to be. And *you* need to know, even more than I do."

"I do know, I guess. I just don't like it." I paused to take a drag on the cigarette. I instinctively blew the smoke out of the corner of my mouth away from Heidi; she couldn't stand cigarettes.

"Heidi, I have to go on doing . . . well, what I do. It's about the only thing left that I'm able to do."

She grinned slyly. "Well, not the *only* thing. . . ."

"Now who's not being serious? Look, I had a bad time of it in Portugal. I never should have taken that job. But that doesn't mean I should give it all up. It just means that from now on I'm only going to take the jobs that I want to take, and I'm only going to deal with people who know what they're doing. Nothing in the world can protect you from other people's stupidity, so I'm going to be damn sure that I don't work with any more Portuguese comedy acts. For now, I'm just going to lie on the beach and think pure thoughts. But when the time comes, you won't have to worry, because it will be safe and professional."

"But why do it at all? I'm not trying to talk you into becoming an accountant or anything, but maybe you could find some other way to live."

"Is that what you want?"

"I want what you want. I just want to be with you. But I like you better the way you are."

"As opposed to what?"

"As opposed to in ten million pieces."

*   *   *

Stover found us at Tillie's that night. Tillie was a plump, attractive Englishwoman in her forties who had bought a small bar in Torremolinos. Tillie was always behind the bar, all smiles, singing along with Vikki Carr records. She turned up the volume on the stereo during the instrumental bridges, then lowered it for the vocals so she could drown out Miss Carr. Her voice was round and robust, and she could reach most of the high notes. Heidi and I enjoyed her performances, and Tillie always greeted us with wicked winks and lewd jokes.

Stover sidled up next to us at the bar and ordered a scotch. He looked much better with all his clothes on. He wore a yellow knit shirt with the inevitable alligator over his heart, and seemed trim and relaxed. He looked relatively harmless, even friendly, and completely at home with a drink in his hand.

"Do you want to talk?" I asked him.

"Here?"

"Anywhere you want."

Stover smiled at me. He was not a very good-looking man, but his smile was toothy and not entirely unpleasant. "You seem almost eager, Boggs. I thought you would put up a little more resistance."

"You haven't got me yet."

"Oh, I've got you, all right."

"What would you do if I told you to go take a flying fuck at the moon? Just hypothetically, of course."

"I'd be hurt, Boggs. Deeply hurt. And then I would go out and find someone else to do the job. After that, *you'd* be deeply hurt."

"I assume you're not simply referring to my professional pride."

Stover laughed. "It's such a nasty business we're in, Boggs. You don't like it, and I certainly don't, but neither of us make the rules."

44

"Who does?"

He finished his drink and turned to look at me. The smile and laugh were gone now. "I don't know who makes the rules. I don't even know who pays the bills. But they get paid, and that's the important thing."

"I need to know more."

"That's what I'm here for."

"Is that all?"

"One of the things."

Heidi had been listening quietly. Now she put her hand on my right knee and said, "Sam? Don't forget to tell him." I nodded.

"Look, Stover, whatever it is, it includes Heidi. Any objections?"

From his face I could see that he had a lot of objections. "What does she do?"

"She mops the sweat from my brow while I'm assembling hydrogen bombs."

Stover shook his head in disgust. "I'm truly amazed that you've lasted this long, Boggs. Can she keep her mouth shut? For that matter, can you?"

I kept my mouth shut. Heidi bit her lips.

"Jesus," said Stover, shaking his head again. "Your place in fifteen minutes. Try not to invite the neighbors." He dropped a bill on the bar and left in a hurry. Tillie waltzed over to collect it, singing along with the Beatles. She wanted to know if we'd still love her when she was sixty-four.

"Always," I told her.

"I suppose you have moral objections to building an atomic bomb," said Stover.

"I suppose I probably do," I agreed.

He nodded. "That's one of the reasons we wanted you. Listen, Boggs, we both know that there's nothing particularly difficult about building a simple nuclear device. I couldn't do it, but I know people who could, and so do you. There are thousands, maybe hundreds of thousands of people who could do it, given the materials. With your knowledge and experience, your bomb would probably be better than most, but that's not why we want you."

"Are you going to tell me why you do want me?"

Stover had another scotch in his hand. He had the look of a man with a great capacity for holding liquor.

"We know about your record, and we know that you're very proud of it. And we know you're good; you've worked for us before, whether you realize it or not. You know what explosions will do, and you're very respectful.

"You would do it right, Boggs. I told you we want a nuclear weapon. What we don't want is a nuclear explosion. We think we can count on you to know the difference."

"Let me get this straight. You want a bomb, but you don't want it to work?"

"Oh, we want it to work. We don't want there to be any doubt in anyone's mind that the thing will work. We just don't want to use it."

"I don't understand," said Heidi.

Stover looked at her, annoyed.

"You might as well spell it out, Stover," I told him. "Maybe I don't understand either."

He finished his scotch and held out the glass toward Heidi. She let him hold it there for a while, long enough to let him know that she was not just a barmaid, and didn't appreciate being treated like one. They glared at each other for a long moment, then she took the glass and refilled it.

Stover waited for his scotch, took a healthy slug, then started talking. "What you have to realize is that we are businessmen now. I don't care what you saw in *The Godfather,* we don't go around firing tommy guns at each other."

"If that were true, I'd be unemployed."

"Okay, let me put it another way," he said patiently. He was trying hard to present the image of a man with inexhaustible funds of patience and good will. "There is still an occasional need for hits on people and property," he continued, "but it's just that: an *occasional* need. That's precisely why you get work. If we have a problem that needs fixing, we can go to someone like you, lay out five grand, and get the job done right. We don't have to keep a lot of Damon Runyon characters on the payroll. We don't like to have people like that hanging around. We're respectable now. Do you know what I did before I went to work for my present employers? I was a bond salesman. Not bail bonds; muncipal bonds. In fact, I *still* sell bonds."

"Only, now they're phony or stolen or something."

He smiled. "Sometimes."

"Okay, so you're respectable. You go to the finest restaurants, and the waiters know you by name. What does that have to do with an atomic bomb?"

"Everything. Maybe it won't surprise you to learn that way over half of the business we do is completely legitimate. We own hotels, theaters, radio stations, restaurants, real-estate syndications, you name it. We even own two major-league baseball teams."

"Say it ain't so, Joe."

"Boggs, what I am trying to tell you is that we are part of the establishment. We've got banks, buildings, and ball parks to protect. We don't want them blown up."

"So you're building up your own deterrent force?"

"In a way. We live in a dangerous age, and as a part of the establishment we want to see those dangers minimized. Someday, almost certainly within the next ten years, somebody somewhere is going to steal some plutonium and build a clandestine atomic bomb. With the growth of commercial

47

nuclear reactors, there will soon be literally tons of plutonium floating around. Already they have problems accounting for all of it. We're talking about *tons* of the stuff, Boggs. How much does it take to make a bomb?"

"About two kilograms. Call it five pounds."

"Five pounds. Not much, is it?"

"It's frightening," said Heidi.

"Indeed it is. Sooner or later, someone is going to get his hands on that much plutonium. The safety regulations are a joke. Two midgets with slingshots could knock over most of the plutonium storage facilities in the States. It's pathetic. They guard liquor stores better than they guard plutonium.

"Why, you ask? Because the power companies and the AEC are hot to sell the public on safe, clean nuclear energy. Everyone is afraid of it at first, so the power people spend more money on public relations to get people to believe it's safe than they do on actually making it safe. If they suddenly started putting armed guards and pillboxes around every reactor, they'd blow the whole thing. People would ask, 'If it's so safe, why do you need all those guns?' Armed convoys just to transport a few pounds of plutonium would alarm the public. They'd get scared and vote against nuclear power. So the power companies say to the AEC, 'Look, we've got a lot of money invested, so kindly soft-pedal the security regulations. Let's not rock the boat.' And the AEC goes along, because they've also got a vested interest in nuclear power. And the result is that right now there is one hell of a lot of plutonium just sitting around waiting to be stolen."

"I don't quite see how my building a bomb for you is going to make things any safer. What the hell do you want, a first-strike capability?"

I got up to mix myself a scotch. As I walked by her, Heidi grabbed my hand for a second; this conversation was unsettling both of us.

Stover waited for me to get my drink, then continued. "In a way," he said, "we do want a first-strike capability. The thing is, when somebody does finally build their own bomb, and maybe even uses it, there is going to be one incredible stink. Many heads will roll. Fingers will be pointed. The AEC will blame the power people for being lax. The power people will say they were just following existing regulations. Politicians will hold televised hearings. The people will scream. And the result will be that there will be new, stringent security regulations. Every gram of plutonium will have to be accounted for. Every storage facility and reactor will be armed to the teeth. In other words, after the horse has escaped, they finally bolt the barn door shut."

I nodded; he was making sense. "What you're saying is that you can steal plutonium and build a bomb once, but you can't do it twice."

"Exactly. The second time around, it will be a lot more difficult. But the first time, almost anyone could do it. The question is, who's going to do it first? Black September? The IRA? The Symbionese Liberation Army, if they still exist? The Black Panthers? The Weathermen? Or some right-wing kook? Or some group nobody's even heard of yet? It could be any of them. Tell me, Boggs, you've worked with radical groups. Would you build a bomb for them? Would you trust any of them with a nuclear weapon?"

I had to laugh, it was such a horrible thought. Most of the hard-core radicals, for all their blather about power to the people, really want power for themselves. People who spend their lives reading Lenin and Mao are rarely altruists.

"You've made your point. I suppose I'd trust you a little more than I'd trust Mark Rudd. But am I supposed to believe that you want to build a bomb as a public service?"

"No, but we are responsible. And as I said, we've got a lot to protect. This would be one way of doing it."

"Come on, Stover I'm not that naive."

Stover sloshed his scotch around in the glass for a moment. "I never said that we didn't expect to make a profit out of the deal."

"Now you're becoming a little more believable. Go on."

"Well, as I said before, having a bomb and using it are two different things. While you have it, you've got a tremendous amount of leverage. If you use it, all you've got is a large hole in the ground."

"And someone would be willing to pay a lot of money to make sure that the hole in the ground isn't in their backyard."

He smiled, ear to ear. "A *lot* of money." Stover laughed expansively, just a good old boy at heart.

"Enough money to pay me a million dollars."

Heidi gasped. "A million dollars! Sam, you never told me. . . ."

"I didn't want to upset you."

"But a million! Sam, that's not exactly spare change!" Heidi sank back into the couch and thought about it.

"What about you, Stover?" I asked. "What will you get out of it?"

"Me? Personally, I'll get the satisfaction of a job well done. And possibly some fringe benefits."

"I don't doubt it. But I meant, what do your, uh, employers get?"

"You don't really need to know that."

"I might."

"I don't see how. But I can tell you this. It won't simply be a billion dollars in small, unmarked bills. There are a lot of things we want that money can't buy. As far as the public is concerned, we'll get the billion dollars. But the reality will be a little different."

I didn't like to admit it, but Stover was impressing me. They had thought this out very carefully, and they knew exactly what they wanted. We weren't going to argue about money and targets in the back seat of a Toyota. I suppose I should have been happy to be dealing with professionals again, but I wasn't. Lurking beneath Stover's calm, reasoned approach was the fact that he had already told me too much to let me back out. We both knew it, and nothing else mattered.

"Who gets the honor of being the victim? The Feds, I presume."

"The thought of a nuclear explosion in downtown Washington, D.C., would probably be more effective than a threat to blow up New York or Boston."

"Undoubtedly. But how do you get them to take you seriously? You can't just tell them you've got a bomb and expect them to believe it."

"Of course not. So instead of just telling them about our bomb, we're going to give it to them. That's why it has to work."

"Wait a minute. I thought—"

Stover cut me off. "Give it to them *intact*, I mean. We are going to steal enough plutonium to make two or three bombs. Then we'll give them the bomb we actually build and let them sweat about the rest of it. They'll know we stole it, and they'll know how much we stole. When they look at the bomb we've built, they'll take us seriously."

"And what happens to the rest of the plutonium?"

"When we get what we want, we'll give it back. We're honorable people, Boggs. And we wouldn't want all that fissionable material sitting around, although we'll take much better care of it than the power companies do."

I didn't really believe that, and I doubted if Stover expected me to. They would keep that plutonium the same way a blackmailer keeps the negatives.

I sipped my scotch and pondered the situation. The story was certainly plausible, but on general principles I didn't believe all of it. People like Stover dissemble out of sheer habit, if nothing else. On the other hand, what he had told me so far made a great deal of sense. The truth, whatever it was, probably was pretty close to Stover's story. I looked for holes in it.

"With your clout, why do you have to steal the plutonium? You could probably just buy the stuff outright."

"No doubt. But the plutonium theft and the bomb threat are going to appear to be the work of a dangerous radical terrorist group. At least, that's the story that you'll read in the New York *Times*. Privately, certain key people will be told what they need to know about who really has the bomb. But for public consumption, we need to steal the plutonium."

"Interesting. And what happens to the terrorists? Do they get away scot-free?"

Stover shrugged. "I rather doubt it. It's not our problem, really, but I expect that the government will arrange something. It will all be pretty melodramatic, I imagine, but the public will buy it."

"You're not making me feel any more comfortable, Stover. How do I know I won't end up as a dead terrorist? Notorious underground bomber, and all that. It would make the story more convincing."

Stover was enjoying telling the tale. He reached over to me and slapped me heartily on the shoulder.

"Come on, Boggs! You're smarter than that, and we know you are. You'll cover yourself. A letter in a safe-deposit box, something like that. If you turn up dead, Woodward and Bernstein get another scoop, right? Hell, you're no fool. That's why we want you."

"I'm flattered. I'm also not convinced."

"Look, anybody who gets to play the role of the martyred terrorist will have to be completely ignorant of what's going on. If it were you, there might be some way to connect you with us. That woman in the bar noticed us together, maybe. We can't take any chances like that."

"Can you take the chance of leaving me alive?"

"Small risk. You'll behave, Boggs. That million isn't all going to be in one lump, you know. You weren't planning to spend it all in one place, were you?"

"I trust you, and you trust me."

"Exactly. And we both have ways of protecting ourselves."

"Assuming I say yes, I would want the first installment in advance. Just in case anything goes wrong."

"If anything goes wrong, you probably won't get a chance to spend it. But you'll get it in advance. This is big-time stuff, Boggs. We're not going to try to cheat you out of a lousy million."

"A lousy million!" Heidi shrieked.

"Your friend seems unduly impressed by money," said Stover.

"Well, who wouldn't be?" she demanded. "You people are really crazy. You too, Sam. I mean it, this is really insane." She jumped to her feet and began pacing around the room. She was wearing a brief halter top and hip-hugging Levi's and looked as if she had just stepped out of a surfer movie. Stover regarded her with a mixture of disgust and hatred.

"My God, Boggs—"

"It'll be all right."

"If she does anything to screw this up—"

"I said it will be all right!" For a moment I was angry enough to tell him to take his bomb and shove it. But you don't say things like that to people like Stover; they have a way of remembering. I calmed down and mumbled, "Give me a chance to think about it."

He rose to his feet slowly and took his time walking to the door. He paused as he passed Heidi.

"Kid," he said, "you had better do exactly what he tells you to do. Because he's going to do exactly what I tell him to do. This is not a game."

"Yes it is," she said. "It's all a game."

For a moment I thought one of them was going to slap the other. Stover reddened under his sunburn, and Heidi stood rooted in one spot, barely shuddering with anger.

"Okay, sugar, it's a game," Stover told her evenly. "But if you make one wrong move, you won't ever pass Go and collect your two hundred dollars. That's the kind of game it is. You're in it now, and so is he. And nobody gets out of this game. Keep that in mind."

Stover slammed the door behind him. I got up and went to Heidi, but she wouldn't let me touch her.

"Sam? I meant what I said."

"What was that?"

She shook her head. "You're crazy. You're both crazy."

"I know. I know, but what difference does it make? You said it yourself. It's all a game."

In a little-girl voice she said, "I think I like hide-and-seek better."

"Who knows? We may play that, too, before we're through." In fact, it seemed almost certain.

4

The first man who ever asked me to build a bomb for him was Colonel John Harschorn, United States Air Force. He strode into my cramped little office in the chemistry building at Berkeley one afternoon and told me he needed my help. He had a crisp military air about him, even though he wasn't in uniform; he wasn't foolish enough to wear it, not at Berkeley, not *then.*

Harschorn waved government money in my face. In those days I was easily impressed by money. I am today, too, but there was a period in the middle there when I turned up my nose at it.

"There's a war on," he informed me.

"I've heard something about it."

He looked out of my one lonely window at the passing parade of students. Their hair was long, Harschorn's was short.

At the time, that was a fairly accurate political indicator. My hair was medium.

"I hope you don't think it's old-fashioned to work for your country. A lot of people do, these days. But whether they like it or not, we're fighting a war, and we intend to win it." He looked ready to go out and storm a bunker all by himself—fit and tough. Handball during lunch hours at the Pentagon probably accounted for it.

"Colonel," I said, "please spare me the politics. I'm a chemist. What can I do for you?"

What I could do for him was to help the Air Force build a new type of bomb. I told him regretfully that while I had no particular objections to working for the Air Force, I knew virtually nothing about bombs.

"But you know a lot about plastics. At least, that is what we have been led to believe." He left the impression that he didn't quite believe it.

"You want to build a plastic bomb?"

He nodded smartly. "That is what we want."

It wasn't exactly what he wanted. The bomb itself didn't have to be plastic, just the shrapnel. In Vietnam, it seemed, the Air Force was having problems with their conventional bombs, which were designed to knock down buildings and bridges and such. Vietnam had a shortage of such artifacts, which left primarily people as targets. Conventional bombs did a fine job of killing them, but those who were only wounded had a tendency to recover and get back into action as soon as the shrapnel was removed from their bodies. It was fairly easy to remove the shrapnel, because the metal fragments showed up bright and sharp on X rays, making them easy to locate.

What Colonel Harschorn and the Air Force wanted was a new kind of shrapnel which would not show up on X-rays. If the Vietnamese doctors couldn't find the shrapnel, they couldn't remove it. Plastic seemed like a good candidate for the job.

I was immediately fascinated by the problem and forgot all about the obnoxious Colonel Harschorn. In effect, I took his money and told him I'd call him when I had something.

I needed to find a plastic that met a number of very stringent requirements. It had to be able to withstand the high temperature of the bomb explosion without melting or losing its shape; it had to behave properly at high velocities; it had to be hard enough to penetrate the human body; and it had to be transparent to X rays. As I had told the colonel, I knew nothing about bombs, but I decided that I would have to learn about them if I hoped to help build one. The Air Force obligingly supplied me with several reams of classified documents: the making of a mad bomber. I may be the best-educated underground bomber in the history of the profession.

The project was secret, of course. The problem with secrecy is that everyone immediately finds out that your work is classified, because you stop talking about it.

I lived then in half of an old wooden frame house in the hills above campus. I had a fiancée who sometimes shared the house with me. The rest of the time she lived with her roommates in a grad-student dorm; she didn't want her parents to think that she was living with a man.

Susan was also in the Chemistry Department, working on her doctorate. She was a lot brighter than I was, but she would have made a worse chemist, because she cared about too many other things. She was hot on the trail of the cosmic secrets locked up in the DNA helix. It was that aspect of her work, I think, which gave her a philosophical turn of mind. Delving into the micromysteries of life, she became concerned with much broader questions about the quality and meaning of life. She worried about what would happen if someday she actually did unlock the genetic code: who would use that information, and in what ways? She was haunted by visions of a genetically engineered brave new world. Her own responsibilities obsessed her. "You have to be aware of the implications of your work," she told me over and over again.

She was also obsessed with the implications of *my* work. I never told her what I was doing, but the very fact that I couldn't talk about it meant that I was doing something for the government, and most likely for the Pentagon. Susan was appalled, angered, and agonized over my work, even though she didn't know what it was.

I don't know how I felt about it. I try to remember, and it's like thinking about a movie you saw years ago. It's all two-dimensional, faded, and blurred.

Susan was small, dark, delicate, energetic. Her hair fell, black and straight, all the way to her waist, in the manner of Joan Baez. She also played the guitar, badly, but her singing voice was pure and sweet, in contrast to the shrill intensity with which she berated me for contributing to the genocide of the Vietnamese people. She joined her anger with that of others and marched and shouted and got arrested; she sat down in front of doorways, she refused to be moved.

Somehow, I was moved. A few memories remain, frozen instants of history, turning points. A friend of Susan's calling me a fascist, asking me why I didn't just go to work for Krupp. Susan herself, asking me why I didn't care. About what? I asked her. About the struggles of oppressed peoples, she told me, but what she really wanted to know was why I didn't care about *her*. How could I go on supporting the war machine when she was ready to lie down in front of it?

We all had our reasons, I suppose, for joining the movement. I wonder how many of us, at rock bottom, were really concerned about what happened in Vietnam. There were many who simply didn't want to be drafted, and there were many who were enthralled with the adventure of being gassed and beaten on national television, and there were probably many more who just went along with it all because that was what was happening. If I first became involved because I didn't want to lose Susan, at least my motives were clear and uncluttered. I wasn't trying to destroy my parents or become another Lenin; all I wanted was peace—in my bedroom, if not in the world.

But still, there was Lyndon Baines Johnson, smiling and scowling from on high and talking about lights and tunnels. And Robert McNamara with his charts and maps of "Veet-Nam"; and Walt Rostow, with his reasoned professorial blood lust. There was Westy Westmoreland and Chesty Puller and Robin Olds, and big bad Curtis LeMay; Kahn and Ky and Thieu; tiger cages, defoliation, napalm, Zippo lighters, and thatched roofs; and Walter Cronkite telling us all about it.

They all had their reasons, too.

One night I stayed late in my office, bundled up my notes, and burned them. It didn't make any difference at all. The Pentagon got their plastic bomb from someone else; and Susan left me.

Soon after she received her Ph.D., the serpent came to Susan in the form of a drug-company executive, just as he had come to me disguised as an Air Force colonel. The drug people had a lot of federal money to use in the crusade against cancer, and they wanted her to come to work for them. She told me that she knew it was dirty money but a cancer cure was above politics. She couldn't turn it down. She crammed all her belongings into her Volkswagen, and we promised each other that we would get together whenever we could. Then she drove off to Maryland. Her letters stopped coming a few months later.

We had argued about politics, because it was obvious and convenient, but after I converted, we didn't have anything left to talk about. Lyndon Johnson and Ho Chi Minh were removed from our relationship, and the two of us alone could not sustain it. She was my reason for joining the movement, I was her reason for leaving it. But motives don't matter; we are what we are now. Susan will save the world from cancer if I don't blow it up first.

I thought about Susan as I lay on the beach next to Heidi. She would have been appalled at what I was doing. Heidi was merely distressed. She didn't understand the world in the same way that Susan and I had. The difference between us was time, a dozen years of it. Heidi could not remember a world where there was no Vietnam, no bomb, no television. Her world was founded on an icy sheet of ambiguities and uncertainties, and mine had been based on the granite of unshakable institutions and morality. Mine had crumbled, but hers could do no more than splinter, break, and reform.

I had grown up with a capacity for outrage and disillusionment, for I had been told that certain things were unquestionably right, and it followed that certain things must then be wrong. When Vietnam happened, my generation felt betrayed. It was an undisguisable wrong done in the name of all the things we had been told were right. They had lied to us about Vietnam—what else was false? Lots of things, as it turned out. Clean-cut American boys murdered babies. LBJ was cruel to dogs. The betrayal was overwhelming. We became enraged. Some of us built bombs to smash the betrayers.

Heidi grew up in the midst of all of it. No one could tell her what was right and what was wrong, because nobody really knew for sure anymore. There was nothing left for her generation to believe in. And where there is no belief, there can be no betrayal. Instead of becoming angry, her generation became cynical and turned inward. They came to terms with as much of the world as they felt they had to in order to survive, but no more. Heidi managed it better than most, and learned to believe in only the things which could touch her. I could touch her, but an atomic bomb could not.

So Heidi was just upset, while Susan would have been appalled by my monstrous betrayal. In time, Heidi would accept the situation, because it was just something temporary, grafted onto the world by madmen. She would permit me my own reality, as long as it didn't destroy hers.

Susan would never accept it, because she had gotten off the roller coaster too soon. If she had stayed, she would have understood that rage ultimately gives way to disillusionment, and then it doesn't matter who or what is betrayed.

Heidi was lying next to me on the beach towel, facedown. The top of her bikini was undone, and the bottom was pushed down so far that it revealed most of her tanned cheeks. She was an extraordinarily erotic woman when she wanted to be, which was most of the time. Perhaps her own body was the limit of her reality, and even I was just a persistent fantasy.

I spread baby oil on her back, sliding my hands over the sensuous ridges and depressions. She had said she would stay with me as long as I wanted her. I couldn't imagine not wanting her.

But I could lose her. Sooner or later, some Portuguese revolutionary or small-time hood could lose it all for me. If I kept on meeting true believers on dark street corners and blowing up strategic outhouses of the world, someday my luck, as they say, was going to run out. The more hands you play, the greater the odds of getting aces and eights.

With a million dollars, I could get out of the game. One more high-stakes pot, and it would be all over—one way or the other.

Or I could get out now.

I could take what I had and run as far and as fast as I was able. I could buy a sheep farm in the remotest corner of New Zealand and sit and wait for the day when Stover would show up to close the account.

"Heidi," I asked her, "what do you think of New Zealand?"

She rolled over onto her back, not bothering to put on her top. She squinted in the sun and asked in a sleepy voice, "What do I think of *what*"

"New Zealand. You remember, eighth-grade geography. Sheep. Wool. Kiwi birds."

"What do I think of it?" She shook her head. "I don't think I'd like it very much. It seems so far away from everything."

"That's the whole point."

She concentrated on picking some sand out of her navel, retreating back into her body. New Zealand was not on any of the maps of her world.

"Don't let me interrupt anything."

I looked up and saw Stover, eclipsing the sun above us. Heidi whirled over onto her stomach, not out of modesty but out of contempt for Stover.

Stover wore plaid Bermuda shorts, another alligator shirt, and a golfer's hat with the brim turned down to protect his face and the back of his neck. I couldn't see his face well in the shadow, but I thought he was smiling.

He hunkered down next to me. "I'm getting an awful bad sunburn. Do you suppose we could talk over there in the shade?" Stover pointed to one of the beachside bars, where the tables had thatched sun umbrellas. No one was there at the moment but the bartender.

We walked over to the bar and ordered three beers while Heidi fastened her bra and adjusted the bikini bottom. Stover stole a look at her and let out an audible sigh. "Maybe you've got the right idea, Boggs. Be a beach bum. I wouldn't—" He caught himself, looked at me without humor, and told me, "Forget what I just said."

We sat at the table farthest from the bar and drank our San Miguels from the bottle. It was the local brand, bottled down the road in Málaga, and it wasn't very good.

"Well," said Stover cheerfully, "I hope you had a good night's rest."

"How could we?" Heidi asked, her eyes challenging him.

Stover ignored her. That was obviously going to be his strategy for dealing with her from now on.

"I need an answer today, Boggs. We have a timetable."

"What happens to it if I say no?"

"Take my advice. Don't say it."

I took a slow, cold pull at my beer and looked off into the distance, at the gleaming mountaintops above the low haze of Malaga.

"What the hell," I said finally. "When do we leave?"

Stover flashed that quick grin of his. "I knew you were an intelligent man, Boggs. We leave in the morning."

"First, the money."

He chuckled knowingly, as if I had just told an old and private joke. "Come on, Boggs. Let's not kid each other. If you got the money before we reached the States, why, you might just decide to get on the wrong plane. I think it's better for both of us if I remove that temptation. After we get where we're going, you'll get a bank statement showing that a half-million dollars has been deposited in your account. Trust me, Boggs."

"I suppose I have to, don't I?"

"Now you're getting the idea." He turned to Heidi, who was staring at her beer bottle. "And you, my dear Heidi, you might as well stop pouting and enjoy the ride. You're coming along, and you're going to stay right by Sam's side all the way through it." He gloated.

"I wouldn't leave him anyway. You don't have to worry about that."

"Just don't give us a reason to worry. That's all I ask." He finished his beer and stood up. "Get your things packed, Boggs. We've got a nine-A.M. flight to Madrid. I'll pick you up at eight."

"I'll be there."

Again, he grinned. "I know you will," he said. I watched him as he walked up the beach. I didn't want to look at Heidi.

She put her hand on mine and said, "Sam? If this is our last day here, let's try to enjoy it. Okay?"

I didn't say anything. "*Okay?*" she persisted.

I looked into her Mediterranean-blue eyes and wondered what color they would be under the gray, heavy skies of America.

"Okay," I said. We lifted our San Miguels to toast the remaining hours in Torremolinos.

"Here's looking at you, kid," she said in an extremely bad Bogart voice.

"Bombs away," I answered.

5

A 747 goes as far as humanly possible toward totally insulating you from the incredible adventure of flying seven miles above the Atlantic Ocean. Heidi and I sat together in the middle section at the rear of the airplane, while Stover glided along in the luxury of the first-class lounge. I didn't mind at all. Those of us in the back had to struggle along with only our newspapers, magazines, drinks, meals, movies, and seven-channel stereo to keep us amused. From our vantage point it was impossible to tell that we were in an airplane. I wouldn't have been surprised to see people playing shuffleboard in the aisles.

Somehow the preprogrammed entertainment failed to captivate me. I preferred to look out the window and watch the cloud mountains sail past us. Since we had no windows of our own, I spent my time leaning on the emergency door and looking out through its window. It gave me a giddy feeling, resting my weight against that door; seven miles is a long way to fall. Of course, at thirty-five thousand feet, I would freeze to death or die of oxygen starvation long before I completed my swan dive. So I put my trust in Boeing and enjoyed the view. There was not much to see except the tops of cumulus clouds and the slate-gray pavement of the Atlantic; still, it was preferable to all the things TWA had provided to take my mind off oxygen starvation.

The stewardesses were distressed to see me spending so much time at the emergency door. They kept asking if they could get me anything, and I kept assuring them that I was doing just fine. Finally, one of them, a Barbie-doll blond with a button nose, told me that the movie was about to begin and I would have to close the window shade.

"I don't want to see the movie," I told her pleasantly.

"Yes, sir," she answered sweetly, "but many of the other passengers do want to see it. That window lets in too much light. I'm afraid you'll have to shut the window shade."

I wanted to argue with her, but I checked myself. You can never win when the officious little minions of the bureaucracy start talking about the greatest good for the greatest number.

I have a theory about revolution. My Marxist friends would never agree with it, but I think it explains a lot of history. Revolutions are not caused by oppression or starvation; these are things which people learn to expect and endure. They don't inspire anger.

Revolutions are caused by people like my cute little stewardess, people who know the rules and believe in them. The revolution, if it ever comes, will begin not in some dark conspiratorial hideaway, but in an angry line at the Department of Motor Vehicles.

I just smiled my cynical smile at my stewardess and returned to my seat. Revolution no longer interested me.

I had seen too many revolutions, most of them confused and abortive. In the early days at Berkeley none of us knew what we were doing, and if we had, we probably never would have gotten started. The outrage of Vietnam led us into the labyrinths of revolutionary politics and theory, but there was no one around who could tell us what to *do*. It was all trial and error, mostly error.

Very few of us jumped all the way from anger to anarchy. Rather, it was a step-by-step kind of thing, and we were seldom even aware of the steps we took or the direction we were moving. By 1968 I had become a bomber, an underground fugitive on the ten-most-wanted list. I didn't stay on the list long, because they soon discovered people they wanted worse than they wanted me. As far as my life was concerned, it made no difference whose list I was on; we were all on somebody's list. And we were making lists of our own.

My first bomb was small and symbolic. We still thought in terms of "protest" then, but our protests were becoming more and more emphatic. We discovered that the authorities drew no distinction between a symbolic act and a revolutionary one, and soon the distinction disappeared for us as well. Somehow, we found ourselves past the point of no return.

The hard-core types insisted we were making progress. Things had to get worse, they said, before they could get better. When conditions became intolerable, the working class would rise up and destroy the capitalists. But I noticed that whenever revolutionary idealists tried to establish an alliance with the workers—the factory laborers and hard hats—they invariably got the shit beat out of them.

And I also noticed that my comrades were becoming tougher, more doctrinaire. Revisionist thinking was condemned. All counterrevolutionary activites within the movement had to be rooted out and suppressed. Factions formed, and soon we were spending more time fighting each other than the capitalists.

Once I was in Seattle, brought in furtively by a group that wanted to blow up a tanker that was bound for Vietnam. With any luck, the sunken hulk of the ship might block the harbor and tie up movement of troops and matériel for months. The leader of the group was known simply as Ilyich, which happened to be Lenin's patronymic. He seemed quite serious about the name, and about everything else.

When he had explained the job to me, I told him I didn't want it. The explosion of a tanker in a crowded harbor would inevitably result in deaths, and I wanted no part of it. Maybe the truth is that I just didn't have the stomach for it.

Ilyich did have the stomach for it; he had a passion for it. He launched into a tirade against me and the people in his group who agreed with me. He accused us of crimes against the people and revolution.

During his ravings, one of my supporters, a guy named Rick, turned to me and said, "You know, after the revolution, people like that will shoot people like us." I had to agree, and it seemed like a good reason for turning my back on the revolution.

It wasn't as easy as that; you don't just walk away from the shadowy world of conspiracy and sedition. My talents were in demand, and I had nowhere else to go.

But I began to take money for my work. The thrill and the romance were gone, and it didn't seem wrong to be paid for what I had been doing all along for free; thus is a prostitute born.

Eventually it didn't matter who came to me with a job offer. As long as they could pay, I would work.

*   *   *

Heidi, child of the electronic age, was plugged into her headset and staring at the movie. I glanced at the screen and saw a lot of well-groomed people racing around from place to place with no apparent purpose.

I turned to the newspaper for amusement. The news was of still more well-groomed people racing around from place to place with no apparent purpose.

There was another congressional investigation of the CIA. A Senator Preston was racking up a lot of points with the press for his let-the-chips-fall-where-they-may attitude. He pledged to "put an end to the CIA's continuing perversion of the American ideal," whatever that was. I could have told him a few things about that continuing perversion. On more than one occasion I had done small jobs for the CIA. I wasn't supposed to know it, but you get a feel for the style of your clients. Targets, methods, language, and personalities add up to patterns of behavior. When they don't add up the way you expect them to, it usually means that you're not working for the people you thought you were. I came to recognize the CIA jobs; my contacts always seemed to be tense, paranoid, and relentlessly professional. The CIA also paid more promptly than the revolutionaries, although not as quickly as the Mafia.

Senator Preston might turn out to be a huge pain in the ass to the CIA, but I doubted if he would pose any real threat. The CIA was in business for itself, and I was confident that they were well equipped to deal with any interference from vote-hungry politicians. Preston would get tidbits, false leads, and a few spectacular but unimportant sacrificial lambs, and that would be the end of it.

The newspaper was also concerned with the sad state of the economy, and the sad state of practically everything else. Things were falling apart all over the place: mad dictators here, starvation there, war, inflation, disease, everything but

69

plagues of locusts, which weren't due until next year. The way things were, a trifle like nuclear blackmail probably wouldn't even make the front page.

The movie finally ended, and I returned to my post at the emergency door. The ocean was behind us now, and we were sliding down the northeast coast of North America. It had been almost five years since my last visit to the New World. So many peculiarly American institutions had infiltrated Europe that it was difficult for me to be sure just what I had missed and what I would be glad to see again.

I recognized Boston, passing almost directly beneath us. It was a city I knew well, from the days when Cambridge, across the river, was a center of the revolution, as practiced by upper-class Harvard men. The New England weather was sparkling clear, and as we began to make our descent for New York, I was able to pick out the familiar landmarks of the Hub.

I played bombardier. From about this same altitude, the *Enola Gay* had delivered its package of death to Hiroshima. Twenty kilotons' worth of devastation; what would it do to Boston?

The golden dome of the State House stood out clearly, a beacon on Beacon Hill. That would be my aiming point. At noon on a clear day, my bomb could probably kill 150,000 Bostonians outright and another 100,000 from radiation. A fireball fifteen hundred feet in diameter would vaporize most of the buildings along Tremont and Beacon. All of the wood and brick buildings on the Hill would collapse. Hundred-mile-an-hour winds would sweep through Back Bay, knocking all the glass out of the Hancock Building and the Prudential Tower; all of the people in those buildings would probably die from direct radiation. Suburbanites who happened to be looking in the wrong direction would receive retinal burns up to thirty miles away.

Twenty kilotons would do all that. Today, they don't bother making bombs that small. They think in terms of megatons. A twenty-megaton bomb, an even thousand times larger than the Hiroshima bomb.

Drop it on the same spot, and the thermonuclear fireball obliterates all of downtown Boston, from Fenway Park to Southie. The great banks and insurance companies along State Street cease to exist. Up the river a couple of miles, the Charles boils and Harvard Square disappears in the firestorm. Twenty miles away, in Concord, exposed suburbanites are charred. Beacon Hill is now a crater a half-mile in diameter and 250 feet deep.

Jack it up to the fifty-megaton horror that Khrushchev bragged about. Now you can knock down houses in Framingham, set ablaze the peaceful trees around Walden Pond, and shatter windows in Worcester and Providence. They'll feel the shock wave in Philadelphia.

My bomb would not be of the same order. If I made it well, it might pack about one or two kilotons. Only a tenth the size of the Hiroshima bomb; puny. But two kilotons is two thousand tons of TNT, or four million pounds of high explosive, all going off in a millionth of a second.

Two kilotons would vaporize the State House and knock all of the glass out of the Hancock Building. Blast damage would not be great, but direct radiation would kill thousands. Explode it under the World Trade Center in downtown Manhattan, and you could probably bring down both towers and give Wall Street a lethal dose of gamma rays.

Put the bomb in the back of a small van and take it other places to see what you can do. With a little imagination, you could destroy the Golden Gate, the Eiffel Tower, or the Astrodome. Park the van in Washington, D.C., and you could wipe out the national monument of your choice.

71

I was playing an absurd and dangerous game. The thousands of blackened corpses my imagination produced might become reality at the hands of a deranged bomber: me. I balked at building bombs that would kill a single person, yet I was ready to build one that could annihilate thousands. Why?

Professional pride might have been the reason, I decided. This would be my Sistine Chapel, my Mona Lisa. All right, then: the atomic bomb as art. I could paint a landscape to end them all.

It seemed pretty hollow, even to a mind that was hungry for rationalizations. Greed was a much more basic emotion. With a million dollars, I could get out of the game for good.

Fear, of course, was not to be ignored. If I didn't build Stover's bomb for him, he would see to it that I wouldn't be around to observe the results when someone else built it. Maybe the Nazi rocket engineers felt the same way; politics change, but technology goes on forever. The bomb was going to be built, and the only question was whether it would be built by me, or by someone with more pride, greed, and fear.

Heidi and I checked through customs at Kennedy with no problems. A kid ahead of me in the line was returning from three months in Nepal, where he had undoubtedly been doing extensive research on the local vegetation. They let him go through without even checking his backpack. Sam Dobbs went through with only a cursory examination of bags and belongings. My demolition gear was safely stored in a waterproof box at the bottom of a rocky Mediterranean grotto, and I hoped that it would remain there until the sea dried up. I didn't expect to need it again.

We took a limousine into midtown Manhattan and checked in at a hotel not far from Times Square. Our instructions were to wait there until Stover contacted us, probably within a couple of days.

The hotel was faded and slightly seedy, and must have been reasonably fashionable back in the fifties. We had a bedroom and a drawing room furnished with nicked and cigarette-burned artifacts from another age. It was styleless and sterile.

Heidi and I flopped down on the springy bed as soon as we arrived and tried to sleep off our jet lag. Neither of us felt like making love or conversation. We were out of phase with the world, and our bodies and minds seemed to belong to someone else, far away.

We awoke refreshed, but frustrated to find that it was still only five in the morning and the rest of New York was sound asleep. We couldn't even get breakfast for two hours. Together we found a way to fill those two hours; it was all sad and depressing, somehow. Heidi's golden body looked forlorn and out of place in the gray dawn of the dirty city. Horns sounded in the distance, buses changed gears with an angry growl, and Heidi's soft moans and my urgent grunts blended in with all the other lost and lonely voices. When it was finished, we clung to each other and listened to the empty noises and the sad song of New York.

Manhattan in August is only slightly less tolerable than Manhattan at any other time of the year. Heidi had never spent much time in New York and wanted to explore. I told her that I had work to do, but she should go out and enjoy herself. The truth was that I just didn't want to stare down at the city from the top of the Empire State Building. If I did, the nuclear fantasies would begin again; Boston was already gone, and I had no wish to send New York to join it.

Instead of fantasies, I concerned myself with facts. While

Heidi went off in search of the Staten Island ferry, I walked to the New York Public Library.

I had homework to do. I knew something about nuclear weapons and what they could do, but I had to have very exact statistics and details in order to build a bomb. The library contained all the information I or anyone else would need to build an atomic bomb. There are no nuclear secrets. The only secret there had ever been was that a bomb was possible at all, and the U.S. government revealed that secret on August 6, 1945, rather spectacularly. The principles of physics and chemistry cannot be classified, and anyone with an understanding of those principles can build a bomb. The technical data to go along with those principles were listed in hundreds of different books, there for the taking.

A nuclear bomb can be made out of uranium or plutonium. Uranium occurs in nature, mostly in the form of U-238, an isotope which cannot be used to make a bomb. At the atomic weight of 235, however, uranium can level a city. U-235 makes up a small percentage of all natural uranium, and it can be extracted from the U-238 by various enrichment processes.

Plutonium does not generally occur in nature. It is a manmade element, first discovered at Berkeley, ironically enough. If U-238 is subjected to a neutron bombardment, some of it will capture a free neutron and become U-239, which is unstable. Within about a half-hour, half of the U-239 will decay into neptunium-239; the decay process involves the spontaneous transformation of a neutron into a proton and the creation of an extra electron. It's a mysterious thing to think about; a nuclear physicist could try to explain why the transformation happens, but I don't think anyone really knows. These impossibly small particles are the building blocks of the universe, and nowhere is it written that man is supposed to understand the universe.

Soon after the neptunium-239 is created, it too decays by an identical process and becomes plutonium-239, which is relatively stable; it takes twenty-four-thousand years for half of it to decay. But it takes only a millionth of a second for it to become an explosion.

Plutonium was going to be the material for my bomb. You can make a bigger and better bomb with plutonium than you can with uranium, and you don't need as much of it.

Nuclear-power plants generally use uranium as a fuel. In the form it takes in reactors, it is not very likely to start a chain reaction and become a bomb. But while it is in the reactor, a significant part of the U-238 becomes plutonium. After the nuclear fuel is spent in the reactor, the fuel assemblies are removed and transported to a fuel-reprocessing facility. There, the uranium and plutonium are chemically separated, and the uranium is then "enriched" again and sent back to the reactor.

The plutonium presents a problem, however, since it is not generally used in commercial reactors. After the so-called breeder reactors come into use in the eighties or nineties, plutonium will be abundant and useful. Now, a lot of it simply sits in storage facilities.

The problem with plutonium is that it is difficult to handle. Plutonium is about twenty thousand times more toxic than cobra venom. It shoots out alpha particles, which are low-energy particles that can penetrate only a few millimeters of human tissue; you can hold metallic plutonium in your hand with no danger. But if even a thousandth of a gram of plutonium gets into your lungs, you'll die of fibrosis of the lungs within a few days. Still smaller amounts can cause cancer.

Metallic plutonium is the safest to work with, but we would not be getting it in that form. During the reprocessing of nuclear fuel, it is combined with nitric acid in order to separate the uranium and the plutonium. The result is plutonium nitrate, a liquid solution. In that form it is highly dangerous but not suitable for bombs. I would have to precipitate the plutonium out of the solution,forming a powdery substance known as plutonium oxide. I could use that for a bomb, but as a powder the plutonium is just too dangerous to work with. At least, too dangerous for me. But the process of converting plutonium oxide into metallic plutonium is not difficult; and once you have the stuff in metallic form, you are set to build your bomb.

I looked up from my books, took off my glasses, and peered around the reading room of the library. Randomly scattered among the heavy wooden tables were hunched-over scholars and students absorbing the accumulated knowledge of mankind. Two tables down from me a Hasidic Jew was poring over a thick, musty-looking tome. He had a great, gray, biblical beard and looked ready to climb atop the mountains of books and prophesy plagues and devastation for all sinners.

I wondered what he was reading. I wondered what he would have thought if he had known what I was reading. His secrets of matter and energy had nothing to do with mine, yet they were equally mysterious.

He had probably spent his life pondering the meaning of it all, searching through the ancient manuscripts for the key to existence. But all I had to do was take a quick glance at my book, and I would see that key to existence, horrifying and glorious in its simplicity: $E = mc^2$.

Energy equals mass times the speed of light multiplied by itself. My bomb could be small and unimpressive because of that equation. The mass of the plutonium I used could be very low, and very small indeed would be the percentage of that mass that actually became energy; m in the equation was a trifling number. Because the speed of light is an incomprehensibly large number, squared it is a number so large that the mind cannot accept it. So multiply that very small number by the inconceivably gigantic number, and you will get a value for E so large that the temperatures generated by that tiny mass will exceed the temperatures in the interior of the sun.

I closed my books and stared at the Hebrew scholar. I envied him, in a way, because he had the courage to reject unacceptable answers. He would continue squinting and staring at those hoary records in search of the answers that he wanted. But I had an answer, and it terrified me.

6

My philosophical musings didn't last long. That evening, Stover called us and told us to check out.

"Darn," said Heidi. "I didn't even get to see Grant's Tomb or the UN or anything."

"This isn't a sightseeing tour, you know."

"I know," she mumbled, suddenly sullen. She sat down on the edge of the bed and began inspecting laundry before tossing it into her suitcase.

I sat down next to her and put my arm around her. She continued to sort laundry and didn't look at me. I found myself feeling very protective and paternal.

"Heidi, from here on, there's no going back. It's me they want. You don't know enough to hurt them. While I'm going out the front door, you could be leaving by the back, or hiding somewhere in the hotel. We could work out something."

She still didn't look up. "Is that what you want?"

"I want you to be safe."

She didn't say anything, and I couldn't think of anything else to tell her. I didn't want to drag her into something that could become very ugly, and I didn't want to lose her.

"Look," I said, "you could go back to Torremolinos. When this is over, I'll meet you there and we can buy a yacht and sail to Tahiti. How about it?"

"I get seasick." The corner of her mouth flickered upward for a split second, but she quickly brought it back under control. I knew it would be okay. She was having her mandatory sulk—she'd earned it—but soon she would be back to her normal free-spirited self.

"Are you scared?" she asked.

"Yes."

"So am I," she said; then she put her arm around my back and rested her head against my chest. "I guess we might as well be scared together, then."

"I guess so," I said.

Nine P.M. was an unusual time to be checking out, but the desk clerk didn't seem terribly interested in anything except his money. Heidi and I carried two bags apiece, and got a dirty look from an idle bellhop. I smiled at him as I walked by.

We emerged from the air-conditioned lobby into the fetid night air. It had rained for an hour around sunset, and the streets were black and gleaming. Passing cars made whizzing noises on the wet pavement.

Stover pulled up to the curb in a new cream-colored Buick. He was on the passenger's side, and I saw that he had a driver, who quickly hopped out and went around to open the trunk. Stover got out and opened the rear door for us.

"Take care of these bags, would you, Billy," he said to the driver. Billy nodded and grabbed two suitcases in each arm with no apparent effort. He was a tall, angular man with a sunken face and, long, closely trimmed sideburns. He was dressed in a drab charcoal suit but looked as if he belonged in boots, Levi's, and a stetson.

Stover held the door for us wordlessly while Heidi and I climbed into the back seat. Billy was finished with our bags and back in the driver's seat before Stover had even closed the door on us.

Billy moved us out into traffic with the practiced ease of a cabdriver, turning left at the first intersection to take us crosstown toward East River Drive.

"I called you in the afternoon," Stover said without bothering to look back at us. "You weren't there."

"That's right," I said.

Now he did turn around, and stared evenly at Heidi and then at me. "You should have been," he said. "I don't want either of you roaming around where you could get into trouble. Is that understood?"

"No, it's not understood. Nobody's looking for Heidi, and after five years, I doubt if they're still looking for me. Let's get something straight right now, Stover. We have a business relationship; I'm not part of your family. You hired me as an independent contractor. I have responsibilities toward you as a client, but that's all. You don't own me."

Stover half-smiled, half-sneered. "The last of the red-hot bigshot independent operators, is that it? Fine, Boggs, play it any way you want. But until this job is finished, I want you where I can see you. And that goes for Little Mary Sunshine, too."

He turned toward me, dismissing Heidi from sight and probably mind as well. "Look, Boggs," he said, in a voice that dripped with reason and rationality, "for a million dollars we expect a little cooperation from you. Is that really asking so much?"

"I'll cooperate. You don't have to worry about that. But don't crowd us. I need a little room to breathe."

"Granted. I won't push, just as long as you don't pull."

We took the Triborough Bridge and angled across the Bronx to the Hutchinson Parkway. Behind us the long narrow strip of Manhattan glowed like the lights of a stately old ocean liner steaming across the night sea; like the *Titanic,* perhaps. Billy kept his cowboy eyes on the road and swung us smoothly from lane to lane without jerk or jiggle. I guessed that we were headed into the wealthy wilds of Westchester County.

"I wonder if you would be so kind as to oblige us by putting on these blindfolds?" He handed me two plush strips of black velour.

I handed them back. "You read too many cheap paperbacks, Stover."

He smiled indulgently and dropped the blindfolds in my lap. "On the contrary, I don't get much chance to read anything but *The Wall Street Journal* these days."

"I prefer the *Police Gazette,*" I told him. "Okay, Stover, we'll play along." I helped Heidi tie hers in place, then slid my own into position. The velour felt positively luxurious against my face, sensuous and restful. I might even have fallen asleep, but I soon felt a precise, even deceleration as Billy brought us off the parkway. We turned right, but after that the ride was an endless series of curves and hills, and I quickly gave up all hope of plotting distance and direction. I couldn't see what difference it would make anyway.

I felt Heidi's hand searching for mine. I locked my fingers around hers and gave her knuckles a little pat with my free hand. "Just a ride in the country, babe," I told her.

"I love the scenery."

"You're not missing much. Just manicured greenswards and spooky estates. You probably couldn't find a place within ten miles of here that would go for less than a hundred grand. Am I right, Stover?"

"No peeking, now, Boggs. But as it happens, the figure is probably closer to a quarter of a million. Maybe you two will want to settle down here after it's all over."

"Sorry," I said, "I'm choosy about my neighbors." There was no reaction from Stover, not that I expected there would be. I was fishing for any information I could find, but if Stover was a happy resident of Westchester, he apparently wasn't bothered by my aspersions.

We might have been into Connecticut by the time I felt us make a sharp left turn into a driveway; I could tell it was a driveway because it seemed better paved than the road we had been on. After another minute we coasted to a comfortable stop; if we had been on a plane landing, we wouldn't have known we were down. Billy was the consummate driver, and I hoped the rest of the team measured up to his standard.

We removed the blindfolds without waiting for Stover to tell us to. Billy ran around to get the door for Stover, but let us open our own. I got out, and Heidi slid across to my side and emerged with a look that made me think of Dorothy walking out of her Kansas farmhouse and into the land of Oz. We were at the front portico of a mansion that looked like the White House would have if they hadn't run out of money. It was immense, shadowed, and very private behind an army of towering trees. Some railroad baron or traction-trust titan had probably built the place after a junket to Versailles. Charles Foster Kane would have felt at home there.

In spite of myself, I suddenly felt very shabby. I was wearing a ratty old brown corduroy sport jacket and faded blue jeans, and the scene demanded Gatsbylike finery. Heidi, in her yellow cotton sundress, probably felt the same way. Say what you will about egalitarianism, we poor mortals are unfailingly cowed before the majesty of unabashed opulence. It is why there will always be slaves.

We followed Stover up a short flight of marble steps and through a pair of massive oaken doors that might have been scavenged from a medieval fortress. I expected to find a suit of armor, possibly occupied, standing guard, but there was only silent Billy, holding the door for us.

Inside, it was dimly lit and smelled like some of the ancient ruins I had seen in Europe. Stover led us through a cavernous hallway decorated with classical statuary, then up a magnificent winding staircase carpeted in a rich claret at least an inch deep. Heidi started to say something, but it died in a sort of awed mumble.

At the top of the staircase we turned right and went down a long hallway that reminded me of the Louvre. All along both walls there were dark paintings of madonnas and nymphs. I didn't see any noticeable consistency of style or period, and it confirmed my suspicion that the mogul who had caused this palace to be constructed had been some kind of unlettered hick; everything I'd seen so far could have been picked up at a fifteenth-century clearance sale.

We went all the way to the end of the hall and stopped at another thick and ornately carved door. Again Billy maneuvered into the lead and opened the door for Stover. He strode into the room, followed by Heidi and then me and Billy.

The inside of the room was as much of a surprise as the outside of the mansion. It was furnished like the boardroom of an electronics conglomerate, all done up in blond wooden panels, Design Research furniture, and soft fluorescent lighting. A large round table, not quite large enough for King Arthur, dominated the center of the room. Black leather swivel chairs on polished chrome mountings were evenly spaced around it. Four of them were occupied.

The four men got briskly to their feet, like General Patton's staff at the entry of the great man. Stover nodded to them, and they sat down again. Billy took a chair next to the closest of the four.

Stover turned to me and swept his arm toward the men in an inclusive gesture. "Boggs," he said, "these are the men you'll be working with. You've already met Billy Wynn. Next to him is Kemper, then Morrison, Locatelli, and Serino. Gentlemen, meet Sam Boggs and his lovely friend, Miss Heidi Wallace. Please, sit down."

Stover planted himself next to Wynn, and Heidi and I sat on his right. We were about a hundred and eighty degrees away from Serino, who was small and dark and reminded me too much of the Portuguese. Locatelli was huge and looked like a college linebacker gone to seed over the last ten years. His hair was long and thin, getting thinner. Morrison looked like a computer programmer, average in every way except for his flaming red hair and his unblinking blue eyes. Kemper was another monster, bigger than Locatelli and uglier than the bad guy in a wrestling match. His nose appeared to have been broken frequently and thoroughly. Billy Wynn was the oldest of the lot, perhaps forty, although his eyes were surrounded by the kind of wrinkles most often found in rest homes. He had stared at a lot of highways. They all gazed back at me, making their judgments, all of them except Serino, who seemed more interested in Heidi. I turned back to him and furrowed my brow a little in what I hoped was a threatening expression. Serino defiantly kept his eyes on Heidi for another moment, then turned toward Stover with a self-satisfied little motion that seemed to say, "I seen better."

Stover looked at Serino and nodded. Serino produced a black attaché case and opened it, removing some papers. He passed them on to Locatelli, who took a sheet. When the last two copies reached me and Heidi, I saw that they were Xeroxes of a floor plan. A second sheet, stapled on, contained what seemed to be a timetable. Each copy was numbered.

"This," said Stover, tapping his copy, "is a diagram of the plutonium-storage facility of the Pennsylvania Atomic Control Authority, known as PACA. It's located near the town of Rogers' Crossing, about thirty miles from Scranton. It is used to store plutonium produced by commercial reactors in fourteen eastern states. Boggs, the others are already familiar with the site and our operational plans, but we're all going to go over them again for your benefit and ours. If you have any suggestions, feel free to make them."

"Fine," I said. "Let's hear it."

Stover cleared his throat and launched into it. He looked very much at home giving a briefing.

"The PACA facility is seven-point-three miles from Rogers' Crossing, and twenty-two miles from a state-police barracks. It's located on a two-lane blacktop road at the base of a three-thousand-foot mountain. The surrounding land is hilly and used mainly for pasture. The nearest building is a tavern, two-point-three miles down the road in the direction of the town. The facility was constructed there because no town wanted the plutonium stored close to residential areas. This isolated site was thus ideal for PACA's purposes, as it is for ours as well.

"Tomorrow afternoon at about five-forty, a truck carrying ten canisters of plutonium will arrive. The canisters are known as birdcages, and are five feet high and two in diameter. Each birdcage weighs approximately four hundred pounds. They contain one plastic, steel-sheathed bottle, in which is stored a solution of plutonium nitrate. Each bottle will yield two-point-five kilograms of plutonium. Boggs, how much plutonium will you need to construct a bomb?"

"You could do it with as little as one birdcage, but it would have to be awfully well designed. I think I could make a bomb in the kiloton range with about seven or eight kilograms. Three birdcages would probably be enough, but four would be better."

Stover nodded. "That is about what we figured. In any case, we're going to take all ten of the birdcages."

"What about their security?"

"Unimpressive. If you'll refer to the diagram, you can see that the building itself is surrounded by an eight-foot chain-link fence with barbed wire at the top. The fence is at a mean distance of one hundred and ten feet from the building. The enclosed area is well-lit and patrolled by a single night watchman, provided by a security firm in Scranton. He carries a gun and has a walkie-talkie for communicating with the internal security guard.

"The inside man handles the electronic systems. The fence and gate are wired. The building is protected by a silent alarm system and monitored by a number of television cameras. Any intruder will register on the guard's board, and the alarm signal is transmitted to the state-police barracks. The alarm goes out through an underground cable, but there is also a radio link. The inside man is armed."

"How long is the response time?"

"From Rogers' Crossing, about twelve minutes minimum. However, the Rogers' Crossing police force consists of six underpaid and badly trained young men and a chief who has been there since the thirties. At any given time, no more than three men are likely to be on duty."

"And the state police?"

"Forty-five minutes from the barracks, over winding mountain roads. If a car is in the area at the time of the alarm, the response time could be as low as ten minutes. However, as you'll see in a moment, we don't have to worry about either the state or the local police.

"As I mentioned, the initial alarm goes out over an underground cable. The exact location of that cable is indicated by the dotted line. At a point about a hundred yards from the facility, you are going to blow that cable."

I gave an ironic little internal laugh that came out as a muffled "hmmpf." So my career as a conventional bomb specialist was not yet ended.

"How deep is it buried?" I asked.

"Four feet. We have all the equipment you'll need. Serino will be there to assist you."

"What about the radio?"

Stover gestured in the direction of the expressionless red-haired man. "Morrison's department," he said. "In such a mountainous region, effective radio communication is not possible without a high aerial. PACA's aerial is forty feet high and mounted on top of the building at the point marked A. Morrison is an expert marksman. He'll cut down the aerial with a high-powered rifle and special explosive bullets."

I studied Morrison. He was square-jawed and steady-looking, and his cold blue stare was a little unsettling. I could easily imagine him with a rifle in his hands.

"What if he misses?"

Stover looked toward Morrison. The man still had not blinked, and showed no sign of resenting my expression of doubt.

"He won't," Stover said flatly. I had to believe him.

"What happens to the guards?"

"Don't worry, Boggs. We know you've never killed anyone, and you won't have to tomorrow night. No one is going to be harmed. Strange as it may seem, we want to have witnesses. Remember, the cover story is that the facility is attacked by a gang of radical terrorists. We'll give the guards some false tidbits—accidentally mentioned names, radical jargon, that sort of thing—and it should be enough to divert any investigation from our trail. Also, we want to help promote the inevitable cover-up of the incident, and that would be more difficult if the guards were killed. If the public finds out about this too soon, there will be an uncomfortable amount of pressure on the government. We don't want that."

"Nobody gets killed?"

"Not unless someone gets careless." He made a slow survey of the men at the table. "I trust that won't happen."

"How do we handle the guards?"

He glanced in the direction of the two monsters. "Mr. Locatelli and Mr. Kemper will tend to that. Locatelli does a very convincing drunk act. He will stagger up the road from the tavern and engage the outside man in some sort of conversation. At some point in the conversation the guard will be made aware of the fact that Kemper has a gun pointed at his head. We expect that he'll be more than willing to open the gate for us.

"When we have the guard taken care of, Morrison will eliminate the antenna. When you hear the shot, you'll blow the cable. That will isolate the inside guard. We will then contact him via the walkie-talkie and explain his situation to him. Since he is armed with a standard pistol and we will be carrying automatic weapons, I doubt if he'll try anything."

"And you're sure that there's no other way he can communicate with the outside?"

"None. Believe me, Boggs, all of our information is accurate. If everyone does his job correctly, we should have no problems from outside law-enforcement personnel. After we open the gate, Wynn will bring in the truck. It is a tractor trailer and will be able to accommodate all ten birdcages of plutonium.

"Using the guard's keys, we will gain access to the loading dock. On the dock will be the ten birdcages delivered in the afternoon."

"Hold it, Stover," I said. "I've done some reading, and I know something about plutonium storage. It's *shipped* in birdcages, yes, but after reaching a storage site, the birdcages are inserted in a concrete casing that weighs at least a ton. The plugs for the casings weigh three hundred and fifty pounds. We couldn't possibly move the plutonium from those casks."

Stover was unfazed. "It won't be in the casks," he said with a trace of smugness.

"How do you know?"

"Because the truck delivering the plutonium from South Carolina will be delayed en route. It's scheduled to arrive at four, but it will be late. The two workmen who handle unloading normally leave at six. They'll stay to complete the unloading, but they'll go home when they're finished. The birdcages will remain on the loading dock overnight. The next day, the workmen will come back to insert the birdcages in the concrete casks, but they will find the plutonium gone."

"I assume you've arranged all of this."

"You don't need to know any more than I've told you, Boggs," Stover snapped. "When you get there, the birdcages will be ready to go. You can count on that."

"After we get inside, what next?"

"Locatelli and Kemper will handle the loading operation. As you can see, they are well equipped for the job." Kemper was impassive, but I thought I could detect Locatelli blush slightly; he, too, had been looking at Heidi.

"Morrison," Stover continued, "will tend to the guards. Serino will be at the gate, acting as a lookout. And that reminds me." He learned forward to look around me, at Heidi. He smiled pleasantly. "You, Miss Wallace, will also have a place in our little operation to keep you out of mischief. You will be parked in a car along the side of the road, about a mile away from the facility in the direction of the town. The show

90

will begin at two A.M., and there should be no traffic at that hour. But if anyone does come along, you'll play the part of the distressed lady motorist. I don't think you should have any difficulty in getting someone to stop."

Heidi's eyes were bright and interested. I was hesitant about having her get directly involved, but it might be the best thing for her. She would feel like less of a fifth wheel, and the job of lookout probably wouldn't be dangerous.

"You'll have a walkie-talkie with you. If anyone does appear, just send a quick signal. If they get by you, relay that information. Serino will be in communication with you and will let you know when the operation is completed. Do you have any questions, Heidi?"

"Sounds okay to me," she said.

Stover beamed. I could see that he still couldn't stand her, but he was making an effort to be pleasant.

"On Serino's signal, you'll drive to the gate and pick up him and Boggs. The others will stay with the truck. Serino will then give you instructions on where to drive to."

"What if Serino is no longer around?" I asked. "Something might go wrong, you know." I flashed a quick smile at Serino.

"In that case, follow the truck. But if everyone does his job, nothing will go wrong."

"And what about you, Stover? Where will you be during all the fun?"

"Elsewhere," he said. "But I'll be with you in spirit, Boggs."

"That's comforting. So who's in charge?"

"I am, of course."

"That won't do. If we have to alter our plans, we need to have someone who's there make the decision."

"Okay, Boggs. You want to be in charge, you got the job."

I nodded to my playmates. "These gentlemen will concur with that?"

91

"They'll follow you into the very jaws of hell, Boggs."

Somehow, I doubted it. The problem with conspiracies is that they are made up of conspirators. At some point in every conspiracy, there are thoughts of double crosses, betrayals, and defections. It's unavoidable, and sometimes it can be fatal.

Since Stover had mentioned my million dollars in the presence of Wynn, they were all probably aware of it and they all probably resented it, even though they would no doubt get a few hundred grand themselves. The money would have to be big to get anyone to participate in this caper. I didn't know what my teammates had done in the past, but even if they were all hit men, this had to be something beyond what they were used to. I wondered if they were aware of the provision of the Atomic Energy Act that mandated a twenty-thousand-dollar fine and up to life imprisonment for anyone found guilty of possession or manufacture of nuclear materials or weapons with the intent to injure the United States. If the case ever came to trial, they would be sure to get the maximum.

I hoped they were unfamiliar with the Atomic Energy Rewards Act, which provides for payment of up to a half-million dollars for anyone blowing the whistle on a clandestine nuclear operation. I decided that if they didn't already know about it, I certainly wasn't going to tell them.

But there was something else about this setup that bothered me.

"I don't understand something, Stover. Why hit the PACA facility at all? From what you've said, it's obvious that you have somebody on the inside. You have access to schedules and shipping information, and you say you can delay the truck. Why not just hijack the truck? You'd get the ten birdcages and do it without all this James Bond nonsense."

Stover looked as if he had been expecting the question. His answer was ready.

"Boggs, you have to keep the scenario in mind. The attack on the PACA facility is to look as if it's been engineered by radical terrorists. That should not be very difficult to accomplish. But a truck hijacking can be done by virtually anyone. It might be more effective, but it would certainly be less impressive. It's extremely important that we give the government that red herring."

"I don't see why you couldn't make it look as if the radicals had hijacked the truck."

"It could be done, I suppose, but it would be less convincing. Boggs, do you have any idea how many trucks are hijacked every year in this country? Thousands. And do you know who is involved, directly or indirectly, in most of those thefts?"

"I can guess."

"And you'd be right, I'm sure. Everyone has a modus operandi. If the truck were hijacked, the FBI would inevitably say, "That fits the M.O. of organized crime." But knocking over the PACA site fits the M.O. of terrorist groups. It may not fool them completely, but they'll certainly concentrate their efforts on the radicals. After a hijacking, they would tend to concentrate on people who have been associated with what the authorities insist on calling 'organized' crime. I'm sure we'd all be much happier if they turned their attention elsewhere."

I wasn't satisfied by his answer. "I don't know," I said, shaking my head, "it just seems to me that you're making this a lot more complicated than it has to be."

"Believe me, Boggs," said Stover, an edge of hostility creeping into his voice, "this *is* the way it has to be."

That seemed to end it as far as he was concerned. I prefer to plan my own operations, and I never feel completely comfortable when someone hands me a script and tells me which part to play. If I were an actor, directors would call me temperamental.

"Does anyone else have any questions?" Stover asked. No one did. I had yet to hear a single word from any of my five fellow felons. Perhaps they were mutes; that might make for a more pleasant operation.

"Fine," said Stover, standing up suddenly. "You all know what has to be done. Keep the plans and timetable overnight and study them. You can return them to me before we leave."

The five men got up and left the room in silence. They seemed to have been very well trained.

"Well," said Stover, "what do you think?"

"Of what? Them? They'll do, I suppose."

"You don't need to worry about them, Boggs. They're good men, and they know what to do. But I meant, what do you think of the plan?"

"Does it matter?"

Stover smiled. "No," he admitted, "it doesn't matter one little bit. But still, I'd be interested in your professional opinion."

I studied the Xeroxed diagram for a moment. "It depends," I said, "on how good your information is."

"It's solid."

"Then you do have someone on the inside."

"Let's just say that we have reliable sources."

I folded the two sheets and slid them into the breast pocket of my jacket. "You know, Stover, I'd like this whole thing much better if you would stop playing your little games of intrigue."

Stover scratched his balding dome briefly. "I hate to say it, Boggs, but what you like or don't like is another thing that doesn't matter one little bit. And I'd still appreciate hearing your evaluation of the plan."

"It should work," I told him. "As long as there are no fuck-

94

ups. But I still say that it makes much more sense to go after the truck."

"Just do your job, Boggs." He started to walk toward the door, but I hooked his elbow.

"One more thing," I said. "The money."

"You'll get it."

"When?"

"After the operation. We're paying you to build the bomb, and you can't do that without the plutonium. When we've got it, you'll get your first installment. If something goes wrong and we don't get the plutonium, you won't be likely to need the money. One thing at a time, my friend. And by the way, your room is at the far end of the hallway. Your bags are already there."

"Many thanks."

"Get a good night's sleep, Boggs." He glanced at Heidi and added, "You too, my dear. And may I suggest that you not wander around the grounds? You could be lost for days in this place. We wouldn't want that."

I closed the door behind us and turned to survey the room. I had thought that this monument to robber-baron capitalism had used up all its surprises, but I was wrong. The room was dominated by a bed that was large enough to play football (or other team sports) on. It was canopied, and each of the four posts was elaborately carved with little cherubs and woodland sprites. The sheets and canopy were of bright red silk, with intricate baroque patterns woven into them. I felt as if I were in a New Orleans whorehouse.

Heidi breathed a subdued, "Oh, wow," then quickly kicked off her sandals, stepped out of her skimpy yellow dress, and peeled off her panties. The entire operation took about five seconds.

95

She turned to face me, spread her arms in a gesture of welcome, or something, and grinned brightly. I shook my head and started to laugh. Heidi flounced over to me and began twisting the buttons on my shirt. In her best Mae West voice she asked, "What's so funny, big boy?"

Still laughing, I asked, "Did you remember the Reddi Whip, Ruby?"

"Well I'm ready," she purred, "if you've got the whip." She hooked her left leg around behind me and started a slow, sinuous massage. Her hands performed other interesting tasks.

I gave her a long, tongue-twirling kiss that seemed to last for hours. Finally I gasped, "How much for all night, sweetie?"

"A mill-yun dollahs," she replied, still doing Mae West. "That's COD."

"COD?"

"It means 'Come on, Darlin'!'"

"Would you take a check?"

"Honey, I'll take anything you can give me."

And she did.

7

Heidi and I sat facing each other on the floor of an Econoline van. Headlights from the highway played across her eyes from time to time, causing her to squint against the glare. Aside from that, she had been motionless for an hour.

In the front, Serino was driving, and Morrison sat next to him. Morrison still had not uttered a single sound, but Serino had become surprisingly chatty. He had nothing of consequence to say, and I thought that he was talking out of nerves and anticipation. I let him rattle on without trying to engage him in conversation.

We all have our ways of trying to deal with tension. Heidi's was to go into an almost catatonic state; she hadn't spoken since we had gotten into the van. Morrison, on the other hand, seemed to be catatonic virtually all of the time, so it was difficult to tell if he felt the tension or not. It was possible that he felt nothing at all.

My own way of dealing with bad nerves was to go over the details of the plan again and again, putting myself in the shoes of every man in the operation, including the two guards. I imagined what I would do if I were a night watchman with a wife and two kids in Scranton, getting paid to patrol a lonely warehouse somewhere in the mountains. A powerfully built man sticks an M 16 against my neck and tells me to open the gate. I'm surprised as hell. I've never had the slightest problem on guard duty before. What do I do? I know there are stockpiles of plutonium inside I'm paid to protect; I know that if I don't open the gate I get my head blown off and the gate gets opened by someone else anyway. I'm not getting paid much; I've probably never fired my gun in anger. What do I do?

I let them in, that's what I do.

It made sense. That part of the plan, at least, made sense.

There were other parts that didn't.

We had been blindfolded again as we left the mansion in the back of the van. We were allowed to take them off as soon as we reached Route 95, headed into New York. There was no way for us to tell where we had been. We couldn't tell what we didn't know.

But Serino knew where we had been. And Wynn. And the others, I was sure. If Heidi and I were caught, it stood to reason that the others would also be nabbed. What sense did it make to keep us in the dark if the rest of the team shared the same risks?

Maybe they all had cyanide capsules implanted in hollow molars. Or maybe Stover had some kind of hold over them and was sure that they couldn't be made to talk.

Or maybe there was another reason.

I had spent the afternoon wandering around that immense pile of stones, looking for some small clues—to what, I didn't know. Stover had told us to stay inside and on the first floor. That still left me a lot of ground to cover.

The house did not look lived-in. There were drawing rooms and grandiose ballrooms and rooms that served no apparent purpose at all, but there were no signs that anyone had occupied those rooms since the days of Fisk and Gould. Yet it didn't have the feel of a museum, like one of the grotesque Vanderbilt estates in Newport, where they let the common folk browse around and see how the other tenth of a percent lives.

I searched for a telephone. There was no one I wanted to call, but I wanted to find the number. That could be as valuable as a street address if the time ever came when I would have to put pressure on Stover. But there were no telephones.

I wanted something I could use for leverage. Stover knew that I would write an insurance letter—he'd even encouraged me to—but unless I could put some hard facts into that letter, it would be a cheap policy indeed. All I had were names—almost certainly false—and a mammoth estate somewhere in Westchester County or Connecticut.

After an hour of fruitless investigation, I wandered back into the main hallway and found Heidi talking with Serino at the foot of that Busby Berkeley staircase. Serino appeared to be enjoying the chat. Heidi was dressed in an outfit which she said would be sure to stop any motorist on that mountain road. Her Levi's looked like they had been applied by an aerosol can. She had on a sheer white blouse with the sleeves rolled up, knotted at the waist and unbuttoned. Her nipples were dark and obvious under the thin fabric. I didn't doubt that she would catch the attention of any late-night drivers; she had caught Serino's.

They noticed me as I approached them and looked up. Serino stared at me for a moment before grinning and extending his hand. He was about five-seven, a couple of inches

shorter than me, but he was solidly built, with arm muscula-
ture that stood out like the diagrams in an anatomy book. He
had long bushy sideburns and hair that was shiny black and
carefully arranged. His tanned good looks were the sort that
reminded me of the gigolos you'd see on the beach in Spain.

I shook his hand. "Hi," he said, "Marty Serino." He
pronounced it "Mahty," in the unmistakable accent of work-
ing-class Boston.

"Hello, Marty," I said, "I'm Sam Boggs."

"Heidi's been telling me a lot about you." He glanced at
Heidi, who seemed not to be paying attention to our exchange.
"You're really gonna build an A-bomb, huh?"

"That's the plan."

He grinned again and shook his head. "Hoo-eee, that's really
fah-out." He was wearing a tight body shirt that was unbuttoned as far as Heidi's blouse. Serino, I decided, was a punk.
How he'd gotten to the big leagues, I didn't care to guess.

"Listen, Marty," I said, "just how much do you know?"

The grin disappeared. "Enough to do my job. That's all I
need to know. And it's all you need to know."

"That's what Stover keeps telling me."

"Believe him. He's a good man."

"You've worked with him before?"

The smile reappeared, but now it was a wary smile. "Oh, no,
Boggs, don't try to pump me. There's not much I could tell
you even if I wanted to. But Stover's a good man, and he takes
care of his people. You don't need to worry about him."

"What, me worry?"

He slapped me on the bicep. "You're okay, Boggs." He
turned to look at Heidi again. "Nice talking to you, Heidi. I'll
see you later." He gave me another slap, then walked off into
another part of the mausoleum.

"What did he want?" I asked her.

"Oh, just the usual, I guess." That much was pretty obvious.

Heidi's bizarre taste in clothing, or the lack of it, tended to attract the Serinos of this world in depressing numbers. I had grown used to it, and Heidi knew how to handle them.

"Did you find out anything from him?"

"Like what?"

"Like what the hell is going on around here."

She inserted her fingers into the tops of her front pockets, pulling the Levi's down another fraction of an inch. "All that happened," she said, "was that I told him I thought this was all a big game, and he asked me if I liked to play games."

"And what did you tell him?"

Heidi frowned and looked hurt. "Are you checking up on me, Sam?"

"I'm checking on Serino. I need all the information I can get."

"I'm sorry, Sam. I told him that you and I have been together for a long time. He just sort of nodded and said that it was a shame that he hadn't met me before you did. And that's when you got here. If you don't want me to talk to him, I won't."

"No, no, go ahead. You might find out something. He seems to be the only one around here with vocal cords."

"You sound worried. Do you think there's something wrong?"

"I don't know, kid, I just don't know."

Eight hours later, I still didn't know.

We had taken the George Washington Bridge and then gotten onto Route 80, cutting across northern New Jersey. A few minutes before midnight Serino pulled over into the exit lane and rolled us into a service area. He parked in an unlit corner of the lot, as far as possible from the gas pumps and restaurant.

"Okay," he announced, "this is it. Last chance to take a shit. Heidi? Sam?"

101

"I'm fine," she said. Serino didn't even ask Morrison; evidently he was immune to normal human functions, as well as emotion.

Serino opened the door on his side and beckoned to us. "This is where we make the switch, ladies and gentlemen. It's the car next to us."

We followed Serino out of the van and paused to walk around on the concrete and stretch our muscles. Serino watched with undisguised satisfaction as Heidi stuck her arms skyward and wriggled out the kinks.

At least she was comfortable. I had been given a pair of dark green work pants and a black turtleneck to wear. They itched, and the turtleneck was already sopping with perspiration. The night was thick with humidity and the sky was hazy, but there was no threat of rain. A yellow quarter moon was a few degrees above the horizon, inching upward. It could have been worse, but by the time Serino and I were out in that field rigging the explosives for the cable, we were going to be fairly well illuminated.

Serino opened the driver's door of the Ford station wagon that was parked next to us. "I'll drive," he said. "You two can ride in back if you want. Your bags are already inside. The extra suitcase has the demolition crap."

Heidi got in and slid across to the right side of the seat; I sat behind Serino. Morrison was going to stay with the van and wait for Locatelli and Kemper, who were in the truck with Wynn. The three of them would go on together in the van, and Wynn would handle the truck alone.

Serino backed out of the parking slot, gave a wave to Morrison, then gunned it back out onto the highway. He immediately took us up to sixty-five and settled permanently into the left lane.

"This isn't a race, Marty. Let's try to get there without getting stopped for speeding."

Serino shrugged and eased up on the accelerator. According to Stover's timetable, at fifty-five miles an hour we would be at the facility by one-thirty. That would give us about twenty-five minutes to set the charge.

I settled back into the seat and tried to relax. Heidi was curled up in the corner of the back seat, arms crossed and feet propped on the transmission hump. I wondered what she was thinking. It was early Friday morning; Sunday afternoon, she had been splashing in the warm waters of Torremolinos.

And I had been basking on the beach. Stover had swooped down out of nowhere like an eagle stealing a baby from its crib, and now I was hurtling along through the darkness toward Rogers' Crossing, Pennsylvania. I didn't trust Stover, I loathed Serino, and everyone else mystified me. I didn't really want to build an atomic bomb, not for anyone. And I had no idea what the hell I was going to do with a million dollars even if we did manage to pull this thing off.

I considered reaching for Serino's chunky neck, putting my hands around it, and telling him to keep on driving, right past Rogers' Crossing, PACA, the plutonium, Stover, and all the insane things that had come into my life. Keep on driving, until he brought me back to Berkeley and the year 1965, where I could go back to Susan and plastics and the Chemistry Department; where I could try again.

But Serino couldn't drive that far. And I wouldn't know what to do when I got there. So go with the flow, Boggs. Play the game. Build the bomb. You have nothing to lose.

The PACA facility gleamed like an industrial diamond under the glare of a hundred spotlights. Serino slowed the car as we came down out of the mountains, and we rolled past the gate at a conservative twenty miles an hour. The building was about a hundred and fifty feet wide and perhaps three hundred deep. It was constructed of heavy steel panels, painted green, and didn't look as if it contained anything of value. Gram for gram, plutonium is about the most expensive thing there is in the world—and the most dangerous. The PACA building should have looked like Fort Knox. Stover was right; it was only a matter of time until somebody stole enough plutonium to build a bomb. It might as well be us.

The land sloped up sharply to the east, in the direction we had come from, and fell away more gently as we continued past the fence. Beyond the fence there was an open field a hundred yards wide. At the far edge of the field a line of trees and a wooden rail fence marked the beginning of pastureland. As we drew even with the trees, we passed a yellow highway sign that announced an S curve ahead.

"There it is," said Serino. He drove on around the first limb of the curve and pulled to the side of the road. "Get the black suitcase, Boggs. And don't forget this."

He tossed me a garishly striped ski mask. Wool. That was going to feel just great. I stuffed it into my back pocket as I got out of the car. Heidi slid across to me, and I reached for her hand and helped her out. I leaned back in and lifted the suitcase out of the rear.

"You've got the walkie-talkie?"

"In my purse," she answered. I looked into her eyes and tried to find some reflection of what was going through her mind. She ought to have been scared or nervous, but all I could see was a kind of unfocused calm. She kept saying that it was all a game; maybe she really believed it.

I kissed her, then drew her into a tight embrace. "If anything goes wrong," I whispered, "if you hear a lot of shots, take off. Don't wait around for anything. Go back to New York and check in at the same hotel. If you don't hear from me by Sunday . . ."

"Don't worry, Sam. Everything's going to be all right."

I should have been reassuring her, but somehow the tables had been turned. It was just one more thing that didn't make any sense.

"You ready?" Serino asked.

I nodded. "Heidi, you know what to do?"

"Go down the road a mile, turn the car around, watch, and wait. I think I can handle that," she said with a hint of a smile.

Heidi got back into the car, threw me a kiss, and rolled off into the night. I lugged the suitcase over to the side of the road and immediately stepped into a ditch and nearly broke my ankle. There was water in the ditch, and I got my right leg soaked almost to the knee.

"Good start," Serino observed.

I picked myself up and started out again, this time sticking to the gravel shoulder. We came back around the bend, within sight of the PACA facility. I squinted into the glare of the floodlights and tried to spot the outside guard. There was no sign of him. The moon was high in the sky now, to our right; that was good, since our shadows fell on the field and blended in with the random night shapes.

Serino removed a large surveyor's tape measure from his back pocket. I took the end of the reel and knelt down by the post of the road sign. "Two hundred and ten feet, right?"

"Right," he answered. He held the spool in both hands, hopped over the ditch, and began trotting backward, uncoiling the tape. I held my end of it against the signpost and nervously glanced over one shoulder, then the other. I was more or less out in the open, and if a car had come by just then, I would have been hard pressed to explain what I was doing holding the end of a tape measure against an S-curve sign at one-thirty in the morning.

Serino was also clearly visible, but he could have ducked into the shadows of the trees, about ten feet to the left of the line. He was hunched over like an infantryman reeling out a phone line across a battlefield. He suddenly slipped on something and plopped abruptly on his ass. I heard an angry whisper of "cowshit" floating on the mild night breeze, and allowed myself a smile. I would hear no more criticism from Serino.

At last I felt a sharp tug on the tape. I held it between thumbs and forefingers as Serino pulled it taut. The pressure suddenly relaxed, and I looked up to see Serino waving to me. I let go of the tape, grabbed the suitcase, and took a quick look for the outside guard. There was still no sign of him. I carefully stepped over the ditch and made my way out to Serino, taking particular caution about where I put my feet.

When I got there, he was laughing. He didn't offer an explanation, but simply pointed. About three feet away from the position he'd marked, there was a short metal sign. "Danger," it said, "Underground Cables—Do Not Excavate."

"My God"—Serino chuckled—"these people are really begging for it." I had to agree.

We unlatched the suitcase and laid out the items we would need. Our digging tool consisted of three interlocking steel rods, two and a half feet long and an inch in diameter. One of the rods had a spiraled screw bit at the end of it. I inserted the other end of it into the middle of the perpendicular crossbar and spun the two rods until the connection was tight. The third rod was simply an extender which we would put between the first two after the hole was started.

I handed the assembly to Serino. "Get it started. I want to check the charges."

Serino took it by the crossbar of the T, stuck the point into the ground at the spot he'd marked, then leaned on the crossbar with all his weight. The tip of the shaft sank about three inches into the ground. "Pretty soft, so far," he said. Now it was simply a case of screwing the bit into the earth, using the crossbar for leverage. It was like winding up the rubber band of a toy airplane by turning the propeller.

I looked at the explosives. We were using C-4, packed into metal tubes an inch in diameter. When the holes were finished, we'd simply drop the tubes into them. The only thing that really required checking was the wiring. I threaded it between my fingers, looking for breaks or corrosion in the insulation, but found none. While I was involved with the wire, Serino attached the third section of the rod and went back to sinking the shaft.

I remembered that we had forgotten to reel in the tape measure. It wouldn't have been wise to leave it behind, but it would have been awkward trying to run with two hundred and ten feet of tape trailing out behind us. I started to wind it up, keeping my eyes on the building.

There was a sudden motion at the rear corner of the building. I shielded my eyes against the glare of the lights and saw someone walking slowly in our direction.

"Down!" I breathed to Serino. He looked up in surprise, turned to check the building, then flattened with the catlike quickness of a football player doing an up-and-down drill.

A hundred yards away, the guard walked straight at us for a few seconds, then turned to his left and strolled on along the side of the building, going toward the road. Unless he had some reason to turn his head to the right, he would never see us.

"Okay," I told Serino. "But keep low." He went back to turning the rods, and I picked up the tape-measure reel and continued winding. It had an annoying squeak once every revolution, but it wasn't loud, and there was nothing I could do about it anyway.

When I had the tape almost in, Serino announced, "Got it. Right on the button."

"You're sure? Let me check." I scrambled over to Serino on my hands and knees and grabbed the crossbar. I lifted it a few inches, then let it drop. It didn't penetrate any farther. I tapped it up and down a few times; there was definitely some obstruction down there, and from the feel of the vibrations, it didn't seem to be a rock. About a foot of rod remained above the ground. We were down four feet, the depth of the cable.

I nodded to Serino. "That's it. Make the other holes about six inches to either side of this one, and about that much deeper."

I wanted to use three separate charges, one directly above the cable and the others on both sides, just below it. If they all went off together, it should catch the cable in a whipsaw action and sever it neatly. To make sure, I was using about twice as much explosive as I needed. The cable was the key to the entire operation, and I wanted to be absolutely certain that it was gone. Otherwise, we might find ourselves in a shootout with the Pennsylvania state police.

The guard had reached the front gate. We wouldn't have to worry about him for another lap.

The second hole struck a rock about two feet down. Serino flexed his impressive muscles and tried to grind right through it, but had no success. He withdrew the rods, and I stuck a penlight into the top of the hole. I couldn't see much.

I told him to try again, three inches farther along the line of the cable. "Make sure you don't cave in the original hole. I don't want a crater." Serino made no comment, but went to work on the new hole. This one went more smoothly, and he had it down to the right depth by the time the guard reappeared at the corner of the building.

I checked my watch. "Plenty of time," I said. "We might as well wait until he's out of sight."

Serino rolled over onto his back and flopped his arms out in a Christlike pose. "Whew!" he sighed. "Don't work too hard, Boggs."

"You just keep on doing what you're good at, Marty. I'll mention to Stover how hard you worked."

"You do that. Hell, the money I'm getting paid, I'll dig holes all day long. A hundred thousand dollars a hole. Christ, what a job!"

"Nothing like it back in Boston, huh, Marty?"

He lolled his head in my direction and grinned. "You can tell, huh?"

"You might as well wear a sign. Let me guess—Dorchester?"

"Nah," he said. "Revere." He pronounced it "Revee-ah." "You ever been there?"

"The beach, once. Not much of a beach."

"I suppose you're used to all those classy beaches in Europe. When this is over, maybe I'll check them out. When were you in Boston?"

"Years ago. In my Ivy League days. So tell me, how's old Sonny Dee?"

He started to answer, but suddenly caught himself. He gave me one of those cautious grins that he seemed to have learned from Stover. "I don't know who you're talking about," he said. I could tell that I'd learned as much as I was going to from Serino, for the moment, at least.

Sonny Dee was one Salvatore Dibiase, also known as the Treasurer. He handled the Mafia's cash flow in Boston, and he kept himself well hidden from public view. He knew how to launder money and keep himself squeaky clean in the process. I had once performed a modest task for him, for which he had paid well.

If Serino had any connections at all with organized crime in Boston, he would know Sonny Dee. He said that he didn't, but that was meaningless. The real answer had come in the split second before he realized that he shouldn't tell me any more. For that brief instant, I was sure that Serino was about to say, "Who?"

I was guessing at too much. I didn't really know what Serino had been about to say. Maybe he was going to tell me that Sonny Dee was an old girlfriend. I told myself to file away my doubts and concentrate on the job at hand.

The guard had disappeared from view again. Serino started the third hole. I went back to sorting wires.

The hole was finished by the time the guard emerged from the shadows behind the building. Serino left the rods in the hole, wanting to avoid the clanking of metal as he disassembled the tool. I began inserting the wires into the tubes of plastic explosive. My last time at bat, I thought. After this one, I was hanging up the old detonators.

We watched as the guard performed his ritual of checking the gate. "Next time around," I told Serino. I glanced at my watch; it was one-fifty-four. Somewhere behind us on the road, Locatelli was getting ready to stagger up to the gate. Kemper and Morrison were in the trees on the other side of the road, checking their rifles. Wynn was up on the mountain, all set to come barreling down in that big rig. And Stover was probably sitting comfortably in that ridiculous mansion, having a drink.

I checked the wires again, making sure they were firmly embedded in the tubes. "Okay," I said. "Here we go." One by one, I lowered the explosives into the holes, playing out the wire at a steady, even pace. Serino gently tamped them down with the steel rod. From the amount of wire I had uncoiled, I could tell that the tubes were snugly settled at the bottom.

As Serino hastily put the rods back in the suitcase, I concentrated on not getting the wires tangled as I strung them out in the direction of the trees. Twenty feet from the holes, I sat down behind a gnarled oak tree and began connecting the wires to the detonator switch. Now that harmless gray putty was as dangerous as a bottle of nitroglycerine. Serino joined me behind the tree, carrying the suitcase with him.

"Now we wait," he said. That was always the toughest part of any operation for me. I wished that I could light up a cigarette.

I thought of Heidi, whose entire job consisted of waiting. Alone in that car, she would have plenty of time to worry. But somehow, I didn't think she would. A strange part of Heidi was beginning to emerge, something I had not seen before and didn't understand. The average California beach bunny would have been freaked out by this operation, but Heidi seemed more calm the more deeply she became involved. Perhaps she was adjusting the narrow limits of her own reality in order to accept the bizarre world I had thrust at her. Adaptability; that was the secret of survival. Heidi would be okay.

Serino suddenly stuck out his arm and pointed silently. The guard had rounded the corner and was headed slowly toward the gate and his rendezvous with Locatelli. I heard an incoherent voice from the road and looked, to see a thick, shadowy form lurching along unsteadily. It was Locatelli, doing his drunk act, and he appeared to be carrying a bottle in his left hand. With a tavern two miles down the road, the guard would probably find nothing suspicious about some

111

anonymous tipsy character appearing out of the early-morning darkness. He might even welcome the intrusion.

I examined the building more closely. The loading dock was facing us, about a hundred feet down the side wall from the corner nearest the road. There was a blacktop parking area with ample room to maneuver a big truck. The radio antenna was on the roof, extending up into the blackness; it was difficult to see against the looming hulk of the mountainside.

Locatelli was at the gate now, raucously singing some unidentifiable song. He started shaking the fence. The guard picked up his pace a little and advanced to meet Locatelli. His gun was not drawn. Why should it have been? This was just some sodden bastard wandering around on the highway.

The guard made gestures expressing patience and understanding. Maybe he was hoping Locatelli would offer him some of his booze. They talked for a few more seconds. Then, with a suddenness that surprised me, even though I was expecting it, Kemper leaped out of the bushes and leveled an automatic rifle at the guard.

Serino flashed me a thumbs-up signal. I wasn't so sure. If I were the guard, it would take me a few seconds to realize the situation I was in; during that time, I might do something foolish.

But this man was too smart to try anything. Kemper, wearing his ski mask, had advanced to point-blank range, with the barrel of the rifle poking through the mesh of the gate and tucked under the guard's chin. Morrison appeared now, also masked, cradling a hunting rifle with a telescopic sight.

I heard the low tones of Kemper issuing instructions. The guard reached very slowly for his keys, then obediently unlocked the gate. Locatelli, moving with surprising agility for such a huge man, bounced through the opened gate and relieved the guard of his gun. The guard flattened on the pavement of the driveway, his hands clasped behind him. Locatelli produced a length of rope and began binding up the guard.

Now it was Morrison's turn. With the unhurried precision that marked all his movements, Morrison eased the barrel of his rifle through one of the holes in the chain-link fence. With the barrel braced and balanced, he took his time sighting on the rooftop antenna. This was as crucial as blowing the cable, and I held my breath while he aimed. It would have to be one hell of a shot.

I saw Morrison jerk abruptly, and a split second later I heard the potent crack of the high-powered rifle. It was followed immediately by a ringing *wham!* from the explosive bullet.

"He got it!" Serino exulted. I motioned for him to get down, then twisted the detonator switch. The ground in front of us bounced convulsively, and we felt the shock in our feet before the muffled sound of the explosion reached us. There was a pitter-patter of raining dirt, and then nothing except the smell and the sight of smoke drifting lazily upward from out of the earth.

"That's all?" asked Serino, disappointed. It had been a pretty unimpressive event, considering all the work he had put in on those holes.

"What did you expect, a mushroom cloud?" I gathered in the loose ends of wire, wrapped them around the detonator switch, and threw it into the suitcase.

I was interrupted by the ringing crack of Morrison's rifle and another sharp thunderclap.

"The son of a bitch missed it the first time!" I kicked a clump of loose sod. Morrison had given the inside man an extra fifteen seconds to get off a message.

"Come on," I said, "let's get this thing over with." I picked

113

up the suitcase and trotted diagonally across the field toward the front gate. Serino, not carrying anything, dashed past me.

"Hold it!" I shouted. He stopped short. "Your ski mask, Serino."

I fished my mask out of my back pocket and pulled it down over my face. There were large holes for ears, eyes, nose, and mouth, but the damned thing was still as uncomfortable as an iron maiden. Wool and sweat do not mix.

By the time we got to the gate, the guard was back on his feet, hands tied behind him, and Kemper was pushing him ahead toward the building, using the barrel of his M 16 as a prod. Morrison stood, blank-faced, holding his rifle at port arms.

"What the hell happened?"

At last Morrison spoke. It was a flat, unconcerned voice. "The first one hit but didn't bring it down. I got it with the second one. See for yourself."

I peered at the roof and saw a jagged stump of antenna rising about a dozen feet into the air. There was no sign of the rest of it.

"Morrison," I said, "you'd better hope that he didn't get off a signal."

"He didn't have the time."

I turned to Locatelli. "Have you contacted him yet?"

"It's all yours." He handed me the guard's walkie-talkie.

I paused for a moment. I couldn't think of how I should address him. "Hey, you in there" would have sounded faintly ridiculous. I finally settled on a weak "Hello."

"Yeah, Jim," crackled the response.

"This isn't Jim," I told him. "Jim has an M 16 pointed at his head right now. Your communications are cut off, and there is nothing you can do. Come on out . . ." (I almost said "with your hands up") ". . . the front door. Keep your hands in

114

plain sight, away from your gun. We'll be waiting for you. If you do exactly as I tell you, nobody will get hurt."

I waited for him to reply. He was probably checking his equipment.

"Your radio works, but the antenna is down. No one can hear you. And the underground cable is cut. We can get what we came for with you dead just as easily as with you alive. Be smart and do it our way."

After a few more seconds of silence, he answered, "Okay. I'm coming out. The front door, just like you said." I handed the radio back to Locatelli.

"You and Kemper and Morrison cover the door. I don't want any shots fired." Locatelli pulled a deadly-looking pistol out of the waistband of his pants and nodded to me, then sprinted down the driveway.

"Serino," I said, "you mind the gate. Close it as soon as Wynn gets in with the truck. And keep out of sight."

"That was the plan, wasn't it?" Serino eyed me contemptuously. Even behind the black-and-yellow ski mask, he had the air of someone who knows he's smarter than his boss.

I was supposedly the leader of this Halloween party, but I realized that no one was really paying the slightest attention to what I said. I didn't particularly care if I was the leader or not, but if I wasn't, I wanted to know who was.

There was a sudden roar of a diesel engine, and Wynn emerged from the mountainside shadows in a monstrous tractor trailer. I though he was going too fast, but I wasn't giving him enough credit. He downshifted and braked smoothly, swung wide, and executed a perfect turn into the driveway. Without bothering to check to see what was happening, Wynn rumbled straight down the drive, veered left, and whipped the big rig around the corner. I figured that he would be in position at the loading dock before we even got there.

Serino pulled the gate shut and sat down in the tall grass at the base of the fence. "Go get it, boss," he said.

I dogtrotted toward the front door of the building, still lugging the heavy suitcase. The mask was so unbearable by now that for a moment I thought that if we killed both guards, I could take the fucking thing off. And I suppose people have been killed for a lot less.

Locatelli, who was the only one of us without a mask, stood against the wall at the side of the door, pistol ready. Kemper was directly in front of the door, with the first guard on his knees and the rifle at the back of his neck. Morrison stood idly by, fondling his hunting rifle.

A muted shout came from inside. "I'm coming out!"

The door opened slowly, revealing a portly man in his fifties, dressed in a drab gray industrial security uniform. The first thing he saw was Kemper, raising the barrel of his M 16 to gut level. His eyes widened a little, and before he could raise his arms, Locatelli grabbed him and removed his gun from its holster.

"Okay," I said. "Around back." They were moving even before I said it.

Locatelli tossed me a set of keys. I grabbed at it but missed, batting it into the grass at the edge of the driveway. I retrieved the keys and trotted after the others, the very picture of leadership in action. I resolved not to open my mouth again.

As I expected, Wynn had the truck backed up to the loading dock and was already opening up the trailer. Though we had never spoken, I liked Wynn. He was thoroughly competent, and he had the look of a man who had seen enough not to be impressed or upset by anyone or anything he encountered.

There was a windowless door adjacent to the loading area, painted a pale puke-green like the rest of the building. I grabbed the inside guard by the shoulder and held the keys in

116

his face. "Which one?" I asked. There were at least twenty different keys on the ring.

He pointed to one of them. I stared at him for a moment and tried to put myself into his shoes. I would have been scared silly; he didn't appear to be. Perhaps he had been through this before at some musty warehouse in Scranton. The fact that it was plutonium he was guarding, instead of television sets, probably made no difference to him. He was getting paid to punch a time clock, not to get himself blown away by an automatic rifle.

The key worked, and I pushed the door open. I entered the dark building first, even though I was the only one who wasn't armed. I ought to have had a gun, but the things frankly terrify me. High explosives were like old friends to me, but handguns and rifles were out of my realm entirely.

I found a light switch. A short flight of a half-dozen steps led me up to the level of the loading platform. Overhead, unfrosted light bulbs cast sharp, dense shadows. Lined up on the platform in two rows of five were the plutonium birdcages. They looked like elongated oil barrels, about five feet high and two in diameter, painted black. They were decorated with the standard radioactivity warning signs, and Atomic Energy Commission seals were attached to the tops of the canisters.

Locatelli joined me on the platform, followed by Morrison, the two guards, and Kemper. We stared in silence at the deadly containers. It was a moment of reverence and awe, as if we had broken into a cathedral. The great atomic god lay at our feet.

Kemper broke the spell by telling the guards to lie down on their stomachs. While Morrison held his rifle on them, Kemper tied up the second guard. They couldn't move, and I doubted if they felt like talking.

I found the switch that operated the corrugated door of the

117

loading dock. I pressed it, and the door retracted upward into the ceiling, rattling as it went.

The illumination from outside flooded in and made the platform seem less cavernous and shadowy. We were in a receiving room, about thirty by sixty. The concrete floor was empty except for the birdcages and a small forklift that had been adapted for handling the canisters.

Wynn hopped onto the platform from the truck and clapped his hands together, as if to say, "Let's get rolling."

"Okay," I said. "You know what to do." Which was more than I did. There was nothing left for me to do but stand around and watch and stay out of the way.

I slid the suitcase into the truck and allowed myself the luxury of turning away from the guards and peeling off the ski mask. My face was dripping. I rubbed it and scratched it and mopped it with the sleeve of my turtleneck. Then I reluctantly pulled the mask back on and immediately felt worse than ever.

_Kemper and Locatelli struggled with the birdcages while Wynn rolled the forklift into position. It really wasn't that much of a struggle; although each birdcage weighed four hundred pounds, either one of them probably could have handled the job alone. I noticed that there was a small crane at the corner of the dock. The regular workmen probably used it to lift the birdcages out of the truck. Kemper and Locatelli didn't need to bother with it.

While Locatelli tilted the containers, Kemper latched onto the bottom of them; then they gingerly deposited them on the tongs of the forklift. The loading apron of the truck was flush with the platform, and Wynn drove the forklift right into the trailer. In the shadows at the far front end of the truck, Wynn released the birdcages, lining them up in a neat row. Then he backed the forklift onto the platform at a surprising speed. Wynn was one of those natural drivers who can handle

118

anything from a baby carriage to a Sherman tank with the skill and style of a Le Mans veteran.

While Wynn was unloading the seventh birdcage, I walked over to inspect the remaining three. Locatelli and Kemper were breathing hard but seemed to be enjoying their work.

Stenciled across the top of the birdcages in white paint were series of identifying numbers. I knew that the plutonium produced by a number of commercial reactors was stored here, waiting for the coming of the breeder reactors. Presumably each company had its own series of identifying numbers. These read "GP—S.Car. 1-1673," with the final digits varying from birdcage to birdcage. It didn't tell me much about whose plutonium we were stealing, other than the fact that it came from South Carolina, which I already knew. At about ten dollars a gram, we would be walking away with a quarter of a million dollars' worth of plutonium; and we were going to sell it back to them for many times that amount. Such is the curious nature of plutonium.

On the opposite side of the platform, Morrison stood with his back to us, still caressing his rifle. Morrison probably felt the same way about guns that Wynn felt about vehicles; I vastly preferred Wynn's obsession. The two guards lay side-by-side, facedown. They couldn't have moved if they had tried, but Morrison was ready to shot them if they did. At such close range, with explosive bullets, one shot could finish them both.

Wynn rolled onto the platform backward, ready for another load. Locatelli, sweating freely, leaned into the next birdcage, tilting it enough for Kemper to be able to get a grip on the bottom. Locatelli tossed his head to get sweat and hair out of his eyes; Kemper must have thought it was a signal. He lifted his end with a strained grunt, catching Locatelli by surprise. It threw him off balance. Locatelli staggered backward under the sudden load and lost his grip.

The birdcage slipped out of his hands, and Kemper dived away from it to avoid having his feet crushed. It hit sideways with a jarring *clang* and rolled straight at Morrison. He didn't see it coming, but some instinct told him to jump. He did, late. The birdcage caught Morrison's heels and flipped him; the rifle went flying out of his grasping fingers. It hit the concrete and went off.

The bullet ripped into the center of the rolling birdcage and exploded with a blast that made my ears ring. The birdcage kept rolling, narrowly missing the heads of the two guards, then slammed into the concrete wall on the far side of the platform. It bounced, rolled a half revolution back in my direction, then stopped. There was a jagged three-inch hole in the middle of it, just above the floor.

Kemper and Morrison were frozen in place where they hit the floor. We watched, not even breathing, as a viscous black liquid gurgled out of the ripped birdcage and formed a spreading pool on the concrete. It flowed, it expanded, it advanced across the platform like a living thing. I stared at it in horror, as if hypnotized by a cobra. The pool crawled onward, toward the two guards, just a few feet away.

Jim, the outside man, screamed, an inhuman, terror-stricken explosion of sound. He tried to roll away, but was stopped by the bulk of the other guard, who seemed unable to move. He arched his back and flopped like a fresh-caught fish. The black stain flowed under his chin, lapping at the shores of his chest and shoulders.

If he had kept still, he would have been all right. But unbridled horror drove him; he strained against the ropes, his face red, the cords of his neck standing out like the cables of a bridge. He arched his back again, flopped once more, and landed with his face in the middle of the puddle of plutonium nitrate.

The rest of us finally came out of our trance of terror. Locatelli grabbed the inside guard by the back of his belt and lifted him away from the pool with one quick, powerful motion. I raced to the other one, who was trying to hold his head out of the puddle. His eyes were shut tightly, his teeth bared, turning his face into a dripping black gargoyle. I hesitated for a second, then hooked him by the back of his collar and dragged him to the other side of the platform. I rolled the man onto his back. His eyes were still shut, but his mouth was opened wide in a futile, silent scream. I didn't want to touch him.

"It burns!" he shrieked. "It burns, it burns, oh, Jesus God, it burns!"

Locatelli knelt down next to me. He stared at the man's blackened face, then turned to me with a look of helplessness. His mouth hung open, unable to frame the question that all of us already knew the answer to.

He was still screaming. I balled my fist and punched him as hard as I could in the solar plexus. It knocked the wind out of him and shut him up. He lay there gagging.

"Stop it!" I grabbed him by the dry hair on the back of his head and lifted him up. "Listen to me, dammit! Did you swallow any? Did it get in your nose?"

He answered me by retching all over the front of his uniform. I released his hair and let him turn his head and go on throwing up.

"Water," I said. "Is there any water?"

The fat inside guard, his face the color of a dirty sheet, pointed toward the back of the platform. "There's a hose over there," he said weakly. "They use it to wash down the floor."

Locatelli sprang to his feet and brought back the hose. Wynn jumped off his forklift and ran back to turn on the water. I took the hose from Locatelli, nodded to Wynn, and sprayed the guard full force. He tried to squirm away from it, but Locatelli held him in place.

"Sit still, damn it! You can take this a hell of a lot better than you can take plutonium nitrate in your pores."

I kept on spraying him until the last traces of gunk were off his face. His shoulders and chest were soaked dark with the stuff, but that wouldn't harm him. Finally, I gestured to Wynn, and he cut off the flow.

"Listen to me, Jim," I told him. "That's your name, isn't it? Jim, did you get any of it into your mouth?"

He moaned. "It burns, it burns."

"That's just the acid, Jim. They make the stuff with nitric acid. It burns, but it won't kill you. Open your eyes, Jim, and tell me if you got any of it in your mouth."

His eyes opened, and I wished they hadn't. His pupils were shrunk down to almost nothing, engulfed in the white sea of his corneas. I had never seen anything like it; here was terror Poe and Lovecraft never even dreamed of. If he had been struck by a rattlesnake or stung by a scorpion, he could have handled it. The pain must have been terrible, but pain, at least, was familiar. It was the fear of that nightmarish black substance that overwhelmed him.

He could tell me nothing. I took a deep breath, then stuck my fingers into his mouth, grabbing him by the lips and chin like a veterinarian examining a horse.

His gums were black. His tongue was black.

I released him gently and stood up. I felt light-headed.

Morrison stood there, impassively observing the scene, the rifle once again cradled in his arms. I walked over to him, jerked the rifle away, and slammed him in the gut with the butt end. He crashed to the floor and skidded a few inches.

I aimed the rifle at his empty face. There was still not a trace of emotion. He didn't need the ski mask; there was nothing there to hide.

"I don't know a damn thing about guns, Morrison, but I do know enough to leave the safety on. Let's see if you know that much."

I brought the sight up to my eye. It was too close to see anything but a blur. I tightened my finger on the trigger.

"It's not on!" he shouted suddenly. "Jesus Christ, don't pull that trigger!"

I lowered the rifle. There was emotion on Morrison's face now, wide-eyed fear. He knew I would do it. He knew he was seconds away from having his head splattered all over the loading platform. His lips moved silently.

I let him feel the fear. I wanted him to know how that poor bastard guard felt. I raised the rifle again.

Wynn put his palm on the barrel and gently pushed it away from Morrison. He looked at me for a long moment with those creased and worn cowboy eyes of his, and I felt the rage seep out of me. He took the gun from me and clicked the safety into position.

"What about him?" Wynn asked, pointing to the guard.

I peeled off the ski mask and threw it into the back of the truck. I didn't care who saw me now. I was sick of the whole fucking thing.

"It got into his mouth," I said quietly. "He'll be dead within a day or two." I looked at him, sprawled out on the concrete, actually quivering with fright. "Maybe sooner," I added.

"Jesus," said Locatelli.

We all turned to look at him. Radiation poisoning is the worst way to die that the fruitful mind of man has yet devised. A massive dose literally kills every cell in the body. The guard would soon begin to vomit up green bile; it would leak out of his ears and eyes. His hair would fall out, his gums would bleed, he would shit uncontrollably. His lungs would turn into a mass of bloody, fibrous tissue. His brain would fill up with fluid. He would die. It couldn't happen soon enough.

123

Wynn seemed to read my thoughts. He tossed the rifle back at Morrison and drew a .45 service automatic out of his belt. "I'll do it," he said to Morrison. "You'd enjoy it too much."

"What about the rest of the stuff?" asked Kemper.

"Leave it," I said. "We've got all we need." Kemper nodded, and Locatelli seemed to breathe a relieved sigh. They were only too willing to follow my order.

Wynn stood over the guard, pistol in his hand. The other guard yelled, "Hey, wait a minute! There wasn't supposed to be any—"

Kemper picked up his M 16 and aimed it at him. "Shut up, goddammit, or you'll get it too."

The guard opened his mouth again, then closed it. Now, at least, I knew who the inside man was. A vital bit of knowledge, that.

"Well," said the guard, "I suppose it's for the best."

I looked down at the puddle of plutonium nitrate. It had spread halfway across the floor. "Come on," I said, "let's get out of here."

"Don't leave me inside!" wailed the guard. Locatelli grabbed him, picked him up like a sack of flour, and deposited him roughly on the ground next to the truck. Kemper and Morrison walked back into the trailer, glancing uneasily at the seven birdcages.

I turned to Wynn. He was kneeling beside the dying guard. They made a sad little tableau: the cowboy, the doomed young man, and the gleaming black pool.

I walked slowly down the driveway, trying not to think of anything at all. At some point, the truck passed me.

"What the hell happened in there?" Serino asked me when I reached the gate.

"Be happy you missed it."

"Yeah? Well, let's go, Boggs. I signaled to Heidi, and she's on her way." We walked past the gate, and Serino closed it behind us.

"I know one thing," said Serino happily. "We just pulled off the damnedest caper in history."

I knew one thing, too.

I could not build an atomic bomb. Not for a million dollars. Not for anything.

8

Heidi picked us up in front of the gate. Serino got into the back seat while I sat down in front, next to Heidi. She hit the gas pedal even before I had shut the door; we fishtailed for a second on the loose gravel of the shoulder, then straightened out and darted forward, up the mountain road.

I looked at her. There was a thin patina of perspiration on her forehead and upper lip. Her mouth was pursed together tightly. There was an odd look about her; not nerves, but something else I couldn't define. It was in her eyes, mainly, a kind of faraway stare that saw without really seeing. I felt as if I had seen that look before, and ought to be able to identify it, but I couldn't.

"Are you okay, Heidi?"

My words seemed to penetrate very slowly. After a few seconds she glanced toward me, smiled, and said, "Everything was fine."

"No problems?"

"None." I waited for her to ask how things had gone at the PACA facility, but she didn't. Finally, Serino asked.

I told him what had happened, using as few words as possible.

"Holy Christ," he said. "What a thing to happen." He was sobered by it, but I thought that he wished he could have seen it. Heidi said nothing at all.

We followed the twisting mountain road most of the way back to Scranton. Serino told Heidi to get onto the turnpike and head south. It was 3:27 when we stopped at the toll booth to get our ticket.

For the rest of the night we rode in silence. Serino dozed for short, nervous intervals. I wanted desperately to be able to sleep, but adrenaline was still pumping through me. Heidi kept her eyes on the road and seldom even blinked.

Sometime after dawn we intersected with the east-west part of the turnpike. I had to wake Serino to ask him which way we should go. He yawned and said west. Twenty minutes later he instructed Heidi to take the King of Prussia exit. Long lines of commuters were already waiting at the toll boths for their tickets, but we were the only ones getting off the turnpike at that hour.

We drove past a huge General Electric space-research plant and a cancerous shopping mall, then turned right. Serino pointed to a motel ahead of us. "We have reservations there," he said.

Serino checked us in while I unloaded our luggage and Heidi walked around the parking lot stretching her muscles. The sun was shining brightly, and I wanted to sleep.

Our room was next to Serino's, facing the highway and a small blue swimming pool. The rumble of passing trucks actually made the room shake, as if it were built on springs.

Aside from that, it was a standard, pseudo-luxurious motel room, with a color television and magic fingers on the beds. The decor was in rich oranges and browns, and there was a print of a Roman gladiator on the wall between the two beds. Its significance escaped me.

I sat on the end of one of the beds and stripped off the black turtleneck. It was immediately obvious that I needed a shower, but I couldn't force myself to move in the direction of the bathroom, or in any other direction. The entire world seemed to be dissolving into a grainy black-and-white print, and I wanted to get far away from it.

Heidi sat down next to me and began massaging my back and neck. I was so far gone that I couldn't tell whether it felt good or not. Heidi kept on rubbing and stroking, and it gradually dawned on me that this was merely intended as a prelude. I turned my head to look at her. The blouse had come unknotted, and her small, perfect breasts swayed back and forth with the rhythm of the massage. I felt a brief, intense kindling of desire somewhere in the back of my brain, but the groaning weight of my fatigue and depression soon snuffed the fires.

I expended my last reservoirs of energy and kissed her lightly on the cheek. "Not now," I said. She continued the massage for a few moments but saw that it was getting her nowhere. She stood up in front of me, removed the blouse, and then slowly unzipped her Levi's to reveal the small fraction of her body that had been concealed. I crawled up to the head of the bed, as if to get away from her.

"Sam!" she insisted. It sounded like a demand.

Head buried in the pillow, I mumbled, "I'm sorry, Heidi. I really am. Can't it wait?"

"No, dammit, it can't!"

I looked up, surprised by the shrillness in her voice. She was on the bed, nude now, sitting with her legs splayed apart like a *Penthouse* centerfold. Her face was twisted into a strange, angry expression.

My mind was not functioning well at all. I understood what she wanted; I just didn't know why.

"Heidi, I need to sleep. I've had one hell of a night, and I need to sleep."

"*You've* had one hell of a night! Do you think I haven't?"

I didn't know what to think. "I had to watch a man die in the ugliest way you can imagine." I thought that would somehow explain everything.

Heidi started to say something, then stopped herself. She crept forward on the bed, put her hand on my thigh, and began another, more sensuous massage. It had no effect.

"Sam, I *need* it!" She nearly sobbed.

I reached out for her and grabbed her hand. I couldn't think of anything to say. My body, and hers, seemed very distant.

"*Please!*" There were tears in her eyes. Real tears.

I couldn't help her. "I'm sorry, honey. We'll both feel more like it after we sleep. I promise."

She stared at me for a moment more, silently pleading with me. Then she jumped suddenly off the bed, threw herself onto the other bed, and hugged the pillow protectively. She turned away from me.

I still didn't know what to say. I took off the rest of my clothes, slipped in between the heavily starched sheets, and quickly fell asleep, wondering why I didn't understand what was happening.

It was afternoon when I woke. I heard the busy whir of the air-conditioner and strained, dull noises from the highway. For a moment I didn't know where I was.

Heidi's bed was empty.

I remembered that strange early-morning scene and shook my head in wonderment. Memories of the guard lying in that grotesque black puddle flitted around the edges of my mind, but I shoved them away.

I showered and shaved and got into a pair of light slacks and a blue double-knit sport shirt. Feeling almost, but not quite, ready to face Heidi and the world, I left the room and walked along a sidewalk toward the coffee shop I'd seen when we checked in. I saw Heidi in the pool, taking long, languorous strokes through the turquoise water, but she didn't notice me.

They weren't serving breakfast at that hour, but I managed to get some coffee and a bacon-lettuce-and-tomato sandwich. I bought a local newspaper and read it while I ate, searching for any mention of last night's activities. I found none, but that didn't prove anything. It would have been morning by the time someone discovered what had happened, too late for the paper's deadline. I had a second cup of coffee, smoked a cigarette, and declared myself fit to meet the challenges of the new day.

I went back to the room and slipped into a pair of swimming trunks, grabbed a towel, and went out to the pool. Heidi was lying facedown on her towel on the concrete next to the diving board. Also resting on the towel were the insignificant scraps of her unstrung string bikini. I tapped her bare behind with my foot.

"This isn't France, you know. It isn't even Torremolinos."

She didn't bother to look up. "I'm surprised you even noticed."

At the far end of the pool, a pop-eyed businessman type had noticed. His wife was stretched out on a chaise lounge, a magazine in front of her face. Either she hadn't seen Heidi or she was shielding herself from the shame of it all. On the highway, cars seemed to be slowing down more than was necessary for road conditions.

I arranged myself on a patch of concrete a few feet away from her. "What we need right now," I said airily, "is for you to be arrested for indecent exposure. Yep, that's exactly what we need."

Heidi rolled over, sat up straight, and flashed me the finger. I raised my eyebrows a little; it was an unusual sight, right there next to the highway in King of Prussia, Pennsylvania.

She wadded up what little there was of the bikini and threw it at me. Then she grabbed the towel, stood up tall and proud, and marched defiantly back toward our room.

This was amazing behavior, even for Heidi, but now I thought I understood it. Last night had been rougher on her than it was on me. What fearful fantasies had gone through her mind as she sat alone in that car? She might have expected sudden death or long years in a gray prison cell: no more frolicking in the Mediterranean surf, no more sun on her golden body, no more nights of joyful lovemaking.

But she had come through it, and she was still alive and free. And she was announcing it to the world. Or maybe she didn't believe in the rest of the world; she was announcing it to herself.

Heidi reached the door of our room. Fortunately, I had left it unlocked. She opened it and tossed the towel inside, then turned to face me again. I didn't know what she had in mind; for a moment I was afraid she was going to march into the coffee shop like that, breasts jiggling, nether hair glistening with drops of water from the pool. I was relieved when all she did was disappear into the room and slam the door behind her.

Sex is intimately connected with death. The closest we come to that ultimate surrender is in the blind, fearless surrender of orgasm. It takes our selves away from us for an instant, but then it gives us back, more human and more vulnerable than before. Heidi's fears had been greater than mine, and her need for that moment of blissful oblivion, and the return from it, was also greater. I had cheated her last night.

The need for the nearness of another human being after the nearness of death was something I knew well. In my more active days as a bomber, I had felt it often. Every time, in fact.

Except for the last two. Portugal and PACA. Things had gone so wrong that I wasn't interested in affirming the continued existence of Sam Boggs.

Poor, stupid Marcelo had died in Portugal. It wasn't my fault, but Marcelo was nevertheless still dead. And the guard at PACA was dead, too, and that wasn't my fault either. But it happened, and I was there.

I realized that I was shucking myself. My no-hitter was gone. People had died because of what I had done. Many more might die if I built Stover's bomb.

To walk away from Stover's operation was impossible. Aside from the dangers involved, there were too damn many questions I wanted answered. The inside guard had been in the bag. How? We hit the warehouse instead of the truck, a much easier target. Serino didn't know Sonny Dee. Maybe he didn't. Stover wanted me kept in the dark about everything except my immediate tasks.

Patterns. Stover talked about modus operandi. Organized crime has an M.O., radical groups have an M.O. Everybody has one. All of my employers had them. Patterns of behavior.

I thought I was beginning to see a pattern. It was warped and incomplete, but it was there. I thought I knew who was paying the bills.

And I thought I saw a way out.

I lay there in the sun for another half-hour, running my mind through the twisted corridors of the maze. Finally I realized that I needed to know more, and there was nothing I could do now.

Well, there was at least one thing I could do now. Heidi had probably cooled off by now, and I felt myself heating up. With any luck, we might find a mutually agreeable temperature.

I gathered up my towel and walked lazily toward the room. The businessman at the other end of the pool looked at me with what I thought was undisguised jealousy. The marvelous nude sun bunny had walked out of his life and into my room. I opened the door, and the sunlight streamed into the room and fell on the bed.

And there was Serino, between Heidi's legs, thrusting.

They didn't notice me. I watched for a few seconds, observing Serino's rippling muscles and the hungry, rhythmic push of Heidi's pelvis. Then I slammed the door, so they would know that I knew.

I went back to the pool and plunged in, hitting with a belly-slammer that stung my whole body. The shock of the dive and the cold water did nothing to ease my anger. I started doing laps, one after another, plowing furiously through the chlorinated water. I swam until at last I dragged myself out of the pool, gasping and exhausted. When I had waited long enough, I walked back to the room.

Serino was gone. Heidi lay nude on the bed.

"Well?" she asked. "What did you expect?"

"Not that," I answered truthfully. I should have expected it though.

There was no hint of apology on her face, but she sat up. "I needed you, Sam," she said, "but you weren't there. I *still* need you."

"So soon?"

She granted me a self-conscious smile. "You know me," she said, as if entering a plea of guilty.

I did know her, or I thought that I did. Reality for her extended no farther than the tips of her fingers, or the lips of her vagina. She was willing to let me enter that hot, hungry odd little world of hers. I had rejected her, so she let Serino in; it didn't matter, because he wasn't real. But now she wanted to make me real again.

"Sam," she whispered, "don't be angry with me. I don't want you to be angry. I just want you to love me. That's all I've ever wanted from you."

In the end, it was all I wanted from her.

And so I reentered the only reality she understood. I joined my juices with hers and Serino's and created the world all over again. The stroking and sliding and the pulsing need brought us back together at the most real moment of all, and locked within and around each other, we tumbled back into the brand-new universe we had made.

I lifted my head so I could see her face. Her eyes were staring at the ceiling, but not really looking at it. She seemed to see something far beyond it.

That distant, vacant look was suddenly very familiar. I had seen it before, and I remembered where.

In the car. Last night. It had puzzled me then, because it seemed so out of context. It was the look of release, of completion. She'd had it last night when she picked us up.

What the hell had happened on the road? I rolled away from her and stared up at that same ceiling. There were no answers printed on it.

9

Kemper mysteriously appeared at our door the following morning. "We're leaving," he said simply. "I'll meet you in the coffee shop."

As we got dressed, I wondered why Kemper had been appointed as our new escort. I hadn't seen Serino since the unpleasant episode the previous afternoon. Perhaps he had reported the situation to Stover, who judiciously decided to transfer him off this particular detail. It didn't make sense, though, for Serino to tell Stover what happened; Serino was the type who would boast of his conquest to everyone else, maybe, but not to Stover. The switch may have been just another part of Stover's Byzantine master plan. Whatever the reason, I was not going to miss Serino. I would have been strongly tempted to punch him in the mouth the next time I saw him, and he probably would have welcomed the attempt.

Heidi and I didn't have much to say to each other. Silence

had rushed in to fill up the suddenly wider space between us.

We had breakfast with Kemper, who was his usual uncommunicative self. I scanned a Philadelphia newspaper, but still could find no account of the plutonium theft. The death of the guard would have made it more difficult to hush up, but a government experienced in Watergate and the CIA scandals would no doubt find a way. The infinite wisdom of the nation's managers had decreed that the people were better off not knowing that person or persons unknown had made off with enough nuclear material to build three atomic bombs. It might upset them.

In our fourth different car in three days, an Oldsmobile this time, we headed south on Route 202. At Wilmington, Delaware, we picked up Interstate 95. It seemed likely that our destination was the Washington area. That was Stover's intended target, so it would be convenient to assemble the bomb on the spot.

Kemper drove in silence, sniffing occasionally to clear the passages of his mashed-in nose. In the back, Heidi spent her time gazing at the unimpressive scenery of Delaware and Maryland.

Shortly before noon, we arrived at a red-brick warehouse on the docks in Alexandria, Virginia, a few miles down the Potomac from Washington. The sign above the padlocked metal door read "Palmer Engineering Co." The sign was new, but the building was not. It stood in solitary decay near the water's edge, several hundred feet from other, newer warehouses. The building might have been used to store Civil War muskets. It was three stories high, with no windows on the first floor, and it looked like a very tired and forlorn place.

Kemper unlocked the door and led us through a dusty passageway between dark, glassed-in office areas. He opened another locked door and ushered us into a large, open storage area, badly lit by the sunbeams fighting their way in through the filthy third-floor windows. Stover was standing alone in the center of the room.

Kemper did not follow us in. Stover stood rooted in place, waiting for us to come to him. We did, our footsteps echoing hollowly from the bare brick walls and the concrete floor.

Stover's eyes flickered balefully in Heidi's direction, and then, as was his custom, he ignored her existence.

"Well, Boggs," he said, not bothering with his usual *pro forma* smile, "I see you're still alive and well, in spite of everything."

"I hope you're not disappointed."

"Not at all. In fact, from the reports I've received, I'd say you handled yourself quite well in Pennsylvania."

I changed the subject. "This is the factory?"

He nodded and spread his arms in an expansive gesture. "It's not much," he said, "but from now on, it's home. Just remember, Enrico Fermi created the first nuclear chain reaction in an old squash court under the stadium at the University of Chicago. You should be able to do the same with these facilities."

"I hope not. The last thing we want here is a chain reaction."

"Hmmm. Yes, I guess you're right. That's why we hired you."

"Speaking of hiring . . ."

"You want your money."

"That's right."

Stover reached into his right inside breast pocket and handed me a piece of paper. It was on the letterhead of my bank in Zurich, and it verified the deposit in my account of one-half million American dollars, cash.

"You won't mind if I check this out?"

"Go ahead. Just don't make the call from here. Which

reminds me, when I said this was your home, I meant it. We've fixed up a small but adequate room for you on the second floor. Since you'll be spending nearly all your time here, we thought it made sense to provide you with accommodations here. There's no point in having you out in public where someone might recognize you."

"Stover, I come and go as I please."

"Of course," he said, "of course." His eyes narrowed a little. "But now that you have your money, we naturally want to make sure that nothing happens to you. Whenever you leave here, someone will go with you. And I'm not referring to Miss Wallace."

I didn't like it, but I could see that it would be futile and dangerous to argue about the arrangements. I looked around the warehouse. It was gray and empty except for a tarpaulin thrown over some shapeless objects along one wall.

"The birdcages?"

Stover nodded. "It would be expedient," he said, "if we could unload the contents and dispose of the containers as soon as possible."

"I'll need equipment," I said.

"And you'll get it. Anything you need. Just make out your shopping list. We have catalogs from every major scientific-supply house. I suggest that you spread out the orders you make; it wouldn't be wise to get everything from one company. Some bright boy might figure out what that particular combination of equipment could be used for. Wynn is standing by with the truck, and he'll personally pick up everything you need."

"Bills made payable to the Palmer Engineering Company?"

"We have order forms, letterhead, you name it. We even have a tax number. It's a completely legitimate company, Boggs, complete with coveralls with our name embroidered on

140

the back." He seemed rather proud of the Palmer Engineering Company.

I knew that Stover answered only the questions he felt like answering, but I decided to try to squeeze out whatever I could. Any information I could gain, even if it were false, would still be an improvement on complete ignorance.

"I've been checking the newspapers," I told him. "So far, there's nothing on PACA."

"And there won't be. As soon as they found out what happened, the place was crawling with FBI agents and AEC inspectors. They clamped the lid on tight. Unfortunately, it was probably a little more difficult for them than it ought to have been."

"The guard."

Stover nodded his head sadly. "They had to lean on his family pretty hard. It was a nasty business, Boggs. I've spoken to Morrison about his carelessness. It won't happen again." He seemed honestly grief-stricken, but I was sure that it had more to do with the screw-up in his game plan than with any regrets about the dead guard.

"What about the other guard? The one you had in the bag."

He smiled sheepishly. "You figured that out, did you?"

"It wasn't too hard. Why wasn't I told?"

"You—"

"—didn't need to know." I finished the familiar litany for him.

"You're catching on, Boggs. The cable had to be cut and the antenna brought down so that the guard would be able to explain why he didn't call for help. I figured that you would do a more convincing job if you thought it was for real."

"Will he talk?"

"Not if he wants to get paid. I think we can count on him."

It seemed pretty sloppy to me, and that was uncharacteristic

141

for Stover. There was something else he wasn't telling me, but I decided not to press him on it. Now that I had my half-million, Stover was going to watch me like a hawk. I didn't want to give him any reason to be suspicious. I couldn't let him get the idea that I was going to skip out.

I wasn't. I was going to stay right there in that crumbling warehouse and build an atomic bomb.

You don't need a Manhattan Project to build an atomic bomb, not now. Back in the forties, nuclear weapons existed only in the minds of physicists and science-fiction writers. No one knew if a bomb was even possible, and they had only a dim idea of how to go about constructing one. Once they had it, they weren't sure if it would work, or how well. Some scientists in the project worried over the possibility that it would work too well, and ignite the earth's atmosphere. Before the Alamogordo blast, Fermi took bets on whether the device would destroy the entire world, or only the state of New Mexico. No one could say with certainty that it wouldn't touch off Armageddon, but they were willing to take that risk. They didn't bother to ask the rest of us.

Most of the vast Manhattan Project was concerned with producing sufficient quantities of U-235 and plutonium to construct a bomb. Huge gaseous diffusion plants were built to separate U-235 from U-238; they collected it a few grams at a time. Plutonium was also difficult to accumulate. At one point, the world's entire supply of plutonium was stored in a cigar box.

But now there are literally tons of plutonium stockpiled in places like the PACA facility. In a few years, when the breeder reactors become common, there will be so much of it around that clandestine bomb builders will have no trouble getting all they need—unless people wake up in time and insist on adequate safeguards.

The commercial reactors have already taken care of the expensive part of bomb building. After you have the plutonium, the rest is easy.

I was not a nuclear physicist, but I was a chemist, and I understood the ways in which a substance can be changed from one form into another. Specifically, I understood how to turn liquid plutonium nitrate into metallic plutonium, suitable for the core of a nuclear weapon.

I spent two days searching through scientific-supply catalogs, findings the items I would need. Someone who didn't care if he built a good bomb with a high yield or a fiftieth-of-a-kiloton fizzle could have done it all much more cheaply. Professional pride, if nothing else, compelled me to build the best bomb I could.

I ordered a two-thousand-dollar magnetic induction furnace which could produce extremely high temperatures in anything that is resistant to electricity—such as plutonium. I got metallurgical equipment, ceramic crucibles, quartz beakers and tubes, a .03-micron glove box, and an array of tools and gadgets to make the job easier. For materials, I went to industrial-chemical companies and rare-metals works. I bought large quantities of oxalic acid, necessary for breaking down the plutonium nitrate. To that I added quantities of hydrofluoric acid, magnesium oxide, metallic calcium, crystalline iodine, nitric acid, and argon gas. Finally, I ordered some beryllium. At one hundred dollars a pound, it was the only truly expensive item I needed, and I could have gotten by with steel or solder (or even wax) if I had wanted to cut corners.

And from the Ares Corporation, old friend of miners and mad bombers throughout the world, I ordered detonators and a supply of C-4. The impressive letterhead of the Palmer Engineering Company made the transaction seem entirely legitimate. Hell, it *was* legitimate. We paid promptly, and Wynn picked up most of the stuff himself in a big tractor trailer with the name of Palmer painted on the side in bright orange.

Palmer would have been very proud of his company. I wondered who, if anybody, he was.

While I was waiting for the supplies to arrive, I complemented my library researches by studying the two volumes of *The Plutonium Handbook,* which Stover had thoughtfully provided for me at the cost of $81.50. It contained virtually everything anyone would ever need to know about plutonium. About the only secret remaining is the precise amount of plutonium necessary to make a critical mass, and that can be calculated from other data.

Stover also provided me with a variety of pamphlets and data sheets from the Atomic Energy Commission. These were readily available at the AEC, and although they contained no classified information, they were immensely helpful.

No, I didn't need a Manhattan Project. Most of the difficult work had already been done for me. All I had to worry about was putting all the components together in such a way as to guarantee a nuclear explosion upon detonation, while avoiding such a happenstance while I was still working on it.

And there was one other thing I needed to worry about.

I had to find a way to sabotage the bomb without anyone knowing about it.

While I immersed myself in the study of plutonium, life at the Palmer Engineering Company settled into a comfortable routine. Wynn came and went, bearing his cargoes of exotic-sounding chemicals and components. Morrison was there, ironically wearing the uniform of an industrial guard. He was our night watchman, and I had high hopes that someone would mug him in a dark alley. Kemper and Serino were there helping with the unloading, and assisting me with whatever I wanted done. Locatelli, it turned out, had worked for several years in a foundry. He would be valuable when the time came to shape the plutonium and beryllium, since I knew little about the casting and molding of metals. Stover was there briefly for a few days, then disappeared.

Serino and I barely spoke. He was not apologetic about anything, but he had the look of a man who had been thoroughly chewed out. Somehow, Stover had discovered what happened at the motel.

And Heidi drifted around the edges of it all, restless and silent. She didn't know what to do with herself. I didn't know what to do with herself, either.

We shared the same room and the same bed, but since the afternoon in King of Prussia, we had not made love. She didn't ask me, and I didn't volunteer. Lying next to her on a creaky double bed, I remembered the look I had seen on her face, and it scared me. I wondered if maybe she had been freaked out, after all, by the operation. Instead of screaming that it was all a stupid game, as she had done in the beginning, she now seemed to have turned inward, toward something that was not visible to me. I tried not to worry about it. When it was all over, we would sail off to Tahiti, and everything would be as before.

That was what I told myself. I don't think I ever really believed it.

10

Locatelli was sweating again. Beads of perspiration the size of raindrops formed on his forehead and neck. The warehouse was warm and muggy, because in September Washington is still warm and muggy, but it wasn't the weather that was making Locatelli sweat. It was plutonium nitrate.

We had opened the birdcages and removed from them seven slender cylindrical plastic bottles, four feet long and six inches in diameter. Each one contained ten liters of plutonium nitrate. Locatelli knew what it could do. So did Kemper and Serino; they stepped back several paces as Locatelli lifted the first heavy container into position.

I had chosen Locatelli to assist me throughout the entire operation. Having worked in a forge, he was at least accustomed to functioning under potentially dangerous conditions. He had a good mind, and I didn't dislike him nearly as much as I did Serino and Kemper. I could tell that he wasn't

147

wholly pleased by the honor of working with me, but I thought I could count on him to follow my instructions. Serino wouldn't have trusted me any more than I trusted him, and Kemper was still an unknown quantity. So Locatelli was my man.

He hoisted the bottle up onto the workbench and fit it carefully into the brace I had built for it. Now it couldn't fall or be knocked over.

After the incident at PACA, I was going to take no chances with the plutonium nitrate, or with anything else that contained even a speck of plutonium. I had adapted a siphon to fit the top of the bottle. The tubes extended down from about seven feet in the air to another workbench slightly lower than the base of the bottle. I could have simply poured the contents of the bottle into other containers, but that would have been inviting another accident. This way, all I had to do was turn a valve and let air pressure and gravity drain the plutonium nitrate into five separate two-liter beakers.

I checked the position of the tubes. The tops of the receiving vessels were sealed tightly.

"Okay," I said. "Here we go."

I twisted the valve, and Locatelli involuntarily stepped back as the potent black liquid snaked down through the tubes and began trickling into the beakers. I wanted to step away from it, too, but I kept close to the valve in case anything went wrong. I had worked with dangerous chemicals for most of my life, but for sheer morbid fascination, I had never seen anything like plutonium nitrate. It may have been that I had seen it kill a man. But it could also have been the awareness of the lethal secrets hidden in that dark, viscous soup; it was as if we were pumping the waters out of the Black Lagoon, knowing that ultimately we would uncover a monster.

"That's all there is to it, huh?" asked a relieved Locatelli.

I laughed. "My friend," I said, "this is the easiest thing we'll do all month."

"Oh," he said flatly, eyes still fixed on the dribbling plutonium nitrate. The beakers were nearly full, the plastic bottle down to the last inch of liquid. I wanted to get as much as possible out of the bottle, for we were going to have a problem in common with the nuclear reactors that had produced this stuff in the first place: waste disposal. Inevitably, as the trickle slowed and stopped, random dribs and drabs of the solution clung to the insides of the tubes and the dregs of the bottle. Those tiny droplets were enough to kill all of us.

Wearing a pair of plastic surgical gloves, I closed the valve and unhooked the tubes from the five beakers. I bent the tubes to keep their ends pointed upward, then carefully disconnected them from the main valve and deposited them in a plastic garbage bag. For the moment, it would do. I then plugged in a tube that ran from a water faucet on the wall. Locatelli turned the handle, and water spurted back up through the tube and emptied out into the bottle. The water would flush the plutonium nitrate out of the tubes and dilute the solution that remained in the bottle.

What remained could not simply be drained into the Potomac. The problem with radioactive waste is that it doesn't break down into harmless chemicals the way other compounds do. No matter what you do with it, the plutonium will go on shooting out alpha particles for the next twenty-four thousand years. Longer, really. The only safe thing to do with radioactive waste, ideally, would be to put it aboard a rocket and shoot it into the sun. That doesn't happen, of course, because it would be too expensive. Instead, the waste is usually sunk in huge concrete blocks and then buried. That is not a very good solution to the problem, because over the next twenty-four thousand years there will be earthquakes and volcanoes occurring in places we can't predict. The result will be that some of those concrete blocks will be split open. But it's not likely to happen soon, so no one gets very upset about it. Our remote descendants, however, are going to have a real problem on their hands—the twentieth century's gift to the future.

With a small twinge of guilt, I was going to add a few more grams of plutonium to the growing mountain of nuclear waste. When we were through with the bottles, they and the garbage bags would be put into a block of cement. I had assigned that task to Kemper and Serino, who didn't much care for the idea.

We repeated the process with a second bottle of plutonium nitrate. I hoped that it would be all I needed. My bomb design called for about three and a half kilograms of plutonium; from the two bottles, we should have been able to extract five kilograms.

My overriding concern was to make sure that the bomb did not predetonate. At any step along the way, it was possible to accidentally assemble too much plutonium in one place at one time and get a premature chain reaction. It wouldn't be enough to cause an actual explosion, but the shower of radiation would kill us just as dead as a nuclear fireball.

It was a nerve-racking business, this. Kemper and Serino remained as far away from the scene of operations as they reasonably could, and even avoided Locatelli, as if he were carrying the plague. I avoided Heidi, for other reasons. And Stover avoided the entire warehouse; I hadn't seen him since the first week. There was little conversation at the Palmer Engineering Company. Even during the nightly poker games, we all kept one ear tuned to the monotonous, random clicking of the Geiger counter that was left on continuously. It was like living with an invisible, murderous ghost.

The second floor of the warehouse, along the west wall, had been turned into a dormitory of sorts. Kemper and Locatelli shared a room next to mine, and farther down the balconylike hallway, Serino alternated with Morrison in a room that had once been a janitor's equipment locker. Morrison spent the nights patrolling the grounds, inside and out, and slept during the days. It was a good arrangement, because it kept him out of my sight. At the northwest corner of the second floor was a rude bathroom, with a cracked toilet, dirty sink, and concrete shower stall. The accommodations were not inviting, and we were all usually smelly and unshaven.

Food was prepared on a hot plate. Heidi, being the only woman around, was given the job of keeping us well fed. The male-chauvinist assumption that Heidi could cook soon backfired on us, and after a day-long epidemic of diarrhea (which strained our facilities to the limit), Heidi was relieved of her duties by unanimous agreement. I exempted Locatelli and myself from the cooking chores because of the small chance that we might have some toxic chemical on our fingers. That left Serino, Kemper, and Morrison, none of whom had any intrinsic culinary talent.

Finally, we decided to stop torturing ourselves. Serino and Kemper alternated on food runs to nearby Burger Kings, delis, and Chinese restaurants. The only exception to this routine came when Wynn was with us. He was usually gone on some mysterious errand for Stover, but once or twice a week he would return and bunk in with Serino. Wynn had a knack for whipping up stews and nameless concoctions that stuck to the ribs and satisfied the palate; without those periodic feasts, we might all have killed each other in a Whopper-inspired argument.

Generally, though, we got along. Locatelli and I became friendly because we spent so much time working together. He had a rather pleasant, undemanding personality, and he was eager to learn about chemistry and scientific method. Kemper remained taciturn and surly, but I got to the point where I could talk to him about things like football without getting the feeling that he'd just as soon slug me as speak to me. With Serino, I maintained an uneasy truce, neither of us mentioning Heidi.

The poker games, conducted at a folding table down on the concrete floor of the warehouse, reminded me of old Chicago gangster films: a gang of hard-case characters smoking cigars, sloshing cheap beer, playing obscure variations of stud and draw, all the while looking as if they expected Capone's boys to bust in at any moment and stitch the walls with a tommy-gun barrage. We played for medium-size stakes, and two- or three-hundred-dollar pots were not uncommon. I was easily the worst player at the table, and the fact that I was now on my way to becoming a millionaire had an obvious influence on the pattern of betting. Anytime I stayed in the game, the pot was noticeably larger than when I folded early. I considered simply buying a few pots, but I didn't think that would go down very well. So I went on being an obliging pigeon, redistributing my wealth. After three weeks, I was down by almost four thousand dollars. Serino played a flashy, dangerous game, and on any given night he was likely to win or lose as much as a grand. Kemper was a steady small-stakes winner, and Locatelli broke even. Most of my money seemed to go to Wynn when he was in town; Cowboy Billy had been around.

One night, after dropping a large pot to Wynn, I asked him how he had gotten into this business. "With your obvious talents," I said, "you should have been able to do all right in Vegas."

He was stacking his chips and didn't look up. "I needed a job," he said. I waited for an elaboration, but there was none. Wynn was no more talkative about his past than anyone else in the employ of the Palmer Engineering Company. I thought some more about patterns of behavior.

152

When I wasn't playing poker, I was busy building our bomb. Working with no more than a few hundred grams of plutonium nitrate at a time, I began the tedious process of extracting metallic plutonium.

I added oxalic acid to the nitrate. That produced a precipitate of water-laden plutonium-oxalate crystals. Heating removed the water, leaving a fluffy, yellow-green cake of anhydrous plutonium oxalate. This was the stuff that made my heart beat quickly and unevenly; a sudden breeze or sneeze could waft that innocent-looking powder up into the air and then down into our lungs. We wore industrial filter masks for protection, but I had no real confidence in them.

I did have confidence in the glove box, and I did as much of the work as possible inside the aquariumlike walls of the box. Plastic gloves were built into the sides of the box, so I could reach inside and work with the plutonium with a minimum of danger. My freedom of movement was restricted, but it was a small price to pay.

I put the plutonium-oxalate crystals into a sealed crucible and ran a tube from it to a quartz container that held hydrofluoric acid. Then I heated the assembly up to 500 degrees Celsius and baked up a new concoction, plutonium fluoride.

When I had accumulated 500 grams of plutonium fluoride, I was ready for the next step. I mixed a magnesium-oxide paste and used it to line the inside of a crucible. Then, with the precision of a gourmet chef, I added to the recipe the 500 grams of plutonium fluoride, 170 grams of metallic calcium, and 50 grams of crystalline iodine. On top of that, I added argon gas, enough to fill the crucible. Then I shut the lid.

All that remained was to stick the crucible in the oven and wait. At 750 degrees Celsius, the mixture reacted. It was an exothermic reaction, and in the space of a minute it raised its own temperature to 1600 degrees. After about ten minutes it

153

cooled to a mere 800, and I removed the crucible from the oven and let it cool to room temperature, like a tray of brownies.

Finally, I opened the crucible and washed away a precipitate of iodine flakes and calcium-fluoride salts with a solution of nitric acid. What remained in the bottom of the crucible was a small, amorphous lump of plutonium.

I picked up the lump. For its size, it was the heaviest thing I had ever handled. And by all odds, the scariest. I handed it to Locatelli.

He took it cautiously, holding it by his fingertips. "It feels warm," he said wonderingly.

"Alpha particle decay," I told him. "It won't hurt you, as long as you don't swallow it. Alpha particles only penetrate a few millimeters. You could carry it around with you all day and it wouldn't bother you. Oh, I wouldn't recommend that you wear a plutonium-dial wristwatch, but for short periods, its perfectly safe."

"No kidding?" Locatelli held the plutonium up to his eye and examined it more closely. Kemper and Serino had been keeping their distance, but curiosity drew them toward us. They passed the heavy little metallic blob around, shaking their heads and speaking in near-whispers.

"That's the stuff that does it, huh?" Serino sounded as if he didn't quite believe it.

"That's the stuff," I affirmed. "We'll keep each batch of it in separate containers until we're ready to shape it into the bomb core. It's dangerous only if we accumulate too much of it in one place."

"What happens then?" asked Kemper.

"You don't have to worry about what happens then. None of us do."

*   *   *

When we had accumulated about two kilograms of plutonium, Stover showed up again. He examined the plutonium
with clinical interest, like a jeweler appraising a diamond.

"Good job, Boggs," he said, as if he had determined the
purity of the plutonium simply by hefting it. "How much
longer?"

"Maybe a week. Ten days. Locatelli is already working on
the beryllium casing. We should have the rest of the plutonium
in a few more days. Now that I'm sure of my procedures, I can
work in larger amounts."

"And the bomb design? You're sure it will work?"

"You've seen it yourself. What do you think?"

"I'm not the expert in this field," he said.

"No, but I'm sure you have access to experts. Don't bullshit
me, Stover. You're not laying out a million bucks without
double-checking to make sure you're getting your money's
worth."

Stover glanced over his shoulder. Serino and Kemper, as
ever, were standing nearby. One of them must have been
feeding Stover. Or not. I didn't know and wasn't sure I
cared.

"Let's find a better place to talk," he said. I put the
plutonium back in its container and followed Stover across the
floor of the warehouse. We went back into the glass-partitioned
office area and sat down on squeaky swivel chairs.

I took out a cigarette and lit up. I was smoking more these
days, as they used to say in the ad, but enjoying it less.

"So," said Stover. "You want to know if I'm checking your
work?" He sounded like a foreman discussing a raise with one
of his more troublesome employees.

"I want to know that, and a lot more. And kindly spare me
the crap about not needing to know. I'm in this thing as deep
as it's possible to get. It's time I got a few answers."

155

Stover looked thoughtful. "You think I'm holding out on you?"

"I know you are."

"You're right."

"And?"

"And nothing. That's it. I'm holding out on you. It's a fact of life, Boggs. Accept it."

I looked at my cigarette smoke, curling upward through the dusty air of the warehouse. I was glad Stover didn't participate in our poker games; he knew how to play his cards. And at the moment, he seemed to be holding aces.

"How about if I go on strike?" I wanted to see how he would react to a bluff—because that was all it was.

"That would be a big mistake, Boggs."

"Meaning you have someone who could replace me."

"I think that's a safe assumption."

"Which means that you do have someone who can check my work." I watched his face, but he merely smiled.

"Brilliant deduction, Holmes. But the trouble with deduction, Boggs, is that it doesn't really tell you anything you didn't already know. Feel free to deduce all you want, if it makes you happy, but don't expect me to tell you anything new. You've got your money. You don't need to know where it came from."

"I might," I said. "Can the money be traced?"

He shook his head. "It's clean as a whistle. Legal tender for all debts, public and private."

Stover waited, expecting me to ask more questions that he wouldn't answer. But I was at a dead end.

"Anything else, Boggs?"

"Yes," I said. "I'm taking a day off tomorrow."

"Really? What's next? A forty-hour week and Blue Cross?"

I ground out my cigarette on the concrete floor. "You know,

Stover, there are times when you can be a real horse's ass."

He smiled innocently. "It's part of my job," he said. "What's this about a day off?"

"I have some business to tend to. I haven't been out of this place since we got here. I want to breathe some fresh air. And I want to confirm the bank deposit."

"Fine. Go ahead. But remember, you'll have a friend along to make sure you don't get lost."

"Naturally."

"As long as we understand each other."

We got to our feet and walked back toward the main floor of the warehouse.

"Christ, Stover, you really picked an incredible dump for this operation, you know that?"

"I thought it was a nice little building, myself," he said, tilting his head back so he could inspect the rafters.

"You don't have to live in it."

That night Heidi and I tried to make love for the first time in weeks. I knew what would happen, and I was right.

I rolled away from her and lit up a cigarette, tossing the match at the green metal wastebasket on the floor next to the bed. It missed.

Heidi reached over to me and began playing with the hairs on my chest. Her hand was very cool.

"Sam?"

"I'm sorry," I said.

"Sam? What's wrong?"

"Nothing's wrong."

"Well, *something's* wrong!" Her voice was suddenly shrill.

I flicked ashes onto the floor and didn't answer her. She made a fist and thumped me solidly.

"Goddammit, Sam! Don't do this to me!"

157

"I told you, I'm sorry. I've got a lot on my mind."

"And you think I don't? At least you've got something to do around here. All I do all day is read old magazines and listen to the radio. Can't I at least expect something at night?"

"Do you want out?" I asked. "You knew it would be rough."

"I didn't know it would be like *this!*"

I looked at her in the dim light that came in from the street through our lone filthy window. Her long blond hair seemed somehow dull and stringy, and the Mediterranean blue of her eyes had become hard and gray. In the shadows, her round face looked stark and angular. I thought about Torremolinos, and then I thought about the white, endless beaches of Tahiti, but mostly I thought about Rogers' Crossing, Pennsylvania.

"Heidi, on the night we hit PACA, what happened?"

"Nothing happened! I told you that before. What's this all about?"

"I'm not really sure," I told her.

"Well, what does it have to do with you and me? I know you had a bad time of it back there, but I don't see why you can't—"

"Let's just forget about it, shall we?"

"How can I forget about it? You keep asking me about it."

She turned away from me with a sudden movement that started the springs bouncing. I stifled an urge to reach out and bring her back to me. What had to happen now was not what I wanted, but it was necessary. Maybe later it would all be okay again.

I leaned back against the pillow and blew a few smoke rings, trying to find the best way to phrase what I had to say.

"Heidi," I said, "I know it's been rough on you, and I'm sorry, but right now I just can't help you. I know you have strong . . . uh, drives, and this isn't fair to you. Why don't you go back to Serino?"

She whirled around and looked at me in amazement. "What did you say?" she demanded.

"Until this is over, maybe you'd be better off with Serino."

"Are you going to hold that over my head forever? I told you—"

"It's okay, Heidi! Really. I understand, and I don't mind. You are what you are, and I am what I am, and right now it's just not working for us. When this is all over, we can pretend none of it ever happened. But for now, maybe you'd be happier with Serino. Wynn's out of town, and he's got the room to himself."

She stared at me for a long moment, then said slowly, "You really wouldn't mind?"

"I want you to be happy."

"But, Sam . . ."

"Don't say anything more. It's for the best, for now. Go to him."

She paused for another moment, then kissed me lightly. "I'll be back. I promise." She kissed me again, then crawled over me, picked a shirt off the floor, and tiptoed silently out the door.

I lit another cigarette from the butt of the old one. For a long time I stared at the orange glow and tried to keep from thinking about anything. But thoughts kept intruding. I put my palm down on the sheet in the empty place next to me and felt the fading warmth from Heidi's body.

People had been using me ever since the start of this thing; now I was using Heidi. I wondered if everything would cancel out in the end.

Probably not, I decided. Books almost never balance.

But equations do, and at last I was sure that I had plugged in all the right variables. X equaled plutonium plus Stover plus an inside man plus a lonely mountain road plus Serino's

Boston accent, multiplied by secrecy, all of it divided by behavior patterns and the speed of light squared.

I thought I had the answer.

The next morning, Kemper and I ventured out of the womb of the Palmer Engineering Company. Driving north along the river, we passed a large complex of buildings about a mile away from the warehouse, and suddenly another piece of the equation fell into place. The buildings belonged to the Global Armaments Corporation. They were the world's leading supplier of old Sherman tanks, B-26's, captured Czechoslovakian automatic rifles, and similar goodies. Global was to coups and revolutions what Spalding was to baseball; they supplied the bats and balls to semipro organizations in every league. Their corporate history was interesting, indeed, and I wondered how much of a coincidence it was that the Palmer Engineering Company was located just a mile away from them.

We parked at Washington's National Airport, right across the river from all the old familiar landmarks. I found a money changing booth in the terminal and bought a roll of quarters. Kemper followed me, keeping about two paces behind. He was there to keep me honest or to break me in half if I tried anything.

All of the phone booths were occupied, so Kemper and I spent a few minutes watching the planes come and go, and pretending that we didn't know each other. When one of the booths was freed, I grabbed it quickly, just ahead of a sailor, who looked as if *he* would have liked to break me in half. It was a nice booth, as phone booths go, with a little wooden seat and a push-button phone.

I got the international operator and gave her the number of the bank in Zurich. She waited patiently, counting the bongs as I fed quarters into the machine.

"Is that right?" I asked.

"One more," she said pleasantly. I inserted the coin. "Thank you," she replied. "Your call will take about five minutes to go through."

"Fine," I said. "I'll be at this number."

She disconnected, but I held onto the receiver. I opened the door and called to Kemper, who had stationed himself about ten feet away from the booth.

"It's going to take a while," I told him. "You might as well find a place to sit down."

Kemper looked at me suspiciously, since it was his job to be suspicious. "I'll be right here, Boggs," he said. He didn't bother to warn me not to try anything foolish; I think he was hoping that I would try something.

I smiled and closed the door, holding the receiver next to my ear, as if listening to someone. Out of the corner of my eye, I kept track of Kemper. After a couple of minutes, his attention strayed to the activity on the runway. I pressed down the bar, then quickly slipped another quarter into the slot. I punched "O."

"Operator," said a flat, mechanical voice.

"Would you connect me with the Senate Office Building, please?" She wouldn't. Instead, she gave me the number and returned my coin. I checked Kemper again and found him still staring at a 727 out on the runway. I punched in the number, got a secretary, and then had a long wait while they put me through to my party.

I had no intention of calling the bank. Either the money was there or it wasn't, and there was nothing I could do about it. Since Stover had encouraged me to confirm the deposit, I assumed that the money was actually there, or that Stover had fixed things on that end.

I had something else in mind.

161

"Senator Preston's office," a female voice said into my ear.

"Let me speak to the senator, please."

"I'm sorry," she said. "Senator Preston is on the floor at the moment."

"I have a message for him. Can you be sure that he gets it?"

She paused for a moment. "Who's calling, please?"

"Never mind about that. I want you to tell the senator to be in his office tonight between midnight and one. I'll call him then."

"What is this in reference to?"

"You can tell him that I have some information for him."

"About what?"

I took a deep breath. Last chance. But no, dammit, I was sure.

"Tell him it's about the CIA. You be damned sure he gets that message, you hear?"

I hung up without waiting for her to reply. I glanced at Kemper; he was still watching airplanes.

It was still hot in Washington, but I sat there in the phone booth and shivered.

I had just come in from the cold, and I didn't feel one bit warmer.

11

I returned to the warehouse with a fresh supply of magazines and paperbacks for Heidi and a pad and paper and an envelope for myself.

Heidi was asleep on our bed. Evidently she had not gotten a lot of sleep during the night. I felt a stab of jealousy, or something, but told myself to ignore it.

I dropped my load of magazines onto the bed next to her. She jerked convulsively and flew up to sitting position before she was even awake. She blinked a few times and finally managed to focus on me. I smiled at her.

She tried to return the smile, but it quickly became a long, weary yawn. It was odd, but I suddenly liked her more than I had in a long time. With sex at least temporarily removed from our relationship, I felt much more friendly toward her.

Heidi conquered another yawn and stretched her arms

luxuriously. "What's happening?" she asked in a thick, sleepy voice.

"Brought you some magazines." I pointed to the stack on the bed. She started thumbing through the pile.

"Oh, wow!" She laughed. "*Modern Screen! Inside Hollywood!*"

"I thought you might be homesick for California."

"I just love this stuff! I've got a real taste for trash, Sam."

"I've noticed." She tried to punch me in the stomach but missed and got me in the hipbone instead.

She rubbed her knuckles and went back to the magazines. "Great! Jackie and Liz and Dick and Cher—boy, I'd forgotten all about those people. And what's this? *Scientific American?*"

"That's for me."

She tossed it down to the foot of the bed. "You're welcome to it," she said.

"Thank you. Look, why don't you take your scandal sheets and go somewhere else for a little while? I've got some work I have to do here."

She bundled up the magazines and got to her feet. "All right," she said huffily, "I know where I'm not wanted." She took a couple of steps toward the door, then stopped.

"I'm sorry, Sam," she said. "I didn't mean that the way it sounded."

"I know you didn't." She stared at me for a moment, leaned toward me and gave me a sisterly kiss on the cheek, then took her magazines and left the room.

I stretched out on the bed for a few minutes and glanced at the *Scientific American*. I read the "Science and the Citizen" column. It was about the need for stricter measures to protect the ozone layer from the effects of fluorocarbons. I was all in favor of that.

Finally, after skimming an article on the small Martian channels, I threw the magazine aside and picked up the pad of notebook paper. It was time to write my insurance policy.

Mick Mahoney was a movement lawyer I knew from the early days at Berkeley. The last time I'd seen him, he had shoulder-length hair to go with his three-piece suit and Phi Beta Kappa key. Mick was fourth-generation Yale, and he knew all sorts of interesting things, like how to choose a brandy or how to choose a jury. In his somewhat warped scheme of things, one was about as important as the other. He lived a life of upper-class hedonism in his opulent San Francisco townhouse, while defending an incredible collection of frothing Marxists. He was aware of the contradiction and even seemed to revel in it, but in spite of his divided loyalties, he was a damned good lawyer. The dyed-in-the-wool revolutionists never completely trusted him, even when he got them off. But I trusted him; right now, I had to.

I assumed that our attorney-client relationship was still operative, although I hadn't seen him in years. That was important because it meant that no one could force him to reveal what I told him. On the other hand, as an officer of the court, he might be obligated to blow the whistle on me. That possibility didn't trouble me very much, though, since Mick never paid much attention to the bar association, except when it suited his purpose. On the great, green golf course of the law, Mick played winter rules.

Without much preamble, I told Mick what I had gotten myself involved in this time. Mick would no doubt be more intrigued than shocked, but he would know what to do with the information if something went wrong.

First, I gave him a complete list of facts, things I knew for certain. Then I added my theories and suppositions; I noted, unhappily, that the theories took up far more space than the facts. Nevertheless, when I reread the letter, it all seemed to make sense.

I told Mick to sit on the information. If he didn't hear from me within six weeks, he was free to do whatever he thought best. And if there was an unexplained nuclear explosion anywhere in the world, he should come forward immediately. Knowing Mick, I was sure that would mean a calculated leak to the press; he was too smart to let himself be tied in directly.

By the time I was finished, the letter filled both sides of ten sheets of paper. It didn't explain everything, but it would provide a lot of leads for anyone who wanted to investigate this particular conspiracy. The letter gave me a certain amount of protection from Stover, who couldn't be sure exactly how much I had deduced; it would make him at least a little reluctant to do anything rash, such as kill me. At the same time, the letter also provided minimal coverage of my own ass in case of a bust. In court, it would at least show that my heart was with the good guys. Beyond that, I was counting on Preston.

I folded the pages and stuffed them into the envelope; it made a bulky package. Using block letters, I carefully printed Mick's address and marked it personal. No need to let some efficient secretary get a look at it.

I glanced at my watch; it was already three-thirty in the afternoon. I had no idea what Locatelli and the others were doing with their day off. Whatever it was, I hoped it tired them out; I wanted them in bed early tonight. That reminded me that I wasn't going to get any sleep at all. I stuck the envelope into the *Scientific American* and rolled over on my side. To my surprise, I fell asleep almost immediately.

I awoke, to find Heidi sitting on the edge of the bed. "Hi," she said.

"Hi yourself."

"Have a good nap?"

"Just fine."

"Good. You've been working too hard. Sorry to wake you up, but Kemper's going out for food. What do you want?"

"Where's he going?"

"Kentucky Fried."

"I'll take ribs if they've got them. Otherwise, chicken is okay."

She nodded. "I shall place your order, sir." She started to rise, but I grabbed her hand. I was only half-awake; I almost never remember my dreams, but I must have been having a good one. Heidi seemed to blend right into it.

I pulled her down to me and kissed her. My hands strayed toward her lush southern regions.

"Well," she said when we paused for air, "that nap really did you a lot of good. Are you trying to tell me something?"

My body certainly was, but my mind suddenly snapped to attention. I was sending out the wrong message.

"I'm just trying to tell you that I still think you're a great broad."

"Is that all?"

"For the moment, I'm afraid. Heidi, it will be over soon, just a few more days. Then we can start fresh. Scout's honor."

She pulled away from me and studied my face for a few seconds. "You mean," she said, "that you want me to stay with Serino again tonight."

"I think that would be best."

"Is there some reason you don't want me here?" Her brows were knit in an expression of doubt.

"Yes, there is a reason why I don't want you here."

"Are you going to tell me what it is?"

"Yep. I don't want you here because if you stay any longer, Kemper is going to leave, and I won't get my ribs. So get moving, woman." I slapped her on the flank.

She stood up, moving with that fluid grace of hers. Somehow, I kept myself from going after her. She paused at the door. "Sam Boggs," she said, "you are a very strange person."

167

"And a hungry one. Go," I commanded, pointing to the doorway. She shook her head, apparently baffled, then turned and left.

I got to my feet and paced around the dingy little room for a few minutes. Finally I kicked the metal wastebasket hard enough to send it clanging off the wall.

It might have been easier if I had told Heidi what I was going to do. It would have been less frustrating, that much was certain. My glands refused to understand the devious reasoning of my brain. But I had to keep my surfer girl in the dark, at least for now. My rationale was borrowed from Stover: she couldn't tell what she didn't know.

A few minutes after midnight, Heidi padded silently out of the room. I wondered what Serino thought of these shadowy assignations. Heidi probably told him that she sneaked away after I was asleep; Serino's massive ego would have no trouble accepting that story. It was plausible enough.

In fact, it was so plausible that I suddenly wondered if it weren't true. For all I knew, Heidi could have been creeping off to Serino every night for the last three weeks. The thought produced a strange set of conflicting emotions. She had been betraying me; yet even if she had been, she was now doing exactly the same thing with my blessing.

I made an effort to push the ambiguities out of my mind. There was work to be done.

I got dressed in the dark outfit that I had worn at PACA. The nights were a little cooler now, in late September, and I didn't think it would be quite so uncomfortable.

Turning up a corner of the mattress, I retrieved a coiled-up length of heavy-duty extension cord that I had ripped off from our equipment. I knotted one end of the cord around a leg of the bed. The knot was secure, and there was no chance that the cord would break, but I worried about the bed. Unfortunately, the room offered no alternative belay. The bed would just have to do.

I went to the window and waited for Morrison to make his appearance. I had a bad angle looking down, and couldn't hope to see him if he stayed close to the building. If I didn't see him in ten minutes, I decided I would have to risk opening the window to get a better look.

After just two minutes, though, I heard muffled footsteps on the uneven brick pavement. The steps came from the direction of the river and moved steadily in my direction. My window was about twenty feet away from the front corner of the building, facing an unilluminated open expanse of perhaps two hundred feet. If Morrison didn't see me, then no one would.

I wasn't able to catch sight of Morrison as he passed, but it could only have been him. I checked my watch, then sat down on the bed and waited for Morrison to come back.

The *Scientific American* was on the floor next to the bed. I picked it up and flipped through it, trying to make out the illustrations in the weak light. The letter to Mick slipped out of the magazine and dropped to the floor. "Good work, Boggs," I told myself. I picked up the letter and jammed it into my back pocket.

Morrison came back in four minutes and twenty seconds. I wanted to time him again, for safety's sake, but it was already twenty after twelve. Preston wasn't going to wait around all night.

I slid the window open and stuck my head out. Morrison was not in sight. Taking care not to let the heavy plug smack into the wall, I unreeled the cord. There was thirty feet of it in the coil, and I had used six or seven feet for the knot and the segment from the bed to the window. I estimated that I was about twenty-five feet from the pavement.

The cord played out, and the plug dangled a few feet above the ground. A quick glance at my watch showed I had a little over three minutes left.

I lifted my legs through the window and sat on the ledge for a few seconds, running through the entire plan one more time. If I had forgotten anything, this was the time to think of it.

There was nothing else to do that I could think of. I grabbed the cord with both hands, ducked my head and shoulders through the window, then let myself drop from the ledge.

The bed immediately screeched across the floor and tried to follow me out the window. I dropped five feet in a hurry. The bed banged into the wall with a hollow thump, and my downward progress ended in a jerk so sharp that I nearly lost my grip.

I was too appalled by my own stupidity to have any reaction other than an abrupt increase in heart rate. To my ears, the bed had made a screaming racket as it lurched across the floor. Of course, I was tuned to hear every small bump in the night. The others might not even have noticed it.

Either they heard it or they didn't. This was not the time or place to ponder the matter, dangling like an acrophobic spider twenty feet off the ground. I went down rock-climber style, hand-over-hand, feet braced against the side of the building. I dropped the last four or five feet and immediately checked my watch. I should have more than a minute before Morrison rounded the corner.

I looked up at the cord. It was in the shadows, but anyone who really looked at the wall couldn't miss it. I wanted to hide it somehow, but I would need that cord to get back in. I would simply have to count on the boredom and monotony of the night-watchman rounds to protect me.

After another glance at my watch, I decided I could risk a straight dash across the open space. I put my head down and started running. My sneakers made virtually no noise on the broken brick pavement; I ran on my toes, as my high-school track coach had taught me. But my last track meet had been nearly twenty years ago, and five thousand packs of cigarettes had taken their toll. The sprint to the side of our neighboring warehouse shouldn't have taken more than ten seconds, but it seemed to go on for hours. I imagined Morrison's delight to see me huffing and puffing across the open space, and the un-alloyed joy with which he would take aim at the center of my spine. I waited for the crack of his pistol.

It didn't come, and I staggered to a halt at the corner of the building. Sweat was already dripping off my forehead. I leaned against the wall and looked back at the home of the Palmer Engineering Company. Morrison had already come around the far corner; I must have been in plain sight for two or three seconds. Somehow, Morrison hadn't seen me. I felt better; if he missed me, but wasn't likely to notice the cord, either.

At a quarter to one, I found a phone booth across the street from a bar that was still open. It was a seedy section of town, and I didn't feel very comfortable about roaming around the dark streets.

I dropped a coin into the slot and dialed Preston's office. At this hour the secretaries were gone. Preston answered it himself.

"Senator Preston?"

"Yes," he replied. "Are you the man who called this morning?" He had a nice rich baritone voice, perfect for committee hearings and press conferences.

"Senator, I have some information for you. Do exactly as I tell you, or I'll have to give this to someone else."

"What do you mean?"

"Just what I said." I wanted to frighten him with the possibility that some other politician might get to drop this particular bombshell.

"What is this all about?" he asked.

171

"I can't tell you now. I want you to go to a pay telephone and call me at this number. 555-4732. Have you got that?"

"I've got it," he said angrily. "Is this cloak-and-dagger nonsense really necessary?"

"Come on, Senator. You know as well as I do that your phone is probably tapped. Just find a safe phone and give me the call. I'll be waiting." I hung up the receiver.

This phone booth wasn't quite as nice as the one at the airport. There was no seat, and most of the glass had been smashed. I was mildly surprised that the phone worked at all. I leaned back against the one unbroken wall and lit a cigarette.

Preston was an ambitious politico on the make. His Senate hearings on the CIA had made him quite a reputation as a liberal slayer of right-wing monsters, and there was a lot of "inside-Washington" talk in the columns that Preston had his eye on the White House. That was hardly newsworthy, since anyone who ever came to this comic-opera city had his eyes on the White House. But Preston's flashy media style made him a serious contender, and that made him vulnerable to midnight phone calls. One more spectacular bit of muck for him to rake personally could make him a household word.

A few minutes later the phone rang. I grabbed it at the first tintinabulation. I wanted to get this over with as quickly as possible, before whoever was almost certainly tapping Preston's phone got around to tracking down the location of the number I was at.

"Preston?"

"Yes. I'm at a pay phone, so maybe now you can tell me what this is all about."

"Sorry, Senator. Not now. I'd rather tell you in person. I want you to drive to the Lincoln Memorial. Walk halfway up the steps on the side facing the Reflecting Pool. I'll meet you there if you're alone. If you're not alone, don't even bother to show up. If I'm not there when you arrive, wait. I'll be there shortly. Do you understand?"

"I understand that I'd be a damned fool to do as you say. I don't know who you are or what you want. For all I know, you plan to kidnap me."

"That's the chance you'll have to take if you want this information."

Preston was silent for a moment. He was probably weighing the potential benefits against the risk. He may even have been thinking that a kidnapping wouldn't hurt at all, as long as he survived it. An assassination attempt might be valuable, too. If Preston wanted the presidency badly enough, he would be willing to take the chance.

"Can't you at least give me some kind of hint about what you've got?"

I knew I had him. "Senator," I said, "this is just too big to talk about on the phone. I'm taking a chance too, you know. Either we trust each other, or I deal with someone else."

There was another pause. Then he spat out, "Okay. The Lincoln Memorial."

"See you there, Senator. Alone."

I risked one more call from that booth and dialed the number of a cab company. I gave them the name of the bar across the street and told them I wanted to be picked up there. The dispatcher called one of his cabs, then told me it would be about ten minutes.

Hanging around in the booth for another ten minutes didn't appeal to me, so I decided to go into the bar and have a quick beer. It was a small, dark place, and I immediately discovered that it was a black bar. Several sets of eyes followed me as I walked from the door to an open spot at the bar.

I had that crawly, paranoid feeling that you get when you find yourself where you know you ought not to be.

173

The bartender took his time getting around to me, even though he didn't seem to be busy with anyone else. He was short and heavyset and looked as if he knew how to take care of himself.

"What'll it be?" he asked, his voice thick with the burr of the southern ghetto.

"Beer. Whatever you have on tap. And I wonder, would you happen to have any postage stamps?"

"Would I happen to have any postage stamps?" he said, eyebrows raised, mocking me. I kicked myself for the way I had phrased it. It made me sound like some kind of Ivy League fop.

"That's right," I said.

He turned so he could address everyone sitting at the bar. "Gentleman here," he announced, "wants to know if anyone would *happen* to have a *po*-stage stamp." There were sly grins and snickers.

A discussion ensued about whether or not anyone happened to have a postage stamp. It was hard for me to follow the quick, slurred talk, but I fully understood that I wanted to get the hell out of there.

My beer arrived, I shoved a dollar bill at the bartender. "Look," I said. "We both know I'm in the wrong place, but I'd really appreciate it if you could get that stamp for me."

His eyes widened, the picture of innocence. "Wrong place? Why, shit, man, this is an equal-opportunity bar!" That set off a fresh round of laughter. I sipped my beer and stared at a calendar on the wall.

A young black man sort of danced his way toward me. He grinned at me, displaying several empty slots.

"Hey, my man," he said, "I hear you want a *stamp*! What you need it for? You gonna *mail* yourself outta here?"

"No," I answered calmly. "It's an important letter to my

stockbroker. I want him to sell all my cotton plantations and buy stock in Aunt Jemima's pancakes and Uncle Ben's rice."

That produced a moment of stunned silence. I sat there and waited for something to happen.

My main man slowly drew his features into a broad, happy-darkie smile. "Why, *sho*, boss!" he drawled. "For a letter like that, I do believe I got a stamp." He reached slowly for what was going to be either his wallet or a switchblade. With a move that would have done Walt Frazier proud, he whipped his hand out of his pocket up to a point about an inch from my eyeballs.

It was his wallet.

"Got one right here," he said. He brought the wallet back down and dug out a stamp. I reached into my pocket for change, but he shook his head.

"Don't need no money, my man. Always glad to help."

"Thank you very much," I said. "You're a fine fellow. Perhaps you'd like a job on my cotton plantation."

"Shee-it, man, you ain't got no cotton plantation!"

"No," I answered, smiling for the first time, "but I got a stamp."

He laughed and slapped me on the shoulder. "Man," he said, "you just completely crazy."

My cab came a few minutes later. I waved good-bye to my new friends, and got into the cab, shaking and scared. I'd been away from home for too long; I'd forgotten that in this great land we're all afraid of each other. That's why people like me get so much work.

On the way into Washington, I had the cab stop at a mailbox. The letter felt too heavy for one stamp. Mick was going to have to pay the additional postage himself. He could afford it.

175

We came in across the Key Bridge. I looked across the river and saw the Kennedy Center, which was new to me, and the Watergate complex, which was not. I had known it back in the days when it was the home of John and Martha Mitchell, a fun couple if ever there was one. I was in Europe when Watergate gained its real fame, and like most people in Europe, I watched from a safe distance, utterly fascinated. We may not have Nixon to kick around anymore, but it was fun while it lasted.

The taxi let me out on the Potomac side of the Lincoln Memorial. It was a quarter to two, and the streets were virtually empty. The memorial and the Washington Monument in the distance were only perfunctorily lit, not like the pre-energy-crisis days when they gleamed brightly all night long.

I climbed the dirty marble steps, impressed by the edifice in spite of myself. Despite all the un-American things I had done, it was impossible not to feel a touch of awe and admiration when in the (symbolic) presence of Lincoln. Perhaps I had chosen the location out of some subconscious desire to atone for my sins in the presence of old Honest Abe. But that was bullshit; if I had wanted to atone for my sins, I certainly wouldn't have been meeting with a political hack like Preston.

He was there. From the top steps, I could see him standing alone, facing the Mall. He was halfway up the steps, and I could see no one else anywhere in the area. If he wasn't alone, his friends were well hidden. And they had probably seen me by now.

I walked around to the front of the memorial on the level I was at, then descended to meet Preston. My sneakers (aptly named, I suddenly realized) enabled me to make a silent approach. He didn't know I was there until I was directly behind him, one step up.

176

He spun around in a movement that betrayed eagerness and a certain amount of fear. With the practiced discipline of the trained public figure, he quickly regained his composure and met my eyes with a sincere, probing stare. Preston was in his mid-forties and still had all his hair and teeth—perhaps even some extra teeth, from the dazzling glare of his public smile. He wasn't smiling now, however. He had that wrinkled-brow, down-turned-mouth-corners look that politicians use when they are viewing with alarm.

"Glad you could make it, Senator," I said. Out of reflex, he started to extend his hand, but caught himself in time. If he had the savvy I thought he had, he was aware of the possibility of hidden cameras. A midnight handshake on the steps of the Lincoln Memorial with a disreputable character would make a pretty picture.

He studied me in silence for a few moments, then said, "Okay. Who are you, and what is this all about?"

I made a sweeping gesture to encompass the memorial. "Welcome to my office, Senator. Won't you sit down?"

He looked at the thick marble steps, decided they were clean enough, then lowered his expensively tailored behind to the step. I sat down next to him and lit up a cigarette. We didn't look at each other; we were both busy looking back and forth at the trees and shadows, searching for anyone who wasn't supposed to be there. If anyone did see us, we must have looked like two birds on a wire.

"Before we start," I said, still not looking at him, "I'm going to need some guarantees."

"Such as?"

"Immunity. And I'm also going to need a presidential pardon."

Preston looked at me now, in amazement. "What do you think I am?" he asked incredulously. "I couldn't possibly

177

guarantee you a pardon. I don't even know what you've done."

"That didn't stop Ford from pardoning Nixon. But I'll concede that you're still in the dark on this. Once you've heard what I have to say, you'll see why a pardon is not only necessary, but possible. In the meantime, I'll settle for a promise of immunity."

"From prosecution? I can't even give you that. I will offer you conditional immunity if you testify before my committee."

"Conditional on what?"

"On the basis of what you have to say. So far, you've told me absolutely nothing."

I looked at the shimmering waters of the Reflecting Pool and decided that I had gotten as much as I was going to at this stage of the game. "Okay," I said. "I'm willing to work with that—your promise of immunity before the committee, and your promise that you will pursue the pardon."

"I'm agreeable, if—and only if—you have something important."

"I do, believe me. But listen, Senator, if you give me any reason at all to doubt you, that's the last you'll see of me."

"I'll stand by what I've said. Now it's your turn."

After years of guarding my every word, it was difficult to get started. I decided it would be best if I introduced myself.

"Do you know who I am, Senator? Do you recognize me?"

He looked at me for several moments. I have a rather unremarkable face, but at one time it was prominently displayed in newspapers and post offices.

"Can't say that I do," he said. "Should I?"

"My name is Sam Boggs. Does that do anything for you?"

"Sam Boggs? It rings a ... Wait a minute! Back in the sixties?"

You're on the right track. With all due modesty, I was the leading underground bomber of that turbulent era."

He snapped his fingers. "Right! I remember now. You used to be a chemistry professor someplace."

"Berkeley."

Preston spent another moment staring at my face. Now he knew that he at least had something, but he wasn't sure if he liked it.

"I never approved of the likes of you, Boggs. You gave the whole antiwar movement a bad name. Killing innocent people—what was it supposed to prove?"

"My bombs never killed anyone. I was very careful about that. But that has nothing to do with why we're here. I don't care if you approve of me or not, Senator. I just wanted you to know who I am, so you'll believe what I have to tell you."

"Which is?"

"What do you know about the incident at the plutonium-storage facility at Rogers' Crossing, Pennsylvania?"

Preston's eyes widened. "You were involved with *that*?"

"How else would I have known about it? The government hasn't said a word."

"And they're not going to. Everyone in this town who knows is scared silly. A lot of people have taken sudden vacations. Boggs, if you have solid information about this, I'll guarantee your immunity."

"And the pardon?"

He thought about it for a moment. "I don't know. It would be difficult, but I think the White House is so eager for a lead on this thing that they might go for it. I'll try, I promise you that."

"Fine," I said. "And to show my appreciation, I'm willing to handle this in a way that will make you look like Jack Armstrong, All-American Boy."

Preston allowed himself a narrow little smile. "Of course," he said, "that would be a pleasant spin-off. But the important thing is to recover that plutonium and get the people who stole it."

"Naturally. But it won't be easy, and you're just going to have to play this my way. There are complications. That's why I came to you."

"The CIA?" I nodded. "Boggs," he said, "you can't be seriously suggesting that the CIA stole that plutonium. That's just plain ridiculous."

"It's ridiculous, but I think it's true."

"You *think* it's true? You mean you don't know?"

"Senator, I was offered a million dollars to build an atom bomb. I wasn't told where the money came from or whom I was dealing with. I'm just a hired hand. But I've put the few pieces I have together, and it looks to me like they spell CIA. I did some small jobs for them in Europe—your committee might be interested in the details—and I think I got to know their pattern of behavior. It's the same pattern I'm seeing in this operation."

"And that's all you have to go on? Don't you have any solid evidence?"

"I'm afraid not. What I do have is an atomic bomb that's a week away from being functional."

"You've actually built it?"

"I didn't have much choice. The other side of that million dollars was a boat ride down the Styx."

Preston examined his thumbnail; it was neatly manicured. "Will it work?"

"Yes. It should yield two kilotons."

"My God, Boggs! Don't you realize what you've done?"

"Senator, the fact that I'm here should tell you something. The bomb is not completed yet, but when it is, I'll have taken steps to sabotage it."

"Effective steps, I hope."

"The best I can do. The problem is, an atom bomb is so damned simple that there aren't many ways to fix it that won't be noticed. I'm the only one in the team who knows what's involved, I think. But I know that they have people I haven't met who are checking my work. So I can't do anything obvious. There's nothing I can do about the plutonium or the basic bomb design, which is what they are probably checking. But I think I can manage to disable the detonators in a way that they won't notice."

"But the detonators could be replaced."

"I know. But you have to remember that they have other people who could build a bomb. The only way I can do anything to sabotage it is if I stay in their good graces. I'm taking a hell of a chance just being here."

Preston got to his feet and walked away from me for a few seconds. Maybe he thought I was radioactive.

"All right," he said. "I believe you. But what makes you think that the CIA is involved?"

"You might as well sit down, Senator. This will take a while." He did as I suggested.

"Shoot," he said.

"Senator, when I first became involved in this, I thought I was dealing with the Mafia. That's the way they came on. They said they didn't plan to use the bomb, they just wanted it for blackmail purposes."

"That's a relief, I suppose."

"Don't bet on it. There were holes in their story. We hit a guarded plutonium-storage facility. I suggested that it would be much, much easier to hijack a truck, something they have experience in. But they didn't go along with that. Their cover story was that the hit was to be made by a radical terrorist group. We were supposed to make all kinds of leftist noises when we were at PACA—but nobody did. For all the extra

181

trouble they went to in order to establish the story, they didn't even bother to follow through on it. And another thing: they had an inside man at the facility."

"The dead guard?"

The live one. Has he disappeared yet? If he hasn't, he will. And that would be another strike against the terrorist story. I have to believe that the radical business was mostly for my benefit, to get me to believe in certain aspects of the operation which wouldn't have made sense otherwise. I keep coming back to the truck. They had accurate information on when the delivery would be made, and they claimed they were able to delay the truck en route. So why not just grab it? If they were really Mafia, it would be a snap for them. And I've done enough work for the mob to know that the whole business of the cover story is totally uncharacteristic. The Mafia's idea of a cover story is being in a barber chair in Miami while somebody is being hit in Detroit. Look at the Hoffa thing. They could have tried to make it look as if anybody had gotten him—he certainly had enough enemies. But they didn't bother. The cover-story business just doesn't wash, not if they're the Mafia."

"So far, that's just supposition. What else have you got?"

"More supposition, I'm afraid. But it hangs together. There were five others in the group that hit PACA. None of them talks about anything more revealing than the weather. That would make some sense, on the basis of keeping me from knowing more than I have to. But what good does it do to keep me in the dark if we get busted? *I* can't tell anything, but they could, and probably would. So they're specifically trying to keep me ignorant. Why? Maybe because I wouldn't like it if I discovered I was working for the CIA.

"And another thing. The one time I managed to pry some information out of one of them, it didn't jibe with the Mafia

182

story. He didn't seem to know somebody he would have had to know if he had come out of the Boston mob; and from his voice, that's clearly where he came from."

"Okay," said Preston. "You don't think they're Mafia. That's certainly a possibility. But what makes you think they're CIA?"

"First, they've got money. Whoever they are, they've got the capital to put on a well-financed operation. They deposited a half-million dollars for me in a bank account, or at least I think they have. That rules out any real terrorist organization. Even someone like Black September doesn't have that kind of bread to throw around. And they certainly wouldn't get it from Egypt or Syria; the last thing they want is nukes going off all over the place. If that happened, the Israelis would use their own bomb."

"You know about that?"

"Doesn't everybody? Anyway, I just can't believe that they're an actual terrorist group with that kind of capital.

"And I have to be careful on this one for the moment, but I think there's at least circumstantial evidence of a link with the Global Armaments Corporation."

Preston scratched his chin thoughtfully. "Hmmm ... they're CIA, all right, or were. They started up in the fifties as a CIA proprietary, but at least in theory they're on their own now. But you know the old saying, there's no such thing as an *ex*-CIA agent. That's one thing we've learned for sure from the hearings. Anything else?"

"Nothing specific. Just a feeling. The money had to come from somewhere, and the CIA has to be a strong candidate."

"Assuming it is the CIA, it still doesn't make sense. They could get all the plutonium they wanted from other sources. And what would they do with a bomb, anyway?"

"With the CIA, who can tell? I think that if they wanted to

supply some group with nuclear weapons, they would take elaborate precautions to make sure their tracks are covered. Every nuclear explosion has a characteristic 'signature.' By analyzing the fission products in the fallout, you can pretty well tell how the bomb was built and even who built it. This way, the bomb can only be traced back as far as PACA and the unknown group that stole the plutonium. And that could be anybody. Also, a professional bomb design would be apparent, so they got themselves a good amateur to build it—me. They may even plan to blame it on me, somehow. More likely, they just wanted a bomb that would be efficient, but homemade. As to what they plan to do with it, take your choice. Africa, Asia, South America, you name it. There are plenty of people who would like to have one, and maybe the CIA wants to help."

"And maybe they don't. Boggs, this is a fascinating story, but you still haven't proved that it's a CIA operation. I'm no longer surprised by anything the CIA dreams up, but this is pretty extreme."

"I agree. I just don't have any other logical candidates. Do you?"

"I think it could still be the Mafia. This isn't a typical operation, so there's no reason to expect them to act true to form."

"It's possible," I admitted. "But I just don't think so."

Preston stood up again. He was a tall man, in good shape; he got a lot of female votes.

"Boggs," he said, "regardless of who is building the bomb, the important thing is to prevent them from using it. If you seriously want to help, I think you and I should go straight to the FBI."

I stayed where I was on the step. "Wrong, Senator."

"Oh?"

"If we blow the whistle now, you get one half-assembled bomb and a gang of hoods. The rest of the plutonium we grabbed has been moved. I don't know where, and I doubt if anyone else in our little group does either. I think they're all nearly as ignorant as I am. If this operation gets blown, they'll just start all over again somewhere else with the remaining plutonium. And they'll be more careful the next time."

"Well, then what do you suggest?"

"I'm going to go back and finish the bomb and pretend to be pure as the driven snow. When I know more, I'll contact you. In the meantime, I'll throw some names at you. Check them out, but for God's sake don't let them know you're checking. If they get wind of it, they'll know there was a leak, and they'll know where to look for it."

"Give me the names," he said.

"The man who seems to be in charge says his name is Stover. It's probably not, but check anyway. He's in his forties and claims to have been a muncipal-bond salesman. Billy Wynn is a truck driver. Marty Serino is the one from Boston. The others, all I have is last names. Kemper, a muscleman. Morrison, a gun freak. And Locatelli, who used to work in a foundry."

"Is that all?"

"And me, of course. By all means, check me out." I hesitated for a moment. "Preston? There's one other name, but she's not really involved. She's a friend of mine."

"Even if she's not directly involved, tell me anyway. I'll run a quick check."

"I don't know. But there are so many loose ends, I'm not really sure of anything. Her name is Heidi Wallace, she's twenty-two, and she comes from Venice, California. That's all I know."

"Okay, I'll check her out."

"Go easy."

Preston stared at me for a long moment. "Boggs, I'm taking an awfully big risk on this. I should just flatten you and drag you back to the Justice Department."

I stood up and faced him. He was considerably larger than me. "Why don't you?" I asked.

"I'm not sure. If that bomb goes off and anyone finds out that I met you, they'll tar and feather me. There are a lot of people who'd like to, anyway."

"Senator, if you don't do this my way, you'll never get the rest of the plutonium."

"And if they find out that you've talked, we won't even be able to find you and your bomb."

"That's the chance we're both taking."

He turned and looked at the Washington Monument and the Capitol Building, with the spotlighted flag fluttering limply in the night air. "Imagine what it would do, Boggs."

"Believe me, I have."

"If anything goes wrong," he said, shaking his head, "God help us all."

"Senator, if anything goes wrong, God will pretend he doesn't even know us."

12

It looked like a shining metal basketball. Inside it there was another metal sphere the size of a baseball.

"Goddamn," said Locatelli in a voice that bordered on reverence. I knew how he felt. Locked up in that silvery orb was the secret that all our lives had been a secret shared only by powerful and distant men who controlled the fate of the planet. The nuclear genie did their bidding, and theirs alone, and the rest of us waited helplessly in the background.

Now we had harnessed the genie for ourselves.

"I just can't believe it," Locatelli muttered.

"Why not?" I asked. "You helped build it."

"I know. But somehow, I don't think this is what they had in mind back in tenth-grade metal shop."

I laughed. "I don't think Mr. McLish, my eleventh-grade chemistry teacher, would be crazy about it, either." In a strange and frightening way, I was proud of the damned thing. And I was appalled by what I had done.

The plutonium sphere (two hemispheres, really) had weighed in at 3.5003 kilograms. Now nestled inside a beryllium casing two centimeters thick, the plutonium should have been slightly below critical mass; the fact that Locatelli and I were still standing there at least proved that it wasn't yet *above* critical mass.

Critical mass was difficult to calculate, and I had made sure that if I erred, I did so on the down side. You reach critical mass when enough neutrons are bouncing around within a given volume and density of plutonium to be able to start a self-sustaining chain reaction. The point at which that happens depends on a number of factors.

One is the plutonium itself. There are several different kinds of plutonium, and it's extremely important to know which kind you've got. As a metal, it can be either dense alpha phase or somewhat less dense delta phase. Inside a beryllium shell, alpha-phase plutonium goes critical at four kilograms, delta phase at eight kilograms. What we had was mostly alpha phase.

Another thing you need to know about plutonium is what isotope you have. In military bombs, it is almost entirely plutonium-239. But the kind of plutonium produced by commercial reactors contains a significant percentage of plutonium-240, a very different breed of cat. Unlike 239, plutonium-240 fissions spontaneously, spraying out neutrons without any help from bomb designers. Without the 240, you need what is known as an initiator at the center of the plutonium sphere. That consists of two materials, usually lithium and polonium, which emit neutrons when rammed together; the initiator provides the neutrons which get the chain reaction started. But if you have plutonium-240 in your bomb, you already have neutrons flying around, and your problem then becomes predetonation. If your chain reaction begins too soon, you can get a fizzle. You can also get a dead bomb maker.

My measurements were not as precise as I would have liked, but I estimated that we had about twenty-percent plutonium-240. For my purposes, that was unfortunate. If we had needed an initiator, I would have had a subtle but effective way to disable the bomb. Instead of putting in an actual initiator, I could have substituted a wafer of some element such as boron, which absorbs neutrons instead of emitting them. But knowing that Stover had people looking over my shoulder, I couldn't take a chance on faking the need for an initiator. Even worse, if the switch was discovered and they tried to replace it with a real initiator, the bomb could go off right then and there.

The beryllium casing was also crucial in determining critical mass. Our basketball-like shell served as a neutron reflector. Any neutrons escaping from the plutonium would tend to bounce off the beryllium and go right back into the chain reaction. Without the neutron reflector, you would need a much greater quantity of plutonium to get a critical mass.

Beryllium was the optimum choice for the neutron reflector, but we could also have used steel or aluminum, or even about six inches of wax. As the fourth element on the periodic table, beryllium is one of the lightest substances there is. But as a metal, it is also the densest element, with more atoms per cubic centimeter than any other element. That is what makes it such a good neutron reflector. It is also highly poisonous, brittle, and difficult to work with. Locatelli had had a hard time shaping the reflector, but his final product was flawless.

So good, in fact, that it worried me. The steady background beat of the Geiger counter picked up noticeably in frequency and intensity after we put the plutonium inside the casing. It wasn't at a dangerous level yet, but I still had to pack on a layer of high explosives. Plastic explosive is another good

189

neutron reflector, and by the time it was added to the bomb, we would be uncomfortably close to a critical mass. If my calculations were wrong, the whole thing could blow up in my face, literally, while I was adding the C-4.

The Geiger counter would be my best friend during that operation. The second it took a jump, I would strip off every ounce of the C-4. Then the whole thing would have to be recalculated.

I took another precaution to make sure that nothing that could contribute to criticality would get too close to the bomb. The whole contraption was suspended from wires inside a tubular aluminum framework. When it was finished, the detonators and wiring could be hidden inside the framework, which would then be covered by plastic panels and mounted on wheels. My atomic bomb was going to look like an unimpressive plastic box, four feet on a side. The wheels would make it easy to move, which was a definite advantage for Stover, but it also eased my mind. My memory of Locatelli and Kemper dropping the birdcage was all too vivid.

"Well," I said, "I suppose I might as well get started." Locatelli lifted a box of plastic explosive up onto the workbench. We had a couple of hundred pounds of the stuff, far more than we would need. I expected that Stover would somehow manage to find a use for the surplus.

Locatelli started unpacking the C-4. It came in strips, a foot long, four inches wide, and two inches thick. That was too thick for my purposes, so I couldn't simply slap the strips onto the beryllium globe, like someone working in papier-mâché.

"You ought to get out of here, Locatelli," I said, tapping his ample gut. "You make too good a neutron reflector."

"Whatever you say, boss." He picked up a few of his tools, then walked off to the far corner of the warehouse, where Kemper and Serino were playing gin. I liked Locatelli now, and I enjoyed having him working with me. But there was nothing more he could contribute now, and I didn't want him standing next to me if I accidentally put on too much plastic explosive.

I tore off a piece of the C-4 and began working it around in my hands as if it were modeling clay. When it felt right—and I have no idea how I determined that—I stuffed the gray gunk into a small mold I had constructed. It served the same function as a cookie cutter.

I wasn't about to just plop the stuff onto the globe and push it around until I had a uniform layer. The mold was precisely shaped to duplicate the curve of the beryllium shell. It gave me an exactly measured piece of a large jigsaw puzzle that, when completed, would cover the entire surface of the shell.

Handling it gingerly, I removed the C-4 from the mold, gripping it lightly by the edges so that I wouldn't mar the smoothness of the inside curve. Then I daubed it with a few drops of industrial glue and set it carefully onto the spot I had marked on the globe. The glue wasn't really necessary, since the plastic would naturally stick to the shell, but I worried about potential sagging at the bottom of the ball. The globe hung from its wires, stationary, at about chest level. I patted the chunk of plastic into place and listened intently for any change from the Geiger counter. There was none. I visually checked the needle on the gauge to reassure myself.

So far, so good. As the plastic covered more and more of the globe, the Geiger level was gradually going to change. I had rigged it to start beeping at a certain level, which I hoped was comfortably below the danger point.

It was asking too much for the wedges of plastic to fit exactly and cover the sphere with complete uniformity. I put each piece in flush with the ones already attached, and tried not to let the pattern get too far out of line. But each small

191

error was cumulative, and by the time I had everything but the sphere's north pole covered, I was left with a large, irregular open space.

I stepped back from my creation and mopped sweat from my forehead. The muscles in the back of my neck were clenched, and my stomach was generating the angry juices of tension.

I checked the Geiger again. It was holding steady at a high but still safe level. Then I glanced at my watch and found, to my surprise, that I had been working without a break for over five hours. Time flies when you're having fun. It was well past the time when someone normally went out for food, but if anyone had, they didn't tell me about it.

The amoeba-shaped empty patch at the top of the sphere stared back at me. I was in no hurry to cover it up, but I had learned a long time ago, as a Sunday golfer at Berkeley, that a putt doesn't get any shorter if you stare at it. I grabbed a glob of C-4 and got to work.

Molding the plastic by hand now, I added it to the bomb in half-dollar-size increments. After each addition, I poked a thin wire into the plastic to check the depth. It was consistently shallow, which meant I had to lay on very thin strips above what I had already put in place. That was a finicky, frustrating process, and more than once I had to pause and tell my shaky fingertips to behave. It would have been much easier to purposely apply too much plastic and then scrape off the excess. It would also have been much more dangerous.

Finally I plugged in the final piece of the puzzle and gently coaxed it into the right shape. The shiny, silvery basketball was now a dull gray medicine-ball-size atomic bomb.

I cracked my knuckles, wriggled around to loosen up my spine, then walked away from the thing. God help us all, the senator had said.

*   *   *

"So this is it," said Stover. "It doesn't look like much."

"We could paint it red, if you like," I suggested.

Stover ignored me and walked slowly around the metal framework. It looked like a very large bowling ball suspended inside a jungle gym. Stover, for the first time since I had met him, was impressed.

He put his pudgy hand up to his chin and scratched it. "How likely is it to go off?" he asked.

"Accidentally?"

"That's what I was thinking of."

"That's about all that anyone around here does think of. The biggest part of the risk is behind us, I think. When I was putting on the C-4, it could have gone at any time. But now I think we're in the clear. Whatever we've got, at least it's not a critical mass. Adding the detonators tomorrow shouldn't add significantly to the danger of reaching criticality."

"And what about intentionally?"

I sat down casually on the corner of the workbench. "What do you care about that, Stover?"

He stopped his pacing. "I don't follow," he said blankly.

"I said, why should you care whether or not it can go off? You weren't planning on using it, were you?"

"What's on your mind, Boggs? You know the plan as well as I do. The bomb has got to be functional, or it has no blackmail value."

"It's functional, all right, or will be when I set the detonators and wiring."

"That's all I wanted to know," said Stover. "And what was it that you wanted to know?"

"Same old thing. What's going on?"

Stover parked his oversized ass on a stool. He had gained some weight since returning to the States.

"Boggs," he said tiredly, "do we have to go through this song and dance again?"

"In the words of Count Basie, one more time. It's pretty late in the game to worry about what I know and what I don't know."

Stover spread his arm. "Then why are you worried, Boggs?"

"I meant that it's pretty late for you to be worrying about it. Me, I've still got some questions."

"You can ask. Just don't expect answers."

"Sorry, but this time I do expect some answers. My part of this operation will be finished as soon as the detonators are in place. That should be finished by tomorrow night. What happens then?"

"You get a good night's rest, I would imagine. And pleasant dreams."

"And then I get up and eat breakfast. And after that?"

"We take you for a ride, and you wind up as the new cornerstone of an Italian restaurant in Jersey City. What did you expect?"

I hopped off the workbench and walked over next to Stover's stool. "You know," I said, "you think you're putting me on, but what if you're not?"

Stover stood up to face me. "Get to the point, Boggs."

"You keep telling me that there are people above you who give the orders. That's the implication, anyway. What happens if they decide they want to save themselves the rest of my fee?"

Stover pondered the question for a moment. I couldn't tell if he was trying to think of a good lie or simply didn't know what to say.

"I don't think that's very likely to happen. There's been no indication of it."

"Christ, Stover, who did you take your public-speaking lessons from? Ron Ziegler? 'No indication of it,' my ass. I've been straight with you, Stover, and I haven't given you any problems that an aspirin couldn't cure."

"And you think I owe you something?"

"Aside from my money, I'd appreciate a little candor. What are the plans for me after tomorrow?"

"Honestly, Boggs, I don't know. I expect I'll receive instructions tomorrow. You can believe that or not, but it's the truth."

I didn't believe it for an instant. "What do you think your instructions will be, just off the top of your head?"

"I would guess that I'll be instructed to put you on ice for a while, frankly. They'll want you available in case we need another bomb for some reason. Also, they'll want you where no harm can come to you while we play out the scenario. I don't think it will be terribly unpleasant for you, Boggs. I wouldn't want to mislead you, but I hear the Bahamas are nice this time of year."

"Well," I said, "that's something to look forward to."

Stover clapped me lightly on the back. I don't know if it was intended to reassure me or to prove that he was a good guy, after all.

"Don't worry about it, Boggs," he said. "You've done a good job here. Nobody's going to screw you for it."

"We can hope and pray," I said.

I was dog-tired that night. My muscles ached, my head hurt, but my mind was still going full-tilt. Heidi lay next to me in the bed, and that didn't help. Wynn was spending the night, which meant that Serino already had a roommate.

I kept telling myself that there was only one day left to go. That thought should have made me relax, but it had the opposite effect. Preston hadn't heard from me in nine days and was probably getting frantic; he was increasingly likely to do something stupid. Tomorrow night would be my last chance to contact him, and I wasn't entirely sure that I wanted to. It might be a lot easier to take the line of least resistance and go along with Stover.

If I did go back to Preston, there wasn't much that I could tell him except that the bomb was finished. That information wouldn't exactly calm him down. On the other hand, Preston might have a pardon waiting for me.

"What's the matter, Sam?" Heidi asked me. "You keep mumbling."

"Am I? I'm sorry, I didn't realize it."

"What were you mumbling about?"

"Nothing much. Stover says that we might be going to the Bahamas in a couple of days."

"Really? That would be great!" The thought of smooth beaches and warm water always turned Heidi on. What would she do if Stover sent us to Minnesota, instead?

She put her arm across my chest and scooted over so that the full length of her body was pressed against mine.

"Sam?" she said. Her voice was as soft and warm as her body. "When we get to the Bahamas, it'll be just you and I again, won't it?"

I ran my fingers through her hair and kissed her gently. "I hope so, kid. I really do."

We held each other in the dark for several long minutes. I didn't want to send her back to Serino tomorrow night. It would be the last time, but it seemed like one time too many.

I had almost drifted off to sleep when Heidi whispered, "Sam, whatever happens, I want you to know that I really do love you. I really do."

"I know. And I love you, too, Heidi."

She hugged me more tightly. "I'm so glad to hear you say that again. It sounds like heaven."

To me it sounded more like good-bye.

*   *   *

I spent the next morning sabotaging the detonators. It was by far the simplest thing I had done since leaving Torremolinos. Plutonium cores and neutron reflectors were new to me, but I could work with detonators in my sleep.

I sat at the workbench next to the bomb and pretended to sort through several dozen detonators. I told my fanclub that I was checking them to make absolutely sure that they were all in good shape, since even one faulty detonator could adversely affect the bomb. No one doubted my word, and no one was anxious to get close enough to the bomb to look over my shoulder.

What I was really doing was disconnecting the wires that led into the detonators. It was easily accomplished, and when the detonators were reassembled it was impossible to tell that there was anything wrong with them.

The bomb design called for twenty-four detonators evenly spaced over the surface of the globe. In an atomic bomb, everything happens with frightening speed; the multitude of detonators assured that all parts of the plastic explosive would ignite simultaneously. If it exploded unevenly, by just a few thousands of a second, the shock wave would be irregular and the bomb would probably fizzle.

In theory, what happens is that the chemical explosion drives the globe inward upon itself. The neutron reflector acts as a piston, compressing the plutonium core. By the time the shock wave reaches the core, the plutonium is precisely at critical mass. The added jolt of the shock wave compresses it still more, kicking it past the point of criticality. The plutonium has such a density by this time, and the atoms are so closely packed, that the random neutrons released by the plutonium-240 have a high probability of splitting the nuclei of neighboring atoms, releasing still more neutrons to split more nuclei ... and suddenly (very suddenly) you have a

197

nuclear chain reaction. The whole process takes about a millionth of a second.

But if Stover and company tried to explode this bomb, it wouldn't happen at all. I thought it unlikely that they would dismantle any part of the bomb just to check the detonators. When it failed to go off, they would realize that something was wrong, but they might be a little reluctant to reenter the blast area to determine the nature of a malfunction. Nothing contributes to a bomber's ulcer like having to check out a bomb that should have gone off but didn't. That's why I always made damn certain that my bombs would go off on the first try. Except for this one, of course.

I was feeling pretty pleased with myself by the time I had inserted the last detonator and sorted out the wiring. The bomb now resembled an old submerged mine that had gotten tangled in seaweed. But as far as everyone else was concerned, it was now a fully operational atomic bomb.

The employees of the Palmer Engineering Company gathered around—at what they judged to be a safe distance—to inspect the fruit of their labors. Even Morrison got out of bed to come down and look at it. Heidi got into the spirit of the day and passed out cans of beer.

There were bad jokes, nervous laughter, and an odd feeling of camaraderie. We were like a dissension-torn baseball team whose players hated one another but had nevertheless just won the World Series. Locatelli even poured a beer over my head. It was a touching gesture, but sticky.

Serino clanked his beer can against mine. "Boggs," he said, "you did okay."

"So did you," I answered. Serino laughed uproariously and stole a quick glance at Heidi, who had come out of her doldrums and was wearing the same outfit she had worn the night we hit PACA. He probably thought that he was the only one who had caught the double meaning of my words.

Heidi went out with Kemper to get food and booze. With Stover gone and the job completed, it was party time.

Five men and one woman don't make for much of a party, but Heidi did her best to make it a memorable occasion. To the blaring beat of top-forty radio, she danced wildly with Serino and then Locatelli. Kemper and Morrison were content just to watch Heidi falling out of her blouse.

Heidi mixed up a potion she labeled Plutonium Punch and got everyone falling-down drunk. With Morrison it was hard to tell, but his vacant stare seemed glassier than usual. By eleven o'clock no one appeared to be capable of anything more demanding than throwing up.

I avoided the punch, and when Heidi forced it on me, I took a few sips and then surreptitiously poured my cup back into the lab basin that was serving as the punch bowl. I planned a late date with Preston, and I didn't want booze on my breath or brain.

Everyone racked out early; Serino and Kemper had to carry Locatelli up to his bed, an imposing task.

Heidi seemed to be pretty well-lit herself, but I pretended to be in a virtual stupor. She didn't even bother to try to get a reaction out of me.

"Just go to sleep, Sam," she said, "and tomorrow we'll be on our way to the Bahamas."

"Right," I mumbled into the pillow.

"Do you mind if I say good-bye to Marty?"

I said something incoherent, and Heidi kissed me on the back of the neck. I heard her close the door as she left.

Getting out of the building was no problem this time, with Morrison still stretched out on the workbench downstairs. I phoned Preston from the same booth, reaching him at the home number he had given me. We agreed to meet again at the Lincoln Memorial.

199

It was a drizzly October night, the kind of weather that made me think again about the Bahamas. If that was really what Stover had in mind.

Preston was where I had found him the last time, standing alone on the front steps of the memorial. He was wearing an overcoat and staring at the raindrops falling into the Reflecting Pool. I descended the steps to meet him; he didn't turn to look, but he knew I was there.

"You're late," he said.

"My apologies, Senator. I had a hard time getting a cab."

"That's an interesting bit of information," he said. "You know, of course, that I could check with the cab companies and find out where you were picked up."

"You could. I doubt if it would help you a great deal."

"Well, it doesn't matter. I've decided that we've played it your way long enough. From now on, we'll do it my way." He turned to face me.

"Senator!" I said, surprised. "I thought you were in favor of gun control."

He lifted his arm, bringing the black barrel of the little .38 up into the light. It was pointed at my face.

"If you shoot me, Preston, I won't be able to tell you very much."

"It shouldn't impair your speech if I blow your kneecap off. Let's go, Boggs. There's a car waiting."

I could see that he meant it. "Okay," I said. "But, Senator, you've just lost my vote."

"Move," he said.

I moved.

13

The car was parked in the shadow of the cherry trees, along the Reflecting Pool. In it were two men, both of whom got out and met us as we approached. One had a gun aimed at me, and Preston handed his own gun to the other one. They didn't waste any time with words. Preston got into the front seat, next to the driver, and the man with the gun pointed at me motioned for me to get into the back. I did, and he followed.

I leaned back against the plush upholstery of the long black government Chrysler and kept my mouth shut. It seldom does much good to argue with men who are holding guns on you. From the look of these two, they were probably FBI agents, crisp and efficient. When we were rolling, Preston turned and said to me, "This is the way it has to be, Boggs."

"You could be making a huge mistake, Senator." He didn't reply, and turned back toward the front.

Actually, from his point of view, he was probably making

the right move. I just wasn't interested in his point of view. I had decided to tell them where the warehouse was, since all of us, bomb included, would probably be leaving in the morning. It would have made me feel a lot better if I was sure that someone was keeping track of the bomb while I basked in the Bahamas. But I wanted to give them the information freely and without coercion; now they intended to beat it out of me, if necessary. And I was no longer sure that I wanted to tell them.

We cruised in silence along the empty streets of Washington and eventually arrived at a building on E Street. There were two lights burning on the fifth floor.

They herded me inside, into the elevator, and up five flights. The elevator doors parted to reveal a large linoleumed office area with gray metal desks spaced at regular intervals. My escorts guided me past the first row of desks and into a private office.

It was a small room, with only three chairs: one for me, one for Preston, and one for the man staring at me from behind another gray metal desk. My friends from the FBI closed the door behind them as they left the office.

I sat down quickly, not wanting to get involved in a prolonged staring match with the man at the desk. He was about forty, with black hair that was getting noticeably sparse on top. His nose sloped down and slightly away from two intense, unblinking brown eyes that were sheltered by thick dark brows. He was unshaven and looked as if he had been up for several days. The desk was littered with empty Styrofoam coffeecups.

Preston sat down without a word of introduction. The man at the desk continued to stare at me. I wasn't interested in playing that game.

Finally he said, "He's Boggs."

"I know that already," I said. "And who are you?"

"McNally. We had some doubts that you were really who you claimed to be." He had a Midwestern twang in his voice, a true product of the heartland.

"Now that we know who we are," I said, "why don't we talk about how stupid you are?"

"Don't try to be glib, Boggs," said McNally, propping up his chin with an elbow on the desk. He didn't seem particularly excited about having me in his office.

"I took a terrible risk with you the last time," said Preston. "I decided it would be much safer doing it this way tonight. You're too important, Boggs. We can't let you wander off into the night again."

"And who is 'we,' Senator? If I'm under arrest, you've already blown your case."

Preston started to answer, but McNally cut him off. It surprised me, because civil servants don't usually interrupt senators.

"Boggs," he said, "you might as well forget about your constitutional rights. No hot-shot ACLU lawyer is going to come rushing in here with a writ of habeas corpus. Nobody from the Washington *Post* is going to make you into a fucking hero. Nobody knows you're here, and if you don't cooperate, nobody ever will. And nobody's gonna miss you when you're gone." ,

"I'll concede the rest of it, but you're wrong about the last. If I'm not back where I came from by morning, the folks I work for are going to miss me. Unless you're a complete idiot, you can figure out what that will mean."

"I told you, Boggs, don't try to be glib." His voice was still flat and unconcerned.

At the rate we were going, we were going to sit there trying to outtough each other until dawn. I decided to try the offensive.

"Preston," I said, "I gave you a chance to be a hero, and

you've blown it. I was prepared to tell you where to find the bomb tonight. I thought you could be trusted to handle it with a scrap of intelligence. Now I'm not even sure if you could piss in the ocean if I gave you a map."

The senator wasn't fazed by it. "You didn't really think I was going to deal blindly with a wanted fugitive, did you?"

McNally listened to the exchange with a look of profound boredom.

"Save us all some time," he said, "and accept the situation, Boggs. We can find out whatever we need to know from you. We can do it the hard way or we can do it the easy way. It's up to you, but you'd better decide now."

"I had already decided to give you all I had. I took a lot of risks to bring the information to Senator Smiles, here, and I thought I was going to get something in return. McNally, you're the one who wants to do this the hard way. You blow the arrangements I made, and all you'll get from me is headaches. Here's one for starters: they're going to move the bomb tomorrow morning."

"We'll have the location out of you long before then."

"No doubt. And all you'll get if you bust them is one bomb and a few low-lifes. The rest of the plutonium has already been moved. And if you decide not to bust them, it still won't help you to follow them, because when they discover I'm gone, they'll run in six different directions, none of which will lead you to the rest of the plutonium. You'll blow it so bad, McNally, that you'll be counting paper clips in Nome by tomorrow night. And as for you, Preston, how do you think your constituents will take it if they find out that their smiling senator was responsible for the escape of a clandestine group with an atom bomb?"

"What makes you think they would find out?"

"A letter I wrote. If you don't live up to the deal we made, that letter will end up on the front page of a lot of newspapers." In fact, the letter I wrote to Mick didn't even mention Preston, but he didn't know that.

I could tell that I had finally reached them. Preston went a little pale, and McNally removed his chin from his fist. He got to his feet, a little unsteadily at first, then rolled his head around to loosen up his neck, the way Roberto Clemente used to do.

"Would you like some coffee, Boggs?" he asked.

"Cream and sugar," I said. "And no sodium pentothal, please."

He smiled as he opened the door. "You won't even get the cream and sugar. Grossman," he called to one of the men who had brought me in, "bring us three coffees."

McNally sat on the one uncluttered corner of his desk; it looked as if it had been kept clear for precisely that purpose. He popped his knuckles, one by one, while we waited for the coffee.

The coffee arrived, black, and Grossman left us as soon as he finished the delivery. The three of us raised the cups simultaneously, as if we were making a toast. Nothing could have been farther from my mind.

"Okay," said McNally, "now we know where we stand. Can we proceed from here in a spirit of friendly cooperation?"

"Not quite," I said. "I'd still like a little quid pro quo here. You can drag some useless information out of me, or you can get my active cooperation. Which way do you want it?"

McNally seemed to sigh, then glanced at Preston. The senator gave a slight nod. McNally went back around behind his desk and removed a paper. He handed it to me.

It was White House stationery. I read it quickly, with growing interest. I raised my eyebrows a little when I saw the signature at the bottom.

205

"It appears to be a conditional amnesty," I said.

"With an emphasis on the 'conditional,'" Preston added quickly. "It means that the government is willing to forgive and forget just as long as you cooperate. And that means by our rules, not yours."

"Fine with me, Senator. That's all I wanted in the first place. But tell me, what's to prevent you from using me as long as you need me, then hitting me over the head with a blunt instrument and tearing up this little piece of paper?"

McNally sat down again and resumed his *Thinker* pose. "That sounds like a great idea to me, Boggs. But naturally, you'll probably want to mail your new diploma home to Mom and Dad. Or whoever you sent the other letter to. That's your insurance."

I started laughing. "McNally, that's exactly the same deal I made with my 'employer.' Are you sure you two haven't worked together?"

"Still think it's a CIA game?"

"Signs still point that way."

"No they don't," said McNally. "*I'm* CIA, and if this bomb caper were a Company project, I'd know about it. It's not, so you can forget about that angle."

I looked at Preston. "Well, Senator, surprise, surprise. By day, you're a courageous defender of liberty, and by night you play footsie with the CIA. Fascinating."

Preston glared at me. "Contrary to what you might believe," he said, "the two are not mutually exclusive."

McNally quickly interjected, "The senator is just helping us clean house, Boggs. It's nothing to get excited about. So why don't we get down to business? We have a lot of ground to cover if we're going to get you back home by dawn."

I saluted him with my cup of coffee. "Very good thinking, McNally. Why didn't you do it this way in the first place?"

"The President didn't want to use that pardon unless it was absolutely necessary. He's understandably reluctant to have his name on any piece of paper that has anything to do with this situation. But you stated your case so persuasively that it seemed like a good idea to haul out the pardon. Forgive us for trying to do it the easy way first."

"Easy for you," I said. "Difficult for me."

McNally smiled slightly, then removed a pen from his breast pocket and shoved a yellow legal pad into position. "Okay," he said, "let's get to it. The senator has already given us everything you told him. The important thing now is the bomb itself. What shape is it in?"

"It's finished. It's also sabotaged."

McNally jotted a few notes. His face remained impassive, as if we were talking about a shipment of defective auto parts instead of an atomic bomb.

"Can it still explode?" he asked. "And how likely are they to discover the sabotage? If they do, can they fix it?"

"One at a time, please. I don't think the bomb can explode now, barring some kind of freak accident. In order to discover what I did, they'd have to remove each of the detonators and take them apart; I don't think they'll do that. But if they do, it will be a simple matter of replacing them."

"That's not very reassuring," Preston put in.

"It was the best I could do under the circumstances."

"You could have refused to build it in the first place."

"If I had, I'd be dead, and someone else would have built it," I told him angrily. I was wishing I had picked some other politician.

Without looking up from his legal pad, McNally raised his right hand in a peacemaking gesture. "What about the plutonium, Boggs?" he asked.

"The bomb contains about three and a half kilograms. We

opened two birdcages to extract it, and we had about one-point-four kilograms left over. We should have gotten an even five kilograms, but a tenth of a kilogram somehow disappeared during the operation. That's a pretty normal occurrence, so don't try to make anything out of it. The industry calls it a MUF—Material Unaccounted For. Plutonium somehow disappears during processing, and nobody really knows what happens to it. But the stuff that was left after processing is still at the warehouse. All the rest of the plutonium that was stolen has been moved. I don't know where."

"Where is this warehouse?"

"On the docks in Alexandria. We go under the name of the Palmer Engineering Company. It's about a mile from the Global Armaments Corporation. I thought that was an interesting coincidence."

McNally put down the pencil and looked at me. "I told you," he said, "the CIA knows nothing about this."

"Are you sure?"

He answered slowly, choosing his words with care. "Boggs, the Company is not involved, period. I will admit to the possibility that some renegade operators are caught up in it, but if they are, it's entirely on their own. The Mafia story makes much more sense."

"Have you come up with anything to support it?"

He shook his head. "The names you gave us didn't check out. None of them."

I sat up straight. "*None* of them?"

"Not a one. Did you really expect them to?"

I had sure as hell expected that at least one of them would. I didn't know what to think now.

McNally continued, glancing occasionally at his notes. "The FBI has been checking out all organized crime activities. They've leaned pretty hard on a lot of prominent people, and have come up with nothing. Either nobody knows about it, or they're too scared to talk."

"Who could scare those guys?"

"Good question. It's a big hole in the Mafia theory, but it doesn't prove anything one way or the other. As you suggested to the senator, whoever is running the show must have access to substantial amounts of money. To me, that points the finger right back at organized crime, whether a lot of people know about it or not. It could be a small group hidden inside a family. It could even be an unauthorized caper, the brainchild of some ambitious Young Turks."

"It seems to me," said Preston, "that the important thing right now is to get that bomb before they move it. We can worry about who's behind it later."

I looked up at the ceiling and let McNally answer. He did it diplomatically, but not without the implication that the senator had marshmallows for brains. "Senator," he said, "I know you're worried about the bomb going off. But I think you'll agree that it's much more vital to find where they've taken the rest of the plutonium."

"All I know," Preston replied stubbornly, "is that there will be hell to pay if that bomb explodes and anyone finds out that we could have prevented it."

"There will be even more hell to pay if we get this bomb and they build several more and detonate *them.*"

"Don't fret, Senator," I added. "If we blow it, I'm sure you'll think of some way to blame it on the Republicans before Election Day."

Preston's face went red. He jumped to his feet and took a challenging step in my direction. "Goddammit, McNally," he bellowed, "I told you we should have—"

"Senator!" McNally, still seated placidly behind his cluttered desk, bit off the word with the sharp authority of a

209

gunshot. Preston stopped, looked at McNally, then back at me. He was seething.

After a moment, McNally calmly continued, "I think, Senator, that we might make more progress here without you. You've already done as much as you can, and there's no reason to get you dangerously involved. Why don't you go home and get some sleep? We'll let you know the minute anything happens."

Preston turned toward McNally, but couldn't think of anything to say. He pivoted briskly and stomped out of the room.

McNally leaned back in his chair and rubbed his eyes. "Keerist!" he said, almost to himself. "And they call *us* incompetent!"

For the next hour we talked about how to handle things in the morning. McNally agreed to have one agent follow me, to the Bahamas or wherever. I wanted to have someone close at hand in case Stover wasn't kidding about Jersey City. It seemed unlikely that I would learn anything else of value about the operation or who was behind it, but I was McNally's only man on the inside. He told me that I would be given recognition codes and a small transmitter, to be used only if I needed to make immediate contact. I was half-expecting an "L" pill, but I didn't get one. That was fine with me.

As soon as I was safely back inside the warehouse, McNally would set up a stakeout—unobtrusively, I hoped. They would follow anyone or anything that came out of the warehouse, but from a safe distance. I didn't expect Stover to move the bomb to the same place he had moved the remaining plutonium, but at least it would be a step in the right direction.

I didn't really care. I felt the tension begin to seep out of me, and knew that it was because it was all over for me. I had done what I could, and now the ball game was out of my hands. My only objective now was to stay alive.

That might not turn out to be easy, but at least it was something I could understand. I had my pardon, I had CIA protection, and (I suddenly remembered) I still had a half-million dollars in the bank in Switzerland.

And I had Heidi. Sweet, tawny surfer-girl Heidi.

McNally's problem was to get the plutonium back. I hoped he would do it, but I had my doubts. He was smart and efficient, and I liked him for the way he had handled Preston. But he was also a CIA man; I trusted him about as much as I trusted Stover.

At three-thirty, McNally got wearily to his feet and put on his jacket. "We ought to get you back home," he said.

I nodded. "Fine with me. But first, I want you to leave me alone for a few minutes. And I want an envelope and a stamp."

"Oh, yeah. Your insurance. Make yourself at home. Stamps are in the top drawer of the desk. Blank envelopes are in the bottom drawer. Don't take too long."

McNally left the room. On a sheet of McNally's legal pad I wrote a quick letter to Mick. There wasn't time to detail everything that had happened, so I concentrated on Preston's involvement and gave Mick a few suggestions about how to use the information if it became necessary. If I knew Mick, he'd probably be anxious to read the next installment of my adventures.

I finished the letter and stuck it and my pardon inside the envelope. Leaning over it to protect it from any prying eyes, I printed the address, sealed and stamped it, then put it in my back pocket.

McNally was in the outer office, making arrangements with the two men who had brought me in. I still thought they were FBI; they had that look about them, right down to their shiny black shoes.

We all went down in the elevator together, but the others

went their own way after we left the building. McNally led me down the street to a nondescript-looking Plymouth.

"Yours?" I asked. "I thought secret agents all had Aston Martins."

"And I thought anarchists all had long, shaggy beards. Get in, Boggs."

I had him drive first to the main branch of the post office. I didn't want to trust my letter to a corner mailbox. The CIA made a habit of reading other people's mail anyway; I didn't think they would balk at hijacking an entire mailbox if they thought it would help them find out where I was sending my insurance policy. At the main branch, though, they would have a tough time separating my letter from all the others, even at this hour. And by the time they could get around to it, my letter would probably already be on its way.

On the way to Alexandria, I went over the recognition codes. It seemed like silly spy business to me, but McNally insisted that it was necessary. The midget transmitter was about the size of a cigarette lighter. I could use it to send Morse code, or a continuous homing signal. McNally said that it had an effective range of about ten miles.

Lights out, we crept slowly along the riverside streets of Alexandria, to within three blocks of the warehouse. I told McNally to let me out there.

As I stepped out onto the pavement, McNally leaned across the front seat and said in a loud whisper, "Boggs."

"What?"

"Don't get your ass shot off." He grinned, then I grinned. My buddy, the CIA agent. I had been making some strange acquaintances lately.

Keeping to the shadows, I trotted along the deserted street and stopped at the corner of our neighboring warehouse. I watched the building for several minutes.

Coming back from my first meeting with Preston, I had made a frantic dash across the open space, but this time I was going to make an easier approach. Morrison was probably still inside, dead to the world. But on the chance that he had recovered, I planned to wait and see if he had awakened to perform his sentry duty.

I waited a full fifteen minutes, but there was no sign that Morrison or anyone else was awake. I forced myself to wait an extra minute. There was still nothing. I started trotting toward the warehouse, keeping low, but not really rushing.

Fifty feet from the building, I lifted my head for some reason. A brilliant white light suddenly flashed in my eyes, then swiftly grew to engulf the warehouse, the earth, and the sky. I couldn't believe how beautiful it was.

Just as swiftly, it faded and became distant, a faraway memory, like the red warmth of the womb. I was sad that it was gone. But I was astonished by how very long it had lasted, and by how much you can think and feel in a millionth of a second.

14

The light was there again. It wasn't as bright or burning this time, and it moved. I followed it back and forth until I heard a muffled voice say, "Good." Then the light went away again and, pleased with myself, so did I.

When I returned, I found myself in a gauzy, soft-focus world colored a gentle green pastel. It took some time for me to realize that I was staring at a ceiling. I tried to move my head to see what else I could discover about this place, but my efforts produced no movement whatsoever. My vistas were strictly limited to the ceiling, and not much of that; I seemed to be viewing the world through a very narrow tunnel.

That amused me. I had finally seen the light at the end of the tunnel.

Curiosity drove me to further experimentation. Okay, I couldn't move my head; what else couldn't I move? The answer was simple: everything. I was a disembodied head, and nothing more.

That didn't amuse me. I abandoned the physical world for the moment and tried to take stock of my mental equipment. I assumed that I was in a hospital, but I had no recollection of how or why I was there. Whatever had happened, it had rendered me completely immobile. For how long?

I remembered hearing about people who remained in comas for many years before mysteriously returning to consciousness. Perhaps I was one of them. It might be the twenty-first century by now. And I could be a paralyzed octogenarian.

It was a sad thought. I wondered what I had missed in the last few decades.

That was a fruitless line of thought. I decided to concentrate on questions that I could reasonably be expected to answer. Questions like: Who was I?

I fielded that one effortlessly. Encouraged, I tried a tougher one: What was the last thing I remembered?

I played with that one for quite a while. The best I could do was a vague memory of being in a hot sunny place where people spoke a language I didn't understand. I suddenly became very angry at myself and my inability to recall anything about myself. Here I was, an eighty-year-old quadriplegic, with nothing to do but stare at a narrow slit of ceiling. I couldn't imagine anything more frustrating.

My anger cooled, and I realized that if my assumptions were true, then I wasn't going anywhere, so I might just as well settle down and really concentrate on trying to remember what had happened.

A hot, sunny place where they spoke a strange language. Okay, then, list every hot sunny place you can think of. I did, ticking off islands and deserts and resorts and places I had heard mentioned in junior-high-school geography class. When I got to Spain, there was a little click of recognition, like the tumblers of a cheap combination lock falling into place. I visualized a map of Spain and zeroed in on all the place names I could remember. Torremolinos clicked another tumbler into place.

Gradually I built up a past. While doing so, I became aware of sensations from my body. I couldn't identify the feelings, but at least they established the fact that I still had a body. I couldn't move it, but it was there.

My right arm felt strange. I tried to analyze the sensation, and broke it down to a combination of itch, heat, and dull pain. I also had the impression that the arm was encased in a cast. If true, that was a useful bit of information. It meant that whatever had happened to me, it had happened recently. With a trace of regret, I bade farewell to the twenty-first century.

It didn't seem nearly as difficult to remember something that must have happened only a few days or weeks ago, instead of half a century back. Memories came flooding back into my mind, too many of them to handle all at once.

While I was trying to sort them out, I heard voices. They were muted, and they had to compete with an insistent ringing that I noticed for the first time. I couldn't understand what was being said, so I ignored the voices and went back to sleep.

When I awoke again, my world was considerably enlarged. I could see more of the ceiling, the ringing had abated somewhat, and I remembered everything. I found myself wishing that I could forget it again.

People came into the room. There was a tall white-haired man whom I took to be a doctor. And there was also McNally.

He had finally gotten around to shaving, but he looked more haggard than ever. He swam over to me, through the green haze, and peered down into my face.

"Don't try to say anything, Boggs," he said, carefully

enunciating every word. "Just blink once for yes and twice for no, okay?"

I blinked once.

"Good. Do you know who I am?"

Blink.

"Do you remember what happened?"

Blink.

"Good, good. You're doing fine."

I felt like Rex the Wonder Horse. I expected McNally to offer me a lump of sugar as a reward for my performance. Instead, he asked the doctor to leave the room. He retreated from my field of view, and I didn't have the energy to try to follow him. I heard the scraping of chair legs on the floor.

"You probably have a lot of questions," McNally began, "but you're in no condition to try to ask them."

I forced out a weak groan. My mouth didn't seem to want to open.

"I told you, don't try to say anything, Boggs."

I groaned again, louder this time. Then I laboriously put together a sentence composed of the few sounds that I was capable of making.

"Ae mmm ae alae?"

"What was that? Try it again." I did, and it sounded a little more coherent the second time, though not by much.

" 'Why am I alive?' Is that what you're trying to say?" I blinked once. McNally hesitated before answering. "That's a real good question, Boggs. Dumb luck, I'd say, but that's not a medical opinion."

I blinked twice. "Uh ohmm!"

"The *bomb*? You think . . . Oh, I get it. Boggs, that wasn't a nuclear explosion, if that's what you were thinking. If it had been, you *wouldn't* be alive, and neither would I. The bomb was removed before the explosion. What went off was the plastic explosive—one hell of a lot of it, too."

I closed my eyes for a few seconds. There had been about a hundred and thirty pounds of C-4 left after I finished the bomb. That would not produce anything to compare with a two-kiloton atomic bomb, but standing at close range you probably wouldn't notice the difference. I certainly hadn't.

"Your next question," said McNally, "will probably be: 'How badly hurt am I?' I ought to let the doctor answer that one, but I don't want to keep you in suspense. You'll live, Boggs, although for a while we had some doubts. You have a bad concussion and a broken jaw, to begin with. Your mouth is wired shut, which is why you can't talk. I hope you'll get used to it and manage to speak a little, because you and I have a lot of things to talk about. Aside from the jaw, your right arm is broken a couple of inches below the elbow, and you have a few broken ribs on the right side. Also a lot of bruises, abrasions, and assorted traumas. They've kept you sedated up until now, but I think you can look forward to a lot of pain for a while. All things considered, you came out of it pretty well. When I pulled you out of the rubble, I didn't even think you were still alive. No, no, don't thank me, Boggs. I was just doing my duty as a public servant."

Thanking him had never entered my mind. He wanted me alive because I was apparently their only remaining link with the missing plutonium. From what he had said, it sounded as if Stover had made a clean getaway with the bomb.

I heard the sound of a match striking. Smoke drifted across my patch of ceiling. I grunted.

"What? You want a drag? I don't think that would be a very good idea, Boggs. If you started coughing, you could mess up a lot of the doctor's work."

I grunted again, more insistently.

"Oh, what the hell," said McNally. He leaned over me and inserted the cigarette between my lips. I took a cautious puff. It wasn't my brand, and it tasted raw and noxious, but I was grateful for it. I was grateful for any new sensation; being sedated is, above all, boring.

McNally let me take a second puff, then removed the cigarette. "You know," he said, "this situation has certain advantages. You've got quite a mouth on you, Boggs. When I told Preston what happened, I think he was disappointd that you weren't killed. I'm glad you're alive, but I can appreciate his point of view. You're a pretty loathsome character, Boggs."

I groaned. No communication was intended; it was just a plain old groan. I didn't feel like listening to McNally lecture me on the evil of my ways. But, it appeared, I didn't have any choice.

"I respect you," he said, "because you're good at what you do. But what you do stinks. I know, if you could talk you would come back with some smart-ass line about how you're no worse than the CIA. But you'd be wrong about that, Boggs. We do some lousy things, I'll admit. I know—I've done some of them. But at least we do them for a reason—a very good reason, in my opinion. But you, Boggs, you just go around blowing up anything that people are willing to pay you to get rid of. We've even used you ourselves. Tell me, is money really that important to you?

"No, I forgot, you can't tell me. But I suppose you'd say that it's not the money, it's professional pride or some such thing. Whatever it is, Boggs, it's not a good enough reason. At the start, maybe you thought you had a good reason. I didn't like Vietnam very much, either. And if you keep it on that basis, maybe you can make a pretty good case that you're just the same as me. Better, maybe, since what you did required a little

220

more dedication to the cause than what I did. But after you got out of the radical business, what was your excuse then?"

"Ugh oo."

"I understood that, Boggs." He gave me another drag on the cigarette.

"Don't misunderstand me," he continued. "I'm glad you're alive, because we need you. And the fact that you came to us—or to Preston—in the first place may mean that you do have some remaining scruples. I certainly hope so, because you and I are going to be spending a lot of time together. You're going to help us find that bomb and the rest of the plutonium, Boggs. And if you screw up or try to skip out on us, I will personally break any of your bones that haven't already been broken. I'll leave you with that happy thought."

He gave me one last drag on the cigarette, then stood up and walked to the door. Several people walked into the room. Some of them started prodding me in various parts of my body, one of them changed the I.V. bottle that was hanging from a metal brace above my left arm, and none of them said a word to me. Evidently McNally had instructed them to keep their minds on their work and not on anything I might have to say.

I didn't have anything to say anyway. After a while they completed their labors and left me alone again.

McNally hadn't said anything new. I had already told myself all the things that he had, and had learned the hard way that building atomic bombs was not a healthy occupation. At least, not for me. But what about the others? They must have helped move the bomb; that much seemed certain. Blowing up the warehouse could only have been intended as a way to get rid of me and leave a body to throw the authorities off the track.

But killing me meant that they intended to kill Heidi, too.

And Heidi was with Serino that night. How could Serino have gotten away without Heidi knowing about it? Maybe she did know about it, and had gone with him. Or maybe he hadn't gotten away at all. It could really have been an accident. But no, that didn't fit in with removing the bomb.

I just didn't know enough to be able to figure out what had happened, or why.

But it did seem likely that Heidi was dead.

I didn't want to think about that, so I slept instead. Drifting off to sleep was the easiest thing I had ever done. They had probably given me another sedative in the I.V., and I didn't mind.

The room was dark the next time I opened my eyes. My little scrap of green ceiling blended in with the blackness, and I felt as if I were floating in interstellar space. I had no sense of distance.

But something was moving, something very close to me. To my left. I managed to turn my head a full inch, and caught a thicker, denser shadow than the rest of the room. Gradually, it came into focus.

A person was standing over me. It had the shape of a person, at least, with a head and arms that were in motion. I heard an odd sound that I couldn't identify; it reminded me of the noise you make unscrewing the lid of a peanut-butter jar.

I didn't think there was any peanut butter in the room. It had to be something else. The noise was coming from the direction of that dark shape hovering above me. I strained to see what it was doing.

It was unscrewing the lid of my I.V. bottle, that's what it was doing. A nurse, then. A silent, efficient nurse. A male nurse, in fact, dressed in a dark suit.

Another noise, now. A muffled, liquid little plop; the sound of a pebble dropping into a pond. And then the screwing noise again.

The dark person took a step back from me and paused. It seemed to be waiting for something. I heard the sound of measured, regular breathing. It was my own, I realized.

There was another motion now, but it didn't come from the black shape in the shadows. It came from inside the I.V. bottle. Something was making bubbles inside that bottle. Soon, whatever it was would drip down the tube running from the bottle and into the vein in my left arm. That had to be what the person was waiting for.

And suddenly I knew what was happening, and that I would be dead in a few more seconds. I couldn't move and I couldn't speak; all I could do was lie there and wait for the poison to mix with my blood and kill me. I had come to terms with death a long time ago, but I never dreamed it would happen like this. The sudden, violent flash of a bomb gone wrong was what I had expected, maybe even wanted. But this was a brand of death that I couldn't accept.

I felt my sphincters loosen and my lungs contract. I couldn't breathe. The poison was already in me, and I was scared out of my mind. There was nothing I could do. I couldn't move.

I could groan. I did, in despair and fright, and the dark figure above me moved suddenly. I groaned again, as loudly as I could. It was a horrible, strangled sound. The person in the shadows hesitated for a second, then walked quickly away from me. I saw a light flash briefly when the door opened, then disapper when it closed.

The poison hadn't caused my sphincters to let go; it was blind fear. The foul smell drifted up into my nostrils and sickened me for a moment.

The I.V. bottle was bubbling like a pot of coffee; the capsule hadn't completely dissolved yet. I might have a few seconds left before the stuff slid down the tube and into me.

My left arm was strapped to the side of the bed. The idea was to prevent the patient from accidentally unplugging the I.V. It was a great idea—it worked.

But my right arm was free. It was sheathed in a cast up to the bicep, which felt old and weak. I lifted from the shoulder and managed to hoist the incredible weight of the cast a few inches into the air before my strength was used up. I tried again, feeling pain this time, sharp and insistent. I used the pain, telling myself it would be over just as soon as I lifted that arm up and across my body.

I jerked suddenly, pushing up and over from my shoulder and ribs. The pain stabbed from my broken ribs now, driving the air right out of my lungs. Bright white dots appeared like starbursts around the corners of my vision. When they faded, I saw that my arm was resting on the right side of my torso.

Very carefully, making sure that the arm wouldn't slip back to the bed, I inched it across my body toward the needles that were stuck into the crook of my left elbow. At last, my arm reached its destination, but it was still no good. I couldn't bend my arm far enough to be able to reach the needles. There was just no way. I sobbed in frustration.

Any second now, the poison would be coming down the tube. *The tube.* I had been concentrating on the needles. I took a deep breath and pushed myself over until I was resting on my left shoulder, my right arm draped across my left forearm. With another quick jerk, I managed to flip my arm a few inches into the air; coming down, I hooked my fingers over the metal railing at the side of the bed.

Using my fingers, I dragged the arm along the railing, toward the translucent yellow tube. I snared it, finally, between my first two fingers. I tried to squeeze it shut, but I couldn't get my fingers to work the way they had to. The strength just wasn't there.

I thought of one more thing to try. It had to work, because I didn't have the time or stamina to try anything else. Fingers still hooked around the tube, I shoved my arm forward across the railing until it was balanced a few inches below the elbow—the point where it had been broken. The tube was stretched taut, running parallel to my arm.

One last time, I managed to lift the arm. Only an inch this time, but it was enough. I brought it down on top of the tube, squashing it between the metal railing and the heavy weight of the cast.

I was soaked with perspiration and sticky with the excrement of blind panic, but I was thankful for it. The smell of my own shit had gotten me moving.

I couldn't lie there like that all night. I tried to shout through my wired-shut, swollen mouth. The sound was incoherent, but at least it was a sound. I tried again and produced a louder, uglier noise.

After a few minutes of grotesque grunting, I heard footsteps in the hall. My door opened, and the lights came on, blinding me for a few seconds.

"What are you doing?" demanded the nurse. She must have been horrified by the sprawled, stained body in the bed.

I grunted unintelligibly. She strode toward me.

"Ae ee!"

"What's that? I can't understand you."

I flicked my eyeballs repeatedly in the direction of the I.V. bottle. She finally glanced toward it and immediately went pale.

It was still bubbling like a witches' brew. "What in the world. . . ?" She stared at it, fascinated. When she reached out to unscrew the top of the bottle, I screamed again, louder than ever. I forced out something that sounded like "No!" If they had put cyanide, for example, into the bottle, the gas would kill us just as dead as a direct flow into the veins. I got my message across, and she drew her hand away from the bottle as if it were red-hot.

The nurse ran out of the room, but reappeared in less than a minute with two doctors and an orderly. They stared at the bubbling concoction for a full minute before they thought to take the needles out of my arm. I grunted in gratitude, then collapsed back onto the bed.

"It's the best thing that could have happened," McNally said two days later.

"Right," I replied. "It's the second time in a week they've tried to kill me. That's just great, all right." I leaned back against the pillows and thought dark things about McNally.

I could talk now, after a fashion. The doctors had removed some excess braces and paraphernalia, and the swelling had gone down, permitting me to speak more or less intelligibly through my clamped-down teeth. They had also dispensed with all of the intensive-care gadgets that constantly monitored my condition; as if in compensation for the loss, I had been provided with an around-the-clock marine guard outside my door.

"You shouldn't take it so personally," McNally said airily. "Their taking a chance like that means that you're still important to them."

"I'm still important to me, too, dammit."

"Boggs, you're not thinking. Why should they make such a high-risk move against you? Obviously, it's because you must know something that could damage them. Now, all we have to do is find out what it is."

"And maybe they just wanted to get rid of me out of pure

nastiness. McNally, I don't know anything that I didn't tell you the night of the explosion, and that's a fact."

McNally looked thoughtful. He was seated on a folding Samsonite chair, legs crossed, his omnipresent yellow legal pad in his lap. "Perhaps," he suggested, "it's something very small, something that seems unimportant to you. It might tie in, somehow."

"Like what? The color of Stover's socks?"

"Look, Boggs, you've got a right to be pissed off. We blew the security the other night. I'm eternally sorry about that. It won't happen again. So why don't you calm down and cooperate? Life will be a lot more pleasant for both of us if you do."

"And a wonderful life it is, too." I was already sick of my little green room in Walter Reed, and the uninspiring view out of my lone window. And I was especially sick of the high-octane fruit juices I was allowed to drink with a straw. I had absolutely vetoed any return to the I.V., and that had limited my nutrition intake to vitamin-enriched liquids that forced me to urinate ten times a day. I had filled enough chamber pots to float a small aircraft carrier.

"What's eating you, anyway? Is it the girl?"

McNally might as well have kicked me in my broken ribs. It was, indeed, the girl. Heidi was strange and scary at times, and I no longer believed that it would have worked for us in Tahiti or anywhere else. But if I hadn't gotten her involved at least she would still be alive.

After a few moments of revealing silence, McNally reached into his briefcase for some papers. "I don't know if this is good news or bad news," he said, "but I might as well tell you. We've combed the rubble of the warehouse. So far, we've recovered four, maybe five bodies."

"*Maybe* five?"

"It was one hell of a bang, Sam. There wasn't very much left."

"Jesus," I said softly. The thought of Heidi's lithe brown body was almost more than I could take.

"The good part," said McNally, "if you can call it that, is the fact that the three bodies that were more or less in one piece were all male. The fourth body was blasted almost to atoms. We've found pieces of it, and it's very difficult to tell whether we're dealing with one body or two."

"What about the first three?"

McNally handed me some photos. I looked at them and felt like gagging, but when your jaws are wired shut, you learn to control the gag reflex. The only alternative is a tracheotomy.

"Kemper, Locatelli, and Serino," I said. They were all badly mangled and burned, but still recognizable. Serino's body intrigued me. It was in somewhat better shape than the others. If Heidi had been with him, presumably her body would have been recovered as well. I decided not to tell McNally about Heidi and Serino; life was already complicated enough.

McNally took the photos from me. "Kemper, Locatelli, and Serino," he said, "are actually Kramer, Leonardi, and Salerno. We got prints from them and ran them through the computers. Want to hear what we found?"

"Please."

"Kramer did time in Illinois on an assault charge. Nothing big, and he was out in a few months. His occupation was listed as construction worker. Last known address was Alaska; apparently he worked on the pipeline. Leonardi's prints we got from the Army. Served two years, was a tank mechanic. Spent most of his hitch in Europe. Tax records show that he worked for several years in a foundry in Trenton."

"Tax records?"

"I told you before, you can forget about constitutional rights on this one. We're pulling out all the stops. There are times when all those computer files you read about actually do come in handy. Without them, we'd never have identified the man you knew as Serino. Never did time, wasn't in the service. But he did apply for a hack license in Boston, once upon a time. That's where we found his prints. Salerno worked for a fuel-oil distributor in Boston."

"That's all very interesting. How do we tie them together?"

"We're working on it. We've got people checking out every move they made from the time they were ten years old. There has to be some connection, and sooner or later we'll find it."

"What about the Palmer Engineering Company?" I asked.

"A real company, set up by unreal people. Nobody connected with it seems to exist. They owned the building—bought it from a now defunct real-estate company whose employees are now deceased or missing. They cover their tracks well."

"And the guard at PACA?"

"Disappeared. He had a wife and two kids, but he either ran out on them or was wasted. No leads."

"Sounds like you're doing a real bang-up job, McNally."

He didn't bother to respond. Instead, he reached for his briefcase again, returned the photos, and lifted out a small tape recorder. He placed it on a side table next to my bed and fiddled with the knobs and buttons.

"Sneer if you want, Boggs," he said, "but we're busting our asses on this. It's difficult, because it's top-priority, but we can't tell anyone what it's all about. Even now, there are probably only two dozen people who really know what's going on, and you're one of them. That's why we're going to take it from the top and get it all down on tape. You know something important, even if you don't know what it is."

I could see that he was serious. The CIA has a mania for collecting gobs of useless details, just for the sake of having them. Somewhere at Langley there is a room filled with literally tons of undigested intelligence reports. When this was all over, the tapes of my strained voice would probably wind up in the same room.

McNally tested the recorder and was satisfied with the results. "Okay," he said, "let's get to it. I want every detail, from the initial contact to the business with the cyanide the other night."

I couldn't think of any way to avoid it. "In the beginning . . ." I said.

We went over everything that had happened at Torremolinos. I tried to remember every word that Stover had spoken. When I got to the part about the money, McNally became very interested.

"He knew the number and size of your account?"

"That's right. I don't know how he could have gotten the information. That's another reason why I thought it might be a CIA operation."

McNally laughed. "You give us too much credit."

"Or not enough," I said. I was still not convinced that the CIA had nothing to do with what was happening. Sometimes their right hand doesn't know what their left hand is doing.

McNally pressed me on the bank account, but I refused to give him any more details. If the money was really in my account, it would have been laundered so well that they could never trace it. If it wasn't there, it didn't make any difference. Either way, it was my business, not McNally's.

I closed my eyes and tried to describe every baroque detail of the opulent pleasure dome in Westchester. I didn't think it would help very much; they could spend a year checking out every mansion in the area before they found the right one. And if they did, it probably wouldn't lead to anything.

The plans for the PACA operation I could have recited in my sleep. Halfway through them, McNally had me pause while he changed the tape.

"Let's continue," he said after a moment. "Who did what? Give me a breakdown on the individual assignments."

"Wynn had the truck. He was parked on a turnoff up the mountain while we were breaking in. Kemper and Locatelli— or Kramer and Leonardi—took care of the guard at the front gate. Ser . . . Salerno and I were in the field to the west of PACA, blowing the underground cable. Heidi was down the road about a mile, acting as lookout."

McNally scratched his chin. "You mean it was *Heidi* who killed those two cops?"

I looked at him. "What did you say?"

"The two policemen who were shot. Their bodies were found about a mile from PACA."

"Oh, my God," I said weakly.

"You mean you didn't know about it?"

I turned away from him and stared at the wall. No, I thought, I didn't know about it.

Sweet, sexy little Heidi. At first I couldn't believe it, but then I knew it had to be true. The look I had seen on her face that night, the look of postorgasm release—it was something else entirely. Or maybe, I realized, it was exactly the same thing. I had often thought about how other people never seemed to be real for Heidi, but the implication had escaped me: if other people weren't real, then it didn't matter what you did to them. You could fuck them or kill them, and it didn't matter which. Heidi did both, and enjoyed both. For six months, I had been sharing my bed with a psychopath, and I never realized it.

"Are you all right, Sam?"

"Fine," I said, "just fine."

"You really didn't know, did you?"

I shook my head. "She was just a girl I met on the beach. I liked her. Maybe I even loved her. If I hadn't gotten her into this, she might have had a normal, healthy life. She might never have killed anyone. Maybe, somehow, the whole thing triggered something inside of her. I don't know. She kept saying it was all a game. Maybe she thought the cops would get up and go home after the game was over."

"They didn't," McNally said flatly.

"Christ, I just can't believe she did it, but she must have. She wasn't even *supposed* to do anything like that. All she was supposed to do was call us on the walkie-talkie and let us know if anyone was coming. I didn't even know she had a gun. I can't even figure out how she could have gotten one, unless . . ."

"Go ahead, say it."

I turned to face McNally. "Unless," I said, "she was a part of the operation from the beginning. But I can't believe that."

"Don't be too sure," he said. "She didn't check out with the information you gave us. And there's something else I didn't tell you about the bodies in the warehouse. They all had traces of chloroform in them. Somebody gave them a Mickey."

"Heidi," I said. I knew it was true. "She made a fantastic punch for us that night. Plutonium Punch, she called it. And she practically forced it on everybody. Including me."

"But you didn't drink it?"

"I faked it. I was meeting Preston that night and didn't want to be drunk. Everybody racked out early, and everybody was pretty drunk."

"She wouldn't have had any of her own punch, knowing it was loaded," McNally pointed out. "But she thought that you were as doped up as everyone else. Boggs, how the hell did you get out that night without her knowing about it?"

Reluctantly I told him about Heidi's midnight meetings

with Serino. It didn't seem to matter now. I had been using her to be able to get out at night; apparently she had been using me for the same purpose.

McNally listened sympathetically. "Don't take it so hard," he said. "Just be thankful that you didn't let her know you were sneaking out. She obviously intended for you to be in the warehouse when it went up. While everyone else was out cold, she and someone else—Wynn perhaps—moved out the bomb. After the explosion, we were supposed to find your body and one and a half kilograms of plutonium. That would link you to the bomb and probably send us off on a wild-goose chase among the radical groups. And it would have worked, too."

"It's still hard to believe."

"Believe it."

"But I met her months before Stover came along."

"Naturally. She was setting you up. Her job was to make sure that you took Stover's offer. If you had tried to back out, she would have steered you right into it. You're not the first man to get taken to the cleaners by a woman, Boggs."

An hour ago, I had been feeling bad because Heidi was dead. Now that I knew she was probably still alive, I felt even worse.

McNally didn't let me dwell on it. He led me back into a description of the events at PACA. I told him about the relentlessly efficient way we had handled the guards, one of whom was on our side anyway. I told him about Kemper and Locatelli loading the birdcages onto the forklift, and described in unpleasant detail what happened when they dropped the eighth birdcage.

"That must have been pretty rough," he said.

"You can't even imagine what it was like. After it happened, all we wanted to do was get the hell out of there. We didn't even bother with the last three birdcages."

McNally held up his hand suddenly. "Wait a minute," he

said. "You loaded seven birdcages before the accident, then left?"

"That's right."

"So you've got seven birdcages in the truck and three left on the platform?"

"Yes."

"Then what the hell happened to the other twenty birdcages?"

We stared at each other. I didn't know what in the world he was talking about.

"Boggs," he said intensely, "twenty-seven birdcages full of plutonium nitrate were stolen that night. You've accounted for only seven of them."

Somebody, somewhere, had enough plutonium to build seventeen atomic bombs.

15

After I finally convinced McNally that I knew nothing of the other twenty birdcages, he snapped off the recorder, leaned back in his chair, and lit up a cigarette. He stared thoughtfully at the wall for several minutes.

"Well," he said at last, "this is very interesting."

"To me, it's just confusing. This must be my day to be stupid."

"No, I think they've been counting on your stupidity, or ignorance, for the last month."

"Thanks," I said.

"I should thank you. This has to be the thing that they wanted to kill you to keep you from spilling. The question is, how does it all fit in?"

"What I can't understand is what difference it makes. You've known all along that twenty-seven birdcages were taken. In fact, I was probably the only one in the entire operation who *didn't* know it."

McNally absently flicked some ashes onto the floor. "If that's true," he said, "there has to be a reason. They wanted to keep you in the dark about it. Why?"

"Why not? They were keeping me in the dark about everything else."

"So let's think about how they did it. There were only ten birdcages left on the platform when you got there. The other twenty had to have been removed earlier."

"Which means that both guards were in the bag."

"Right. They needed active cooperation to come in there with a big truck and load twenty birdcages. And after it leaves, everything goes back to normal in time for your operation."

I motioned with my left arm for McNally to give me a cigarette. He lit one, then handed it to me.

"The obvious conclusion," I said, "is that the second operation was staged entirely for my benefit. Why?"

McNally thought about it. "I'd say that it was necessary to keep you in the game. Stover conned you with a story about a gentlemanly blackmail operation. If you had known they were going to swipe that much plutonium, you'd have seen through the story. You probably would have turned him down."

"So what? They could have gotten somebody else to build the bomb for them."

"Yes, but they wanted you. And don't forget, the charred body of Sam Boggs was supposed to turn up in the ruins of the warehouse. With your radical connections, it would have led us in the direction of underground terrorist groups. That's obviously the wrong direction."

"But what is the right direction? If it is the Mafia, they've got a hell of a lot more plutonium than they need for a blackmail scheme."

"I know. That's been our primary worry. I would guess that they plan to sell the stuff."

"Then why go to all the trouble of having me build a bomb? Why not just kill me and drop the body in the warehouse?"

McNally dropped the cigarette to the floor and ground it out. "Apparently they wanted a bomb. They might want to use your bomb for the blackmail operation and sell the rest of the stuff."

"There's another possibility," I said.

"What's that?"

"They may want to sell finished bombs, not plutonium. I designed and built a workable atomic bomb for them. They could use it as a prototype to build others from the same design."

"A comforting thought. Using your design, they could build what? Sixteen, seventeen bombs?"

"At least. A ready-made bomb would bring a much higher price than raw plutonium nitrate."

"Much, much higher," McNally agreed. "And the other bombs wouldn't have defective detonators."

I stared at the glowing ashes of my cigarette. I felt sick to my stomach. They had a total available kilotonnage about twice as great as the bombs used at Hiroshima and Nagasaki. We were no longer talking about blowing up buildings; we were talking about destroying entire cities.

McNally got to his feet. "There's still something missing," he said. "They planned this very carefully to throw us onto the wrong track. But there must be something in all of this that will lead us to the right track. All we have to do is figure what it is."

"Correction," I said. "All *you* have to do. It's your ball game now, McNally. I've given you everything I have."

McNally walked over to the window and looked out at the

green lawn of Walter Reed. I sensed that he was about to tell me something that I didn't want to hear. I was right.

"I almost hate to tell you this, Boggs," he said, still gazing out of the window. "Your insurance policy has been canceled."

"What do you mean?"

"There was a radioactive tracer on your pardon. We followed it to San Francisco and intercepted it. But it wouldn't have helped you anyhow. Mick Mahoney is dead."

It had been a bad day.

"He was murdered," McNally said, turning to face me. "His office was ransacked. Whoever did it was looking for something."

"My letter."

"Obviously. How did they know?"

I closed my eyes and remembered Heidi coming into my room to wake me up the afternoon I wrote the letter. It was already in the envelope, addressed, stuck between the pages of the *Scientific American.*

"Heidi," I said. "Who else?"

"It figures. She's turning out to be one hell of an interesting lady. I'd like to meet her. I hope I get the chance. And if I do, you'll have the opportunity for a happy reunion. Because you're going to be with us on this, every step of the way."

"Why, for Christ's sake?"

"You built that bomb, Boggs. I'd say you have a certain responsibility for what happens to it, wouldn't you? We may need you at any time, for information on the people or on the bomb itself. If you want that pardon, you're going to have to earn it this time."

"What happens if I decide I don't want to help?"

"You can figure that one out for yourself, Boggs, You're still wanted on a half-dozen different state and federal charges. You could be shot while attempting to escape."

"Or while lying peacefully in my bed."

"I'm sorry, Boggs, but you're a dangerous man. You know too much, and we can't afford to let you go wandering around on your own until this thing is over, one way or another."

"And then?"

"And then, we'll see. If you help us recover the bomb and the plutonium, you'll get a new 'Get Out of Jail Free' card."

"And what if we don't get them back?"

He walked to the door and rested his hand on the knob. "If we don't get them back, Boggs, I am going to wish I had never been born. And I guarantee you, I won't be the only one."

McNally left the room, leaving me alone with a lot of unhappy thoughts. I wanted to shout out a string of obscenities, but it's difficult to cuss effectively when your mouth is wired shut.

After another two days at Walter Reed, McNally sprung me. I was still a mess: my face was swollen, lopsided, and discolored. I looked as if I had gone fifteen rounds with Ali. And felt it. I walked out of my room with all the practiced grace of a syphilitic old man.

McNally provided me with new clothes, which didn't fit very well. He also gave me the keys to my very own apartment, in a building across the street from the offices on E Street. The apartment next to mine, not surprisingly, belonged to one of McNally's assistants, an energetic young go-getter named Jim Gardner. Gardner's mission was to make sure that nothing bad happened to me. Considering the way things had been going, it looked like a formidable task.

The E Street offices actually belonged to the Interior Department, but the CIA had pressed a few buttons and commandeered the entire fifth floor as an operations center for the current emergency. My apartment also happened to be on the fifth floor, so McNally was able to keep tabs on me just by looking out of his window. Technically, I wasn't a prisoner, but I never lacked companionship. Technically, in fact, I wasn't anything at all; I fell into a gray limbo, somewhere between the status of a captured spy and an unindicted coconspirator.

During my first few days out of the hospital, I spent most of my waking hours being endlessly debriefed by McNally and then by two FBI men, Carter and Polonski. They were humorless, unimaginative men who seemed to have been mass-produced by a factory somewhere in Kansas. I was never quite sure which was Carter and which was Polonski. They bored me, but not as much as the tapes of my own distorted voice that they made me listen to over and over again. They wanted me to think of anything I might have left out.

Once, McNally called me at three in the morning. He asked me one question, and I answered it. The next day I didn't even remember what the question had been.

I returned to Walter Reed briefly to get myself unwired. It was an honest thrill to graduate from Hawaiian Punch to Gerber's strained carrots. My doctors advised me to stay away from rock candy for a while.

A week after I got out of the hospital, McNally called a meeting to review our progress. It could easily have been a very short meeting.

Nine of us gathered around an oblong conference table. McNally and Gardner represented the CIA, Carter and Polonski represented the FBI, and I didn't represent anyone but myself. Three of the remaining four were from the AEC, the Pentagon, and the White House. The fourth was Senator Preston, representing the fools on the Hill. I tried to smile pleasantly at him as he entered the room, but the condition of my face must have made the attempted smile look more like a burned-out jack-o'-lantern.

The meeting was grim. Gardner led off, reciting the CIA's bootless contributions to the investigation. They had checked out all the major international terrorist organizations and turned up exactly nothing. Carter (or perhaps Polonski) described the Bureau's thorough but inconclusive efforts to find someone connected with organized crime who might know something. He also went over the investigation of Kramer, Leonardi, and Salerno. That, too, had led nowhere; it figured, since the bodies would not have been left behind if there was any way to link them with the operation. As for Morrison's shattered corpse, it had never been put back together sufficiently to permit any kind of identification.

The man from the AEC had nothing to contribute except the fervent hope that whoever had the plutonium knew how to handle it. The Defense Department representative said that they had prepared a list of foreign countries which might be in the market for plutonium and/or nuclear weapons. It was a depressingly long list.

Preston had nothing to say. He was there only by virtue of the fact that I had been foolish enough to come to him in the first place. Also, I guessed, he was present as a token of the administration's efforts to "consult with the Congress."

The president's man at the meeting was a study in controlled panic. He alternated between trying to kick some asses and begging everyone to *please* come up with *something*. He was also very insistent that security be maintained until the crisis had been "managed."

The presentations completed, McNally peered through the dense blue smoke that hovered over the table and asked me if I had anything to say.

I did, but not in the presence of the people at that table. I had some ideas that I wanted to talk over with McNally, alone. I was even more afraid of a security leak than the man

241

from the White House. If this mess ever hit the press, a lot of people were going to be looking mighty hard for a scapegoat. It seemed highly probable that I would then be trotted out as Exhibit A.   .

"I don't have anything to add," I mumbled.

"Neither do I," he said. "Does anyone?"

No one did. The meeting broke up, and people slunk away in scared silence. They knew what was going to happen. They were powerful men who, for the first time in their lives, were suddenly powerless. The bombs would bang, and they could only whimper.

McNally stayed at the table, sorting through his notes. Long yellow sheets were scattered about as if dropped from an airplane. I got up and walked over to him.

"Can I see you?" I asked.

He didn't look up. "Not if you're going to hassle me about something."

"Who, me?"

"I think I liked you better when your mouth was wired shut. What do you want?"

"I have some random thoughts about the situation. I want to discuss them with you. But not here."

McNally shoved some papers aside. "I have some random thoughts, too. I've found that random thoughts are often the best kind." He bundled up the notes, threw them into his briefcase, and stood up. "I have also found," he said, "that alcohol is capable of increasing the essential randomness of one's thoughts."

"As a chemist, I'd be happy to verify that observation."

"As a chemist, Boggs, you are a crock of shit. Let's go."

We walked down E Street a few blocks to a dark, wood-and-leather kind of place. It was midafternoon, but the bar was fairly crowded; Washington is that kind of city. We ordered, bourbon for McNally and scotch for me, then found a booth in a corner. McNally looked and acted about as crippled as me, and nobody had even tried to kill him.

"Why the hell don't you go home and get some sleep?" I asked him.

"The most I could do would be to go home and lie awake all night. That freaks out my wife, so I just don't go home much these days."

"What does she think of all this?"

"She doesn't know. But she can tell that something big is happening. She's dying to ask, but she never does. She knows that if she did ask, I'd probably tell her. So she doesn't ask. She's a hell of a woman, Boggs."

"The all-American marriage," I said.

McNally put his drink down and pointed his finger at me. "Are you being snide, Boggs?"

I looked at him; his eyes were bloodshot and dangerous.

"No," I said, "no, I'm not being snide. I think I really meant it. That sort of domestic tranquillity has eluded me somehow."

We sipped our drinks in silence for a few moments.

"Any kids?" I asked.

"Two," he said. "A ten-year-old daughter who is going to be beautiful and a twelve-year-old son who has a jump shot that is going to make me prosperous in my old age."

"I suppose it must be nice to have a family. My family was the brotherhood of the revolution. None of that extended-nuclear-family shit for me, nosiree."

"What's this, Boggs? Regrets?"

"I suppose red-hot CIA agents don't have any."

McNally sighed and took a big slug of bourbon. "Yeah," he said, "I've got regrets. Remind me to tell you about some of the things I did in the Congo in sixty-one. But I can live with those things, Boggs, I really can. You know why?"

He waited for a response. "Why?" I asked dutifully.

"Because I'd have a hell of a lot more regrets if I hadn't done those things. I'm not what some people would call a patriot, Boggs, but I do believe in protecting the things you have. And what I've got is a family I love and a small piece of a nation that provides me with a lot of good things. So I do what I can, and if that means fucking over innocent Hottentots and Eskimos, so be it. Things are bad out there, and they're going to get a lot worse. The Company is just trying to keep us from going down the drain with everyone else. And we're not even succeeding. I'm afraid for my kids, Boggs. The last part of this century is going to be no fun for anyone, you can bet on it. So what does that make me, I wonder? A little Dutch boy frantically sticking my various appendages into a million different holes. What was it Louis the Fourteenth said? 'After me, the deluge.'"

He laughed, took another drink.

"So what are these random thoughts of yours, Boggs?"

"They're pretty random," I admitted. "We agreed that the business with the extra twenty birdcages was most likely the reason they tried to kill me in the hospital. Yet that information hasn't really led us anywhere. Maybe we're looking at it in the wrong way."

"How do you mean?"

I paused for a moment and tried to organize my thoughts. I still wasn't sure if it all made sense.

"Okay," I said, "take it step by step. I was being set up to make it look as if a radical terrorist group was behind the operation. And your guys haven't found any evidence to indicate radical involvement. So let's eliminate the radicals.

"Stover represented himself to me as a part of the syndicate. I began to doubt him almost immediately. It just didn't fit the pattern. The FBI hasn't been able to find a single informer anywhere in the rackets who knows anything—and that also doesn't fit. Mafiosi tend to be compulsive braggarts, to each other, at least. And none of the people at the warehouse ever said a word about their activities in the mob. They were a bunch of well-disciplined clams. So let's eliminate the Mafia, too.

"What's left? You've already eliminated the CIA. A foreign country? I'd say that's still a strong possibility, except for the fact that it's too elaborate. Any country that really wanted to get some nukes could simply have gotten a reactor from us or the Russians and then diverted a few kilograms of plutonium the way the Indians did. That would be far less complicated than arranging the PACA operation, and safer. That applies to the larger countries, anyway. The really small or unstable ones couldn't have gotten a reactor. But they also would have a very hard time running an operation this large and expensive. So I say, let's eliminate active involvement by a foreign country."

"Wonderful," said McNally. "You've just eliminated all our suspects."

"Not quite. But now we're down to a different class of suspects. We still need someone with a large organization and a lot of money. After eliminating everyone else, that only leaves big business."

McNally made a sour expression, then took another sip of his drink. "I'm tempted," he said, "to ignore your proposition because it sounds too much like left-wing paranoia. But at this stage of the game, I'm even willing to listen to that. Go ahead."

"Maybe you need a little left-wing paranoia. So far, you've all been acting out right-wing paranoia, chasing down anarchists and communists, and it hasn't accomplished anything."

"Granted."

245

"So turn it all around. We've been concentrating on who stole the plutonium. Why not look at who it was stolen *from*?"

"You mean PACA? Boggs, that's just a state agency. You're welcome to your paranoia, but I really don't think Pennsylvania is out to conquer the world."

"Not PACA. While we were loading the birdcages, I noticed some numbers across the top of them. 'GP—S.Car.,' then a series of numbers in sequence. I assume that refers to the reactor that produced the plutonium."

"Right. General Petroleum's South Carolina reactor. Boggs, I hate to disappoint you, but we've already checked out the people at GP. The truck driver who delivered the plutonium from South Carolina has disappeared. No one knew very much about him, and he hadn't been working for them very long. Obviously, there were people on the inside in this operation—the guards, the driver, and possibly some others. But that doesn't mean that GP stole the plutonium from itself. It doesn't even make sense."

"A lot of things don't make sense. Again, why not just hijack the truck—particularly if the driver is your man? Or steal it right out of the reactor?"

"Why not indeed?" McNally asked. "Boggs, you're shooting down your own argument."

"No, I'm setting it up. Listen, whoever stole the plutonium—the Mafia, the KGB, or the munchkins, whoever it was—logically, they should have hit the truck. It would have been the easiest thing in the world, even without an inside man. Those trucks are not guarded, and they make radio checks only once every two hours. It would have been a piece of cake. Yet they hit PACA and went to elaborate lengths to make it look like a radical group. But the radical stage dressing could have been added to a truck hijacking, too. I pointed that out to Stover, and he just brushed it off with some nonsense about how truck hijackings fit the Mafia M.O. It seems to me that they not only wanted to steal the plutonium, they also wanted to steal it from PACA and nowhere else. So why PACA? The only thing I can think of is that PACA is the point on the plutonium cycle *farthest removed from the owners of the plutonium.*"

McNally polished off his drink, then got to his feet, taking my glass with him. A few moments later he returned with refills.

"You're beginning to intrigue me, Boggs. Go ahead, corrupt me with more left-wing drivel."

I sipped a little scotch, then continued. "My theory also explains the cyanide incident. From the fact that I didn't know about the initial twenty birdcages, it's clear to all of us that this was at least partially an inside operation. They wanted to get rid of me so that you wouldn't start thinking in those terms. You did, but in the wrong way. You're still looking at it as an inside job carried off by outsiders. Why not consider the possibility that it was an inside job carried off by actual insiders?"

McNally lit two cigarettes, gave one to me. My right arm was still in the cast, and I hadn't mastered the art of striking a match one-handed.

"There are still a lot of angles to be explained," he said. "But this is the first new idea I've heard lately. Hitting PACA instead of the truck bothered me, too. If GP really is behind this, then it begins to make some sense. GP's birdcages are just a few out of the thousand that are stored at PACA; if theirs just happen to be the ones that get stolen, it keeps us from looking too closely in their direction."

"Meaning you haven't."

"Oh, we gave them a once-over, but, as you said, we were more concerned with outside groups." He nodded to himself, then tended to his drink.

I felt a strange sort of subdued elation. It was as if I had just solved a key word in a complicated crossword puzzle. It seemed to fit, and if it did, it would lead us to the other missing words.

And I realized that I was beginning to identify with McNally and his whole convoluted operation. The realization surprised me. My main concern had been to find a way out from under, to get far away, to save my own ass. Now I was getting dangerously close to donning a white hat of my own and joining the posse. Sam Boggs was supposed to be too smart to do anything so obviously stupid.

"What do we know about GP?" I asked him.

"I didn't pay much attention to it, frankly, but I'll give you what I remember. General Petroleum itself dates back to the Oklahoma oil fields of the twenties. They got squeezed out by the big boys and limped along until the sixties. Then they were taken over by one of the go-go conglomerates. They kept the name of GP, but it's now basically an umbrella for a wide range of activities. Petrochemicals, plastics, bug sprays, shipping, you name it. They got into the nuclear field about five years ago. They have small reactors in South Carolina, Georgia, and Florida. Their stock was doing well for a while, but it took a dive in the last couple of years. It seems that their oil fields are nearly played out, and they've had trouble picking up new leases. That explains the diversification. What it doesn't explain is why they would steal plutonium from themselves."

"For the same reason that anyone else would steal it. Money. Black-market plutonium would fetch a nice profit—particularly since it wouldn't be taxable income."

McNally frowned. "And black-market atomic bombs would be even more profitable."

"I think you ought to check the Pentagon's list of potential buyers. Find out if GP does business with any of them."

"I intend to check a hell of a lot more than that. We're going to run GP through a wringer. Maybe there's nothing to this theory of yours, but this time we're going to find out for sure."

He downed the rest of his drink and pounded his fist on the table.

"Goddamn," he said. "I feel great."

I didn't. I felt good, but not great. I had the uncomfortable feeling that McNally wasn't through with me yet.

16

It was a crisp, green November morning in the suburbs of
Atlanta, Georgia. Mr. Alfred Westover paused at the front
door of his small-scale Tara and kissed his wife good-bye. He
took a deep breath of the clean Georgia air, looked up to
admire some squirrels chasing each other through the over-
hanging trees, then walked purposefully toward the beige
Lincoln Continental that was parked on the gravel circle in
front of his home.

Westover was a handsome man, with a tanned patrician face
that complemented a full head of silvery hair. He carried a
rich leather briefcase and wore an expensive light-gray suit.
For so early in the morning, Westover looked remarkably
chipper. He had every reason to feel that way. He was on the
board of the General Petroleum Corporation, and he was
worth about two million dollars.

He opened the door of his car, which was worth about

twelve thousand dollars, tossed his briefcase onto the front seat, and got in. He inserted the key into the ignition switch, but didn't start the car. Before he could do that, he had to fasten his seat belt and shoulder strap. If he didn't, lights would flash, buzzers would sing out, and the car would refuse to start. By buckling the belt, he would complete a circuit that would satisfy all the clever little safety devices.

He also would complete another circuit. Westover snapped the two halves of the belt together.

Abruptly, all four wheels of the Continental shot off their axles and into the cool Georgia air. Deprived of its support, the Continental dropped to the earth like a felled water buffalo. The thump made by so many pounds of metal was even louder than the explosions that had separated the wheels from the car.

Mr. Alfred Westover sat behind the steering wheel of his amputated Continental, stunned.

A hundred feet away, hidden by the towering trees of Westover's estate, I turned to Jim Gardner and grinned. "I always wanted to do that," I said.

He grinned back at me. He was having fun.

Gardner was with me because McNally still didn't completely trust me. He was probably correct in that. If Gardner hadn't been at my elbow, my instincts for self-preservation might have led me to disappear into the teeming wilderness of America.

On the other hand, I had a certain proprietary interest in these "activities." Our game plan was mostly mine now, and I was anxious to see if it would work. As far as Mr. Alfred Westover was concerned, it had worked perfectly.

After our session in the bar, McNally had returned to the office, where he immediately launched a top-to-bottom investigation of General Petroleum. The results trickled in over the next few days; they proved nothing, but were tantalizing.

Serino's Boston fuel-oil distributor, it turned out, occasionally bought oil from GP. It was a microscopically small link, but it was nevertheless a link. Kemper had worked on the Alaska pipeline, not for GP, but at least he was associated with the oil industry. One more potential connection.

The Atomic Energy Commission did its regular sixty-day audit of GP's reactors. They found nothing suspect, aside from the missing twenty-seven birdcages. The GP executives were distraught by the loss of nearly a million dollars' worth of plutonium. That was to be expected.

What was not expected was the discovery that the South Carolina reactor had been operating at a loss of over one and a half million dollars every year. That's not entirely unusual in the nuclear-power industries; reactors are sometimes built before they are really needed, so that they will be ready and running when they are needed. But not even the most optimistic growth projections for that part of South Carolina would give them a profit within the next twenty years. It seemed to be strange economic behavior. The losses provided GP with lucrative tax breaks, but there were much easier ways to lose that much money, if that was your aim.

But the word among oil people was that GP was in trouble. Their domestic oil fields were, indeed, running out. Efforts to obtain foreign oil leases had been largely unsuccessful. The problem for GP (and for everyone else) was that all the "easy" oil had already been found. What remained in the earth's tortured crust was generally to be found in out-of-the-way places like Alaska and the North Sea. It required a gigantic operation to get the oil out of such places, and as oil companies go, GP was not gigantic.

They couldn't compete with titans like Standard and Gulf. Countries which possessed oil reserves wanted to be sure that the companies they dealt with would be able to extract the oil efficiently and economically. GP could give no such assurances. The rich new leases went to the huge multinationals, and GP ended up with scraps or nothing at all.

"It must add up to something," said McNally, "but I'm not sure what."

"They're getting desperate," I suggested.

"But are they desperate enough to start peddling black-market nukes?"

"How desperate do they have to be? Fat cats like Shell and Standard have been known to knock over a government here and there when it suited their purposes. What would a lean-and-hungry cat do?"

"I know, I know," he said tiredly. "The possibilities are endless. They could sell the nukes for market value alone. Or they could use them to scare somebody into giving them oil leases. Worst of all, they could *trade* the nukes for oil leases. Imagine what that might mean. San Salvador wasting Costa Rica. Dahomey obliterating Chad. Idi Amin nuking everyone in sight. Boggs, seventeen atomic bombs could turn the Maldive Islands into a world power. Think about that."

I shuddered involuntarily. "I have," I said. "Believe me, I have."

"The hell of it is, we don't even know if we're on the right track!"

McNally was right, we weren't sure. And because we weren't, the whole GP investigation had to be a kind of sub-rosa affair. GP, like every other oil company, had excellent connections within Washington. If someone like Preston or the man from the White House found out that GP was under suspicion, the news would almost certainly get back to the people at General Petroleum.

"I don't think it's possible for them to have built very many bombs yet," I said. "Five or six at the most. But by the end of the year, they could have a full arsenal."

"You're suggesting that we ought to do something soon," said McNally. He looked as if he had aged ten years since the night I met him.

"I think that's pretty obvious."

"What did you have in mind? You know better than anyone how well insulated these guys are. If we just go in there and lean on them, all we'll accomplish is to scare them into strengthening their security. We don't have one solid fact to implicate GP, and I doubt that we'll find one. Without a definite case, we're helpless. They'll just get on the phone and complain to the White House about harassment, and we'll be told in no uncertain terms to stay away from GP. Sure, Boggs, we have to do something soon. Just tell me what."

McNally's gloom was infectious. I went back across the street to my apartment and fixed myself a strong drink.

The doorbell rang. I answered it, knowing who it had to be; I wasn't exactly swamped with visitors.

It was Jim Gardner. "I heard the sound of ice cubes," he said. "I thought I'd better investigate."

I fixed a drink for him. He had heard the ice cubes because he heard literally everything that went on in my apartment. I was bugged, and no one made any attempt to hide the fact. The rationale was that if someone took another go at killing me, Gardner could be with me in seconds. Not incidentally, Gardner would also know if I tried to sneak away in the middle of the night.

Gardner was in his early thirties but still looked as if he were about to suit up for his last football game at Princeton. His hair was blond and modishly long, and he had the arresting blue eyes of a Paul Newman. He was, in fact, a gorgeous

255

specimen. I normally don't take the golden boys very seriously, but Gardner turned out to be okay. He had a good mind, and if he shared McNally's lingering contempt for me, at least he hid it well.

He sprawled out on my couch, his feet dangling over the armrest. I settled into an egg-shaped Naugehyde chair opposite the couch and propped my feet up on the coffee table. "What do you think?" I asked him.

Gardner massaged his forehead with the icy glass. "I think I wish that I'd never been assigned to this case. That's what I think," he said.

"Why were you assigned to it" I asked. "For that matter, why McNally?"

Gardner laughed. "We were too damn dumb to turn it down, that's why. McNally has a good record and a lot of nuts-and-bolts experience. He's high in the organization, but not too high. By being where he is, he protects the director. If we blow it, McNally gets axed but the big boys come out of it pretty clean. In other words, he's expendable. And so am I. And so are you."

That wasn't exactly news. I fumbled around in my pocket and dug out a stick of gum. My doctor had suggested that I chew it to strengthen my jaw. I pushed it into my mouth, then took a swig of my drink; I'd discovered a new flavor for Baskin-Robbins—scotch and spearmint.

"It's got to be GP," I announced, as if I'd just uncovered proof positive.

"Sure," said Gardner. "Why not?"

"And McNally knows it."

"Knowing it and proving it are two different things. GP is just about untouchable unless we can come up with a hell of a lot more than we've got."

"How do we do that?" I didn't think Gardner knew the answer; I was simply thinking out loud.

"We don't," he said lightly. "All we can do is sit back and wait for them to make the next move." He tilted his glass back and swallowed some more scotch.

"The next move," I said, "is likely to be a nuclear explosion. Is that what we're supposed to sit back and wait for?"

"Do we have any choice?"

"No," I answered, "I don't suppose we do."

We drank in silence for a while. Waiting for Armageddon was likely to make alcoholics of us all.

"I've got to admit," I said a few minutes later, "I'm disappointed in the CIA."

Gardner looked up. "How do you mean?" he asked.

"I don't know. I guess I just had the impression that the all-powerful Company could ride roughshod over anyone and anything. It's disillusioning to see you hung up by a crummy little oil company."

"You've been spoiled, Sam," said Gardner. "You've been your own boss for so long that you've forgotten all about a little thing called responsibility. If you screw up, nobody's going to haul you before a congressional committee. But if we moved in on GP and it turned out that we were wrong, everybody from the director on down would spend the rest of their lives telling Preston's committee how sorry they were. The Agency has enough problems already—we don't need that. When you get right down to the nub of it, we're just like all the other government bureaucrats. Nobody wants to risk his job on a wrong guess. What you want, Sam, is a *Mission Impossible* team. Your mission, should you decide to accept it, is to scare the shit out of GP and force them to make a mistake. Then capitalize on it and recover the bombs and plutonium before they can use it. All in sixty minutes, less commercials. If you should be caught or killed, the secretary will disavow all knowledge. Good luck, Sam. This planet will self-destruct in five seconds." Gardner downed the rest of his drink and got up to make another.

He was right, of course. The CIA does not function like a TV drama. That should have been comforting to know.

Gardner returned to the couch with his drink. After a few more moments of silent brooding, we both did a theatrical "take": simultaneously, we looked up at each other. Gardner pointed his finger at me.

"You!" he exclaimed.

"Yes!" I agreed immediately. "I could . . ."

I stopped. We were both thinking exactly the same thing, but my enthusiasm suddenly evaporated. I was helping, willingly now, but there were limits.

Gardner caught my hesitation. "Why the hell not?" he demanded. "You're perfect for it."

I grumbled something unintelligible, then took another swallow of scotch.

"Come on, Sam," Gardner persisted. "You were thinking the same thing I was. *We* can't do the *Mission Impossible* trip, but *you* can. You're better qualified for it than anyone. It's exactly what you've been doing for the last ten years."

"I've retired," I told him.

"Bullshit. You want to get that bomb back just as much as we do. More, even. You're the one who came up with the GP theory in the first place. This is your chance to prove it."

"Or get myself blown away. These people play rough."

"They've tried to kill you twice, and they missed both times."

"Not by much. Why should I give them a third shot at me?" I shifted my gum to the other side of my mouth and tried to look firm and unyielding. "They've been two steps ahead of me the whole way," I said. "What makes you think it would be any different this time?"

"Because," said Gardner, "now you know who you're dealing with, and they don't know. For once, you've got the advantage."

"Maybe," I admitted.

"There's no maybe about it. And you wouldn't really be working alone, either. We'd be right behind you."

"And I'd be right in front of you, with my neck stuck out a mile."

"You've been there before. You took a hell of a risk going to Preston in the first place; and if you hadn't, you'd be dead now."

"Okay," I said. I felt somewhat better: Go ahead, doctor—amputate.

Gardner looked delighted, his tanned features pulled up into a smile that showcased a set of teeth that gleamed like the white cliffs of Dover.

"Now," he said, "there's only one more problem."

"What's that?"

He grinned. "You," he said, pointing a finger at me, "will have to get McNally to go along with this."

"Why me?" I asked; it was a question that seemed to be on my lips quite often of late.

"McNally still has his doubts about you, Sam. You're not officially one of the good guys. Unless he's convinced that you really are with us, he's not about to let you go off on an unofficial and illegal operation. You're the only one who can sell him on the idea, because you are the only one who can guarantee the loyalty of Sam Boggs."

The next morning I sat in McNally's undersized office and

laid out the plan for him. He listened impassively, chin on fist, while I described what I intended to do, and how.

"The key thing," I said, "is to shake them up in a way that they're not prepared to deal with. They undoubtedly have contingency plans for dozens of scenarios, but I seriously doubt that they'll know what to do about a series of clandestine raids on each of the directors of the company. It would be a totally random stimulus, and it might produce some interesting reactions."

"And it might get you arrested, blowing this entire operation."

I smiled modestly. "In ten years, no one has laid a glove on me. I'm not worried about getting arrested. But I am a little wary of being so far out in front on this thing. After I've hit two or three of the GP brass, if they are in any way involved in this mess, they'll realize that I'm behind it. Clever explosions that could kill but don't will shake them up, but it will also be like leaving my calling card on their doorstep."

"If that bothers you so much, why are you so hot to do this?"

"It would be a great opportunity," I said, sounding like a fly-by-night real-estate salesman. "If they think I'm on the prowl again, they'll have to do something. And anything they do is bound to give you a little more leverage. As long as they stay buttoned up tight, you don't have a thing to latch on to."

McNally gave a barely perceptible nod. "True," he said, "but they must realize that you've been in contact with us. Your little raids might just make them button up even tighter."

"Maybe, maybe not. The way I see it, they would have just two options. One—do nothing, and try to ignore me. But I intend to make it very difficult for them to do that. Which leads to the second option—get rid of me. They've tried to do it before, and they'll try again if they think I'm still dangerous. And that's why I'm nervous about this plan. I'd be like one of the native brush beaters on a safari. I could flush out the game for you, but I'd be making a target of myself in the process."

McNally removed his chin from his fist and looked at me the way someone might appraise an abstract painting—trying to puzzle out the meaning, estimating the cost, and imagining how it would look on a wall.

"Boggs," he said finally, "you are many things. But a martyr, you're definitely not. I can't picture you setting yourself up like that."

"If you cooperate, it will be GP that's being set up, not me. I won't bullshit you, I don't enjoy the prospect of offering myself as bait. But if that's the only way I can get out from under this madhouse, then I'm willing to do it. But I've got to be sure that you folks will be on your toes. Otherwise, forget it."

McNally drummed his fingers on the desk for a few moments. "You're sure you can pull this off?"

"Certain."

"And you're willing to accept the risks?"

"Yes."

"You really think it's a good idea?"

"I think it's our only hope, at this stage of the game."

Honest?" McNally had a curious expression on his face. I didn't recognize it at first, it was so alien to him. Then I realized what it was, and what it meant.

The bastard was smiling.

Westover's Continental was the first victim of my campaign. We had drawn up a list of the board members of GP, together with all available background information. Based on that and a lot of guesswork, we selected Westover and several other board members as targets.

261

The operative assumption was that even if GP were behind the plutonium theft, not everyone in the organization, even at the top, would necessarily be aware of it. In fact, it seemed unlikely that security could be maintained if all nine directors were party to the caper. Three of the directors, in fact, were also on the boards of competing conglomerates. The odds were that no more than three or four men in the inner circle were involved. The dossiers on the directors revealed nothing incriminating about any of them, but two of them, Westover and Franklin Peters, my next target, had a reputation for playing hardball. They were corporate thugs, tough and successful. They were far from unique in the world of big business, but they were the only suspects we had.

Actually, it was absurd even to think of them as suspects. Westover and Peters were simply at the wrong end of a long and tenuous chain of theories, assumptions, and hunches. We still had no hard evidence that in any way implicated GP. All we could do was yell "Fire!" and then stand back to see which window people jumped out of.

But Westover didn't jump. He didn't do anything at all. He didn't even call the police.

McNally, Gardner, and I waited all day in a hotel room in Atlanta. Our contacts in the Atlanta and suburban police had nothing to report. And the team that was tailing Westover came up with nothing. Westover drove his wife's Mercedes in to his office that day. The taps on his office and home phones produced nothing out of the ordinary.

And that in itself, all things considered, was extraordinary.

McNally clapped his hands together. "It strikes me as pretty damn strange," he said. "A man's car gets blown up and he doesn't call the cops, he doesn't tell his friends, he doesn't even call the garage. That is not normal behavior."

Gardner, who had been staring out the window at the

twinkling nighttime skyline of Atlanta, turned back to face McNally. "It still doesn't prove anything," he said.

"Why not?" I asked. I was proud of my little performance that morning, and I thought that Westover's reaction was suggestive of a man with something to hide.

McNally answered me. "All it means," he said, "is that Westover is afraid of something or someone. In the oil business these days, that's not exactly uncommon. Right now he may be thinking that the bomb was planted by someone he's crossed in the past. The Mafia, Arabs, the competition. He obviously doesn't want to bring the police in on it, but that doesn't mean that what he's hiding is necessarily the plutonium theft. A man in his position probably has a lot to hide."

It made a depressing amount of sense. We still didn't know anything for certain.

"All the same," I said, "I think it's an interesting reaction. If he is our man, he's in a hell of a quandary. He's got to contact his friends, and I would bet that he already has, on a safe phone line. They probably told him to sit tight. But they all have to be worried; from out of left field, somebody just dropped a stink bomb in their living room, and they don't know who or why."

"Then," McNally said, "I think we ought to give them a clue.

Franklin Peters lived in the Spring Branch section of Houston, near the home offices of General Petroleum. He had a modern, elaborately architectured home that looked out over the sixteenth fairway of one of Houston's best golf courses. Peters was the kind of man to whom golf ranks just below breathing on the cosmic scale of priorities. Each morning, before going to work, he religiously hit a bucket of balls into a ten-by-ten-foot net in his backyard.

I watched through binoculars one cloudy morning as Peters lugged his clubs out to his private tee. He wore a blue alpaca sweater and looked fit and ready to tackle Augusta or Baltusrol.

He started with his seven iron, displaying a smooth, clockwork swing that must have cost him several thousand dollars in lessons. After a few shots, he switched to a five iron, then a three. The solid *tock* of his shots reached me a few seconds after he hit the ball.

At last, he pulled his driver out of the bag. He teed up a ball, then stood over it, waggling the club. He took an easy practice swing, then stared at the club head wonderingly for a second or two; it must not have felt right. I just hoped that he wasn't upset enough to examine the club too carefully.

Peters shrugged, dismissing the odd feel of the club, then addressed the ball. I had to admit, he had a sweet swing—perfect leg action and a powerful rotation of the hips. The club head described a precise inside-out arc, accelerating toward the instant of contact with the ball.

He smacked it, all right. It would have gone a long way if the club hadn't exploded.

But Peters was a damn good golfer—he kept his head down the whole way. His follow-through was high and graceful, even though he now held only about two feet of club shaft. He held that classic pose for an instant before slowly lowering his arms and stepping back from the tee. He glanced at the splintered stump of a club in his hands, then stared at the smoking crater where the tee had been. It was one hell of a divot.

Peters calmly replaced his other clubs, then picked up the bag and walked slowly back to his house. The man was either unbelievably cool or simply freaked out.

I put the binoculars back into the case, got back into my car, and drove away. I was all alone this time. McNally didn't want any risk of CIA exposure, and was willing to trust me for a change. It occurred to me that this was the first time in months when I was completely free; I could head for the hills if I wanted to.

I wanted to, but I didn't. In all probability, someone was watching me, just as I had watched Peters.

I returned to our hotel room and found McNally shouting into the phone. "Equipment failure?" he bellowed in disbelief. "What kind of fucking amateur are you, anyway? You get that line tapped! I don't care if you have to use a tin can and a piece of string, just do it!" He slammed down the receiver and looked up at me.

"Boggs," he said, "you may be an anarchist asshole, but at least you're efficient. We just lost the bug on Peters' phone. There's no way of knowing whether or not he called anyone."

"Cops?"

He shook his head. "He definitely hasn't called them. Maybe he called his golf pro instead."

"Or Westover," I suggested.

"Or no one. Maybe your methods are too subtle. Maybe they're just not getting the message."

"They're getting it, Mac. Both of those explosions were too precise to be the work of anyone but an expert, and they know it. They've got to realize by now that I'm the one who's bombing them. I think one more job ought to force them to do something."

He sighed. "Christ, I hope so."

My third target was not so easy. We watched Caldwell Haskins for a week and found him to be a very cautious man. He traveled with a beefy bodyguard and was never out in the open for more than a few seconds. His home, also in Houston, was protected by a spanking-new burglar-detection system. Someone else started his car for him, and he didn't play golf. He did very little, really, except work, eat, and sleep. McNally had declared the GP offices out-of-bounds, so that left me with eating and sleeping. There didn't seem to be very much opportunity for creative demolition inherent in those two activities.

It's difficult to surprise a man who's expecting it, and Haskins was definitely expecting it. He was as well-protected as the U.S. President. Still, I told myself, he puts his pants on one leg at a time, the same as everyone else.

That clichéd thought gave birth to another one, and suddenly I had my plan.

Haskins sent his laundry out. I followed the truck after a pickup one morning. When the driver made his next stop, I sneaked up to the back of the truck and lifted the suit that Haskins had sent out for dry cleaning.

It was a dark blue suit, with thin yellow pinstripes. The pinstripes would come in handy.

I made some free alterations on Mr. Haskins' pants. A very thin, lightweight yellow wire replaced the pinstripe on the inside of the right pantleg. The wire connected the zipper with a tiny detonator hidden in the cuff, which I impregnated with a small amount of black powder. I repeated the process with the left leg. Finally, I wired the metal clasp at the waist to the zipper on one side. The other half of the clasp was wired to a miniature battery sewn into the waistband.

It was an artistic job, and I was proud of it. The alterations would be noticeable, but not immediately, and Haskins wasn't going to have the chance to wear those pants for very long. The instant he zipped the zipper and fastened the clasp, his pants would explode.

I thought it was a gag worthy of Laurel and Hardy. My one

regret was that I wouldn't get the chance to see it happen. The following morning, I followed the laundry truck again and replaced the suit, then caught a plane back to Washington.

We waited several days. The taps on Haskins' lines produced nothing, not that we expected them to. By now we were certain that GP was our villain, but we still had no proof. We couldn't go before the committee and tell them that we were convinced General Petroleum stole the plutonium from itself on the basis of the fact that one of the company's directors failed to call the police when his pants exploded.

"Hell," said McNally five nights later, "how do we even know if his pants did explode?"

"Take my word for it," I told him, "it was foolproof."

McNally slammed his fist on his desk. "Then why haven't they reacted? This whole scheme was supposed to drive them out into the open. Maybe it's backfired and they've gone farther underground. They could be willing to put up with all this nuisance bombing to protect their overall plan, whatever the hell that might be. They could let us go on blowing up golf clubs and trousers until doomsday!"

McNally was getting ragged around the edges again. We were into early December now, and we had still come up with nothing. All other lines of investigation were as fruitless as ever. The White House was frantic; and worse, rumors were beginning to circulate around town that something nuclear and nasty had happened or was about to. It was only a matter of time until the press got hold of the story.

I tried to reassure McNally, not that I felt very confident myself. "They'll do something soon," I said. "They have to. Put yourself in Haskins' place. He takes every possible precaution to protect himself, and then one fine morning as he's getting dressed, his pants blow up. At worst, he got some minor flash burns on his calves, but think of the psychological

267

damage. If a man's pants can be detonated, what's safe? Underwear? Hmmm ... you know, I could even get underwear. Body heat would do it. Problem is, it would produce some pretty bad burns, and we don't want that. The idea is to scare them, not hurt them. They're smart enough to realize that I could have killed them if I'd wanted to. And right now, they have to be wondering when I'll get tired of fooling around. The directors who haven't been hit yet must be going out of their minds. They've got to do something, and soon."

"You're wrong," said McNally. "*We've* got to do something, and soon."

I nodded, knowing he was right. Time was running out on us. By now, they could have built a dozen or more bombs. How much longer until they used one?

I left McNally in his office and went back across the street to my apartment. It was late, and I was tired. I considered knocking on Gardner's door and inviting him in for a drink, but decided against it. I fumbled with my key for a moment, then swung open the door, stepped inside, and reached for the light switch. But someone beat me to it.

I turned to see a gun barrel pointed at me. Then I saw the person who was holding it.

"Hello, Sam," she said. "It's good to see you again."

17

Heidi shut the door and smiled at me. "You're looking well," she said.

"No thanks to you. I had a broken jaw, and my mouth was wired shut. And the cast on my arm just came off this week."

"They were very upset when they found out you were still alive, Sam."

"Yes, I know. That wasn't you in the hospital, was it?"

She shook her head. "If it had been me, this reunion wouldn't have been necessary. Why don't we sit down and talk about old times?" She motioned toward the couch.

I sat down on the right side of the couch, and she took the left side, letting the gun enforce a safe distance between us. Heidi looked glorious, no longer the shabby hippie I had known in Spain. She wore a stylish beige pantsuit and a sheer white blouse, with the top four buttons undone. Her small, dark nipples poked out against the thin fabric as she scrunched

269

around to get comfortable. Her blond hair dropped in graceful waves to her shoulders. She was beautiful, but it was like admiring a lioness at close range; I felt no desire.

"So," I said, "have you been keeping busy?"

"From time to time," she said. "And from what I hear, you've been working pretty hard yourself."

"Yep, busy as a beaver. But I suppose that's going to end now, isn't it?"

She smiled, a thin little smile. "I'm afraid so, Sam," she said softly.

"You seem to enjoy your work," I observed.

"I do enjoy it, I'll admit. Is that really so terrible? You enjoy blowing up buildings."

"Somehow, I don't think it's quite the same. Buildings can be replaced."

"So can people, and much more cheaply. They replaced you with no trouble at all, Sam."

"And what happens when they decide to replace you, my darling psychopath? It's bound to happen, you know."

Heidi shook her head, laughing. "No it isn't," she said. "After tonight, it's all over for me. When I leave here, I'll get on the first plane to Zurich and the half-million dollars."

"*My* half-million dollars?"

"Uh-uh—*mine*. You won't need it, and I can use it to disappear. Maybe I'll even go to New Zealand."

"How do you intend to get it? It's in my account, after all."

"Oh, that's no problem. You took care of that yourself, Sam. Don't you remember the letter you wrote to me from Portugal?"

Suddenly I did remember it, and I groaned. I had given her all the information she needed about my account, including a letter authorizing her to make withdrawals. I had expected to intercept the letter before she could read it, but the pounding I took in Portugal made me forget all about it.

"Foolish me," I said. "That's how Stover knew so much about my account, isn't it?"

"Now you're catching on, Sam."

"Better late than never," I said. "But I still have a few questions, if you don't mind."

"Fire away," she said obligingly.

It was an unfortunate choice of words. Her gun looked small but efficient. There was a silencer on the end of the barrel—very professional.

"Tell me, GP is behind this, am I right?"

"Who?"

"GP. General Petroleum."

"Is that who's running things?"

"Isn't it?"

"I wouldn't know. I work for Stover, and he never told me who he works for." She had nothing to gain by lying about it, so it was probable that she was telling the truth. On the other hand, when it came to judging Heidi's veracity, I didn't have a very good track record. I snapped my gum and looked at the ceiling for a moment.

"Who gets the bombs?" I asked.

She hesitated for a moment. "I don't think I should tell you that," she said.

"Why not? I assume you're not planning on letting me walk out of here."

"Nevertheless, you might have some kind of bug in here. Anyway, I don't really know for certain. I don't even care, to tell you the truth. Too much curiosity isn't healthy."

"So I see." But I was curious, because there was indeed a bug in my room. Heidi might talk freely with me because she expected me to be dead very soon, but Gardner would be picking up the entire conversation. I hoped he had enough sense not to do anything until Heidi had a chance to do some more talking. At the same time, I hoped even more fervently that he wouldn't get so engrossed in the conversation that he'd forget to arrive in the nick of time to save me. In the meantime, I tried to draw Heidi out.

"That was a neat trick you pulled off at the warehouse, kid, I'll give you that."

"You made a pretty good move, yourself. I should have checked to make sure you were really unconscious. Stover was very annoyed with me."

"Who moved the bomb out? Wynn?"

She nodded. "And some others."

"Where did you take it?"

"Sorry, Sam. That little bug might be listening."

I tried to reassure her. "What bug? If there were a bug in here, you'd have had several guns pointed at your head by now."

She smiled again, and her eyes seemed to sparkle. "Wrong again, Sam."

"How so?"

"Because if this conversation is being taped, it still doesn't make any difference as far as you are concerned. Right now, there's no one to listen to your bug. They'll play the tape back later, perhaps, but by then it won't matter."

"What do you mean?" But I thought I knew what she meant.

"Sam, I hate to ruin this conversation for you, I really do. But I suppose you should know. That cute man next door isn't going to help you, Sam. He's dead."

"That cute man next door was a friend of mine."

"I know. It seemed a shame to have to do it. When he opened the door and I saw those big blue eyes, I wanted to keep the gun in my purse and have a little fun first. But that would have been a mistake."

"Don't kid yourself," I said bitterly. "You had your fun anyway."

272

Heidi shrugged innocently. "I told you, I enjoy what I do."

"Did you enjoy killing Mick Mahoney?"

"That was a little different. He took a long time to die. We couldn't just do it. We had to find out some things first."

"And what about me?"

"Don't worry, Sam. It will be quick, and it won't even hurt. We might as well get it over with now. I know the tension must be killing you."

"Was that supposed to be funny?"

"I guess that's what they call 'gallows humor.'"

"You'd knock 'em dead at Forest Lawn, sweetheart."

"Now you're doing it."

"What the hell. Might as well die with a smile on my face and a song in my heart. But would you mind if the condemned man had a last cigarette? Don't your union rules require that?"

She moved a few more inches away from me and raised the gun a little. "Go ahead," she said. "but remember, smoking can be hazardous to your health."

"How could I forget?" I slowly eased my hand into my jacket pocket and withdrew a pack of cigarettes. I held it up for her to see. "Nothing up my sleeve," I assured her. I lit one and put the pack back in my pocket.

"Somehow," I said, "cancer doesn't frighten me anymore."

Heidi leaned back against the armrest of the couch.

"Sex and death," I said. "You specialize in the fundamentals, Heidi."

"And I'm pretty damn good at both of them."

I leaned over to reach the ashtray on the coffee table, moving a good six inches toward Heidi in the process.

"When I die," said Heidi, "I hope it comes right in the middle of an orgasm. What a trip!"

"I wouldn't mind that myself," I admitted. "Do you suppose it could be arranged?"

She chuckled appreciatively. "That's a nice idea, Sam, but I'm afraid not."

"Why not?" I cautiously extended my left arm and put my hand on her thigh. She let it linger there for a moment.

It must have been the thought of sex that gave me the idea. Under other circumstances, I'd have dismissed it as ridiculous.

"You'd better keep your hands to yourself, Sam, if you want to finish that cigarette."

I lifted my hand away from her leg. "Sorry," I said. "I suppose I shouldn't get carried away before they carry me away. Look, I'll even transfer the cigarette to my left hand to keep it occupied, okay?"

"Fine," she said. "And sit on your right hand, while you're at it."

I did as she said. The cigarette, in my left hand now, had burned about a third of the way down. If I was going to do it, I had to do it soon. I took another drag, cupping my palm around the bottom part of the cigarette to shield it from Heidi. I shifted my gum and pressed it up against the plastic filter with my tongue. Then I removed both cigarette and gum. She didn't notice.

"If it's any consolation to you," she said, "I really did like you."

"I stand consoled," I said. I stared at the gaping barrel of the gun and tried to visualize precisely what I was going to do.

"You know . . ." I began. I made my move, praying that my hands were as deft as I like to think they are. With a short, quick movement, I jabbed the cigarette directly at the barrel of the gun. I was dead on target, and the cigarette slid right in, with the gum globbing up the end of the barrel.

Heidi reacted by jumping back from me, at the same instant I dived away from the couch. I rolled over the coffee table, sending the ashtray skittering over the edge. I landed in a kneeling position five feet away from Heidi, who still had the gun trained on me. I could see her finger tighten around the trigger, then stop.

"What the hell have you done?" She looked in amazement at the blob of spearmint on the end of her gun.

"Don't pull that trigger, Heidi," I warned. "The gun will blow up in your beautiful face."

She glanced hurriedly from me, to the gun, then back to me. "What ... how ..."?

"There's a cigarette down the barrel, and gum on the end of it, Heidi. And you already have a silencer on it. What do you think that will do to the muzzle velocity of a bullet?"

Eyes wide in confusion, Heidi started to reach for the barrel to remove the gum, then stopped when I made a move in her direction.

"You can't remove the gum and shoot me at the same time, Heidi."

"You *bastard*!" Tears of frustration were welling in her eyes. "That wasn't *fair*!"

"Against the rules of the game, huh?"

"Yes, goddamn you!" She sounded like a little girl pouting because she'd lost at hopscotch.

She threw the gun at me. It missed, bouncing heavily off the wall. Amazingly, it didn't go off.

I grabbed her by the wrists as she struggled to get away from me. She drew her leg back, but I saw it coming and did a neat veronica as her foot flashed up to crotch level. I released her wrist and snared the ankle as it went by me. A quick upward jerk with the ankle deposited Heidi on her ass. She pounded the carpet with her fist and sobbed.

I retrieved the gun and unplugged the barrel. I found the ashtray and replaced it on the coffee table, snubbing out the cigarette. I wanted to save it, and the gum; someday I might dip them in bronze.

Holding the gun in my left hand, I reached down with my

right and grabbed Heidi by the wrist again, tugging her back up to standing position. Her azure eyes had clouded over, and she glared at me, her face a map of hatred.

"You wouldn't shoot me," she said defiantly. "You have this big thing about killing people, remember?"

"Don't worry, Heidi, I'm not going to kill you. We have some talking to do. But you could still talk with a shattered kneecap. Think about that before you try anything."

"Fuck you," she said.

"Not a chance." I balled up my right fist and swung at her with all the force I could muster in my weakened arm. I connected with her jaw, snapping her head back. She collapsed like a rag doll. I rubbed my knuckles and found myself wishing that Heidi had appeared a few days earlier, when I still wore the cast.

McNally arrived a few minutes later with the two FBI men. We found Jim Gardner crumpled on the floor of his apartment, facedown in his own blood. McNally was pale and trembling, just barely managing to contain his anger. I had to lead him away from the room so we could tend to Heidi and let the FBI agents handle the body.

Heidi was still out cold. For a moment I wondered if I might have broken her neck with that punch, but then I saw the slow rise and fall of her chest. At worst, she might have a broken jaw. As much as I would have enjoyed that, I hoped that she was all right; I knew from experience how difficult it is to talk with a wired-shut mouth.

I told McNally what had happened. He couldn't quite believe the cigarette up the barrel, but I showed him the gummed butt in the ashtray.

"Only you, Boggs," he said, shaking his head.

"What do we do about her?" I asked.

His jaw muscles twitched as he contemplated the prone form on the floor. "I could tell you what I'd like to do with her," he said. "But first, we're going to pump that bitch for everything she knows. We might as well wake her up and do it here. If she doesn't come through, we'll take her out to Langley and dig up a few specialists in the art of coerced conversation."

McNally filled a small plastic wastebasket with cold water from the kitchen tap, then dumped it on Heidi. She shuddered convulsively, her eyes opening like unlatched window shades. She saw us standing above her and came to a slow realization of her situation. The defiance in her eyes faded away, and she tried a new ploy.

"I think my jaw is broken," she whined plaintively.

I looked at it, but noted only a slight swelling. Taking her chin between my thumb and forefinger, I wiggled her jaw back and forth. She squealed in pain, but I wasn't impressed.

"Take it from an expert," I said, "it's not broken."

"But it *hurts!*"

McNally grabbed her wrists and pulled her upright. He slapped her smartly on her sore jaw. "You might just as well get used to pain," he told her. "If you don't tell us what we want to know, pain is going to be your constant companion."

Heidi could tell that she wasn't going to get any sympathy from us. She decided to try her most reliable weapon.

"You didn't have to use such cold water," she said. She disengaged herself from McNally and pushed a wet strand of hair away from her face. Her blouse was plastered down against her breasts, soaked and transparent. She wiggled out of her wet beige jacket, taking care to thrust her chest in our direction.

"I've already seen your body, Heidi," I said uninterestedly. "Half the people in the Western Hemisphere have probably seen your body. You can stop trying to sell it, because the market value just went down."

277

It took her aback. She stared at us sullenly, looking like a cornered blond water rat.

Heidi chose not to cooperate. She sat there glumly for two hours, trying her best to ignore us, saying virtually nothing. I brewed some coffee while McNally kept at it with Heidi, threatening and cajoling, and getting nowhere.

Finally he left her on the couch and joined me in the kitchen as I was pouring the coffee. We could see Heidi through the doorway, but she didn't look as if she were going anywhere.

McNally sipped his steaming coffee, black. "This isn't doing any good at all," he said.

"What's next? The shock shack?"

He gave me an intense, level gaze. "Christ, Boggs, you've sure changed. Aren't you going to complain about how we're violating her civil rights? No lectures on the evil of an unregulated secret police? No humanitarian appeals for moderation and leniency?"

"Drink your coffee, McNally, and shut up."

He put his cup down on the counter. Something in his eyes seemed to change, to soften. "I'm sorry, Sam," he said. "You didn't deserve that."

I shoveled some sugar into my own cup. "No," I said, "I deserved it. You know why? Because all that bullshit about civil rights and secret police is true. In the long run, McNally, you are a hell of a lot more dangerous than all the Stovers and Westovers put together."

"You really believe that, don't you?"

"I do."

"Then why are you on our side? Is it still just to save your own ass?"

"That, and something else. Penance, maybe."

"You think that if we can keep those atomic bombs from going off, it will somehow erase all those other bombs you were responsible for? Is that it?"

"Something like that. I'm still dirty, but that doesn't mean I have to go on wallowing in the mud forever."

"Like me, you mean?"

"Like you," I agreed.

He took another sip of coffee. "Hell, I don't know. Maybe you're right. After this is over, maybe we should both join a convent."

"Who would take us?"

We went back to Heidi. I brought her a cup of coffee, but she didn't want it.

At four in the morning, McNally tried appealing to her enlightened self-interest. "What do you think you have to gain by protecting them?" he asked her. "They can't help you now, and they can't hurt you either. We're the only ones that can do that, Heidi, and I promise you, if you don't cooperate, we will. Hurt you, I mean."

"But you won't help me."

"You're the only one who can help yourself now."

"Bullshit," she replied. It was about the hundredth time she had used that particular word.

McNally collapsed onto the couch. We had invented a new form of third degree: the cops talk until they drop, at which point the bad guy takes pity on them and confesses.

McNally sighed slowly, hissing like a steamboat with a ruptured boiler. "Heidi," he said, "what's going to happen to you after we leave this room, I wouldn't wish on Lucrezia Borgia."

"You're right," said Heidi suddenly. "Let's make a deal."

I had nearly fallen asleep, but my head snapped up abruptly. Heidi was on her feet, looking trim and energetic. I wondered if she was planning to overpower us both—she probably could have done it.

McNally shoved himself up to a more vertical position. "You mean that?" he asked hopefully.

McNally's response made me realize what Heidi's strategy had been. We hadn't been wearing her down—it was just the reverse. Three hours ago, McNally would have told her that she didn't have anything to deal with. He would have been tough and unyielding. Now he was merely glad that she was willing to say something besides "Go fuck yourself."

Heidi smiled triumphantly. "I'll show you where they took the bomb and the plutonium. I can't tell you, but I will show you. But after that, you let me go."

"What?" McNally was on his feet; Heidi had overplayed her hand. "If you think we're going to let you go free after murdering a CIA agent in cold blood, you can just forget it."

"Fine," she said, sitting down again. "Find the bomb yourself."

"Okay, Heidi," McNally said with an air of finality. "That was your last chance. Now we're going to take you to a place where you'll talk and talk and talk. In between screams."

It didn't faze her. "You could find out what you need to know," she said. "But it would take you quite a while to do it. And in case you don't know it, you don't have that much time."

"What do you mean?"

"I mean that there are only four days left, and you'll need all four of them."

"Four days until what?"

Heidi threw her arms up into the air in a fair approximation of a mushroom cloud.

McNally considered this for a moment. "Still no deal," he said. "We have ways to get you to talk in a few hours. That much time won't make any difference."

"It might," she said. "Can you afford to take that chance?" Anyway, it would take you longer to get me to talk than you think. Isn't that right, Sam?"

McNally looked at me. "What the hell is she talking about?"

"I think I understand," I said. "Heidi is trying to tell you that pain would not be a very effective way to get information out of her. Heidi is a woman of unusual tastes. She enjoys killing. Conceivably, she also enjoys pain."

McNally looked lost. He looked back and forth from Heidi to me and didn't say anything.

"All I want," Heidi said, "is the same deal you offered Sam. I help you find the bomb, and you let me go free."

"It's not the same, dammit." McNally wasn't ready to give in—not quite.

"Why isn't it the same?" she asked.

"I'll tell you why," I said hotly. "I didn't kill anyone."

"Is that so? Tell me, Sam, how many people do you think that bomb of yours would kill if it went off in downtown Manhattan?" McNally started to say something, but Heidi quickly added, "Or Los Angeles."

There was a pregnant silence in the room for several minutes. Heidi finally broke it with two words that settled the matter.

"Four days," she said.

18

Heidi was wrong. We didn't have four days. We didn't even have one.

McNally organized an early-morning convoy; we were going wherever Heidi led us. She and I sat in the back seat of the lead car, side by side, hating each other. She wouldn't tell us where we were going; she simply told us to get on I-95 and stay on it until she said to get off. We drove north, fighting the traffic through the gray and stinking garbage flats of Baltimore and the high-speed confusion of beltways and parkways. The highway was slick with a thin, frigid drizzle, and the dirty sky hung low and oppressive.

Thirty-five FBI agents in seven cars followed us into the industrial haze of Wilmington and over the monotonous, rolling landscape of southern Pennsylvania. McNally kept in touch with the other cars by radio, but there was little to report. We stared blankly out the windows and watched without comment as the rain changed to snow and then back again.

"Next exit," Heidi said as we traversed the flat marshlands south of Philadelphia. McNally relayed the word to the other cars. It seemed almost a shame to have to abandon the stuporous hum of the highway.

Following Heidi's terse directions, we wended our way past the lifeless maze of oil-tank farms that grew like weeds along the banks of the sluggish Schuylkill River where it emptied into the Delaware. The waterways were dotted with slow-moving tankers gliding through the gray waters like bulky ghosts, scarcely leaving a wake to mark their passing.

We passed warehouses and row houses nestled among the cracking plants and storage tanks, looking like abandoned colonies on a hostile shore. Heidi pointed to one of the warehouses. "That's it on the left," she said.

McNally ordered the driver to take us by it, then we circled around and parked under the concrete pillars of the highway. The other cars joined us. It was a deserted, forgotten place, and our presence would have been readily noticeable if there had been anyone around to see us.

We got out of the cars and milled around in the damp, bone-chilling wasteland. I looked at my watch; it was 8:57.

"Where is everybody?" I said to no one in particular.

"It's Sunday," one of the agents said, as if it surprised him, too.

McNally conferred with about ten of the agents while I stuck close to Heidi, although it hardly seemed likely that she would try to escape. She had no coat, and she drew the jacket of her suit around her protectively. We watched the boats on the river for a while.

"Okay," said McNally, coming up from behind us. "We

need some more information. How many people are there in
that warehouse?"

Heidi turned and glanced vaguely at McNally. "I don't
know," she said. "I never spent much time there. It could be as
many as a dozen or as few as three."

"Are they armed?"

Yes."

"With what?"

"Atomic bombs."

McNally started to say something in response, but stopped
himself. He took a deep breath, then said in a low, reasonable
voice, "You're not being very helpful."

Heidi shrugged and turned back toward the river. "I told
you I'd help you find the place," she said. "After that, it's up
to you."

He stared at her shoulderblades for a moment, then gestured
for me to follow him. We walked back to the cars, leaving
Heidi with an FBI agent.

"Boggs," he said, "you know the setup they used in Alexandria. What do you think we're likely to find in there?"

I considered it. "You might find nothing at all," I said.
"These people have a habit of folding up their tents and
disappearing into the night."

"Great. But assume they're still there."

"In that case, I think you'll find four or five heavies, armed,
possibly with M 16's. And if this really is their bomb factory,
there could be another four or five technicians."

I thought another moment. "You could take them, I'm sure,
but I'd be careful about it if I were you."

"Why? The bombs?"

I nodded. "If a stray bullet touched off any of the plastic
explosives in there, you'd almost certainly get a nuclear

285

explosion, assuming they have at least one finished bomb inside."

"How big would the explosion be?"

I waved my arm around the horizon.

McNally's eyes widened. "That big?" he asked.

"Or bigger, depending on how many bombs they have. With all these oil tanks around here, even a fizzle would probably touch off everything in sight. They'd never put it out; there would be radioactivity and intense heat. You might even get a small firestorm. I'd say that a nuclear explosion of one or two kilotons at this location would burn down this entire section of the city."

"Maybe that's part of their plan," McNally said. "That warehouse could be booby-trapped."

"It's possible," I admitted. "But if that were the case, I don't think Heidi would have wanted to come along for the ride."

"She might not know about it. That would be their style, wouldn't it?"

Indeed it would. It wasn't difficult to imagine the inferno that would be created if we guessed wrong.

"I would suggest that before we do anything, you evacuate this part of the city."

McNally shook his head. "Impossible. It would take all day and alert the people in the warehouse. And it would cause a panic if anyone discovered the reason. We don't want anyone to know what's going on here, if we can help it."

I kicked at a pebble in disgust. "Same old CIA mentality, huh? What they don't know can't hurt them, even if it kills them. You'd keep the end of the world secret, wouldn't you, McNally?"

"If I thought it necessary. Boggs, the most we can do is call in the Philadelphia police and have them stand by to block off the area. And we can't even tell them why."

"You might alert the fire department, too," I added. "Just in case."

"Right. We'll tell them there's a gas leak or something."

"One other thing."

"What?"

I pointed to the throng of federal agents. They were holding enough small arms to equip an infantry company. "If I were you, I'd get rid of all those guns. One numskull could kill us all."

"I see what you mean. But we'll need firepower to take the warehouse."

"No, you need the threat of firepower. If you actually use it, I don't want to be around. Let them keep their guns in sight, but have all but a couple of your best men unload their magazines."

McNally went back to the cluster of feds. A few moments later I heard the sharp noises of magazines being ejected. It was a small, cheerless victory.

We waited there for an hour. Philadelphia police arrived, and there was an extended, heated conference. The cops were not happy about having so many feds appear unexpectedly on their turf. They didn't like not knowing what was going on. And they most especially didn't like being ordered around by McNally. They appealed to the mayor. McNally one-upped them and placed a call to Washington. Fifteen minutes later the mayor told the cops to cooperate, and they did, grudgingly. Helicopters fluttered overhead like indecisive dragonflies, and the radios crackled with ten-fours and cryptic code words. I watched it all unfold, feeling like a war correspondent on the eve of D day.

Heidi kept to herself, pondering the shallow mysteries hidden in the waters of the Delaware. I pondered the larger mystery of Heidi. How did she get to be the way she was?

And how did I get to be the way I was?

Heidi stood rooted and immobile, facing the river like an isolated, rockbound watchtower. She looked fragile and lonely. In spite of everything, I felt a sudden surge of tenderness for her. I remembered watching her in the waters off Torremolinos, golden in the sun, alive and hopeful.

I stood next to her for several minutes, silently gazing at the same muted vista. Finally I asked, "How's your jaw?"

"It hurts," she said.

I looked at it. There was a discolored lump low on the left side of her chin; it didn't diminish her beauty.

"I'm sorry I hit you," I said.

"Forget it."

"I'd like to forget that and everything else. It's a hell of a thing when you can't even slug a murderer without feeling bad about it."

She turned to me. "Does it matter so much that I've killed people?"

"Yes," I said.

"Why?"

"I don't really know. It just seems like it ought to matter. Back in Torremolinos—"

"Don't think about Torremolinos. It's too late. We should have taken off to Tahiti. But we didn't, and now it's too late. We did what we did, and now it doesn't matter what we should have done."

"I suppose not."

A foghorn sounded on the river, a lost and dying moan.

"We're all going to die," Heidi said.

After two hours of planning and bickering, everyone was in position. The police blockaded an area around the warehouse a half-mile in diameter. Inside the circle, they quietly began rounding up people and telling them to leave. It was a futile gesture, because if a bomb exploded, a half-mile wouldn't be nearly enough.

The feds surrounded the warehouse and peered at it cautiously from behind parked cars and other buildings. The warehouse was very similar to the one in Alexandria, four stories high and cracking with age. There were three doors and one large truck entrance, all closed. If there was anyone inside, they were not in evidence. The feds, on the other hand, were all too obvious. McNally was counting on surprise, but he was fooling himself—and probably knew it.

Six agents crept up to the side of the warehouse, moving in fits and starts from doorways to parked cars to the slim shelter of stop signs. They reached the building and flattened themselves against the walls, moving sideways, crablike, toward the doors. From my vantage point I could see four of them, two to a door. When they were ready, they reported in whispers via walkie-talkie.

The FBI man signaled his troops to check the doors. All three groups quickly reported that they were locked. That was expected.

"Open them up," ordered the supervisor. In other circumstances that might have been the signal for his men to barge in, tommy guns blazing. Now it was the signal to commence picking the locks. One man in each team got down on his knees and leaned close to the doors; they worked delicately and silently with their burglar's tools.

The sudden, staccato chatter of an automatic rifle caught me by surprise. It surprised the feds, too. I looked back at the warehouse. The two men at the door nearest me were lying still, sprawled out on the street like dark inkblots. The door slammed shut.

McNally grabbed the walkie-talkie from the FBI man.

"Hold your fire! he shouted. "And get the hell away from those doors!"

The FBI supervisor tried to pull the walkie-talkie away from McNally, unsuccessfully.

"Dammit!" he barked. "I've got to get those two men out of there!"

"Leave them," McNally said coldly. "We can't risk any more gunfire."

"Those are my men out there," the agent protested. "Do you know what it's like to have a man down and not be able to do anything about it?"

McNally gave him a look that could have frozen a tidal wave, then pivoted sharply and walked away. I touched the agent's sleeve. "He knows," I said. It had been less than twelve hours since we found Gardner's body.

We settled down for a protracted siege. The FBI supervisor, a florid, high-voiced little man named Colton, wanted to launch a gas attack and smoke them out. McNally rejected the idea; the gas canisters could start a fire, as had happened at the infamous SLA shootout in Los Angeles. But this fire could be considerably larger.

People came and went with noses red and runny. The police provided us with thermos bottles full of coffee and rubbery sandwiches. Food and drink were our only advantages, and slim ones at that. Sooner or later, the people inside would get hungry and thirsty. But in the meantime, anything could happen.

We stared at that warehouse and wished we had X-ray eyes. If we knew what was inside, we might be able to figure out what to do. And while we were staring, somewhere plans were being changed, targets were being selected, bad guys were getting away. You never catch the big boys in sleazy warehouses.

McNally finally turned to Heidi. "Your only hope," he told

her, "is that we finish this quickly and cleanly. You know that, don't you?"

"What happened to our bargain? I showed you where to find them; from now on, it's your problem."

"If we don't get in there, we'll all have problems. That includes you."

"What do you expect me to do about it? If you can't take the warehouse with all your men and guns, how could I manage it?"

"They know you. You could go in and talk to them."

"I don't think I want to go in there," she said. "They might not let me back out. And what would I say to them, anyway?"

McNally answered her haltingly, as if each word drew blood. "You are a very persuasive young lady," he said. "You could make them see that they don't have a chance."

Heidi gave him a short, snorting laugh.

"You could try."

"I could also get killed. After I get inside, you might decide to storm the place. It would be a good way to get rid of me while you're at it. That's what you want, isn't it?"

"Nothing," McNally said through clenched teeth, "nothing would give me greater pleasure."

"Is that how you get your rocks off?"

"Listen," McNally persisted, "they would trust you more than they'd trust one of us. You could . . . you could find out what they want."

"A deal, you mean?"

He exhaled heavily, sending a plume of steam into the air. "That's what I mean," he said. McNally had clearly had his fill of deals, but he knew it was necessary.

"And what about me?" Heidi asked.

"Your deal stands. Help us recover the stuff, and we'll let you go."

"How do I know you'll live up to your end of the bargain?"

It was a good question; I knew, because it was the same question I'd asked myself a million times.

"It's the same offer we made Boggs," said McNally. "He's done what he said he would, and we'll honor our promise."

Heidi turned to me. "What about it, Sam?" she asked. "Do you really think he's going to let you go?"

I looked into Heidi's eyes and saw the same trust that I'd seen there before. It was real, I thought. She'd take my word for it. McNally stood there, waiting for my response. He had trusted me before, though not very far. But lately he almost seemed to have forgotten that I'd ever been anything but just another agent working with him. He had accepted my word on the GP raids, he had trusted me with a degree of freedom. Now I had to decide how far I could trust him. There was absolutely nothing to prevent him from shooting me in the back when the whole affair was finished. If that was what he wanted to do, he could do it. And would.

"I trust him, Heidi," I said. It was a truly visceral response; I hadn't consciously planned to say anything.

Heidi wasn't satisfied. "Maybe you can trust him," she said, "but how do I know that I can? He's got a special reason to double-cross me."

"He won't do it," I said.

"How do I know?"

"Because I say he won't. You don't have to trust him, Heidi, you only have to trust me."

She looked at me for a long moment.

"Okay, Sam," she said at last. "I'll trust you." She smiled suddenly, a warm and honest grin. "How could I not trust you? You're too fucking honorable to screw me."

Heidi walked alone across the empty street to the door of the warehouse. It was the other door, not the one with the two dead agents lying in front of it. Her gait seemed unnaturally stiff and forced; I realized that Heidi was scared. It hadn't occurred to me that she was capable of such a vulnerable emotion.

I had briefed her on what to look for in the warehouse. Her main mission was that of negotiator, but if negotiations broke down, her reconnaissance might be valuable. She was to find out, if possible, the number, location, and condition of any bombs in the warehouse. From her experience at the Palmer Engineering Company, she would at least be able to recognize a bomb if she saw one.

She paused ten feet in front of the door. I thought I saw a face appear at the second-story window, but it was difficult to be sure. Fog was drifting in from the river, cutting visibility.

After another minute, the door opened. A rifle barrel protruded from the darkness inside. Heidi started to go in, hesitated, then continued. The door closed behind her.

I lit another cigarette. It was damp; everything was damp. I leaned back against the fender of a car and waited.

McNally joined me in my vigil. He bummed a cigarette from me.

"You look like you're worried about her," he observed. The clear implication was that I shouldn't be.

"We're all screwed up here, all of us," I told him. "If I deserve another chance, why shouldn't she?"

"Maybe you don't deserve it," he said.

"Look, McNally, don't say anything that's going to shake my faith in you at this late date, okay? If you're planning to shaft me, I'd rather not know about it."

"No, I'm not planning to shaft you."

"Or her?"

He took a long, thoughtful drag on the cigarette. "You gave her your word," he said. "I gave you my word. I guess we just have to trust each other."

" 'Said the spider to the fly.' "

Heidi emerged from the warehouse a half-hour later. I took a few steps to meet her, but McNally grabbed me and pulled me back. We let Heidi approach by herself.

McNally and I sat down inside the car with her, all of us in the back seat. She tilted her head back and rested it against the cushion. Eyes closed, she made her report in a mechanical monotone.

"You won't like it," she said. "The want hostages and safe conduct to the airport. They also want a plane. They said it had to be a military transport. No pilot, just the plane."

"What about the bomb?" McNally demanded. "Do they have one?"

"They've got several. They wouldn't tell me how many. I don't think they trust me very much."

"Did you see one?" I asked.

She nodded. "They've rolled it out into the middle of the main floor. They wanted me to be sure to tell you that. One shot could set it off. And they said that rather than go to jail, they'd just as soon blow it up themselves."

"Do you think they mean it?" McNally asked.

"They mean it. There are only five of them. One of them is the guy who's building the bombs, and he seemed kind of scared. But the others are all tough. They've done some other dirty stuff, so they aren't about to give themselves up."

"What about the one who's building the bomb?"

"I don't know much about him," she said. "I think he's just some atomic scientist who got into some kind of trouble. I think he'd give himself up if he had the chance."

"Do you think he'd help disable the bomb?"

"You'd have to hold his hand, or break his arm, maybe, but he'd do it if there was any way. But I don't see how."

McNally looked at me, his eyes suddenly sharp. I had a queasy feeling about what was coming next.

"Boggs? What about it? If we could get you in there, could you disarm it?"

I said I didn't know for sure, which was true. I asked Heidi to describe the bomb. She said it looked just like the original, except that there was no plastic paneling around the tubular frame. The bomb itself was exposed and accessible.

Very reluctantly, I told McNally that it just might be possible. "You've got to remember," I said, "that this is not a military bomb. There's no switch that will disarm it. The only way to do it would be to cut the detonator wires at the point where they connect with the battery, or yank out the detonators themselves. But there are twenty-four of them, and you'd have to be careful. Anyway, how the hell do you think you'll get me inside? And what good would it do? You heard Heidi. They've got more than one bomb. And even if I did disarm it, they could set it off just by shooting at it."

"One thing at a time, Boggs. Heidi? Is there anyone inside who knows Boggs?"

She shook her head.

"That's it, then," he said. "You'll be one of the hostages, Boggs."

"Bloody hell, I'll be a hostage!"

"Calm down, Boggs. It's the only way to do it. We can't do anything as long as we're out here and they're in there. We either have to get in or get them to come out. This way, we do both. Somewhere between here and the airport, you might get a chance to fix the bomb."

"That's fine for you, McNally. I get into the back of a truck with five killers and an atomic bomb. Meanwhile, you just get to waltz into the warehouse and pick up the rest of the plutonium. Beautiful."

McNally scratched his nose. "It won't be quite that easy, I'm afraid. You see, Boggs, I'll be the other hostage."

I stared at him for a full minute before I realized that he was serious. "You really mean it, don't you?"

"You didn't think I'd let you go alone, did you? It's not that I don't trust you, Boggs. I just worry a lot."

"You mean I'd switch sides again?"

"Temptation is a terrible thing, Boggs. Anyway, someone has to go along. I'll try to create a diversion long enough to let you disable the bomb. It might even work."

"Bullshit." I didn't believe it. Hell, he didn't even believe it. McNally was volunteering us for a kamikaze mission.

I got out of the car and wandered off down the street, toward the barricades. Beyond them, a considerable crowd had gathered, despite the efforts of the police to keep the area clear. I saw a white station wagon with the call letters of a radio station printed on it; the press was here. Too many people already knew we were dealing with nuclear weapons here. Sooner or later, probably sooner, the story would leak. Then the feds certainly wouldn't go out of their way to protect the guy who built the bomb that blew up half of South Philadelphia.

Not that it would matter. I'd be gone. I was wedded to that damn bomb. Wherever it went, I was going along.

I looked at the gray rows of tenements. People lived in them. Real people, with children and dogs and pet goldfish. If the warehouse blew, how many would die? Fifty thousand? The same number as died in Vietnam. That was what got me into this business in the first place, wasn't it? How now, Sam Boggs, you noble defender of peace and freedom?

I might be able to save some of those people, some of those tenements where they lived the only lives they had. I knew what McNally had in mind. Get them out of the warehouse with only one bomb. Then somewhere out in the marshes between here and the airport, make our play, whatever it would be. If the bomb explodes there, all we lose are some ducks. And a couple of agents. A small price to pay.

I walked back to the car. "Okay," I told McNally. "Set it up."

19

We waited another hour while Heidi went back and forth between us and the warehouse, ironing out the details. McNally spent most of the time on the phone with Washington. The Philadelphia cops cleared the route to the airport. The Air Force brought in a plane. Everyone had something to do but me. I just waited.

Finally Heidi went into the warehouse and didn't come out again. When McNally and I began our walk to the warehouse, she was supposed to meet us going the other way; if all was well, we would continue. Heidi had been promised an airline ticket to Brazil. That would be it: Good-bye Heidi, good-bye Sam.

The truck arrived. A large van, it backed up against the garage door and stopped. The driver left it running, and hopped out quickly. He sprinted back to the imagined safety of our side of the street. After another moment, the garage door opened and someone jumped into the back of the van. The truck rolled smoothly into the shadows and disappeared. We heard the horn honk three times.

McNally looked at me. "Well?" he asked.

"Why not?"

We started walking, like the Earp brothers headed for the OK Corral. Our pace seemed unnatural—too fast or too slow, or something. I had to think about moving my legs.

"Something's wrong," McNally said. "Where's Heidi?" There was no sign of her. She should have been on her way by now.

"Maybe she doesn't want to go to Brazil, after all. What do we do now?"

"We keep walking." McNally snorted contemptuously; I think he was probably just sniffing back some mucus. If he had sneezed instead, it would have ruined the effect.

We stopped about ten feet in front of the garage door. It was still impossible to see very much inside. I looked back over my shoulder at the FBI lines and was not reassured. Their guns were up and ready; some of them had to be loaded.

A head peered around the corner of the garage entrance. It was followed by the rest of the body, short and stocky and so tense that if you had plucked him he would have played high C. I had never seen him before. He was wearing a dark navy-watch cap and a CPO jacket and looked like the kind of guy who'd blackjack you outside a bar and you'd wake up in the hold of a freighter bound for Singapore.

He held an M 16 in his hands. He pointed it at McNally's Adam's apple until satisfied that we weren't going to try anything. Cautiously he slung the rifle and started searching McNally. When he was finished, he repeated the process with me, never taking his eyes off mine. His eyes were sky blue, a surprising contrast to his black stubble and swarthy face.

300

"Okay," he said. "Inside."

McNally led the way, with our escort bringing up the rear. He kept swiveling his head like a squirrel on the lookout for hawks or weasels or whatever the hell it is that squirrels look out for.

The garage was dimly lit, but there was enough dirty light coming into the warehouse for me to make out Stover standing there, waiting for me. We locked eyes for a moment and said nothing. Heidi was standing next to him; I thought there was a hint of a smile on her face. Got you again, didn't I, Sam? She had said that no one inside the warehouse knew me. Counting her, she was off by a factor of three. My third old friend was good old Billy Wynn, the A. J. Foyt of the CB set. My impression of him had been that he could drive anything, and I was right. He was going to drive our getaway plane. Those weathered cowboy eyes of his got that way by staring at horizons, not highways.

I was so involved in looking at my associates from the defunct Palmer Engineering Company that it was a few moments before I noticed the rest of our little entourage. A tallish, sandy-haired man in his late twenties was standing off to one side, holding another one of the ubiquitous M 16's. Near him was the man who obviously had to be the skittish scientist. He had a big bald spot on the back of his head, which I could see because he was lying facedown on the oily concrete floor. His brains were leaking out of the bald spot.

"I suppose," said Stover, "I should say something appropriately villainous, like 'So, Boggs, we meet again,' and then twirl my mustache."

"Say what you like," I told him. I was too depressed for clever repartee.

Stover looked at McNally carefully. "Heidi here tells me you volunteered for this mission, Mr. McNally. That's kind of comforting, really. They say that you CIA types are nothing but bureaucrats these days. I'm glad to see that some of the old Wild Bill Donovan spirit survives."

McNally wasn't impressed. "Why did you kill him?" he asked flatly.

Stover shrugged. "Too scared to go, and too valuable to leave behind."

While they were talking, I noticed that Heidi had been less than truthful about another matter. There were two bombs, not one, sitting benignly near the truck. One was mine—they still had only one bomb ready to go.

Stover noticed where I was looking. "Yes, Boggs," he said, "we have bombs. And plutonium. More than we can take with us, I'm afraid. But we're overjoyed to have you along to baby-sit with the two we are taking. Dr. Conroy was reluctant to come along with us. Afraid of flying, I suppose. Which reminds me, Mr. McNally . . ."

"It's arranged. The plane is waiting at the airport. But just where do you think you can go? No country in the world will let you land with those bombs aboard."

Stover smiled. "Oh," he said confidently, "I can think of one or two. Now, what about the route to the airport?"

"There will be a police escort. They'll lead the way."

"Fine. Just don't forget that I already know the way. If you try to lead us out into the swamp, we'll just dispense with the escort. I know what you're thinking, McNally. I had an escape plan mapped out before we ever got here. We'll go over the Penrose Bridge and then straight to the airport. There'll be no detours on this trip. We'll be going through heavily built-up areas, filled with people and other valuable things."

I could see a muscle twitch in McNally's cheek. He was going to have to get used to dealing with Stover.

Stover eyed his wristwatch. "Time's a-wastin'," he said,

nodding to the two gun-toters. They leveled their rifles at us and suggested that we lie facedown on the floor. That didn't appeal to me at all. It would make three of us lying there, and one of us wasn't breathing.

"Don't be difficult, Sam," Heidi told me.

"Wouldn't dream of it." I joined McNally. While the dockside thug held his gun on us, the sandy-haired one tied us up. He stuck my wrists together and wrapped a length of clothesline around them. It was so tight that my shoulders hurt from being pulled backward in a direction God had never intended them to go. He wiggled my hands around for a few seconds just to make sure I wasn't cheating. Houdini might have found a way to swell up his wrists as rope was being wound around them, but it was a trick I had never learned.

After they had finished with us, Stover told us to stay where we were. He added that Heidi had her own gun on us. "Mr. Bell and Mr. Jones have some work to do, now, and so do I. Don't go away, gentlemen."

I heard footsteps, but when I turned my head to look, all I could see was McNally lying next to me. He looked back at me.

"Don't say it, Boggs," he warned. "Just don't say it."

McNally was, as the expression goes, pissed off. I wasn't sure what he had expected once we got into the warehouse, but this was definitely not it. But his anger could be useful; given the chance, he ought to be able to chew his way through my bonds.

I heard the sounds of heavy exertion, grunting, and swearing. They were trying to roll the bombs into the back of the truck. It sounded as if it were taking all three of them; Stover, of course, excluded his own pudgy self from physical labor, and Heidi was holding a gun on us. With just five people, they were a little short of manpower. As far as I could see, that was our only advantage. Of course, our own little task force wasn't exactly rife with featherbedding.

"Any ideas?" McNally whispered.

'You're asking me?"

"Yes, dammit, I'm asking you! Try to turn off your famous wit and use your brains for once."

Under the circumstances, I thought he was asking a lot. Still, I tried.

"What about the airport?" I asked him. "Usually in a hijack, your guys shoot out the plane's tires so it can't take off. Could they do it out at the end of the runway when we're not close to anything?"

"We talked about it. No good. They couldn't take off, but they could taxi right on back to the terminal and threaten to blow up the airport. That would just make things worse."

I suddenly felt something cold and hard against the back of my neck.

"No talking in class, Sam."

McNally made a rude suggestion, and Heidi kicked him in the ribs, hard. "Tell me some more about all the things you had planned for me, McNally. Tell me about how much it was going to hurt." She kicked him again. McNally made the kind of grunt you hear at the line of scrimmage.

"That's enough, Heidi!"

"Is it, Sam? And what are you going to do about it?" She sounded like a belligerent ten-year-old daring someone to say something about her old man.

"You really do enjoy this, don't you?"

"You bet I do!" She kicked McNally again, then walked away.

"Are you okay?"

The wind was knocked out of him. He was gasping, trying to get the engine started again. "Fine," he managed.

Before he could say any more, Bell and Jones came back and lifted him up like a secondhand carpet. A few moments later it was my turn. One grabbed my legs, and the other took hold of my shoulders. They carried me, headfirst, into the back of the van. It was crowded in there, with two bombs and McNally on the floor between them. They dropped me on top of McNally. I was reasonably comfortable, but Mac was not going to enjoy the ride.

Doors slammed, and the engine started. By tilting my head as far back as it would go, I could see Wynn in the driver's seat, naturally, and the sandy-haired fellow riding shotgun—with an M 16. The others must have been sitting on the floor behind us at the back of the van.

"Okay, Wynn," said Stover, "slow and easy."

We lurched forward, into the streets of Philadelphia.

I lowered my head down next to McNally's ear. "Let me know when you're going to create the diversion," I said. "I want to be ready."

From beneath me, I heard McNally's muffled voice tell me to go fuck a rock.

"To get out of here, gladly."

The ride to the airport went as smoothly as a presidential motorcade. I don't think we even hit any bumps in the road. No one did any talking, so I used the opportunity to think, and I didn't like my thoughts. If McNally and I had been two run-of-the-mill hostages, our chances of surviving would have been poor. But since we were who we were, our chances were just about zero. McNally would make a special prize for Heidi, and Stover had already ordered me killed three different times. I rather suspected that the fourth time, he would do it himself, just to make sure.

On the plus side of the ledger, we had apparently broken up whatever plot Stover was hatching. Except for the two on

305

either side of me, they had lost all their bombs and fissionable material. On the minus side, the loss was bound to make them desperate and angry. I tried to think the way they would, which wasn't difficult, since I was desperate and a little angry myself.

Stover, however, was not behaving in a particularly desperate manner. He was a planner, and the only thing I could see upsetting him would be something totally unexpected, out of left field. He had obviously prepared his escape plans well in advance.

But he couldn't have counted on having me along for the ride. I was a wild card in his deck. So was Heidi, for that matter. She had been faced with the double agent's classic dilemma: how to wind up on the winning side when the shooting stops. She had opted for Stover at the moment. If the odds changed, would she switch allegiances again?

I suddenly realized that I didn't want her on my side again. I liked her just fine right where she was.

We slowed down, and Stover shouted to Wynn, "Take us straight into the plane." We speeded up again and abruptly headed up an incline. The bombs began to roll toward the back of the truck. As the one on my right went by, I gave it an extra shove with my foot. I rolled off of McNally and got to my knees.

"Don't try it, Boggs." Stover was pinned to the back door of the van by one of the bombs, but he had his gun out and aimed at me. Heidi and Jones, the swarthy one, were struggling with the second bomb. For a second it was just one-on-one. I could have dived at him. I could have, but I didn't, and then the second was gone. The truck was into the plane and level again. Jones shoved his bomb back toward the front end of the truck, and Heidi pulled her own gun out of a pocket.

I slowly lowered myself back down to the metal floor. Stover pushed the bomb away from him and put his gun away. "That showed good sense," he said. "You'll stay alive as long as you keep your head, Boggs."

McNally had rolled over onto his back to see what was happening. Stover turned his gaze toward him and added, "That applies to you, too, Mr. McNally."

"I never doubted it," he answered.

Stover made his way past the bombs and over McNally to the front of the van. Wynn had stopped the truck and turned off the motor.

"Wynn," Stover said briskly, "you check out the cockpit. Bell, look at everything else in the plane. Check it for booby traps, locked doors, anything that doesn't look right. If you find anyone out there, don't start shooting. Just remind them that we can still blow the bombs at any time." Wynn and Bell did as they were told.

Jones was leaning against the back door, his M 16 at port arms. Heidi had her back to us, her face up against the rear window. For a moment I considered another mad rush at them, and I knew that Mac was thinking the same thing. The odds were not likely to get better, and once we were in the air, the ball game would be over. There are not a hell of a lot of places you can run to on an airplane.

But Jones was sharper than I gave him credit for. Just as I had halfway made up my mind to leap at him, he casually shifted his rifle toward us. "You ever see what kind of damage one of these things can do at close quarters?" he asked. "I did," he went on, as if answering his own question. "Down in the delta, once, we found a bunch of gooks asleep in this little shack, about the size of this truck. We just opened up on them, and after about ten seconds there was brains and shit splattered all over what was left of that shack. And there wasn't much, let me tell you. Place looked like it'd been attacked by giant termites, so many holes in it."

I got the message. I let my muscles relax, or tried to, and Jones went back to port arms.

Wynn and Bell returned to the truck. "Clean as a whistle," Wynn reported.

"Will it fly?" Stover wanted to know.

Wynn nodded. "All fueled up, looks to be in good shape. No problems."

"Radar?"

"I can handle it," said Bell. "It's newer than what I used, but it shouldn't be any hassle."

"Fine. As soon as you tie down this truck, we take off. And somebody tie down these damn bombs, too. I don't want any more atomic bombs rolling around loose. You should have thought of that before, Wynn."

Wynn made no apology. "There's plenty of cargo webbing," he said. "Put Jones to work on it. I have other things to do." Wynn got out of the truck and walked off toward the cockpit.

Stover bowed to Wynn's obvious independence. "You heard him," he told Jones. "Do it."

Jones opened up the back door and got to work, along with Bell. The odds kept changing: now it was two-on-two again.

"You really think you'll make it, don't you?" McNally asked.

"We're doing okay so far," Heidi replied.

"You're still on the ground, kid. There's a long way to go."

"Indeed there is," Stover broke in. "And if you want to be around for the whole trip, I suggest you keep your thoughts to yourself."

Jones returned with an armful of webbing, tough straps that

were not likely to break even in severe turbulence. He ignored us and set about lacing the straps through the metal tubing of the bomb carriages, lashing them tightly to the sides and floor of the truck. I heard Bell outside, doing the same job on the truck itself.

When they were finished, Jones retrieved his M 16 and told us to get up. McNally and I struggled to our feet, balancing ourselves as well as we could with no hands. Heidi opened up the back of the van, and we stepped down onto the cargo deck of the plane.

The transport was not huge, but standing there on the empty cargo deck was like being in a large aluminum cave. The clamshell doors at the rear were still open, revealing the hard gray runway beneath us, but the ramp had been retracted. The other way, there was about thirty or forty feet of open floor between us and the steps leading up to the cockpit. Some foolish impulse made me want to shout and see if there was an echo, but before I could, one of the engines coughed noisily into life.

Within a couple of minutes, all four engines were spinning, and we had to shout anyway, just to make ourselves heard. "Over there!" Jones commanded us, pointing to a spot on the far side of the plane, about midship.

McNally and I obediently went where we were told. Jones gestured for us to sit down. Since there were no seats on the cargo deck, that meant sitting on the floor, which we did. This was definitely going to be a no-frills flight.

From the cockpit, Wynn pulled the lever to close the clamshell doors. We began to move. Heidi and Jones sat down on the floor opposite us. Jones carefully put down his M 16 and removed a .45 automatic from his pocket. The M 16 was a ridiculous weapon for such close quarters; if he had used it, he probably would have shot off one of the wings. I wasn't overjoyed about the pistol, but it seemed like a definite improvement.

Aside from the lack of seats, the major disadvantage in riding in the back of a transport is that there are no windows except for the paratroop exit door at the rear of the plane. So we sat and stared at each other and wondered what was going on outside.

I felt the plane turn sharply to the right, then come to a stop. The engines increased in volume as Wynn brought them up to full takeoff power. There was obviously going to be no waiting around for DC-9's from Cleveland and weekend Piper Apaches; we were number one on the runway.

There is something oddly thrilling about the sound of a powerful prop plane revving up for takeoff. The noise gets inside you and shakes your bones, vibrates your vitals.

Suddenly we were in motion. With no windows, the sensation of speed was missing. Rather, there was just the dull pressure of acceleration and the vibration from the runway. And then the vibration was gone, and we were in the air.

I turned to McNally and shouted, "Welcome to the friendly skies!"

McNally made no reply. I knew what he was thinking. Philadelphia was safe. All those Main Line matrons and boisterous Flyer fans might never know what they had missed, or what had missed them. But the problem was not solved. We were exporting it to God knew where. And McNally and I were going along for the ride.

After we had been airborne for about ten minutes, Stover returned from the cockpit. Stover was not the kind of man who would actually strut, but there was a hint of self-satisfaction in his stride. He seemed to be very pleased with himself.

"Where are we going?" McNally asked him, raising his

voice to make himself heard above the droning engines.

"Cuba," Stover answered. "Surprised?"

"Not really."

"Well, you should be. The Cubans are going to be surprised, I'll tell you that. Cuba's not our ultimate destination, but we'll need to stop there for fuel. I doubt if they'll object very strenuously."

"I wouldn't count on it."

"I would. I do, in fact. The Cubans are as fond of Havana as you are of Philadelphia. They'll cooperate."

"And if they don't?"

Stover smiled. "Always looking at the dark side of things, aren't you, McNally?"

"It's in my nature."

"And you, Boggs?" Stover asked, looking at me with another smile. "What is in your nature?"

"You know me," I said cheerfully. "Always glad to cooperate with anyone who's holding a gun on me."

"I'm glad to hear it. Your cooperation is sort of essential at this point, what with Dr. Conroy gone."

What did we have here, I wondered? An edge? Perhaps, but I was cautious. Stover always knew how to arouse my interest and take advantage of it.

"Tell me about it," I said.

Stover carefully lowered himself to the deck and deposited his large ass on it. He didn't look comfortable, but he was the sort of man who would never look physically at ease in any environment. He seemed to be fighting, and losing, a perpetual war with earth's gravity field.

"I won't beat around the bush," he said, having arranged himself at last. "While we were on the ground, everyone was afraid of us because we had a couple of bombs. Now, up here in the air, we don't have bombs, we only have devices. You know what I'm talking about, don't you?"

311

I nodded. "The nukes aren't really bombs, not the kind you can drop from an airplane. They're worthless to you as a threat, Stover."

"I'm well aware of that fact. If we dropped one of them, it would be just so much falling junk. To make them effective, we need detonation devices. Something that can set them off while they're still in the air. A barometric fuse would be ideal, but I doubt if we could construct one under the circumstances. We need something else."

"And you want me to come up with that something else? Stover—"

He cut me short. "Keep your mouth shut and listen, Boggs. You know what's going to happen to you, I'm sure. You and your friend are cold meat. Your usefulness as hostages has already come to an end. Oh, McNally might be marginally useful on the ground in Cuba, but that's pretty unlikely. And you, Boggs, you never did have any value. If we were to kill you right now, can you think of anyone who would bother to shed a tear?"

I couldn't. Not a soul. I had never really thought of it that way before.

"But you do have a useful skill," Stover continued. "You are a weapons expert, and right now we need a weapons expert. Am I beginning to make sense?"

He was. McNally looked at me sharply and started to say something, but thought better of it.

"What's in it for me, if I may coin a phrase?"

"Isn't it obvious? When we get where we're going, we'll let you go. You'll be free and alive, Boggs. What more could you ask for?"

"I seem to remember hearing that before."

Stover was not in the least embarrassed by being reminded of past duplicities. "That was then," he said simply. "This is now. Before, your dead body would have helped promote our cover-up. Now it means nothing. You still don't know anything, so there's nothing you can tell anyone, even if you want to. You can't hurt us, so there's no reason to kill you. We kill, yes, but not without reason."

"Is that why you wanted to build a dozen atomic bombs? So you could reasonably kill a million people?"

"Our reasons don't concern you, Boggs. But I will tell you this. The bombs were never intended to be used in the United States, or in any heavily populated area. Now that our plans have been disrupted, the bombs in this plane will be delivered to our original client, but I doubt that he'll use them."

"But you want to use them, Stover. Why else would you want me to rig up a fuse?"

He shook his head. "No, Boggs. I don't want to use them. Believe me, that's the very last thing I want. But we have to have a credible threat. We have two bombs. If necessary, we can drop one of them on an uninhabited area, just to make sure that no one bothers us. I don't want anyone trying to shoot down this plane. I think, under the circumstances, that you ought to be able to agree with that sentiment."

I had to admit to myself that he was right. I had no desire at all to get greased by some jet jockey. McNally, though, probably had other ideas. Given the chance, he'd saw off our wings. There was just a touch of the kamikaze in him.

"You're asking me to take an awful lot on faith," I said. "You won't kill me, and if you drop one of the bombs, it'll be over the ocean. Is that it?"

"That's it, Boggs. Without belaboring the obvious, let me point out that if you refuse to help, we'll shoot both of you right here and now. You'll be dead, and we'll still have two bombs. Where's the advantage in that?"

"So I'm supposed to trust you."

313

"It's as simple as that. Oh, I admit that if our roles were reversed, I'd be cautious, too. After all, I have tried to have you killed once or twice."

"Thrice, as a matter of fact. I'm keeping track."

"Three times, then. I don't expect you to like me, Boggs. But I do think you should bow before the inevitable. I'm offering you your one and only chance to live. What other option do you have?"

I chewed on my lower lip for a few moments and came to the conclusion that Stover was absolutely correct. If I said no, I'd be dead a minute later.

"I'm no saint," I told him, "but I don't like the idea of giving you a functional bomb. How do I know you won't drop it on Washington?"

"You don't know. And you didn't know when you built the bomb in the first place. But you did build it. And you're right, Boggs, you're no saint. You're not a martyr, either. You and I both know that martyrs have only one thing in common— they're all dead. What you are is a man who has a very well-developed ability to look out for himself. Don't blow it all with an ill-timed attack of conscience. You can't afford it."

McNally had slowly been turning red while Stover and I talked. If he had suddenly been set free, I don't know which one of us he'd have tried to strangle first. But he had enough sense to keep his mouth shut.

"Boggs," Stover went on, "we both know what you are. You're a twentieth-century version of a hired gun. For a while there, you thought that it might be nice to get to wear the white hat and tin star. But they don't fit you, Boggs, and they never will. Give it up. Be what you are. Be smart."

I thought about it for a moment or two, and then Stover stuck the hook in. "Let me point out," he said, "that you still have a half-million dollars in that bank in Zurich. That's five-hundred thousand more reasons for doing it my way."

"I thought the money belonged to Heidi."

He shrugged. "If she had done her job, it would have. You weren't supposed to be around to claim it. But here you are."

"And there she is," I said, nodding toward Heidi, who was still sitting on the floor on the other side of the plane with Jones.

"Well, it belongs to one of you. Maybe you'll want to split it. That's up to you."

It was not an especially attractive prospect. You don't have to be a mathematician to know that a half-million dollars divided two ways is a hell of a lot less than a half-million dollars divided one way. My old phantom brother, Fred C. Dobbs, would have understood.

"When we get where we're going, could you see to it that Heidi is delayed for a few hours?"

"You want a head start to Zurich? Fine, you've got it. Anything else?"

"Yes. You let McNally go, too."

Stover's eyebrows went up a centimeter. "I didn't think he mattered that much to you."

"I owe him."

McNally finally erupted. "If he does let me go, Boggs, I guarantee that the first thing I'll do is hunt you down and kill you. That's a promise."

"Nevertheless."

"If that's what you want," agreed Stover. "We could let him off in Cuba. That might be safer for you."

"Not likely," McNally snarled. Veins were popping in his forehead.

Stover got to his feet. "Okay, Boggs. Welcome back." He called to Jones, who was up in a second and walked toward us with his pistol ready.

"Untie Boggs. He's going to help us."

Jones allowed himself a moment of surprise, then tucked the

gun in his waistband and reached behind me for my ropes. He wasn't very careful, and took some skin away along with the ropes, but it was a great relief to be able to move my hands. I woodenly smacked them together and flexed my fingers.

"Get McNally, too. He is going to lose both hands if you keep him tied like that. At least retie him in front. I may be wearing a black hat again, Stover, but I draw the line at deliberate torture."

"Fair enough." He took his own pistol out of an inside jacket pocket and held it loosely, aiming it at a point somewhere between McNally and me. Jones went to work on McNally's bonds. Jones allowed him a minute to rub his wrists before he started winding the rope again. McNally ignored Jones's ministrations and kept his eyes on me.

"You're a bigger shit than I thought, Boggs. How many people do you think are going to die because you decided to save your own miserable ass? How many, Boggs? How many?"

"One less than might have been. So close your fucking mouth, or I'll change my mind about you. You make me want to puke, McNally, with your goddamn sanctimonious bullshit about God and country. You ride roughshod over everything and everybody, but you get pissed if anyone else tries to do the same thing. Well, you can just shove it, Mac, straight up your rosy-red-white-and-blue ass. It's *my* bomb, *I* built it, and I'll do what *I* want with it."

McNally spat at me. I walked away from him, out of range.

I didn't know if he'd gotten the message. It didn't seem to make much difference, but when we died, I didn't want him to think I was a shit.

It wasn't even necessary to think about how to rig the bomb—I just *knew*. Call it instinct.

"What altitude are we flying at?" I asked.

"I don't know," Stover said, "but I can find out."

316

On the side of the plane, a few feet ahead of where McNally was sitting, there was a phone jack and a headset hanging from a hook. Stover fumbled with it for a moment before getting the jack plugged in and adjusting his earphones.

"Wynn!" he shouted into the mike, "can you hear me?"

Apparently Wynn could, for a few seconds later Stover was asking him about altitude. Wynn supplied the information.

"We're at seven thousand feet right now. But Wynn says he plans to take it on up to fifteen. Why?"

I closed my eyes and did some rapid calculations, very rough, but close enough for government work.

"Fifty-five seconds," I said. "That's how long your bomb would take to hit the ground, give or take maybe ten or fifteen seconds. It's hard to be precise."

"So?"

"So we take one bomb out of the truck and hook the other one into the truck's battery. Use the dashboard clock for a timer. When you're ready to drop it, set the timer for, say, two minutes, then push the truck out the back a minute later. Use the rest of the time to put the plane in a shallow dive and get the hell away. It ought to work."

"It sounds good to me, Boggs. Go ahead, do it."

"I hope it goes off in your face," McNally growled.

"If it does," Stover told him, "the citizens of Baltimore are going to have one hell of a bad day."

Rigging the bomb was something I could have done in my sleep. I'd done virtually the same thing dozens of times, and the fact that this was an atomic bomb didn't alter the procedure.

I went straight to my own bomb, like a pigeon returning to its nest. Jones pushed the other one out of the back of the truck while Stover kept a wary eye on me. His gun wasn't out, but I knew that it would have been in a second if I tried anything.

317

So I didn't try anything. I did a thoroughly competent job, stringing wires from the bomb to the battery, by way of the clock. The only thing I had to worry about, aside from Stover, was the possibility of letting live wires come in contact. Rule number one of the bomb game.

I let my mind wander in spite of everything. My hands knew what to do.

I thought about elements. There are a hundred-and-some-odd elements now. They'd just found a couple new ones, way up around 125, so that meant that they had some gaps to fill in on old Mendeleev's chart. Given time, I was sure they would. They could predict what those missing elements would be like, and from the predictions, they would know how and where to look for them. They might exist for mere microseconds, but the boys in the lab smocks would find them.

Just like they found plutonium. The ninety-fourth element. In nature, ninety-two, uranium, is as far as you can normally go. But the big brains back in the forties knew that plutonium was out there waiting for them to find it. A brief stopover at ninety-three, neptunium, and then there you were at the big ninety-four.

Plutonium had a distinction. Several distinctions, really. It was the first manmade element to be produced in visible quantities. And it was, and is, the only element ever discovered and produced with the sole purpose of killing people. Enrico and the gang may have had purer motives, but they never would have had the opportunity to do the work except for the fact that the ninety-fourth element was perfect for nuclear weapons.

Ah, but plutonium can also heat your home, light your lights, run your car, even. Our friend, the atom. The friendly atoms inside my bomb had been destined to provide heat and light for some family in Keokuk, Iowa, I supposed. But the folks back in Keokuk were just going to have to get along without them. Because these particular plutonium atoms had been called back to active duty; once a soldier, always a soldier.

Trying to domesticate plutonium is like trying to make a house pet out of an attack dog. Maybe he'll fetch your slippers and chase sticks for a while, but sooner or later he'll tear your throat out.

I taped up the exposed end of the wire leading to the bomb and wrapped it around the steering wheel a couple of times. Then I wiped the sweat off my palms and stood up.

"You're going to leave it like that?" Stover asked doubtfully.

"Yes, unless you want to have to reset the clock once every hour to keep from getting blown up. When and if we have to, all we need to do is connect that wire with the minute hand. The hour hand is already hooked up. Then you set the clock for the amount of time you need, and there you are. When the hands come in contact, you've got yourself a mushroom cloud."

"Ingenious."

"Standard. A Belfast Special. Park the car, set the clock, and walk away. Very effective for killing people you don't even know."

We stepped down out of the truck. "Getting another attack of conscience, Boggs?" Stover asked.

"Don't you recognize cynicism when you hear it, Stover? Mine is a very cynical profession."

"Mine, too," he said. "Are you sure that thing will work?"

"It can't miss."

"Good. I like a man who takes pride in his work. Well, why don't you sit down and relax. We've still got a long way to go."

Stover was acting funny; I couldn't tell just how. But I took his advice and plopped down on the floor and leaned my back against the wall. McNally was a few feet to my right, but he didn't say anything, and neither did I. I didn't want to talk.

But Stover seemed more lively. He bounced up and down on the balls of his feet and looked positively happy. That scared me.

"Yes, indeed," he repeated, "I do like a man who takes pride in his work. I was interested in the way that you went straight to your own bomb, the one you built. Why not the other one?"

"I was familiar with my own work," I said slowly. I was beginning to get an icy feeling in the pit of my stomach.

"That's good thinking, Boggs," Stover said breezily. "Don't trust anyone else's work. They might have done something slipshod."

I nodded. The other shoe was about to come down.

"For example," he continued, "take that very bomb you just worked on. Now, I knew you were a good workman, but just the same, I worried a little. I mean, maybe you forgot to connect something. So to be safe, I had the late Dr. Conroy go over it, just to check things out, you understand. And you'll never guess what he found, Boggs. I know it's hard to believe, you being such a professional and all, but it seems that you forgot to connect all those little wires inside the detonators. But don't worry, Boggs. Dr. Conroy fixed them."

I shut my eyes and wished very fervently that I wouldn't have to open them again. I did, though. Jones was walking toward me with a length of rope in his hand.

Stover smiled benignly. "Nice try, Boggs," he said.

20

Heidi strolled over to gloat. She sat down next to me and didn't say anything for a few minutes. I opened my mouth wide and yawned, trying to get my ears to pop. The plane was not pressurized, and we were climbing up toward fifteen thousand feet. That's not high enough to require oxygen, but it's more than enough to make you feel dizzy and disoriented.

"How's it going, Sam?" Heidi finally asked.

I lifted my bound hands to let her see the rope, then dropped them back into my lap.

"Well, that's an improvement, at least," she said cheerfully. "They used to be behind your back. See how much we trust you?"

"If you came over here to irritate me, you've succeeded."

"No, I didn't plan to irritate you, Sam, I really didn't. I just wanted to chat. It might be our last chance."

"Why? Are you going somewhere?"

"I'm not, but you are." She gestured toward the rear of the plane and the clamshell doors, closed at the moment. "When we get out over the ocean, I think Stover plans to lighten the plane a little."

"Tell me, Heidi, what makes you think that Stover won't throw you out, too? You messed up his plans, and he's not likely to be grateful."

"I can take care of myself, Sam. At any rate, I'm doing a lot better than you at the moment."

"At the moment."

"The moment," she said, "is all there is."

"Go away," I told her. I turned my head and looked toward the front of the plane. Stover was struggling again with the earphones. His mechanical aptitude was improbably low for a man who had coordinated the building of an atomic bomb.

Stover listened to Wynn for a few seconds, then began to shout instructions. "Get on the radio," he yelled, "and tell them to stay the hell away from us. Tell them that if we see another plane on our radar screen, we'll drop a bomb on the nearest city." He pulled the headset off, nearly removing his ears in the process.

"McNally!"

Mac looked up at him.

"Just what did you tell the Air Force?"

"What do you think I told them?"

"If you gave them instructions to send chase planes after us, then you made the biggest mistake of your life. Our flight path is going to take us right down the eastern seaboard, McNally. We'll never be more than a few miles from a population center. Washington, Richmond, Raleigh, Columbia, Charleston, Savannah, Jacksonville, and every place in between. If they try to shoot us down, somebody is going to get nuked. Is that what you want?"

"Is it what *you* want? What makes your slimy hide worth the lives of fifty thousand people, Stover?"

Stover grabbed the headset and thrust it at McNally. "Tell them!" he commanded. "You tell them to stay away, McNally. You know I'll do it if I have to."

McNally studied Stover's face. Both of them looked rockhard, unyielding.

"You would do it, wouldn't you?"

"I will," Stover said flatly.

They stared at each other for another moment. Then McNally put on the headset.

"Patch me in to the radio," he said. There was a pause as Wynn set it up. Stover withdrew his gun and pointed it at McNally's temple. McNally kept his eyes on Stover as he spoke.

"This is McNally," he said. "I'm on the plane. They have two bombs, and one of them is ready to be dropped. They mean business. I want clear sailing from here to Florida. That means no commercial planes in the flight path and no fighters, repeat, *no* fighters flying chase. If they see a blip on their screen, they're likely to panic and drop one on the nearest city. There is to be absolutely no interference with this flight. Acknowledge."

McNally waited for the acknowledgment, then handed the headset back to Stover.

"Very good," Stover told him.

"It won't make any difference. You're as dead as I am, Stover."

Stover replaced the headset on the hook, then squatted down between McNally and me. "Heidi," he said, "why don't you go forward and keep Wynn and Bell company?"

"Why don't you?" she replied.

Stover's gun was still in his hand. His eyes flicked toward it.

323

Heidi said nothing, but got to her feet and walked off toward the cockpit. Jones was still planted on the other side of the plane, out of earshot.

"Now," Stover said, "why don't you tell me why you think we won't make it?"

"Because they'll never let you out of the country," McNally told him. "There are ninety miles of open water between Florida and Cuba. How do you think you'll get across them?"

"We'll make it," Stover said confidently. "We didn't just stumble into this, you know. It's well planned. From Key West to Cuban territorial waters is fourteen minutes of flight time. If we don't have a clear screen, we'll circle Key West until we have one. Key West is pretty crowded this time of year. I don't think they'll want to risk losing it. When our screen is clear, we'll head for Cuba. By the time we could be intercepted, we'd be very close to Cuban waters. No one is going to take a chance on wrecking U.S.–Cuban relations just to splash us at the last possible moment. We'll make it."

"And what do you think the Cubans are going to say about all this?"

Stover laughed. "I think they'll cooperate. They would hate to lose José Martí Airport. They'll give us fuel and anything else we need, and be glad to get rid of us."

"It's possible. It's also possible that they'll just wait you out. Or rush the plane. Those Cubans are very macho. You might find yourself in a Cuban jail, Stover. A lot less pleasant than Leavenworth."

"There is that chance," Stover admitted. "But that wouldn't be any great obstacle. Ask Boggs about Swiss accounts. He'll tell you what handy things they are. I've got over two million dollars in mine, McNally. If I can't buy my way out of a Cuban jail with two million dollars, then I'm just not trying."

"Two million? You executives are well-paid. How much

more on delivery? Another two mill?" Stover didn't respond, but he didn't deny it, either. "Nice," I said. "Hell, Stover, when Heidi led us to your factory, she cost you a cool two million, didn't she?"

There was a brief, hostile flash in Stover's eyes. "She shouldn't have talked, but she did. I'll deal with it later."

"Why did you send her away?"

"Because I'm going to tell you some things that she doesn't need to know. She doesn't know who's in charge, beyond me, and that's the way it is going to stay. I'm the only one in this operation who knows where the money comes from. I'm going to tell you, because you're not going to have the opportunity to tell anyone else. Call it vanity, but I want you to know. When the moment comes, I want you to die with the knowledge that the bad guys are getting away clean."

"That remains to be seen," said McNally.

"But not by you," Stover reminded him. "You won't be seeing anything. That's why I'm going to tell you."

"So tell."

Stover tried to make himself more comfortable on the floor, and then took out a pack of cigarettes. He handed one to each of us, took one for himself, then lit up all around.

"A last cigarette?" I asked. "Pretty melodramatic, Stover. Not your style."

"It just happens that I wanted a cigarette and I didn't want to be impolite. Enjoy it, Boggs. Now, you want to know who the bad guys are. Well, I'm sure you'll be overjoyed to learn that you guessed right. General Petroleum is behind the whole operation."

McNally glanced at me, and I shrugged modestly. That was the only thing I had been right about since the beginning.

"As I'm sure you know," Stover continued, "GP has had some problems recently. Their domestic oil fields have been drying up, and they haven't been able to obtain any good foreign leases. But as luck would have it, GP came into possession of a confidential geological report that originally was to have gone to one of the big international conglomerates."

"I can guess how they got it," McNally commented.

"And you'd probably be right. I wasn't involved with that end of it. But I do know what the report showed. It indicated that there was a huge new oil field waiting to be tapped, the biggest since the Alaskan North Slope. Estimated value of seventy-five billion dollars. So you can see the stakes we're playing for."

"Whose oil is it?"

"That was the problem. It happens to be sitting under a certain white-ruled African nation. At the moment, they don't know that it's there. Were they to find out, the oil leases would go to one of GP's competitors. That would have been a disaster, financially speaking, so other plans were made.

"It seems that a neighboring black-ruled country has long coveted the particular strip of land that contains the oil. The ruler of that country is a man known for his temper tantrums and his erratic behavior. But, in fact, he is a very sly man. We went to him and proposed a deal to our mutual advantage."

"Bombs for oil," McNally said.

"Exactly. We agreed to provide him with a number of atomic bombs, which he would use to conquer his neighbor. In return, GP gets the oil leases, and everyone is happy."

"Are they still happy?" McNally asked.

Stover made a sour expression. "Probably not," he admitted. "When the word gets out, I can think of a few people who are going to be pretty upset. But I don't expect to be one of them. I have my money. Our African friend will be disappointed, but I think he'll be glad to accept delivery of these two bombs. These two may be enough to tip the balance of a war between

326

the two countries. GP may have to renegotiate the oil leases, since the agreement specified a dozen bombs, and there are now only two. But I think an accommodation will be reached. After we reach Africa, I'll simply disappear. You two, however, are due to disappear in the more immediate future."

McNally was more interested in GP. "They won't get away with it, Stover. We're already on to them."

"Where's your evidence?" Stover didn't look especially worried. "You can tear apart that warehouse in Philly, but you won't find one speck of evidence to connect GP with it. Counting the two of you, there are only eight people in the world who know the whole story, and that number is about to be reduced by twenty-five percent. No, McNally, GP will get away with it. I'll get away with it. Can you guess who *won't* get away with it?"

"I hate guessing games," McNally told him.

Stover stood up and pointed the gun at me.

"This is it?"

Stover's finger tightened around the trigger, and I realized that my time was up. I didn't feel any particular emotion, just mild curiosity about how it would feel.

Stover kept me waiting.

"No, Boggs," he said, "this isn't it. Not quite yet. I still might need you, and if you're dead, I can't bring you back. So you have a few more hours. Enjoy them."

He turned to leave, but stopped after two steps. "Oh, by the way," he added, "don't try to tell any of this to Jones or Heidi. You won't have the chance to talk with either of them, anyway. But you're free to discuss it between you." He smiled again, then left for the cockpit.

We didn't exactly discuss it. We brooded about it. I was sure McNally was thinking about the price of failure, about how duty was something you couldn't shirk, about what could be done to right the wrongs—or at least get even. Me, I just tried to concentrate on the pleasant moments. I was surprised to find there had been so many. Studying chemistry back at Berkeley had been pleasant, experiencing the thrill of discovering how the universe was put together. And some of my days in the movement had been pleasant. There was solidarity, a common goal, and a naive optimism about the future. Torremolinos hadn't been bad, either, even if it had been all a sham. Deceptions and deceits are not without their rewards, even for the victim. Someone comes along and helps you to believe the things you want to believe. When the guillotine falls, at least you have memories of something better.

But it wouldn't do to get sentimental about Heidi. She was headed for her own tacky final scene, whether it was in Africa or Zurich or wherever she chose to hide. Stover was keeping her alive because he wanted the money in my account. No other reason, and they both knew it. But Heidi was sure she could finesse it somehow, the way she always had. Maybe she would. I didn't really care who fucked who anymore.

Jones had remained at his post throughout the entire flight. We stared at each other sometimes. Since he was the man who, in all probability, was going to kill me, I wanted to get to know him. After a couple of hours, though, I gave up. I didn't think there was anyone there to know. Jones was simply a golem. Getting killed by Jones would be like getting crushed by a falling I-beam, emotionless and final. Neither one of us would enjoy it.

Heidi would enjoy it, of course, as long as she was allowed to pull the trigger. I wondered if when the time came, she would enjoy her own death. She very well might, I decided.

She spent most of the flight asleep on the front seat of the truck, curled up innocently next to an atomic bomb. I was tired enough to sleep myself, but the idea of slumbering away my final hours was appalling.

It was getting on toward five o'clock when Stover came back from the cockpit and woke up Heidi. She got out of the truck and rubbed her eyes. For a moment, I don't think she knew where she was.

"Coming up on Miami," Stover announced, sounding like a railway conductor. He didn't say it, but this was clearly the end of the line.

Stover called Wynn again on the intercom. While he fiddled with the headset, McNally stared up at him with cold, unblinking eyes. Mac was awash in hatred. I had always expected that the end would come more or less this way, but McNally was probably looking forward to a quick cerebral hemorrhage on the fourteenth hole at Burning Tree. He was not ready to accept such a dingy conclusion.

Stover listened to Wynn for a moment. "Where?" he said suddenly. "How fast?"

I looked at McNally. He pretended not to see me.

"They couldn't wait!" Stover screamed at McNally. "Your hot-shot aces just couldn't wait, could they? We've got four blips on the screen, coming our way. Well, those stupid fuckers have just lost themselves a city!"

Heidi chose that moment to interrupt. "Is there a little girls' room on this plane?" she asked him.

Stover's eyes widened. He was trying to blow up Miami, but she had to go to the bathroom. Vastly different priorities.

"Up front," Stover said, fighting to compose himself. "Under the cockpit."

"Thank you," she said politely. She turned and walked quickly toward the front of the plane.

"My God!" Stover sighed. "How could you stand her, Boggs? How the bloody hell could you stand her?"

"Beats me," I answered truthfully.

He called to Jones. "Start unstrapping the truck! I want it ready to roll!" Jones spread his arms, then pointed to his ear and shook his head. Stover screamed the instruction again, fighting to make himself heard above the continuous roar of the engines. Jones finally got the message and went to work on the cargo webbing at the front end of the truck. Stover turned back to the headset, getting himself slightly tangled in the wires.

"Wynn, listen to me. Get on the radio and warn those planes to get off our screen. Tell them we'll circle Miami until they do. If they're not gone in five minutes, we'll drop a bomb. Open the rear doors. I want them to believe us."

Stover removed the headset and started to untangle himself, but he didn't get very far. McNally was on him.

McNally gave Stover a knee in the base of the spine, knocking all the air out of him and crushing him up against the side of the plane. With his hands still tied together, Mac jerked the headset jack out of the socket and started wrapping the wire around Stover's neck. Stover's hands flew up to his throat, but Mac had already made two loops and was pulling hard, bracing himself with his knees against Stover's back.

Stover turned red, then purple. I watched as his eyes bulged out of their sockets and blood vessels burst in the corneas. Stover died as I sat there watching.

I came to my feet in a rolling start and charged Jones. He had been bent over one of the cargo straps and had missed the action. I was going to give him one hell of a kick in the side of the head as he looked up.

I timed it perfectly, but Jones's head wasn't there when my foot arrived. He was quick, and Mac was suddenly dead. Jones rolled away from me and came up firing as I stumbled past him, off balance. He got McNally in the back with the first shot.

I tried to recover before he could turn, but it was no good. I couldn't stop my forward motion without the use of my arms; I careened into the side of the plane and bounced, turning, back toward Jones. He was waiting for me.

The top of my head came off. They say you never hear the one that gets you, and they were right. I never heard a thing. There was one fractured instant of terrible pain and surprise, and then nothing.

And then ... something. Blurred images and a high-pitched buzzing reverberating in my head. My head ... still there. I felt a curious tingling on the right side of my scalp at the hairline, as if my foot had gone to sleep, except it was my head. It was all very strange for a few moments.

I was lying on my back, my head tilted against the side of the plane. My eyes were open, and I saw two people walking toward me, both of them dressed like Jones. They stopped in unison, just in front of me. Both of them had guns in their hands, and they were slowly raising them.

I aimed for the one on the right.

My foot came up between his legs and connected with soft tissue. The Jones on my right crumpled; so did the one on my left. Both guns fell to the deck and clattered away.

I didn't know which one to go for first. I didn't even know where the second Jones had come from, or why he had fallen when I kicked the other one. I carefully pushed myself up to standing. I had four legs.

"Silly me," I said aloud. "I'm seeing double." Only one Jones, one gun. Now, where the hell was it?

I kept my eyes on the floor and tried to conduct a systematic search, but something was falling into my right eye. I brought

331

my hands up to my face to investigate. Blood, sure enough. Right on the first try.

I found the gun. With my foot, I found it. The gun bounced farther back into the tail of the plane. My vision had started to clear when something slammed into me from behind.

I went down again, and Jones was on top of me.

There wasn't much I could do with my hands tied and Jones clawing at my throat. I tred to shove him away, but my arms were as weak as spaghetti. He was well on the way to strangling me.

But Jones wasn't the type who learned from his mistakes. I rammed my knee into his groin. Jones went *oof* and fell off me.

I wanted to get up, but decided to lie there and think about things for a few more seconds. Normally, I was in pretty good shape, and it bothered me that I was having so much trouble getting around. It was the thin air, I concluded.

The gun was still back there somewhere, and I knew I wanted it, although I couldn't remember exactly why. I pushed myself back up and managed a few steps before I realized that Jones was not where I had left him.

Quite a guy, that Jones. He had crawled after the gun while I stared at the ceiling. His hand closed around the pistol, and I couldn't do anything about it. His movements were painfully slow, but he was fifteen feet away from me. There was nothing I could do this time. Jones wasn't going to come back in range.

I don't think he was capable of it, any more than I was capable of getting to him for one final kick. We both stopped and concentrated on breathing. I sucked the thin air into my lungs and waited for Jones to relieve the need. He was on his side, practically fetal, with one hand clutching his groin, and the other the gun.

He pointed it at me.

"You son of a bitch!" he gasped. "You ruined me!"

Jones fired. I felt the bullet tear through the inseam of my pants. Jones wanted to do the same thing to me that I had done to him. I didn't know which way to move.

He raised the gun and took careful aim. And then he was gone.

Wynn opened the clamshell doors. Jones was lying across the seam and dropped right out of the plane when the floor opened under him. The gaping hole widened, revealing choppy blue waves far below. There was no sign of Jones.

I staggered up as close to the edge as I dared and looked down. Jones and the gun were gone, no doubt about it. I was still alive and more or less intact. I marveled at the fact.

I have never liked heights. Staring out of a pressure-sealed window at thirty-five thousand feet is one thing; standing at the edge of a three-mile drop is quite another. The waves seemed to beckon.

"Get with it, Boggs," I said to myself. I was talking to myself because there was no one else left alive on the cargo deck. If I wanted to maintain that status, I knew that there were things I had to do. I made my way forward, very slowly, back to where Stover and McNally lay tangled in their death dance. Stover had shit all over himself. Mac seemed to have died with a little more dignity.

I pulled Stover's pistol out of his pocket and examined it. The safety was off, and I knew that was good, because there were things I had to do with that gun. There was still someone around that I had to deal with.

Heidi. That was it, good old Heidi, up there in the little girls' room. I resumed my journey toward the front of the plane, holding the pistol between my roped-together hands. My balance seemed to be improving. I didn't even need to look down at my feet as I walked.

So I was looking up when Heidi emerged from the head. She

stopped dead and stared at me, then at the scene behind me.

"What happened?" she asked.

It was such a dumb question that I couldn't think of an appropriate response.

Heidi recovered quickly from the surprise. She was as adaptable as a chameleon.

"What are we going to do now, Sam?"

"We?"

"Why not? There's no one left to tell us what to do. McNally and Stover are dead, so it's just you and me again."

"Just like before?"

"It could be, Sam. If we gave it a chance."

I was swaying back and forth a little. Maybe Heidi thought it meant that I was wavering. I wasn't.

"Heidi, the only chance I'm going to give you is to stay alive awhile longer. Do what I tell you, or I'll shoot."

The only problem was that I didn't know what to tell her. I couldn't think of a thing to do with her. I had to get up to the cockpit somehow, but not with Heidi still free. And I couldn't very well tie her up, not with my own hands tied.

She knew me too well. She knew what I was thinking. Her eyes strayed toward the steps to the cockpit, twenty feet away from her. She was only about ten feet in front of me, but she could get to the steps before I could get to her, that much was certain.

"Don't, Heidi."

"Give it up, Sam," she said. "You can't do it, and we both know it. I've done it before, so I know what it takes, and I know you haven't got it. You won't shoot me. You can't."

I raised the gun.

"You won't do it, Sam. I know you. Years of exploding bombs, and you never once killed anybody. Do you think you can start now?"

"I won't have to kill you."

Heidi laughed at me. "In the leg, you mean? The kneecap? Is your aim that good? Sam, you can barely even hold that gun. Why don't you give it to me?"

She extended her arm. It was a good fake, and I took it. While I was trying to focus on her arm, she darted to her left, toward the steps. Three more good strides and she would be there.

I fired twice. The first shot hit her low in the back, on the right. The second one was higher and to the left, where her heart was.

I stared at her motionless body and tried to feel something. Tried very hard.

I don't know how long I stood there, but I had the impression of the passage of a considerable amout of time. Minutes, perhaps. I was snapped out of it by a pocket of rough air, which sent me reeling to the deck. The coldness of the metal against my cheek had restorative powers. I kept my flesh pressed against it until the flow of heat from me to it had equalized the temperature. For the first time, I understood the medieval practice of bleeding a sick person. Maybe there really are evil spirits and bad humors that can be expelled from the body.

I felt better.

Wynn and Bell were still up there, flying the plane. They obviously hadn't heard the shots over the roar of the engines, or they'd have been back here a long time ago. It would be possible, then, for me to sneak up the steps and surprise them, shoot them in their backs. That was something I knew how to do, now.

Something I didn't know how to do, however, was fly a plane. That was a problem. If I had to, I supposed that I could land a Piper Cub, maybe, if someone in the control tower were talking me down. But I had no illusions about driving a monster four-engine transport. And no one in his right mind would help me land it at his airport, not with two atomic bombs on board. They'd talk me down, all right—straight into the Everglades.

And I didn't think I could frighten Wynn by sticking a gun in his ear. In a normal hijack situation, it's the guy with the gun who doesn't care what happens and the pilot who wants to get home to the wife and kids. But our roles were reversed; Wynn would just laugh at me and fly on to Cuba.

Okay, then, forget about the people in the cockpit and hope they return the favor. They might wonder what had happened to Stover, but I guessed that Wynn would be happy not having to listen to Stover's instructions. It could be a long time before they got curious enough to check out the cargo deck.

That gave me time, and I knew I was going to need it. The cargo doors were still open. All I had to do was wait until we were over open sea, then roll the truck out, followed by the second bomb.

I got to my feet and held steady for a moment to take my bearings. My hands were still tied, and something had to be done about that. And my scalp was still bleeding, but I didn't think that there was much that *could* be done about that.

If I was going to bleed to death, then I had to get my work done in a hurry. I looked around for something to use for cutting purposes, but nothing presented itself.

There was a tool kit in the truck. I'd used it when I rigged the bomb. All I'd used were a pair of pliers and a screwdriver, but I thought that there might have been something else usable.

The tool kit was still there, right next to the bomb. I rummaged around in it, and to my utter amazement found a hacksaw blade—just the blade, no handle. I tried to manipulate it between my thumbs, pointing it backward across the ropes, but immediately dropped the blade. That was not going to work.

A considerable length of wire was left over from my work on the bomb. I found a pair of wirecutters and snipped off two eighteen-inch segments. Working with as much precision as I could manage, I positioned the hacksaw blade along one of the struts of the bomb carriage, just above the floor of the truck. The teeth of the blade extended just beyond the metal tubing. Holding the blade in position with my knee, I started wrapping the first piece of wire around the strut. It seemed to take forever, because I could wrap it around only one side, then had to drop it and pick it up again on the other side, pulling it taut to avoid any slack. After seven or eight loops, I tucked the end of the wire under the wrapping and hoped that it would hold. I repeated the whole process again at the lower end of the blade.

It was a good job; the blade held steady. Just to be safe, I held my knee against it as I started dragging the ropes over the blade. In surprisingly short order, one of the ropes broke, and the whole assembly unraveled. I rubbed my wrists and felt the welcome prickly pain of blood flowing once more.

I set to work on the cargo webbing that held the truck in place. There were two straps under the front axle, two more looped through the bumper, and a couple more in back.

I couldn't get any of them.

"You thought you were so fucking smart," I chided myself. The straps looked simple, but I just could not figure them out. Every time I leaned down to work on them, thinking I knew what to do, I screwed up completely. My hands went their own way, and my vision clouded.

Somewhere inside my head, something was bleeding. When I

337

leaned over, the blood put pressure on something vital, a nerve or brain lobe or some goddamned thing. It was only a matter of time until I blacked out, possibly for keeps. There was just no way I was going to move that truck.

There was an alternative. I didn't like it, but it was the only thing my partially addled brain could come up with. If I kept on fiddling around with the straps, we'd be in Cuba before I had the first one undone. So the thing to do, obviously, was blow the bomb.

We'd be over the ocean, so there was minimum hazard to human life. Fishermen, maybe, but they'd have to take their chances. Yes, it was necessary. Completely necessary. No other way. . . .

Cut the crap, Boggs—you *want* to blow it. The voice of reason and conscience wormed its way out from beneath the blood and confusion and spoke to me. You built it, man, and now you want to see if it works. You want to see it go boom. You've lived with it and damn near died with it, and now you've got to find out if it all meant anything. Go ahead, Boggs, try to deny it.

I couldn't. Yes, I wanted to see it, but that wasn't the only reason. It couldn't be the only reason. . . .

"Dammit!" I shouted, "There *isn't* any other way!"

And the voice of reason said to me: "Go ahead. Do it. Sure it's necessary. But no matter what happens, Boggs, you'll know the real reason, *you'll know* . . ."

I stumbled into the truck and found the wire I needed. The glass covering of the dashboard clock had already been broken, and the hour hand was wired up. The clock read five minutes after five.

While I removed the tape from the end of the wire, I calculated times. Fourteen minutes from Key West to Cuba. We were over water now, which meant that we had to be at least over the Keys. I didn't think we could be much farther than that, even though it seemed like hours since Stover had announced that we were coming up on Miami. I had to guess: ten minutes seemed about right.

I attached the wire to the minute hand and shoved it ahead to sixteen after the hour. At about 5:26 or 5:27, the hands would come together and the bomb would go off.

I hadn't thought about it, but the next steps seemed pretty obvious—get out of the plane. I left the truck and looked around for a parachute. They should have been hanging all over the walls, I thought, but they weren't. Beneath the gaping cargo doors, the waters were turning red with the sunset. It occurred to me that it probably didn't matter whether I had a parachute or not. Soon it would be night, and no one would ever find me down there.

But I wanted to *see* it. And I wouldn't see very damn much of it if I stayed in the plane.

It was then that McNally groaned. For two seconds, I believed very firmly in ghosts.

I went over to him. The back of his jacket was stained red, but there was movement as he breathed. He was one tough son of a bitch, McNally was.

Carefully I pulled him away from Stover's corpse and rolled him onto his back. His eyes opened, and he almost smiled at me.

"What happened?" he asked.

I smiled back at him, almost. "All kinds of things," I said. "But I don't think I have enough time to tell you about it."

"Why not?"

"Because the bomb is set to go in a few minutes. I was planning to make my exit about now. Care to join me?"

"Why not?"

"You're repeating yourself, Mac. Or I'm hearing you twice.

Listen, we have a slight problem. I can't find a parachute. Do you know where they keep them on these things?"

"Try up front, beneath the cockpit. There are storage lockers up there, I think."

I left McNally and went to investigate. I was sort of glad he was alive, bastard though he was. We could drown together, or bleed to death together, whichever came first. And if I couldn't find the fucking parachutes, we'd be vaporized together.

I found them, and more. My lucky day, definitely. I returned to McNally with my booty.

"Mae Wests. The yellow is rather garish with the red you're wearing, but it was the best life vest I could find."

"It'll do," he said. "I think you'll have to help me get mine on. I can't move my left arm." He seemed embarrassed to admit it.

I got him into the vest, moving him as little as possible, but I could see that even that minimum was painful. I didn't see how in hell he was going to survive a parachute jump.

"Now the chute," he said. "Make sure you get everything buckled right."

"You'll have to tell me. I've never jumped before."

He laughed at that, even though it hurt him. "Sam Boggs, international soldier of fortune, has never jumped from a plane? That's really amusing."

"And you skydive on weekends, I suppose. You'll have to tell me about it sometime."

"Jump school at Fort Benning. Made a man out of me."

"I can think of easier ways." I buckled up my own chute and grabbed McNally under his right armpit. "This is going to hurt," I warned him.

"What doesn't? Let's do it."

I put my arm around his back, stuck my head under his armpit, and lifted. It hurt. I was right about that. We grunted in unison.

340

"You'll have to help," I told him. "I can't carry all this deadweight by myself."

"Deadweight?" He sniffed. "You keep insulting me, Boggs, and I won't tell you where the ripcord is."

Together, we made it. I put him down a foot from the edge of the cargo door and then collapsed myself. We spent a moment breathing hard and watching the light play on the water.

"Where are we?" he asked.

Over the gulf, I think. Between Key West and Cuba. Do you think there are likely to be sharks down there?"

McNally reached over and smeared some of my blood on his finger. "If there aren't any now," he said, examining my hemoglobin, "you can bet there will be when we hit the water. Take care, Boggs."

McNally rolled over the side. I watched him get smaller and smaller and waited for the chute to open, but I didn't see it. He disappeared from my field of view, and there was still no chute.

It was my turn. I tensed my muscles and tried to push off, but nothing happened. My body refused to go. I gazed down at the dancing waters and tried to imagine that they were just three meters below me, off the high board. Three miles was too much to think about.

I would have stayed right there, clinging to the edge, if it hadn't been for the bomb. I remembered that I'd given myself only ten minutes, and God knew how long I'd spent getting McNally into his chute. I not only had to get out, I had to do it in one big hurry.

My body must have realized the greater danger in store if I stayed; I found myself rolling out of the airplane without really having planned it.

I began to tumble immediately. Ocean and sky rolled past me, and I didn't even know which direction I was falling.

341

Cautiously, I extended my arms and tried to stabilize myself. That straightened me out; I was on my back, staring up at the orange sky. There were a lot of cumulus clouds, and they seemed very close.

I discovered then why I was so afraid of heights. It's because falling is beautiful. I avoided high, open places because something deep inside of me wanted to soar on out and never stop.

Like hell I never wanted to stop. I was scared to death. I had to get down as fast as possible, but not this fast. I drew in one arm and managed to flip myself over, and suddenly the ocean looked a hell of a lot closer than the clouds. I reached for the handle and pulled.

The shock of the parachute opening snapped my head back and made it hurt even more. But the sight of the canopy billowing over my head eased the pain. It caught the pink-and-orange sunset and looked like a circus tent, complete with the pink-cotton-candy clouds.

I looked down and saw the ocean. It was still far below me. From the time I jumped to the time the chute opened, probably no more than ten seconds had elapsed, despite the way it felt. Idiot that I was, I had managed to leave myself hanging in the middle of the sky with the bomb about to go off.

Yes, the bomb. Now, where was it? I scanned the horizon and the sky beneath the canopy and could see no sign of the plane. There was nothing but empty sea. That was good, at least; we were far from land. The bomb wouldn't do any damage—and I was going to have a long swim.

I tugged at the cords and tried to swing myself around. My efforts set up a pendulum motion, with me as the pendulum, and I knew enough basic physics to know that you can't rush a pendulum. I stopped what I was doing and tried a different motion, a variation on the Chubby Checker twist.

That turned me around, and I saw the plane immediately. And beyond it, I saw Miami.

It took a moment for me to realize the enormity of my mistake. We weren't over the keys, we never had been. We had been circling Miami, waiting for the Air Force planes to get away from us.

Apparently they hadn't.

The lights of Miami were twinkling in the fading sunset, no more than fifteen miles from me. The plane was headed right for the city.

"You had to see it!" I shouted at myself. "You just had to see it! Well, take a look, Boggs! You're going to see four kilotons' worth of bang, right before your very eyes!"

How many people lived in Miami? I wondered. And how many would still be alive two minutes from now?

The plane held its course, steady and true. The perspective was difficult, but it looked as if it would be over the coast in another minute. I had lost track of time, but it had to be soon, now, terribly soon.

I didn't want to see it. Not now. I closed my eyes, closed them tight, and let myself drift downward.

And then, a thought that made me laugh. It seemed as if much more than ten minutes had passed. Maybe it was a dud! A fucking dud! Maybe I wasn't such a red-hot bombsmith after all. It was so funny that I opened my eyes to watch the bomb not explode. That was funny, too.

I was still laughing when I saw the plane. One wing was dipped in a graceful bank. It was no longer headed for Miami.

It was headed straight for me.

That was when I knew for certain that it was no dud. It was coming back to find me—Wynn wasn't flying that plane, the bomb was. We had a rendezvous. I thought of one of the books I had read in Torremolinos: *all this was rehearsed by me and thee a billion years before the ocean rolled.* My own white whale was coming back to get me.

Some internal clock told me it was time. I turned my head.

There was a second sunset that night. But first, a sunrise.

I looked back toward Miami. Between me and it stood a boiling, churning flower, blooming in shades of pink and orange and violet, climbing skyward.

It was incredibly beautiful.

Thoughts of my radical days. Bakunin was right, destruction *is* the greatest expression of the creative force. Here was life, death, love, art, the entire universe, building and blossoming in that fantastic cloud.

We'll do it someday, I thought, we'll really do it. The urge is just too strong. One small taste of Armageddon—and one taste would not be enough. Someday we'd eat the whole goddamn apple.

The shock wave hit me then. I was thrown violently back, away from the cloud, a spider clinging to its web in a hurricane. I heard the sound of ripping fabric blended in with the deep-throated express-train roar of the explosion.

Something else hit me abruptly, with a loud smack. The air rushed out of me, and when I tried to breathe in the darkness, I felt saltwater pouring into me. I remembered the Mae West and started to search for the knob that would inflate it, but I really didn't care whether or not I found it. The sea was warm, and I didn't mind it.

I found the knob, and with some reluctance I twisted it. Almost immediately I was back on the surface, choking and coughing and fighting for air. Something was tugging me back down, and I realized it was the parachute, acting as a huge anchor. I hastily unbuckled the chute and worked myself clear of the tangle of shroud lines.

Above me, the cloud had reached its apex, probably forty thousand feet high, and was beginning to flatten out as the superheated air in it collided with the cold mass of the stratosphere. I leaned my head back against the collar of the life vest and watched. The waves rocked me back and forth as gently as a porch swing on a summer's night. I might have been the only one left in the world.

I wondered if the current would take me to Tahiti. Tahiti would have been nice. Except for a slight queasiness in my stomach, I felt just great.

After a while I was aware of a loud noise nearby. I turned myself around and looked away from the dying cloud. A helicopter was hovering overhead. It annoyed me. I hadn't asked for it, after all.

Somebody leaned out of the copter and shouted at me. I couldn't understand what he was saying, so I waved at him. He waved back. Then he turned on a winch and lowered a sling to me. I understood that I was supposed to get into it. I didn't really want to, it was so pleasant there in the water, but I knew that if I didn't, the guy in the copter would have to jump in and do it himself. So I cooperated. After I was snug in the sling, they hauled me out of the water like a bloated old carp.

Two pairs of hands grabbed me and pulled me into the helicopter. We all stumbled together, and I hit the deck hard. Suddenly, I didn't feel so great. As a matter of fact, I felt lousy. I felt like throwing up.

So I did.

"Jesus!" cried one of the guys who had pulled me from the water. "If you're gonna get airsick, do it out the window."

But I wasn't airsick. I knew better than that. I wasn't even seasick. But I didn't say anything, because I knew they'd probably throw me back in the water if I told them what it really was.

It was radiation.

21

They kept me for three months.

After they were sure that I wasn't going to die right away, they shipped me up to Bethesda, where they could keep an eye on me and nail down the lid. I suppose they must have debriefed me, but I don't remember it. I didn't talk to anyone but doctors and an occasional nurse. Nobody told me anything, and nobody asked me anything.

Not that I was very interested. I was much more interested in watching my body fall apart. My hair fell out, every last strand of it. That was humiliating, but not very important. I threw up a lot, and shit a lot. That was annoying, but not very dangerous. And I hemorrhaged a lot, and that *was* dangerous. I was frequently delirious.

They gave me massive blood transfusions. When that didn't help, they did a bone-marrow transplant. They did all kinds of things to me, then stepped back to wait and see if any of it had helped.

They estimated that I had taken about 350 to 400 roentgens. If you get 600, you automatically die. At the 300 level, about a quarter of the population dies, and the rest just wish they could. I turned out to be in that segment, though not by much.

Gradually, I improved. My hair started to grow back; more of it was gray than before. Radiation will do that to you. So will stress. I'd had plenty of both.

I was told that my life expectancy had dropped by at least ten years. I was now a high cancer risk. The news didn't bother me much; I had been a high-risk case for the last ten years.

Eventually I was well enough to walk around my room. That was as far as I could go, however. I was strong enough to go farther, but the guards outside my door would almost certainly have objected. So I stayed in my room and did a lot of laps around the bed.

One day McNally came to see me. He looked considerably better than I did. He had jumped before me and had enough sense not to open his chute until the last possible moment. When the bomb went off, he just ducked beneath the waves and missed most of the radiation. But he did come close to bleeding to death before the chopper got to him.

He sat down on the edge of my bed and stared at me for a minute or two. "Christ, Boggs," he said, "you look like a marine drill sergeant."

I ran my hand over my fuzzy scalp, across the inch-long scar at the hairline whre the bullet had furrowed me. I was still weeks away from needing a comb.

"It's the new look," I told him. "Haven't you heard?"

"I'm always out of step with the latest fashions, I'm afraid."

348

That seemed to exhaust our fund of small talk. I sat back and waited for him to tell me.

"You nearly blew it," he said.

"Nearly?"

"Eight and a half miles. That's how far offshore the plane was when the bomb went off. Miami is still standing, Boggs. I thought you might like to know that."

"Imagine my relief."

"That's all you have to say?"

"I don't even know what to feel."

"Lucky," he told me. "You should definitely feel lucky. There was an onshore breeze when it went. What little fallout there was dropped at sea. Aside from a few cases of minor retinal burn, you were the only one to get hurt."

"I should feel lucky about that?"

"You lived. What more do you want? Tell me, Boggs, why the hell didn't you just shoot Wynn and Bell, turn out to sea, set the autopilot, and jump?"

I thought about it. "It didn't occur to me," I said lamely.

"Fair enough, I guess. You had a concussion at the time, so I suppose we can excuse a little fuzzy thinking. Even if it did nearly kill a hundred thousand people."

McNally had a way of forgiving that made me feel distinctly unforgiven. And I didn't imagine that the people of Miami were ready to throw bouquets at my feet.

"What is the world saying about all of this?"

McNally sighed. "The world," he said, "has practically forgotten it ever happened. There's a congressional investigation under way. They should issue a report sometime before the turn of the century, optimistically. You'll never guess who's heading it."

"Preston?"

349

He nodded. "None other. That's pretty convenient, really, since he has so much to hide himself. He'll stick to the party line."

"Which is?"

"Terrorists, of course. They're easy to blame, and they can't very well go on *Meet the Press* and defend themselves. Meanwhile, I'm something of a hero because of all the courageous things I did on that plane."

That was a little hard to take. "Strangling Stover, you mean?"

"It doesn't read quite that way in the public prints. And I didn't do it all myself. Agent Bruce C. Milton helped me."

"Bruce C. Milton? Is he someone I should know?"

"He was the other hostage, of course. Poor fellow was killed in the explosion."

"Tough," I said.

"Not so bad," said McNally. "No family, you know. Hard-boiled loner type. Gave his life for his country."

"Ask not what your country can do for you," I heard myself saying. "So what is my country going to do for me?"

McNally laughed and reached into his jacket pocket for a piece of paper. "I bring good tidings. Your presidential pardon." He dropped it on my lap. I didn't bother to look at it.

"It's that easy?" I asked.

"Of course it's not that easy. Haven't you learned anything yet, Boggs? This thing has not been publicized, which I'm sure doesn't surprise you. We've called in all the wanted posters and so forth, but if some bright young deputy sheriff in Bad Breath, Arkansas, recognizes you, there may be problems. We'll do our best to get you out, of course, but don't expect miracles. It might be a good idea for you to find some other place to live."

" 'The man without a country.' "

"That bothers you?"

"Who knows what bothers me? I don't."

"I do," McNally said. "What I'm about to say is going to bother you a lot. You're ours, Boggs, now and forever."

"I don't understand," I said. I did, but I didn't want to admit it.

"You know too much," he said. "And you're too valuable. And too useful. When we need you, we'll come and get you."

"Are you trying to tell me that I've joined the CIA?"

"It's joined you, Boggs. How's that for irony?"

"How do you think you'll find me? Or get me to go along if you do?"

McNally stood up and tried to look official. "Boggs," he said, "I told you before, it's not that easy. A substantial number of people didn't want you to leave this hospital any way but in a box. I talked them out of it. I convinced them that you could be useful to us. And I reminded them that any time you got out of line, your contract could always be terminated. In other words, if you ever cause us any trouble, some-day one of those unsavory little men who live on the fringe of our business will knock on your door. In the meantime, we use you when we need you."

I shook my head. "Not a chance. "I've retired. I have a half-million dollars in Switzerland. I can use it to hide."

"The minute you touch a dime of that money, we'll know where to find you."

"Then I won't touch it. I'm not sure I even want it."

"Wrong, Boggs, You'll use the money. You're human, just like the rest of us. Nobody walks away from a half-million dollars. Nobody. Not even lefty bullshit artists like you."

He was right, of course. Sooner or later, I'd use the money, and they'd have me. I made up my mind that it would be later.

351

"I'm tired of it, Mac. I've heard too many bangs and booms. I want out."

McNally gave me a crooked smile. "You should have thought of that before you got in." he said. "I'll be seeing you, Sam."

"Not if I can help it."

"You can't," he said.

Later that day they let me out. I was free to go wherever I wanted. I reached the end of the hospital sidewalk and stood there for five minutes. The March breeze was cool and unfriendly. I let it make my decision for me. I turned south.

Toward Tahiti.

In Tahiti, I could retire. In Tahiti, there were no Stovers and McNallys. No radicals and no gangsters. There would be only Sam Boggs, retired gentleman chemist, saying good-bye to the whole goddamned world.